Praise for *Love at First Flight*

"A great premise, endearing characters, a racy romance, and a nice dash of suspense… Marie Force knows how to tell an emotionally charged and entertaining story."

—BookLoons

"Sultry and sensual… A touching, heartfelt, and dramatic love story with memorable characters and a plot that will keep you on the edge of your seat."

—The Long and Short of It Reviews

"Captivating… It is an astounding book. I loved every single word!"

—Wild on Books

"What a roman~~ce should be~~ engaging romance th~~at~~ ~~t~~ this genre."

~~nd~~ the Unread

"Marie F~~orce~~ ~~her~~ latest contemporary ~~romance novel~~… Her powerful voice echoes through the characters—Love it!"

—J. Kaye's Book Blog

"[Ms. Force] creates a story and characters the reader can embrace and cheer on whole-heartedly with a smile and a lump in the throat."

—Once Upon a Romance

Praise for *Line of Scrimmage*

"With its humor and endearing characters, Force's charming novel will appeal to a broad spectrum of readers, reaching far beyond sports fans."

—*Booklist*

"Hands down, this is the best romance I've read this year."

—J. Kaye's Book Blog

"Ripe with emotion, steadfast with passion, and downright endearing… the intensity of the story grabs us on page one and carries us to the very last page without a blink of the eye. A must read that will not disappoint even the most finicky romance reader."

—Yankee Romance Reviewers

"An awesome novel. Her characters… are made for each other and their passion simply sizzles as they work through their problems."

—SingleTitles.com

"Ryan… is a good guy desperate to fix past mistakes, a terrific change of pace from the typical reluctant hero."

—*Publishers Weekly*

"Filled to the brim with characters you fall in love with, plot twists you'd never guess, and plenty of action in between. …A fast-paced read that will warm you on the inside and make you believe everyone deserves a second chance."

—Romance Junkies

Also by Marie Force

Line of Scrimmage
Love at First Flight

Everyone
Loves
a Hero

MARIE FORCE

sourcebooks
casablanca

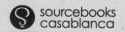

Published by Sourcebooks Casablanca, an imprint of Sourcebooks, Inc.
P.O. Box 4410, Naperville, Illinois 60567-4410
(630) 961-3900
FAX: (630) 961-2168
www.sourcebooks.com

Printed and bound in the United States of America.
QW 10 9 8 7 6 5 4 3 2 1

For Dan, truly one of the good ones.

Chapter 1

COLE OPENED THE EYE THAT STILL WORKED AND struggled to figure out how he had ended up on the floor. Pain radiated from his face and shoulder. All he'd wanted was a roll of Mentos to get him through his next flight. What he'd gotten, though, was a fist to the face. His shoulder throbbed from smashing into a display of Washington Redskins souvenirs, and his face pulsated with pain. That big dude had one hell of a left hook!

He tried to open his other eye—which was swelling shut after being on the receiving end of Big Dude's meaty fist—and blinked into focus a striking young woman hovering over him. She had long dark hair, porcelain skin, and big brown eyes. Over her shoulder, he took in the crowd of whispering, pointing people that had formed around him. No doubt they recognized him, which meant the press would show up any minute. He also saw two airport police officers arguing with a large man in handcuffs, presumably Big Dude.

Cole hadn't seen it coming. One minute he'd been standing in line minding his own business behind a guy having a heated discussion on a cell phone. Then he'd watched Big Dude throw a wad of money at the clerk. Cole had tapped him on the shoulder to tell him he was being rude to the girl behind the counter.

"She's only doing her job," Cole had said.

The next thing he knew, he was looking up at an angel.

"Are you all right?" she asked, hands coasting lightly over his face.

Cole was appalled by his predictably male response to her touch. Before his little problem became noticeable and before the media could show up and turn his life into a circus—again—he quickly tried to sit up. Too quickly, he discovered when he was hit by a wave of nausea that caught him off guard and snuffed out the situation in his lap.

He lay back on the sweatshirt someone had rolled into a pillow for him, closed his eyes, and took a deep breath to ward off the nausea. "How long was I out?" he asked the woman.

"About two minutes or so. It felt like longer, though."

"*Shit*," he groaned, imagining how the press would blow the incident out of proportion. "I need to get word to my airline that I can't fly today, and I gotta get out of here."

"The airport police called someone from your company. They're on their way, along with the paramedics."

"I don't need paramedics," he protested, making a second attempt to sit up.

Her hands on his shoulders stopped him. "Stay still. You might have a concussion."

A veteran of high school hockey, Cole had no doubt about the concussion. *Great. That's just great.* After months on the ground doing "the hero circuit" on behalf of the airline, he didn't need a concussion to knock him out of the air for two weeks just when the whole uproar had finally started to die down.

"What's your name?" he asked, his eyes still closed as he did battle with pain and nausea.

"My name?"

"It's not a trick question."

She laughed softly. "Olivia."

Sticking up for a woman named Olivia had gotten him knocked out and knocked down to earth for at least two weeks. *Damn it!*

"Thank you for what you did," she said.

"No problem."

"Yes, I think it was."

Cole raised his good shoulder in a half shrug. "He was being a jerk."

"Here," a male voice said from above him. "Put this on your eye."

Cole cracked open his working eye to find the store manager holding out an icepack. He reached for it. "Thanks."

The paramedics arrived a minute later, along with a representative from the airline, an older woman Cole had never seen before. She announced she would be accompanying him to the hospital.

"That's not necessary," he said.

"Boss's orders," she replied, full of her own importance. "I'm to stay with you until you're released and handle any media requests."

"*Great.*"

As the paramedics prepared to roll him away, Cole looked around for Olivia and found her in a group of airport employees and customers who were watching the proceedings. Their eyes met, and she stepped forward. He found it refreshing, to say the least, that she didn't seem to recognize him.

"I hope you'll be okay," she said.

"I'll be fine. I've got a hard head."

"I'm sorry this happened."

"It's certainly not your fault."

She tucked a roll of Mentos into his hand. "Take care of yourself."

Amused by the gesture, he said, "Don't put up with any crap from your customers."

Her dazzling smile once again caught the attention of his lower anatomy. "I'll try not to."

"See ya."

Olivia stood back and watched him go. Cole Langston, First Officer, his name tag had read. Why was that name so familiar? She kept her eyes trained on the stretcher until his thick, dark hair was out of sight. Only then did she take a deep breath to calm her emotions.

The whole thing had happened so fast. The obnoxious customer had thrown his money at her while arguing on a cell phone. He had turned around so quickly that she hadn't been able to warn the handsome pilot who intervened on her behalf.

The blow had knocked the pilot backward into the Redskins display, and while he'd lain there unconscious for what felt like an hour, Olivia had willed him to wake up. What she hadn't expected was the jolt of electricity she'd experienced when she placed her hands on his smooth, clean-shaven face. Bringing her hands up to cover her own burning face, Olivia caught the scent of his cologne clinging to her skin.

"Do you *know* who that was?" the manager asked in an excited whisper.

Olivia turned to him. "His name tag said Cole Langston."

"He's the one who landed the plane in a blizzard last winter after the captain keeled over from a heart attack."

"Oh! That's it!" The story came rushing back to Olivia. "Then he saved the captain by performing CPR while the plane sat on the runway."

"You got it. He's been all over the place since then. He was even on the cover of *People* and *Time*."

"No wonder he was so anxious to get out of here before the media showed up."

"He has to be getting sick of all the attention. Anyone would by now."

As she surveyed the mess in the store, Olivia pondered the jolt. Most likely it had been the result of shock and the emotion of the moment. What else could it be?

"The police want to take a statement from you," the manager said. "Do you feel up to it?"

"Of course."

By the time she finished with the police and helped to clean up the store, Olivia's eventful shift had ended. She gathered up her belongings, said good night to the manager, and walked through the concourse to the Metro station. She loved looking up at the night sky through the glass domes atop Reagan National Airport, and she appreciated the elaborate tile mosaics that decorated the marble floors. Every time she studied them, she found something she hadn't noticed before.

She rode the Metro's Yellow Line to Alexandria. The train rattled along on the track as she relived the crazy day that began with a ten o'clock class at American University in the District and ended with her statement to the police.

As the train came to a stop at the King Street station, she wondered how Cole was doing and if the hospital had kept him overnight. Tomorrow, she would check with his airline to see what she could find out about his trip to the hospital. That was the least she could do after what he had done for her. Maybe the airline would give her his address so she could drop him a thank-you note.

She walked home through the crispy fallen leaves that littered the sidewalk. Her plan to get in touch with Cole filled her with enthusiasm as she went up the stairs to the house she shared with her parents on Commonwealth Avenue. Digging her key from the depths of her tote, she let herself in.

"Mom?"

"Back here," her mother called from the kitchen.

Olivia hooked her tote over the banister and hung her coat in the front closet. She made her way to the back of the cluttered house to find her mother unloading a box at the kitchen table. Packing peanuts were sprinkled on the floor around her.

Olivia made an effort to hide her annoyance. "What've you got there?"

"Oh, just the *cutest* crystal mice for my collection." Mary Robison held up one of the tiny mice. "I saw them on QVC the other night and just *had* to have them."

Olivia cast her eyes around the disaster-area kitchen full of stuff her mother "just had to have," a lot of it sitting unused in its original packaging. For reasons she refused to discuss or acknowledge, Mary hadn't left her home since Olivia's high school graduation nine years earlier. But thanks to the Internet and TV shopping networks, Mary managed to keep up an active—and expensive—relationship with the outside world.

"How was your day?"

"Interesting." Olivia filled her mother in on what had happened at work.

Mary gasped. "He just hit him? Right in the face?"

"Knocked him out cold."

"I hope he was arrested."

Olivia reached for a bottle of water in the fridge. "He sure was. I had to give a statement to the police. It was wild."

"Maybe you shouldn't work there anymore." Mary nibbled on her thumbnail and cast a wary glance at her daughter. "It doesn't seem safe."

"It's fine. Nothing like that has ever happened before. Don't worry about it." She took a long drink of water. "So guess who the pilot was. Remember the one who landed the plane in the blizzard and then saved the captain who'd had a heart attack?"

"That was in the paper. Earlier this year?"

"Yep. It was all over the place." Now that she knew who he was, Olivia couldn't believe she hadn't recognized him and his name right away. Chalk it up to the stress of the incident in the store.

"He was a handsome devil, as I recall."

Olivia couldn't have said it better herself, but she wouldn't dare let her mother know that she'd been oddly attracted to him. She'd never hear the end of it.

"Uh-huh. Is Dad home?"

"Not yet. He volunteered to stay late hoping to make a sale."

Olivia's father was a car salesman and had been

successful at it until his dealership switched from Cadillacs to an import he despised. His sales numbers had plummeted, causing the dealer to threaten him with termination if he didn't swallow his opinions and sell some cars.

"You should let up on the shopping, Mom. We can't afford it right now."

"Oh, these little guys didn't cost anything at all." Mary held the glass mice up to the light. "Can you see the prism reflecting off them? I love that."

Olivia knew that disagreeing was pointless. "It's pretty. I'm going up to bed. It's been a long day."

"Good night, honey."

From the doorway, Olivia watched her mother unpack a second box of the crystal mice. Sometimes it was all Olivia could do not scream at her mother to get her head out of the clouds.

Chapter 2

OLIVIA RETRIEVED HER TOTE AND TRUDGED UP THE stairs to her room, which was marked by its lack of clutter.

A white eyelet duvet she had found on the clearance rack at Macy's covered her double bed. The crystal jewelry box her parents had given her for her sixteenth birthday sat on the dresser next to three framed photos—her older brothers, who hadn't lived at home in years, her high school friends, and Olivia with her cousin and best friend, Jenny, before Jenny's wedding. Her cousin's blonde hair and hazel eyes were in stark contrast to Olivia's darker coloring, but there was a hint of family resemblance between them nonetheless.

Framed posters of places Olivia dreamed of visiting decorated the walls—Paris, London, New York, and San Francisco. Her easel was set up by the window in the corner. A TV and boom box occupied the other corner.

The room was the one place in the messy house where Olivia could relax, study, draw, and paint in peace. She had resisted her mother's many attempts to jazz up the space. Mary's obsessive need to surround herself with stuff had made a less-is-more neat freak out of her daughter. Olivia dreamed of the day when she would finally finish school, get a better job, and move into a place of her own. That day seemed light-years away, though, as she chipped away at school a class or two at a time.

Since her parents couldn't afford to help with tuition, Olivia was muddling through with a small scholarship and what she made pulling long shifts at the airport. She could probably make more money in a different job, but she loved the atmosphere at the airport, the excitement of travelers on their way to exotic places Olivia could only dream of visiting, and the opportunities to sketch a wide variety of people.

Her cell phone rang to the tune of "Ode to Joy," and Olivia dug it out of her tote bag. She wasn't surprised to see Jenny's number on the caller ID, since they talked most nights at ten o'clock.

"Hey." Olivia flopped on her bed to settle in for a chat. "What's up?"

"Ugh," Jenny sighed. "Billy's cutting teeth, and he's miserable. Of course that means we are, too. Will just went out with orders to bring back the biggest bottle of wine he can find. I've earned it today."

"Poor Billy," Olivia said. "I hate that he's hurting."

"So do I. The drool is irritating his skin, and he's chewing on his fingers. He's a mess."

"It's a good thing we can't remember getting teeth, huh?"

"No kidding. I hope Will gets back with that wine—and soon."

Olivia laughed. "Motherhood is turning you into a lush."

"A lush and a loony. Tell me something from the outside world. Any tidbit will do."

Olivia relayed the story of the famous pilot who had come to her rescue.

"*Oh*," Jenny sighed. "That's *so* romantic. Your very own knight in shining armor—and he's already a national hero."

"*Puleeze*," Olivia said. "Only you could find romance in a punch to the face."

"Wouldn't that be something? If you could say you met your husband after he took a punch for you?"

"*Husband*? You're a freak—you know that? A total freak."

"Don't tell me it can't happen. Your cousin on your mother's side, Juliana—didn't she meet her husband in an airport?"

"That was different. They sat together on a flight."

"Let's talk about the important stuff. Is he as sexy as he looked in all the pictures?"

Afraid to encourage her cousin, Olivia hesitated. "I guess."

"Either he was sexy or he wasn't. Which is it?"

"He was sexy enough." To-die-for gorgeous was more like it, but there was no way she was telling Jenny that—not when she already had Olivia married to the guy. "It was hard to tell with one side of his face swelling up and turning purple."

Olivia wished she could tell Jenny about the jolt she had experienced when she touched him. Bringing her hand to her face, she was sad to realize the scent of his cologne had faded. She wanted to ask if Jenny had ever felt a jolt with Will, but she didn't want to add fuel to Jenny's romantic fire.

"Tell me *everything*, as if I've never seen a picture of him."

"He had dark hair."

"Dark brown or closer to black?"

"Black, I guess. It was thick and kind of wavy, but not curly."

"But you didn't notice or anything."

"Shut up."

Jenny laughed. "What color eyes?"

That Olivia could answer without hesitation. "Blue." Bright, vivid blue.

"Mmm, I love that combination. Jet-black hair, blue eyes, a pilot, *and* a hero—two times over now. I'm conjuring up Tom Cruise in *Top Gun* over here."

"Is Will back with that wine yet?"

"You're not getting rid of me that easily. Are you going to see him again?"

"Why would I? He came into the store, got punched in the face, and left on a stretcher. I'm sure he'd like to forget he was ever there."

"He'll be back," Jenny said.

"I don't think so. Anyway, I'm going in early tomorrow to see if I can find out if he's okay. I thought that was the least I could do."

"Oh, yes," Jenny agreed a little too enthusiastically. "The very least. It'll probably make the news. Check online in the morning."

"I'm hanging up now."

"Let me know what you find out."

"Good *night*, Jenny. Enjoy that wine."

"I plan to!"

Olivia closed her phone and shifted her eyes to the poster of San Francisco. The image of the Golden Gate Bridge with Alcatraz off in the distance was one of her favorites. If she could visit one place in the world, that's where she would go.

She allowed herself a few minutes to daydream before she sat up and got back to reality. Her life had no room for daydreams or romantic fantasies about pilots on white horses. Olivia had no patience for such foolishness.

—∞—

The next morning, she waited twenty minutes to speak to a supervisor at Capital Airlines. An early-morning scan of the news had yielded a brief mention of the incident but no information about his condition.

"I'm sorry," the woman said in a clipped tone, "but company policy prohibits us from giving out personal information about our employees, *especially* First Officer Langston."

Anticipating that possibility, Olivia handed the woman the note she had written to thank Cole for what he had done. "Can you get this to him?"

The harried woman took the envelope from Olivia. "I'll do my best."

Olivia watched her walk away, wondering if the note would ever find its way to him. "Oh well," she whispered. "I tried."

—∞—

As long as Cole didn't move—or breathe—he could stand the steady thrum of pain. Stretched out in a recliner, he'd discovered that even shifting to use the remote set off bongo drums in his skull that seemed to have a direct pipeline to his stomach. So he kept the TV turned off. With one eye swollen shut, he couldn't see well enough to watch anyway.

"Damn, man, this lasagna is *amazing*," Tucker, Cole's friend and neighbor, said as he plopped down on the sofa, his plate filled to overflowing with food that had flooded in from friends who'd heard about Cole's "accident." Cole didn't have the heart to tell Tuck that the smell made him nauseous. "Where'd it come from?"

"I think Debby made it." Their friend Jeff's wife was known for her Italian wizardry.

"I should've known," Tuck said between huge bites.

When he'd left the Navy after ten years of living and working in squadrons and wardrooms, Cole had worried about making friends in his new home city of Chicago. Through sheer luck, he had bought the place next door to Tucker's, launching a friendship that had led to a whole crowd of friends. Jeff, Tucker's best friend from high school, Jeff's wife, Debby, her sister, Denise, Denise's husband, Paul, and so on. In short order, Cole had found himself on basketball and softball teams, but he had resisted the bowling league, much to Tucker's dismay.

So when the gang heard that Cole was down for the count, they'd responded with enough food and drink to feed an army. Thankfully, Tucker and his endless appetite were around to put a dent in it, because Cole wasn't the slightest bit interested.

"I'm surprised you haven't been inundated with offers of sponge baths," Tucker said with a sly grin. Cole's success with the ladies, especially since "the incident" earlier in the year, was the stuff of legend with Tucker and the other guys.

"There've been a few."

"Like who?" Tucker pounced. At five-feet-ten inches and 220 pounds, Tucker liked to say he lived vicariously through Cole.

"Brenda called from Miami and offered to come up."

"Mmm, Brenda," Tucker said with a sigh. "I *like* Brenda."

If his head hadn't felt so explosive, Cole would've thrown something at Tucker. "What I want to know is how she even heard about it."

"Debby probably sent an email and copied her."

"Further proof that I need to keep my ladies away from you people."

"For the love of all that's holy, please don't do that. You know I have my needs. In fact, what I need right now is a slice of that chocolate cake."

"Have at it." Cole choked back a wave of nausea at the thought of cake. He shifted carefully and sucked in a sharp, deep breath to absorb the waves of pain in his head, face, and shoulder. He'd had concussions before but never one this bad.

"Jeez, you really look like crap," Tucker said when he returned with the cake. "Probably just as well that Brenda won't see you like this. It would break her heart."

"Very funny."

"So she really offered to come up?"

"Yeah."

"And you said *no*? Did you tell her I'd be happy to have her?"

"Your name was never mentioned."

"I bet you were lousy at sharing in the sandbox, too." Tucker stuffed a big chunk of cake into his face. "You must've taken a hell of a hit if you don't want any of your ladies around. I bet Heather would come running."

"She's dating Chuck. They're happy." At least Cole hoped so. He'd flown Heather to cancer treatments at Sloan-Kettering in New York for a year before she went into remission and immediately professed her undying love for him. Realizing she was hearing wedding bells, Cole—who was deathly afraid of the sound of ringing bells—had quickly extricated himself by fixing her up with his friend.

"That may be so, but she still goes all moony when you're around." Tucker batted his eyelashes at Cole.

"You're just jealous."

"You're goddamned right I am. I don't know how you do it, man. Even before your Superman act, your picture should've been next to the words 'chick magnet' in the dictionary. But now we mere mortals can only look on with envy."

In his right mind, Cole would've had a witty retort ready to shut Tucker up, but Cole with a headache the size of the Grand Canyon chose not to engage. "Is it time for more pain pills yet?"

Tucker consulted his watch. "Another hour."

Cole moaned.

"This is why I suggested a sponge bath to get your mind off your troubles."

"Are you offering?"

Tucker almost spit chocolate cake all over Cole's new leather sofa.

"Hell no! But if you're truly feeling desperate, I bet I could get Nutty Natasha over here in less than five minutes."

Cole didn't care about the pain when he sat right up and looked Tucker in the eye. "Don't you even *think* about it!" A surge of nausea took his breath away, and for a brief, heart-stopping moment, Cole thought he might throw up.

Tucker howled with laughter. "Relax, man. I'm just joshing ya."

"That is *so* not funny. I really hope Debby didn't copy her on the email."

"If she had, Nutty Natasha would've been here by now."

"No doubt." Cole grimaced at the thought of it. "I still haven't forgiven you guys for fixing me up with that wack job."

"You can't blame us. We had no idea she was certifiable."

"I can so blame you." Cole didn't even like to think about what he'd been through with that woman. It'd been almost enough to swear him off women forever.

Almost.

"So you're not going to let any of them come nurse you back to health? What about Diana in Phoenix? I bet she gives good sponge."

Cole couldn't help but laugh at that. "Don't make me laugh," he said wincing.

"Don't make *me* beg. I've been having naughty-nurse fantasies ever since you got smacked around."

"I did not get 'smacked around,' and p.s., you need to get your own girlfriend."

"Hello? You think I'm not trying? I mean, I ask you…what woman wouldn't want a piece of this?"

"I can't imagine."

"If you aren't having naughty-nurse fantasies of your own, I'm worried that you suffered permanent brain damage."

"No permanent damage. Don't worry. I'm just not in the mood."

Tucker stared at Cole as if he'd lost his mind. "*You*? Not in the mood for women? Since when?"

Since he'd met a woman named Olivia—and all the others had faded into the background in an instant. Cole couldn't stop thinking about her waterfall of silky dark hair, her searching brown eyes, her lovely smile, and the odd sensation that had coursed through him when she touched him.

"Earth to Cole." Tucker waved his hand back and forth in front of Cole's face. "What has you a million miles away?"

Unlike in the past, Cole had no desire to tell his friend about the woman he'd met. Tucker would assume she was just a flavor of the month and make a joke that would irritate Cole.

All he knew about Olivia was her first name and where she worked, but he wanted to know more. He wanted to rush back to Reagan and find out everything he could about her. That alone was so far out of character it should've scared him half to death. Instead, it filled him with excitement and anticipation.

"I'm dreaming of pain pills. Are you sure it's another hour?"

"You're down to fifty-two minutes."

"Fabulous," Cole groaned.

Chapter 3

"GOOD AFTERNOON ONCE AGAIN FROM THE COCKPIT. This is First Officer Cole Langston along with Captain Jake Garrison." Cole paused to accept the applause he'd received on every flight since returning to work after the incident. As Jake snickered at the outpouring from the cabin, Cole continued the announcement.

"We've begun our final approach for an on-time arrival at Reagan National Airport where it's sixty degrees with high, scattered clouds and an easterly wind blowing at ten knots. We know you have many choices in air travel, and we thank you for flying with Capital Airlines. We should have you at the gate in fifteen minutes. Flight attendants, please prepare the cabin for arrival."

Ten minutes later, Cole eased the nose of the Airbus A320 onto the runway and deployed the thrusters to slow the airplane. Having more than a hundred people along for the ride ramped up the anxiety, and any commercial pilot who claimed not to feel a hint of relief at delivering them safely was a damned liar. In the past, when it was just him and a plane, he'd been too busy being cocky to be anxious. Now the anxiety was part of the routine.

"Nice job," Jake said when they arrived at the gate. At fifty-two, Jake was a seasoned pilot Cole had flown with many times. Unlike some of the other Capital captains, Jake was generous about allowing his first officers to handle takeoffs and landings. "Looks like that concussion didn't have any lasting effects."

Cole grimaced. He had been the target of serious ribbing from the other pilots after his TKO two weeks earlier. Just when the uproar was finally dying down from the blizzard incident, along came Big Dude and a fist to the face.

"Fit as a fiddle," Cole said lightly. In truth, his shoulder was still bothering him. After two hours in the cockpit, he was ready to stretch it out before his next flight. He was ready for something else, too, but he'd spent all day trying not to get his hopes up in case he couldn't find her.

Thankfully, Jake was also generous about taking the shift with the deplaning passengers, knowing that if Cole went out there, they'd never get the plane cleared in time for the next flight. Since he'd returned to work, Cole had received hundreds of phone numbers folded into airplane cocktail napkins. Some of the other captains liked to send Cole out to greet his public just so they could bust his balls afterward.

"I'm going to take a walk," Cole said to Jake when they'd completed their post-flight paperwork.

"Go ahead. We've got forty minutes to kill."

"I'll be back."

"Don't get knocked out."

"Screw you."

Jake's laughter followed Cole out of the plane as he walked quickly up the Jetway into the crowded terminal. He had thought about this—about *her*—for two long weeks and couldn't wait another minute to return to the scene of the crime.

Keeping his head down in the hope that he wouldn't be recognized, he wove his way through a stream of people who seemed intent on keeping him from his destination. An airport transport vehicle beeped its way down the concourse and would have plowed into him if he hadn't leapt to the side when he did.

"Jesus," he muttered. "What *is it* with this place? Do I have a target painted on me or something?"

He looked up to find a young mother staring at him while holding her baby protectively, as if to keep the child safe from the crazy pilot who talked to himself. Then she let out a squeal when she suddenly recognized him.

"Oh! It's *you*!"

Cole offered her a sheepish grin as well as a brief "hello," and kept walking. The newsstand was halfway down the concourse, and as he approached, he was surprised to feel a surge of adrenaline and nerves similar to those he experienced at touchdown.

From outside the store, he saw that the Redskins' display had been returned to its position like nothing had ever happened. Cole absently reached for the shoulder that had connected with the display case and found it still tender to the touch. He took a deep breath and stepped inside. Unlike the last time, there was no line, and the woman working behind the counter was under no duress. She also wasn't Olivia.

The intense disappointment surprised him. *What did I expect? That she'd be exactly where I saw her two weeks ago? Well, yeah...*

"Um, excuse me."

"May I help you?" The clerk was tiny, of Indian descent, and spoke with a charming accent.

"I'm looking for someone who works here. Her name is Olivia."

"I don't know an Olivia. I'm sorry."

"But she was here…" He swept a hand through his hair and looked around the store as if he hoped to find her hiding behind one of the displays. "Two weeks ago. Right here. You're sure?"

Nodding, she studied him. "Someone important?"

He shook his head, thanked her, and turned to leave the store. His stride lost its purpose as he wandered into the main terminal, thinking he might find her at one of the other newsstands. He checked two more but didn't ask for her at either, figuring he would try again the next time he was at Reagan.

Dejected and more disappointed than he'd been in a long time, he started back to the security line. A crowd in one of the waiting areas caught his attention. Since he still had half an hour, he decided to check it out. Over the shoulder of the man in front of him, Cole watched a young woman's hand fly over a sketch pad, perfectly capturing the mischievous expressions of the two boys posing for her.

"Wow, she's so good," a woman whispered reverently.

The artist's long, dark hair was held back in a high ponytail, and something about the curve of her neck was familiar. Cole skirted the edge of the crowd to get a better view.

She looked up at her subjects and made eye contact with Cole. Her mouth formed an O.

His heart tripped with excitement. She was even more strikingly beautiful than he remembered.

"Can we see it yet?" one of the boys asked.

Clearly thrown off by Cole's reappearance, Olivia pulled her eyes off him and returned her attention to the children.

"Almost done," she said. She didn't look at Cole again as she put the finishing touches on the drawing and tore the page out of her pad.

"You totally captured them," the boys' astounded mother said. "You have to let me give you something for this."

"No need. It was my pleasure."

"You're very talented."

Olivia shrugged modestly. "They're cute kids. Thanks for letting me draw them."

"Thank *you*."

The crowd dispersed, and Cole sat down next to her.

"You're an artist," he said, and then felt like a fool for stating the obvious.

"I dabble."

"That was a whole lot more than a dabble."

"It's a hobby."

"I looked for you at the store, but the woman who was working didn't know you."

Olivia's cheeks flooded with color, which he found utterly charming. "I was filling in there, the day we... met. I usually work at that one." She gestured to the store behind them.

"Ah, no wonder they didn't know you."

"It's a big company. So how are you?"

"I'm good. All recovered and back in the air as of today."

"Did you get my note?"

"What note?"

She sighed. "I wondered if it would ever get to you.

The day after, I tried to find out how you were, but your airline wouldn't tell me anything and there wasn't much in the paper. So I gave them a note thanking you for what you did and asked them to get it to you."

Cole fought to hide his disappointment. He would've liked to have gotten that note. He would've liked that very much.

"Sorry, I didn't get it. I refused all requests for interviews this time. Restarting the media firestorm wasn't on my to-do list."

She flashed a small smile that was not quite the dazzling event he remembered from the store, but it stirred him nonetheless.

"What did it say?"

"Um, just thank you for what you did, and I hoped you were feeling okay."

"I got an unexpected two-week vacation out of it."

"Something tells me you didn't enjoy that as much as most people would."

"I love to fly. Being grounded never sits well with me."

She shook her head with dismay. "I'm sorry."

"Why?" he asked, smiling. "You didn't punch me." She blushed again, and Cole couldn't take his eyes off her. "Can I buy you a cup of coffee?"

She consulted her watch. "I have twenty minutes until I have to be back."

"So do I." He stood and held out a hand to help her up. "Shall we?"

He'd come back. Just like Jenny had said he would, and he'd come looking for her! This time, she felt the jolt just by glancing up to find him watching her. Walking to the coffee shop, Olivia stole glances at him and discovered he was even more gorgeous than she remembered. *What is it about a man in uniform? Tom Cruise has nothing on this guy!*

"You look a lot better than you did the last time I saw you," she said. The black eye was all but gone, except for a fading yellow bruise on his cheek.

"I imagine I do. It's been a long two weeks, that's for sure. I almost went stir crazy."

"Are you one of those people who don't know what to do with a vacation?" she asked as they helped themselves to coffee from the urns on the counter.

He loaded his with cream and sugar and paid for both. "Oh, I know what to do with a vacation—when I have time to plan one and when I'm allowed to do more than sit on my ass recovering from a concussion." Leaning in close to her, he added, "I've got to tell you, though, I *love* Dr. Phil. I'd never seen his show before."

She laughed at the goofy face he made and followed him to a table in the food court. "So what happened at the hospital that day? I've wondered how it went."

"I had a CT scan that showed a concussion, which I could've told them, and X-rays of my shoulder, which was just badly bruised. They kept me overnight for observation. The whole thing was a royal pain, especially that woman from the airline. Even though she kept the media away, she drove me totally nuts."

"What about the cops? Did you hear any more from them?"

"They called to say the guy had pleaded no contest to

felony assault. Because it was his first offense, they gave him two years' probation."

Olivia clucked with disapproval. "They should've thrown him in jail. He could've killed you."

"I didn't want to deal with testifying at a trial and all that, so I'm fine with it." He took a sip of his coffee and studied her.

Her face heated under his intense scrutiny. "What?" she finally asked.

"You're very beautiful, but I'm sure you hear that all the time."

Caught off guard by the compliment, she rolled her eyes. "Sure. Every day."

"You don't believe me."

Glancing up at him, she found his bright blue eyes trained on her.

He reached across the table for her hand. There it was again. The jolt. What *was* that?

"I'm not feeding you a line, Olivia. I mean it. I thought of you… when I was sitting on my butt at home. I was looking forward to seeing you today, and when I couldn't find you, I was really bummed."

Her tongue tied in knots, she focused on their joined hands. "Oh. You were?"

"Uh-huh." He checked his watch. "Damn. I have to be back in five minutes, and so do you." With what seemed to be great reluctance, he released her hand. "I'd like to see you again."

Surprised, she stared at him. "You would?"

His deep, rich laugh warmed her from head to toe. "When I came to that day and saw you there…" He shrugged. "I want to see you again. Is that possible?"

"I guess. Sure."

Cocking an amused eyebrow at her, he said, "You guess. Hmm. Okay." He stood up and tugged a pen out of his breast pocket. "I'll leave it up to you." Reaching for her hand, he wrote his phone number on her palm. "If you decide you can bear to see me again, give me a call."

By the time he'd pressed a kiss to the back of her hand, released it, and begun to walk away, Olivia had forgotten how to breathe.

He suddenly spun around. "Hey," he called to her. "What's your last name?"

Olivia untied her tongue to say, "Robison."

"Call me, Olivia Robison." He smiled, waved, and was sucked up by the crowd moving down the concourse.

"Was he talking to you?" a woman at the next table asked Olivia.

"Huh?"

"That was Cole Langston, right? Captain Incredible?"

Olivia wondered if he hated the nickname the grateful passengers had given him. "Uh-huh."

"Was he talking to you?"

Still trying to process what had just transpired, Olivia said, "Um, yes. He was."

"Well, I don't know about you, but if a guy that hot and famous said that to me, I'd already be on the phone."

She grabbed her bag and walked away before Olivia could reply.

Chapter 4

OLIVIA MADE IT TO NINE O'CLOCK BEFORE SHE CALLED Jenny.

"You're early," Jenny said, stifling a yawn.

"I know. Is Billy asleep?"

"Finally! We're just getting around to eating. What's up?"

"Call me when you're done."

"I can talk. Will's pretending not to watch the Nats game anyway."

"He came back."

"Who did?"

"Cole Langston." Olivia felt her face grow warm as she said the words.

Jenny shrieked. "I *told you* he would!"

"I hate to say it, but you were right."

"Did you run into him, or did he come looking for you?"

"He came looking."

"Oh, *wow*." The single word came out as a long, breathy sigh. "What did he say? How did he look?"

Olivia laughed. "He looked good. The bruises were almost all gone."

"Just good? Not great? Not fabulous? Not sexy?"

"All of the above," Olivia said softly.

Olivia had to hold the phone away from her ear when Jenny screamed. "*Oh my God! I knew it!*" To Will, she said, "Liv's hero pilot came back."

"Jenny! Stop! Don't tell him. He'll want to know everything."

"Oh. Um…"

"Of course you've already told him the whole story." Olivia didn't really care, and Jenny knew that. Will had the unique ability to be "one of the girls" with them without sacrificing his manhood.

"We're married. I had to tell him."

"No, you didn't."

"Forget about that, and tell me what he said!"

"He said… I'm very beautiful and he wants to see me again."

"Oh, Liv. *Oh*!"

"He took my hand, kissed it, wrote his phone number on my palm, and said it was up to me if I want to call him."

"That is, without a doubt, the most romantic thing I've ever heard." To Will, she added, "Hush! I'll tell you later." Returning to Olivia, she said, "So you're going to call him?"

"I don't know."

"Olivia! Are you kidding me? Why in the world wouldn't you?"

"I don't even know him. This whole thing is too weird for me. Besides, he must have a million women flocking around him."

"All right, you need to listen to me. Are you listening?"

"Yes," Olivia said, laughing.

"He sounds like a really nice guy. How many people in this day and age would stick up for a stranger the way he did for you?"

"Not many," Olivia conceded.

"Doesn't that and what he did for that other pilot in January tell you everything you need to know to make a phone call? I'm not telling you to have an affair with the guy. I'm just saying… call him. See where it goes."

"I don't know anything about him except he's an often heroic pilot. He could live in Alaska for all I know."

"I can't believe you haven't Googled the hell out of him by now. Are we really related?"

"Very funny. I haven't had time."

"What's the area code on his phone number?"

"Eight-four-seven."

"Already got it memorized?"

"No!" Olivia lied.

"It's Chicago."

"How do you know?"

"I've got my laptop right here, and unlike you, I know how to use Google."

"He's older than me."

"So?"

"And he's…"

"What?"

"Accomplished. Hugely accomplished. I can see that just by the way he carries himself."

"And so you think you're not good enough for him? That's crazy. You've gotten yourself three-quarters of the way through school with no help from anyone. You have no reason to feel inferior to him."

"He's been places, done things… Hell, everyone in America knows who he is. How do I compete with that?"

Jenny sighed. "Don't do this, Liv. It's a phone call."

"There's a jolt."

"A jolt? What're you talking about now?"

"I feel a jolt… of something… when he touches me."

Jenny went silent.

"Jen?"

"Call him. Right now. Tonight."

"I'm too nervous."

"Are your palms so sweaty the phone number is smudging?" Jenny asked, alarmed.

Olivia laughed. "I wrote it down."

"Oh," Jenny said with a sigh of relief. "That's good. If I were you, I'd never wash that hand again."

Olivia would never admit to having had that very thought. "Too late."

"You have to call him. Can you imagine if you don't? You'll wonder for the rest of your life what would've happened if you had."

"I hate when you get all logical on me. I like you better when your head's in the clouds."

"Hey! I resemble that remark!"

Olivia laughed at Jenny's foolishness.

"I'm going so you can call him, and the minute you hang up with him, you'd better call me."

"I'm not calling you back tonight."

"Yes, you are."

"Honestly! Were you always such a pain in the ass?"

"All my life and you know it. That's why you love me. Hanging up. Call me back."

Olivia left the phone on her bed and got up to pace the small room. It wasn't that she didn't want to call him. No. She *wanted* to call him. Badly. But a guy like him could have any girl he wanted—and probably had them lined up hoping to get a scrap of his attention.

What could he possibly want with her, a woman with precious little experience with men, when he had willing women throwing themselves at him? She had stayed with two past boyfriends far longer than she should have, and since she broke up with the more recent one, she had dated only sporadically—and certainly not anyone like Cole Langston.

But he had seemed so… sincere. That was the only word she could think of.

She stared at the phone on the bed.

"Oh, what the hell."

Before she could lose her nerve, she grabbed the phone and dialed the number she had already committed to memory. Her heart pounded while she waited for him to answer.

"Hello?"

Suddenly frozen, Olivia couldn't think, talk, or breathe.

"*Hello?*"

"This is Olivia." She cleared her throat. "Robison."

"Olivia." She heard the smile in his voice. "Are you crank calling me?"

"No!" she said, horrified. "That wasn't my intention anyway."

"What was your intention?"

"I have absolutely no idea." His laugh was so sexy that she dissolved onto the bed. "Where are you right now?"

"Driving home from the airport."

"Where's home?"

"Just north of O'Hare in Des Plaines. Outside Chicago."

"Did you grow up there?"

"Nope. Lafayette, Indiana. How about you?"

"Right here in Alexandria."

"I love the D.C. area. I still remember the first time I was ever there for our senior trip in high school."

"I love the city, too. I spend as much time as I can there."

"So how was the rest of your day?"

"Oh, you know… same old, same old. Nothing as exciting as yours, I'm sure."

"Why do you assume that?"

"Well, flying planes has to be more exciting than scanning candy bars and magazines into a computer."

"Can I ask you something, and will you promise not to be offended?"

"I guess so."

"When you can draw the way you do, what are you doing working as a clerk in a store?"

She didn't want to be offended. Really she didn't.

"Olivia?"

"I work there because I need the money. For school."

"Art school, I hope."

"Business school."

"Why?"

"Because someday I'd like to make some real money."

"Olivia, that woman in the airport today would've paid you hundreds of dollars for that portrait you did of her kids."

Olivia scoffed. "No way."

"Wanna bet?"

"What do you mean?"

"The next time I come to DCA," he said, using the airport's call letters, "we'll find a family for you to draw. When you're done, we'll ask the parents how much they'd pay for it."

"That's crazy."

"What's crazy is you not knowing how exceptionally talented you are."

She hesitated, debated, and decided. "My mother calls them doodles. Olivia's doodles."

"They're so much more than that."

"I'd like to draw you," she confessed. "You have a great face. Good bone structure."

"Is that like saying a girl has a nice personality?" he asked with laughter in his voice.

Olivia's face burned with embarrassment. "I'm sorry. I didn't mean to insult you."

"You didn't. I'm flattered you want to draw me."

She didn't mention that she already had.

"I want to see more of your work."

"Really?"

"Yes, really. I'll be back on Friday. Could I see it then?"

Touched by his interest, she rested a hand on her chest to contain her galloping heart. "Sure. If you want to."

"I want to. How about dinner? I get in at eight, and I'm there overnight."

"Dinner."

"You know, the meal that comes at the end of the day?"

"Very funny."

"Yes, you are. So are you free?"

"I get off work at seven."

"Do you mind killing an hour?"

"No, that's fine."

"How's the Sam Adams place at eight?"

She swallowed hard. This definitely counted as a date. "Good. I'll meet you there?"

"As soon as I can get there. And Olivia?"

"Yeah?"

"I *will* be there. I promise."

"Okay." After a pause, she said, "Can I ask you something?"

"Anything you want."

"How old are you?"

"I just turned thirty-six."

"Oh."

"Is that a problem?"

"I don't know."

"How old are you?"

"I just turned twenty-seven."

"Well, I can see why you would think that's a problem, you know, with me being so much older and wiser than you. Yes, that would definitely put you at a disadvantage."

She couldn't contain a ripple of laughter.

"I like the sound of that."

"What?"

"You. Laughing. You're very serious most of the time, aren't you?"

That he had summed her up so easily, so effortlessly, was unnerving.

"I guess I am."

"Then I'll have to keep you laughing."

"Cole?"

"That's the first time you've called me by name."

"Is it?"

"Uh-huh. What were you going to say?"

"I was just going to ask you… What is this, exactly, that we're doing here?"

"I have no idea," he said, laughing softly, "but I'd like to find out—that is, if you aren't too put off by my advanced age."

"I'm not if you're not."

"No worries on my end. So what do you think? Should we find out what this is? Together?"

Her heart stuttered. This time he had caused the jolt with just the soft cadence of his voice. If she hadn't been so busy trying to breathe, she would've been petrified.

"Yes," she managed to say. "I think we should."

"Good. Friday at eight then?"

"I'll be there."

"Olivia?"

"Yes?"

"I'm really glad I got knocked out in your store."

She laughed—again. "So am I."

"See you soon."

When she called Jenny back, there was more shrieking. At one point, Olivia wondered if her cousin had hyperventilated.

"Take a breath, Jen."

"This is so far beyond cool! We have to go shopping. Tomorrow, we're going shopping."

"For what?"

"You need something new for a date like this. It's required."

"All right, if you insist. Pentagon City?"

"Works for me. I'll make sure Will gets home early to watch Billy. So have you drawn him yet?"

"Maybe."

"I'll need you to bring it."

Olivia sighed.

"What's wrong?"

"It's just…"

"What, Livvie?"

"Scary. I like him. I don't even know him, and I like him. A lot. There was something about him, right from the beginning. Even when he was out cold on the floor, there was something."

"Don't get ahead of yourself. Just think about Friday. The rest will take care of itself."

"Good plan."

Chapter 5

FRIDAY DRAGGED. EVERY TIME OLIVIA GLANCED AT the clock only five minutes had passed. From inside the store, she watched the sky grow dark and stormy. *Perfect!* She wondered if his flight would be delayed—or worse yet, canceled—and wished she had thought to get the flight number from him so she could check.

Oh, well. I guess I'll see if he shows up. He'd call me if he's not coming, wouldn't he? Ugh! Stop thinking about it!

By seven o'clock, she was exhausted from waiting and worrying. Lightning streaked through the sky as she left work and went to the restroom to change into the simple black cocktail dress Jenny had picked out for her. The silk dress was understated yet classy, but the moment Olivia stepped out of the stall to check her appearance in the mirror, she panicked. It was all wrong for dinner at the airport. Far too much skin and cleavage showed.

Unless he's delayed, he'll be here in just over an hour. I can't wear the polo shirt and khakis I wore to work, but I can't wear this either! Why do I let Jenny get involved in these things? When will I ever learn?

She was on the verge of a complete, deodorant-failure meltdown when an elderly woman stepped up to the sink next to her.

"That's a lovely dress," the woman said as she washed her hands.

"Do you think so? I'm having dinner with someone I just met, and it's way too much for that—"

The older woman rested her hand on Olivia's forearm. "Your young man will be dazzled."

"He will?" Olivia wasn't sure how she felt about Cole being dazzled by her.

The woman nodded.

"Thank you." Olivia exhaled a long, deep breath. "I was having a fit."

The woman smiled at Olivia. "Have a wonderful evening."

She left the restroom, and Olivia brushed her long, dark hair until it fell in soft, shiny waves down her back. She applied mascara and lip gloss, and slid on the heels Jenny had loaned her. Tucking her work clothes into her tote, Olivia checked her watch and discovered she still had half an hour to kill. She pulled her sketch pad from her bag and went to check the weather and find some subjects.

Through one of the big windows she saw light rain falling, but the thunder and lightning had moved on. A mother and baby provided the perfect distraction and helped to calm Olivia's out-of-control nerves. She couldn't remember ever being this nervous before a date. At eight o'clock, she put away her pad and ran her fingers through her hair one last time before setting out for the Sam Adams Brewhouse.

On the way, she checked the inbound flights monitor and learned that two of the four Capital flights scheduled to land on or around eight o'clock were delayed. Since she had no way to know if one of them was Cole's, she continued on to the restaurant and found a place off to the side of the main entrance where she could watch for him without being in the way.

She checked her cell phone at eight ten to see if he had called. Nothing. By eight twenty, she figured he wasn't coming. Suddenly, all her nervousness collapsed into disappointment. Nothing exciting ever happened to her, and this, while stressful and nerve-wracking, had been exciting. Leaving her post outside the restaurant, she set off for the Metro station and was about to run her ticket through the turnstile when her cell phone rang.

"Hey, it's me. I'm so sorry I'm late. We were delayed by the weather. I have four minutes of paperwork to do, and then I'll be there, okay?"

Her heart raced at the sound of his voice. "Sure. That's fine."

"Next time I'll have to remember to give you the flight number so you'll know if I'm running late."

Next time? The cloud of disappointment lifted, and the excitement returned. "I'll see you in a few," she said.

"Can't wait."

She tossed the phone into her tote and turned around. As she approached the restaurant, he came jogging into the terminal from the gate, dragging a rolling suitcase behind him. He stopped short when he caught sight of her, and his mouth fell open. With his eyes fixed on her, he took the last few steps.

"You look… *wow*."

She shrugged with embarrassment. "It's a bit much for dinner at the airport, but my cousin made me—"

"Tell your cousin she has great taste."

"I can't. It'll go straight to her head."

He smiled and tucked a strand of hair behind her ear, the tender gesture rendering her breathless. "Sorry to make you wait. I'd planned to get changed…"

"You're fine the way you are," she said softly.

"I'm nervous." He seemed amazed and baffled by the situation. "More nervous than I've been in a long time."

His confession filled her with relief. "So am I."

He released the suitcase handle and held out his arms to her.

With only the briefest of hesitations she stepped toward him and sighed when his arms closed around her. The cologne she remembered from the day in the store filled her senses. Tentatively, she let her arms encircle him, and they stood like that for a long time as the airport hustled and bustled around them.

"How are the nerves?" he asked.

"Better. How about you?"

"Much better. Are you hungry?"

She nodded.

"I'm starving." He seemed reluctant to let her go and kept an arm around her as he reached for his bag and led her into the restaurant.

Seated by a window that overlooked the runway, he ordered a beer and a glass of white wine for her.

"Dicey ride tonight." He stretched the kinks out of his neck. "Really bumpy."

"Where were you coming from?"

"Atlanta. We flew through all the crap you had earlier."

"Is that scary? When it's bumpy?"

"Not for us, but the passengers don't like it. Freaks them out."

"I don't think I'd like it, either."

He crooked an eyebrow in amusement. "Never been on a bumpy flight?"

She hesitated before she said, "I've never been on *any* flight."

The expression on his face was priceless. "What do you mean by that?"

"Just what I said." She smiled at his amazement. "I've never been on an airplane." She picked up the menu and got busy studying it, aware that he was still staring at her.

"There's no way you've never been on a plane."

"If you say so."

"So, by 'never' you mean—"

"*Never*. I've never flown in a plane, a helicopter, a hot-air balloon, a blimp, or anything else that goes up in the sky."

He sat back in his chair. "Well, we're just going to have to fix that."

Wary, she looked at him over her menu. "Define 'fix.'"

"I'm going to take you flying. Soon." He picked up his menu. "I feel like a steak. What about you?"

Over dinner, she learned his mother had died of cancer almost two years earlier, but because he didn't seem to want to talk about it, she didn't press him for details. She heard about his younger brother and sister, both of whom were married and living near their father in Lafayette, Indiana. What she really wanted him to tell her was the story of his heroic action on the January flight, but she figured he was probably sick of talking about it so she refrained from asking.

"What do they do? Your brother and sister?"

"My brother is a supervisor at the Subaru plant, and my sister works for Eli Lilly, the pharmaceutical company. They both went to Purdue, which is right in West Lafayette."

"Where did you go?"

After a long drink of his beer, he said, "Embry-Riddle in Florida for aeronautical engineering."

"I don't even know what that is," she said with a laugh.

"It's the science of designing planes that stay in the air." The simplistic explanation amused her. "Did you always want to fly?"

"For as long as I can remember. There was a general aviation field about a mile down the road from where we grew up. I was about eight when I started riding my bike over there every day after school. I used to sweep the floors in the hangar for free just so they'd let me hang out."

She smiled at the picture he painted of the eager young boy who lived for airplanes.

"When I was fourteen, my parents finally gave in and let me take lessons from the guy who owned the field. I soloed on my sixteenth birthday, and I've been flying ever since. In fact, I had my pilot's license before my driver's license."

"Not many people can say that. How long have you been with Capital?"

"Just over three years. I did ten years in the Navy before that, flying fighter jets, which was really fun."

Olivia was mesmerized listening to him. He had led an exciting life, full of the kind of adventure she craved. "Were you ever in combat?"

"When I was stationed on the John F. Kennedy—that's an aircraft carrier—I flew missions into Iraq enforcing the no-fly zone between the two wars. I got shot at a couple of times but never had any serious close calls."

"What's that like? Flying from a ship?"

"There's nothing more dangerous—or thrilling—than landing a jet on a carrier," he said with a cocky grin. "Big plane aiming at a small, rolling target. It gets the blood pumping, that's for sure."

"And of course you loved the rush," she said with a smile.

"Hell yeah. I miss it."

"Why did you leave the Navy?"

He sighed. "I didn't want to, especially since we were at war. But the Navy was phasing out my program, and I was anxious to get into the private sector. In the airlines, everything is based on seniority. I was already thirty-two, and we face mandatory retirement at sixty-five. If I did another tour in the Navy, I'd be getting a really late start on the second career. It was a tough decision, believe me."

"I can imagine."

"There was this young petty officer on my flight crew, he was maybe nineteen or twenty, and he knew I was struggling with the decision to get out. One day he said, 'Commander, you've done ten years more than most people will ever do. You don't owe your country anything. Go on home now.' It was… freeing to know he felt that way."

"He gave you permission."

"Exactly," he said, seeming pleased that she understood.

"Did you go work for Capital right away?"

"It took a few months to hammer out the details, which was frustrating because I wasn't flying much while I waited to start. But it was worth the wait. I like the job. They're a real pilot-friendly airline—a nice company to work for."

"You were so lucky to know what you wanted to do from such a young age."

"It's my passion, that's for sure." His face lifted into a sexy half grin that melted her bones. "So you've asked me about everything except the elephant in the room."

Olivia felt her face get warm. She didn't dare let on that she'd spent an entire evening online reading every word she could find about what had happened—including his brief but reportedly passionate relationship with one of the passengers. The pictures of him with the gorgeous redhead he'd broken up with months ago had made Olivia insanely and irrationally jealous.

"I figured you'd tell me if you wanted to."

"Well, isn't that refreshing. Everyone I've met since it happened has expected a grand retelling of the story."

"You don't have to…"

He shrugged. "I don't mind." Running his fingers through his hair and leaving it nicely tousled, he leaned his elbows on the table. "We were on final approach to LaGuardia in a nasty snowstorm. The ceiling had dropped much faster than they'd forecasted so we were coming in IFR—meaning we were flying totally reliant on the instruments because we had zero visibility."

Olivia shuddered. "I can't imagine that."

"It's fun," he said with a big grin.

"You have a queer sense of fun."

"So I've been told." He took a sip from his beer. "Anyway, we're on final approach, it's snowing like a bastard, and all of a sudden, the captain just gasps and goes limp in his seat."

"What did you do?"

"I shook him and called his name, but he didn't respond. At that point, my primary concern was getting that plane full of people on the ground and then keeping it from skidding off the runway in the snow."

Filled with anxiety on his behalf, Olivia tried to imagine the situation. "It must've been awful not to be able to do anything for him."

Cole's jaw tightened. "It was. He's a great guy. A good friend." He ran a finger through the condensation on his glass. "Anyway, I got the plane down and stopped right on the taxiway, called for help, dragged him out of the seat, and started CPR on the floor."

"The passengers had no idea any of this was going on?"

"Not until I had to open the cockpit door so I'd have enough room to stretch him out."

"You must've been freaking."

"To tell you the truth, I barely remember. It all happened so fast. By the time the paramedics got to us, the captain's heart had started beating again, and he was breathing."

"That's so awesome," Olivia said with genuine admiration. "How'd you end up all over the news?"

He laughed at that. "Just my luck that it was a slow news week. If Iran had decided to shoot off one of its missiles that day, we wouldn't be having this conversation."

"Oh, I bet you still would've gotten plenty of

attention. The handsome, heroic pilot saves the day and saves a life. It's made for Hollywood."

"You think I'm handsome, huh?"

"Well, you're not *ugly*."

He hooted with laughter. "Gee, thanks."

"Sorry, couldn't resist," she said with a giggle. "So you became an instant celebrity."

"Which was *not* what I wanted. Of course, it didn't help when Bob Greenman went on the *Today* show and told them what a hero I was and how I'd saved his life. He even trotted out the grandchildren to thank me for saving their Papa."

Olivia laughed at his dismay.

"Then they interviewed the passengers who'd coined the revolting Captain Incredible nickname." He shuddered as Olivia continued to laugh. "The end result was months on the dog-and-pony circuit, thanks to the Capital PR people who couldn't resist the opportunity to extol the virtues of their highly trained staff."

"You loved it."

"No, my *father* loved it. He even made a scrapbook of all the coverage. I just tolerated it. For a week or two, it was kind of fun, especially when the president invited me to be in the audience for the State of the Union speech. That was wild."

"Was it so cool to meet the president?"

"It was amazing. Truly. After that, though, it all got *really* tedious, and all I cared about was getting back to flying. In fact, I hope I just told 'the story' for the very last time."

"Thank you for telling me, and for what it's worth, I'm very proud of you."

He seemed taken aback and pleased by the compliment. "It's worth a lot," he said, clearing his throat. "Anyway, enough about me and my passion. Let's talk about you and yours."

"I don't know if I'd call it that. It's just something I do."

"Why do you make light of such an amazing talent?"

His eyes were intense and fixed on her. Olivia found she couldn't look away.

"I don't know," she finally said. "It's just a hobby."

"Did you bring some of your work with you?"

She nodded, reached for her bag, and withdrew her sketch pad.

He took it from her, brushed the crumbs off the table that had been cleared by the busboy, and flipped the pad open.

Olivia watched as he studied each page for what seemed like a full minute before he moved to the next one.

"These are incredible, Olivia. I feel like I know these people. You don't just capture how they look. You get to their spirit, the thing that makes them *them*."

Nothing he could've said would have meant more to her.

He was quiet as he examined the other drawings— until he reached the one she had done of him after their coffee date.

"Wow," he said, laughing. "Do I really come across that confident and cocky?"

"I just draw what I see," she joked.

"My father would love this. He's always teasing me about being cocky."

Reaching across the table, she eased the page out of the pad, rolled it up, and handed it to him. "Give it to him."

"Only if you sign it," he said with a delighted smile. He took a pen from his shirt pocket and passed it to her. "I want him to know he's getting an Olivia Robison original. It'll be worth a fortune someday."

Touched by his faith in her, Olivia wrote her name in the corner. "I've never signed one before," she said as she gave it back to him.

"That's a damned shame. You should take credit for every one of them."

Their waitress came by the table to see if they wanted coffee or dessert.

"Olivia?"

"No, thank you."

"Just the check, please," Cole said, glancing at his watch. "Damn it."

"Are you late for another date?" she teased.

"Nope, but I'm about to turn into a pumpkin. I have to fly at eight in the morning, and I need to go to bed. The pesky FAA requires us to get a good night's sleep." He reached across the table for her hand.

Surprised and unnerved by the jolt, Olivia stared at their joined hands.

"I'm not ready," he said.

She looked up to meet his intense gaze. "For what?"

"For our date to be over. I looked forward to it all week."

"So did I."

Neither of them looked away for a long, breathless moment that was interrupted only when the waitress arrived with their check.

Cole opened it, and his face went blank.

"What's wrong?"

He crumpled up a piece of paper and tossed it on the table. "Nothing."

Olivia reached for the paper, unrolled it, and couldn't believe that the waitress had slipped him her number along with the check.

"Olivia—"

"Does this happen often?"

His face was set in an unreadable expression. "It's let up some, but I'm still astounded by how rude people can be. I'm clearly here on a date. Does she honestly think I'm going to call her?"

"I can't imagine what she's thinking."

"At least she didn't fake a heart attack hoping I'd give her mouth to mouth."

Olivia stared at him, aghast. "Has that really happened?"

"Three times so far."

"Unbelievable."

He drew an American Express gold card from his wallet. "Let me chip in."

"No way. I asked you."

She propped her chin on her fist and studied him. "So if I ask you somewhere, I can pay?"

His grin lit up his face. "Does that mean I can look forward to you asking me out?"

"Maybe."

"We'll negotiate terms if and when you ask."

"Where are you staying?"

"The Sheraton Old Town. The airline has a deal with them, so we always stay there."

"That's right down the road from where I live."

He got up and reached for her hand. "Share a cab?"

"I don't normally do cabs, but since you're pressed for time I'll make an exception." She curled her hand around his and followed him from the restaurant. "Oh, look, honeymooners," she whispered, nodding at a couple across the corridor.

"How do you know?"

"Well, I don't know for *sure*, but I love making up stories for the people I see in the airport."

He released her hand and put an arm around her, drawing her close to him. With his lips against her ear, he said, "What would you guess about us?"

His nearness made her lightheaded. "With you in uniform and pulling your suitcase, I'd say you picked me up in the bar and we're heading to your hotel."

Abruptly, he steered her away from the exit and up the escalator to the second floor, which was all but deserted late on that Friday night.

"Where are we going?"

"Since my hotel isn't an option—at least not tonight—we're going over here."

"Over here" was a dark corner that overlooked the well-lit runways. Across the Potomac, the U.S. Capitol building lit up the night sky.

"Pretty, isn't it?" he asked.

"I never get tired of looking at it."

"Neither do I."

But when she glanced up at him, his eyes were set on her, not the Capitol. And then his hands were cradling her face and his lips were gliding softly over hers. Any jolt she had felt before paled in comparison to what she experienced when his tongue traced her bottom lip. Her hands landed on his chest and then found his shoulders under his uniform coat.

As it was happening, Olivia told herself this was a moment to be remembered. No matter what happened— or didn't happen—between them, she would have this perfect kiss, this perfect moment.

She felt his hand encircle her neck as his other arm tightened around her.

His tongue nudged at her lips, and when she opened her mouth to welcome him, he groaned.

Never in her life had Olivia experienced a kiss quite like this—a kiss that made her want to tear off his clothes and have him. Right here. Right now. She whimpered under the weight of the need that blazed through her.

Misinterpreting her whimper as one of distress, he quickly pulled back from her.

She straightened him out by reaching for him to bring him back.

The second kiss was somehow more than the first. After several long, hot minutes, his fist tightened in her hair and his lips moved to her neck.

"Cole…" Her voice sounded huskier and deeper than usual.

He rolled her earlobe between his teeth. "Hmm?"

She trembled. "You have to go. The FAA, remember?"

"Never heard of 'em."

With a hand on his chest, she held him back. "Flying, eight o'clock. Ringing any bells?"

This time he whimpered as she took his hand and led him to the exit.

The moment they were in the backseat of the cab, he picked up where he'd left off in the terminal. His lips were soft, his tongue insistent, and Olivia gasped when his hand brushed against her breast.

All at once they seemed to realize they were on the verge of losing control in a cab. He wrapped his arms around her and held her tight against him for the remainder of the ride.

"After tomorrow, I'm off for eight days," he said. "I could catch a hop and come back for a couple of days next weekend—if you want me to."

"I want you to."

"Will you have to work?"

"I'll figure something out."

"Remember when you asked me what this is that we're doing?"

She nodded against his chest.

"I'm still not entirely sure, but whatever it is, I'm liking it."

Looking up at him, she said, "Me, too."

Keeping his eyes on hers, he leaned in for a soft, gentle kiss that packed a greater punch than any that had come before. "Olivia…"

"Here you are, folks," the driver said as he pulled up to Olivia's house on Commonwealth Avenue.

Reluctantly, she sat up and right away felt the loss of his embrace. "Thank you for dinner."

"Thank you for the drawing. My father will be thrilled." He reached for the door handle and stepped out to give her a hand. "I'll call you."

She nodded.

With a finger to her chin, he tipped her face up for one last kiss. He watched her go up the stairs and into the house before he got back in the cab.

Chapter 6

"DID HE KISS YOU?" JENNY ASKED THE NEXT MORNING.

Olivia yawned and turned over to hug her pillow. "Uh-huh." She held the phone away from her ear in anticipation of the shriek.

Jenny didn't disappoint.

"Do you think you could take it down a notch? I haven't had coffee yet. And why are you calling so early on a Saturday?"

"It's ten o'clock. That's noon in my world. So define 'kiss'—are we talking a peck or tongue and tonsils?"

"Option B."

"Shut up."

"Fine, I'm going back to sleep."

"Oh, no, you're not."

"*Jenny*. It's my day off. Give me a break, will you?"

"Not until I hear every detail of what happened last night."

Even though she wanted to still be sleeping, Olivia couldn't help but smile when she thought of the evening she had spent with Cole. She wondered where he was at that moment. His eight o'clock flight was long gone. To where, she had no idea.

"Olivia…"

"He liked the dress."

"I told you he would."

"It was too much for dinner at the airport, but he didn't seem to care."

"He was too busy sticking his tongue down your throat to care about what you were wearing."

"Stop. It wasn't like that."

"Then how was it?"

Olivia told her the whole story. When she finished, Jenny was silent.

"Hello? Still there?"

"If you aren't in love with him, I am."

"It was one date, Jenny," Olivia said with another big yawn. "Don't go there."

"He's the one. I know it."

"Oh, for crying out loud! You haven't even met him. How can you say that?" Olivia hated the crazy trip of excitement that rippled through her at the possibility that Jenny could be right. As if the thought hadn't already occurred to her.

"Just a feeling I have. This whole thing is so incredible. When can I meet him?"

"He's going to catch a flight back here next weekend when he's off. Maybe then."

"*He's flying here just to see you?*"

Olivia giggled at Jenny's reaction. "Yes."

"I'm *flipping out* over here!"

"No, really?"

"You guys can come here for dinner."

"I don't know if I'm ready to subject him to you."

"He may as well see what he's getting into right at the very beginning. I come with the package."

"That's true."

"Did you talk about what happened in January?"

"He told me all about it. He's gotten to the point where he doesn't like the attention anymore. You won't believe it, but the waitress actually slipped him her number with the check."

"You're kidding me!"

"I wish I was. He was super pissed."

"I can imagine." Jenny squealed again. "This is ab fab, Liv. I'm so excited for you."

"Don't get too excited. Who knows what's going to happen?"

"You're already thinking about how it's going to end, aren't you?"

"Not really."

"Don't, Liv. For once in your life, just run with it, will you? This could be something really great. Don't ruin it by anticipating disaster."

"I'm not exactly lucky in this department."

"You just hadn't met the right guy—until now."

"*Jenny!* You're going to jinx me. I've got to get going. I've got a paper due in my international business class next week."

"Yawn. You just put me to sleep."

Olivia laughed. "Cole thinks I should be doing something with my art." Using his name felt like an acknowledgement that he really existed, that he had managed to infiltrate her whole life in the course of one unforgettable evening.

"And *who* has been saying *that* for years?"

"*You*," Olivia said with a long-suffering sigh.

"He and I are going to get along just fine. Dinner. Next weekend. Have a good day!"

Olivia showered, got dressed in jeans and a sweater, and went downstairs to find her parents reading the *Washington Post* at the kitchen table.

"Morning, honey," her dad, Jerry, said.

"You were out late last night," Mary said.

"I had dinner with a friend after work. I told you I'd be late."

Without glancing up from the paper, Mary said, "Do you kiss all your *friends* like that?"

Olivia made an effort to keep her anger in check. She couldn't *wait* to get her own place.

"Nothing you want to tell us?" Mary goaded.

"Nope," Olivia said as she poured coffee into a travel mug.

"Leave her alone, Mary," Jerry said.

Olivia sent him a grateful smile. "I'm going over to campus to work on my paper."

"Want a ride?" Jerry asked.

"Sure. That'd be great." Since she felt like she spent half her life on the Metro, the ride was more than welcome.

On the way into the city, Olivia took a moment to appreciate the clear autumn day, the bright blue, cloudless sky, and the colorful foliage. As they traveled parallel to the airport on Route 1, she watched a red-and-blue Capital Airlines plane take off. She couldn't believe Cole, the man who had kissed her senseless the night before, was capable of doing that, of steering an airplane into the heavens.

"Penny for your thoughts," her father said.

Olivia looked over at him and smiled. He was her anchor in the sea of madness that surrounded her mother. "Promising date last night."

"With?"

"A Capital pilot."

"Ah, no wonder why you've got your eyes glued to the action on the runway. How'd you meet him?"

Olivia told him about the fight in the store and what had transpired since then.

"Well, I'll be. So you like this guy."

She sighed. "Am I that obvious?"

"No, but I know my little girl."

"It's kind of scary how much I like him," she confessed. "I've only actually seen him three times, and he was out cold for a big part of the first one."

"The other two times must've been anticlimactic after that."

"Not really. He's very… dynamic. In fact, he's the pilot who landed the plane in the blizzard last winter and then saved the captain who'd had a heart attack."

"Is he now? I remember reading about that." He reached over to squeeze her hand. "Good for you, honey. You need to enjoy yourself more than you do. I hate that you have to work so much while you're in school. Things are starting to pick up some for me, so maybe in the next month or two, I'll be able to help you out."

"Don't worry about it, Dad. I'm doing all right." Left unspoken was the silent truth they both lived with but never discussed—if her mother would quit her obsessive shopping, he would be able to do a whole lot more for Olivia.

"I just wish you didn't have to do it all on your own. When the boys were in school, things were more flush, and I was able to help them."

"No one's keeping score. You've always been right there for me."

When Olivia was five, her mother had miscarried

twins late in her pregnancy. Something in Mary had come unglued in the aftermath of her loss, and years of therapy had failed to put her back together. Mary had slowly withdrawn from life, and without her father's steady presence, Olivia never would have survived growing up in that house. Every ounce of her energy was directed toward the day she would finally be able to move out.

"Can I ask you something?" Olivia asked hesitantly. They didn't talk about this. Ever.

"Sure you can."

"Do you ever think about leaving?"

"She's my wife, you know? Better or worse and all of that."

"You're a saint."

"Nah. You do what you gotta do. That's life."

"I guess." Olivia often wondered if the drama she'd grown up with had caused her to doubt that it was possible to ever be truly happy. She saw how happy Jenny and Will were and how delighted they were with their baby son. They gave her hope. But both of Olivia's brothers had failed marriages behind them, and she was wary enough to be afraid of the feelings Cole stirred in her. He made her want things she was better off not hoping for.

Her dad navigated Ward Circle and pulled into a parking lot by the library.

Olivia leaned over to kiss his cheek. "Thanks for the lift."

"My pleasure." He squeezed her hand one last time before he let her go. "Have some fun with this pilot of yours, Livvie. Don't be afraid to give it a shot. You never know what'll happen."

"You sound like Jenny," she said with a smile.

"My very wise niece knows a thing or two about love. Listen to her."

"She's already got me married to him."

Laughing, her dad left her with a wave, and she headed for Bender Library. She found a quiet corner on the third floor, took out her laptop and notes, and tried to focus on the International Monetary Fund. But thoughts of a dark-haired man with piercing blue eyes kept intruding.

Before she knew it, she was sketching prominent cheekbones, a straight nose, full lips, and the hint of cockiness that should have been off-putting—and would have been on most men—but only added to Cole's appeal.

As he came to life on the page, she was filled with yearning. For what exactly, she couldn't say. For anything other than what she had. She was tired of waiting for her life to begin and sick of being on her way to some far-off destination where all her problems would be solved. The harder she worked and the more she dreamed, the further away that destination seemed to be.

She hated business school. There. She'd finally admitted it. She hated the classes about things that didn't interest or matter to her, the pretentious students who talked about how much money they planned to make after they got their MBAs, and some of the professors who acted like they held the keys to success and would only give them to a lucky few.

Here she was, three-quarters of the way through college, working toward a degree she didn't want. The realization was devastating. What was she supposed to do? Quit? No way would she leave without a degree.

She couldn't let all the time and money she had invested go to waste.

All she could think about was Cole telling her she was exceptionally talented, that he felt he knew the people in her drawings. How had she gotten so far down a road she didn't want to be on? How could a man she had seen just three times finally make her realize that her art had value? Was it possible that if she followed her whimsical heart rather than her practical head she might get all the things she wanted without selling her soul to the devil in the process?

Touching the space bar on her computer, she clicked on AU's website and found the link for the studio art program. Glancing over her shoulder to make sure no one was looking, she felt her heart race like it might if she clicked on porn by mistake. As that thought made her giggle, the studio art page filled her screen. All along, she had known the program was there, but she hadn't paid much attention to it as she pursued the business degree.

She devoured the information on the program and then read about the Katzen Arts Center. The center's website declared, "The Katzen Arts Center stands as a clear statement to the community that at the heart of the city, there exists a place where the arts are honored as the heart of higher education. That place is American University."

Imagining herself a part of the art community at AU was overwhelming and exciting at the same time. Before she could lose her nerve, she sent an email to the contact person for the studio art program, requesting an appointment. After she sent the message, she dissolved into giddy laughter.

"I can't wait to tell Cole about this," she whispered.

Over the next few hours, she ground out the business paper while hoping he would call. She checked the phone twice to make sure she hadn't missed a call and then felt silly for caring so much. By six o'clock, the paper was done, and she gathered her stuff to leave.

Invigorated by the fresh air after being cooped up all day, she had almost reached the Metro station when her phone rang. Her excitement was dashed when she saw Jenny's number on the caller ID.

"Hey," Jenny said. "Did you finish the paper?"

"Just now."

"Want to come over? We're thinking about pizza."

Since she would rather hang out with Jenny and Will than go home, Olivia accepted the invitation.

"Give us a call when you're getting close to Franconia-Springfield, and one of us will come get you."

"Sounds good."

"So, um... did he call?" Jenny asked.

"Not yet."

"He will."

"I wish I could be so sure."

"He's probably busy with work. Don't get all mental over it."

"Who's mental? I wasn't even thinking about it until you asked."

Jenny howled. "Yeah, *right*!"

"I'll see you soon." Olivia hung up and put the phone away in her bag, telling herself that Jenny was right. Cole was working and didn't have time to call her—even between flights. He would call when he could.

But he didn't call that night or the next day.

By the time Sunday night rolled around, their date on Friday seemed like a lifetime ago, and she had given up on hoping she would hear from him. The waiting, the wondering, and the speculating about how she could have been so wrong about him had completely sucked the life out of her. She went to bed early but tossed and turned for a long time before drifting into restless sleep.

When the phone rang at eleven, she thought she was dreaming until the persistent tune of "Ode to Joy" finally woke her. She lunged for the phone and answered without checking the caller ID.

"I *knew* it was too late to call," Cole groaned. "I decided to risk it and woke you up."

Now fully awake and with every sense on high alert, Olivia pushed herself up to a sitting position and cleared the sleep from her throat. "No, it's fine. I'm usually up late."

"But not tonight?"

"I was tired."

"Sorry. And I'm sorry I haven't called before now. This weekend was insane."

"That's okay."

"Were you thinking I was one of those guys who says he's going to call and then doesn't?"

"Of course not."

He laughed softly. "Yes, you were."

"Maybe a little."

"I really am sorry. Some stuff happened this weekend. Well, anyway… it was nuts."

"Do you want to talk about it?"

"No, but thanks for asking. I'd much rather talk about you. What've you been up to?"

"Let's see, I wrote a very exciting paper on the International Monetary Fund, hung out with my cousin, looked into changing my major to art, and cleaned the house."

"Back up, back up. What was that about your major?"

She laughed at his reaction. "I was seeing if you were paying attention."

"I'm very definitely paying attention. Tell me."

"I decided to look into it. That's all."

"What brought this on?"

"It's just… what you said the other night about how you felt like you knew the people I'd drawn. No one's ever said anything like that before."

"Not even in high school? In art class?"

"I didn't show my stuff to anyone back then. That's a recent development."

"So no one had any idea just how good you are," he said, sounding incredulous.

"Except for my cousin, Jenny, and my dad. They've been saying for years that I'm good, but what you said got me thinking."

"Well, I'm glad I said something that got your attention. Are you really going to change your major?"

"I'm going in tomorrow afternoon to talk to the academic adviser in the studio art department."

"That's great, Olivia. That's exactly where you belong."

"The only bad thing is I'll probably have to spend *another* year in school. At the rate I'm going, I'll be lucky to get my degree by the time I'm forty."

"Once you get into a major you love, school will become much less of a chore. I promise."

"I hope you're right, because I'm not sure how much more of the International Monetary Fund I can take."

"That sounds truly dreadful."

"I hate it. Do you know how liberating it is to finally admit that? I *hate* it."

"We'll have to celebrate this epiphany of yours next weekend."

Her stomach fluttered with nerves and anticipation. "I'd love to," she said softly.

"I was going to take a flight from O'Hare on Friday that would get me there around six-thirty. Does that sound okay?"

"I get off work at seven, so I hope you don't mind waiting a half hour."

"I don't mind. I booked a room at the Sheraton, since it's close to your house." When Olivia didn't say anything right away, he asked, "Is this too much for you?"

"No."

"Then what is it? Something's wrong."

"Nothing's wrong."

"Olivia, talk to me," he said in a gentle, cajoling tone. "Come on."

"I'm kind of freaking out," she confessed.

"Why?"

"This whole thing is just…"

"Intense?"

"Yes." That was exactly the word she would've used.

"Is that bad?"

"It would be if you were to suddenly lose interest." She cringed, hating how needy that made her sound.

"Or if you did."

"I won't."

"Then why do you think I would?"

"I can't help but wonder what a pilot who's been everywhere and done everything sees in a perpetual student who works at the airport."

He sighed. "Olivia, why do you do that? Why do you make it sound like there isn't a single thing about you that's interesting?"

"Because nothing about me or my life is all that exciting."

"If that's the case, why have I thought of you constantly since Friday night? Can you tell me that?"

Amazed, she rolled her bottom lip between her teeth. "I don't know."

"I do. It's because you're beautiful and fun and talented and interesting—very, *very* interesting. I loved talking to you, and I can't *wait* to kiss you again. So what do you have to say to that?"

Olivia's cheeks burned and her lips tingled.

His soft laughter rolled through the phone and went straight to her heart. "Nothing at all?"

"How about right back atcha? Would that suffice?"

"Yeah," he said, his voice husky and sexy. "That works."

Olivia wanted to crawl through the phone to him.

"Call me tomorrow after you see the adviser?"

"I will."

"Are you one of those girls who says you'll call and then you don't?"

A burst of laughter took her by surprise. "No. I'm not."

"I know. I've known that since I came to and saw you looking down at me. It's a good thing I found you that next time."

"Why's that?"

"Because I never, ever would've forgotten your face. So don't *you* forget to call me tomorrow, okay?"

It was all Olivia could do to say, "Okay."

Chapter 7

WALKING ON AIR, OLIVIA LEFT THE ART DEPARTMENT. They wanted her to put together a portfolio, and there were forms to be completed and arrangements to be made, but switching her major to studio art wasn't impossible. Wanting to jump up and down with joy, she managed to contain the urge until she reached the quad where she plopped down on the grass and took a long, deep breath. Then she reached for her phone.

"Hey," Cole said. "You called."

"I thought about making you suffer," she teased.

"I guess I had that coming. How'd it go?"

"The good news is they didn't say no. In fact, they promised to help me make it happen in time for the start of the spring semester, provided my portfolio is up to par."

"Congratulations, Olivia. I'm so happy for you."

"Thank you for giving me a push, for encouraging me."

"I'd hate to see talent like yours wasted on the International Monetary Fund."

Laughing, she reclined on the grass and gazed up at the blue sky. The color reminded her of his eyes. Everything seemed brighter today, the hues sharper, the air fragrant with promise.

"How does it feel?" he asked.

"So, *so* good."

"I wish I was there with you. I'd like to see that

amazing face of yours lit up with happiness. I'll bet it's quite a sight."

"You say those things and my heart just…"

"What?"

"Skips a beat," she whispered.

He groaned. "How many more days until Friday?"

"Too many."

"Do you think you could work it out so you could spend the weekend with me? The whole weekend?"

Olivia's feet, which had been skimming through the grass, went still. The heart that had been beating so fast slowed.

"Too much?"

"No," she said. "I'd like to… to stay with you."

He released a long, deep breath. "Are you *sure* it's only Monday?"

―――〰―――

By the time Friday rolled around, Olivia was a bundle of nerves. They had talked every day, sometimes as long as two hours, and she couldn't wait to see Cole again. The afternoon in the store dragged even more than it had the week before when she'd had only dinner to look forward to. This time, they had a whole weekend, and Olivia thought she would go nuts waiting for seven o'clock to arrive.

She had traded shifts with a coworker to get Sunday off and had done extra homework during the week to make sure she wouldn't have to do any over the weekend. Her father had agreed to run interference with her mother and planned to tell Mary that Olivia was helping Jenny with the baby. That was easier than telling her mother the truth and then having to face a hundred questions Olivia wasn't ready to answer.

The only thing standing between her and three nights and two days with Cole was the last hour of her shift. Every minute felt like a year. She was waiting on a customer at six-forty when she did a double take at the sight of him walking into the store wearing a black sweater and faded jeans. He carried a black leather jacket and had a duffel bag slung over his shoulder. Olivia realized she had never seen him out of uniform.

"Can I have my change, please?" the woman at the counter said.

Olivia tore her eyes off Cole. "Oh," she said, flustered. "I'm sorry. Here you go."

"Thank you."

Since they had the store to themselves, Cole strolled up to the counter. "Would you happen to have any Mentos?" A smile lit up his handsome face.

With one hand on each side of that handsome face and without a care as to who might catch them, Olivia leaned over the counter to kiss him. "I thought you'd never get here."

His eyes trained on hers, he turned his face and pressed a kiss to the palm of her hand. "I'm here now."

"I almost didn't recognize you without the uniform."

"Are you disappointed? Did I lose some of my mystique?"

"No," she said, sending her eyes on a journey from broad shoulders to sculpted pecs, to narrow hips and beyond. She licked her lips and turned her eyes back up to find his blazing. "Definitely not."

"That's not fair," he hissed. "Don't look at me like that—at least not yet—and keep your tongue in your mouth."

She replied with a coy smile. "Was it out?"

He glowered at her. "I'll be back in a few minutes."

"Where are you going?" she asked, bereft.

"A quick errand. I'll be right back."

"Hurry."

He left his duffel with her and walked into the terminal.

Olivia took advantage of the opportunity to check out the back of him and once again found herself staring. She still couldn't believe he had come all this way just to see her.

"Mmm." She brought her hands to her face and took a deep breath of the cologne that clung to them. Forever and always the scent would remind her of him.

He came back ten minutes later and pretended to shop while she finished. She looked up at one point to find him watching her over the top of a book. Her face heated with embarrassment and anticipation and a million other emotions. At two minutes to seven, a shift supervisor came to the store to collect Olivia's drawer and paperwork.

The second the supervisor left, Olivia slid into her denim jacket, grabbed her tote and the bag she had packed for the weekend, and led him from the store. Once they were outside, she dropped the metal gate that served as the door to the store and locked it. As she removed her key from the lock, he hauled her into his arms.

"Finally," he sighed, turning his head ever so slightly, just enough to capture her lips. He pressed her to the wall and sent his tongue to find hers.

She clutched handfuls of his sweater and met the

ardent thrusts of his tongue with her own until she remembered where they were.

"Cole," she gasped. "Not here."

He hugged her and took a deep breath. "I wasn't going to do that."

"What? Kiss me? I would've been very disappointed if you hadn't."

Brushing the hair back from her face, he smiled. "I wasn't going to do it the second you finished work."

"I'm glad you did. I couldn't have waited another second."

A tick of tension pulsed in his cheek. "Let's go have dinner somewhere." He put an arm around her. "Anywhere you want."

"How about room service?"

He stopped walking, and when he looked down at her, his face was set in an expression she hadn't seen before. The cockiness was gone, and in its place was something she wouldn't have expected from him—vulnerability.

"Are you sure?"

"I don't know if I'm ready to, you know…" She felt her cheeks heat. "But I want to be with you. Alone with you."

Tugging keys from his pocket, he tightened his arm around her. "Let's go."

"You rented a car?"

He nodded. "That's where I went."

"This weekend is costing you a lot of money."

"Do you think I care about that?"

"I'm guessing you don't?"

"Not one bit. When I was in the Navy, I never had

time to spend a dime of what I made. That, along with the option to my story I sold to Hollywood earlier this year, has given me a nice cushion to pay for things like a weekend in Washington with the lovely Olivia."

"In that case, spend away." She looked up at him. "They're really making a movie about you?"

"They bought the option to the story. From what I hear, that happens a thousand times a year and only a fraction of the movies ever get made. I haven't given it a thought in months, to be honest."

"That'd be so cool."

"I don't know," he said warily. "It would just fire the whole thing up again. I'm ready to slide back into anonymity and just live my life."

On the short walk through the terminal, she saw more than a few double takes from passersby. "I doubt you'll ever be entirely anonymous again."

"Don't crush my dreams," he said in a teasing tone. He led her to a tan Toyota SUV and held the passenger door for her. Before he closed it, he leaned in for another kiss. "I couldn't wait to see you," he whispered. "This week went by so slow."

"For me, too."

He caressed her face. "I want you to know that when I asked you to spend the weekend with me, I wasn't expecting anything. I'd be perfectly satisfied to just hang out with you."

Her hand curled around his wrist. "Thank you for saying that. I feel the same way."

"I wish we lived close to each other and could date like regular people."

"But then we wouldn't have an excuse to spend the

weekend together as our third date," she said with a saucy smile.

"Fourth."

"How do you figure?"

"The TKO counts."

She laughed. "Okay. Fourth then."

His face hovered over hers for a breathless moment.

Olivia urged him into a soft, lush, endless kiss. By the time they resurfaced, she was partially reclined in the front seat and he was pressed against her, half in the car, half out.

His lips touched hers lightly once, twice, and then he simply held her for several long, quiet minutes. "What do you say we take this somewhere more comfortable?"

Overwhelmed by the feelings he aroused in her, she nodded in agreement.

She showed him the scenic route to Old Town, along the George Washington Parkway. He glanced over to find her looking out the window in an unseeing stare. *She's so tense*, he thought, reaching for her hand.

When she smiled at him, it didn't involve her eyes the way her smiles usually did.

He vowed in that moment to do everything he could to make sure she had a relaxing, stress-free weekend. He suspected she hadn't been on the receiving end of much pampering in her life, and he wanted to take care of her.

After years of dodging serious relationships, the re-alization should have terrified him. But it didn't. Being with Olivia felt right, and there was this thing—he couldn't explain it, exactly—that happened when he touched her. The connection between them was nothing short of electrifying.

Go easy, man. You don't want to scare her off by letting her see how badly you want her or how completely she's captivated you. She worried about him losing interest, but could she imagine how he worried that she would? Or that she'd become so afraid of the feelings ricocheting between them that she wouldn't give him a chance for fear of being hurt?

Tightening his fingers around hers, he made a silent promise to be careful with her always.

As he thought about her, his cell phone vibrated incessantly in his pocket. *What the hell is going on?* He had a feeling he didn't want to know.

"Shouldn't you get that?" Olivia asked.

"I'm sure it's nothing. I'll check it later. I'd shut it off, but I never want to be out of touch if my dad needs to reach me." He grimaced when it vibrated again.

"Someone sure wants you for something."

Cole's stomach twisted with anxiety as they arrived at the hotel and parked in the garage. He kept his arm around her and carried their bags to the elevator. After a few minutes of power flirting by the star-struck desk clerk, they were back in the elevator with a key to a room on the fourth floor. Olivia's shoulders, he noticed, seemed rigid with tension.

"I'm sorry about that," he said. "I can't believe she'd come on to me with you standing right there."

"It's not your fault."

"Is everything okay?" *Did she not believe me when I said I didn't expect anything?*

"Of course," she said.

He used the key card in the door and held it for her, ignoring the buzz of his cell phone yet again.

She went in ahead of him.

The small living room was decorated in navy blue and gold. French doors opened into a bedroom with a king-sized bed and a bathroom off the bedroom.

"What do you think?" Cole asked.

Pushing the heavy navy drapes aside, she checked the view of the street. "It's beautiful."

That wasn't the word Cole would've used. He'd stayed in better places—and worse places. But when she turned to him, her eyes bright with excitement, he wished he had taken her to the Ritz. Next time, he decided, he would take her to the Ritz—or somewhere just as fancy.

She crossed the room to him. "Thank you for this."

Resting his hands on her shoulders, he kissed her forehead. "Thank *you* for rearranging your schedule for me."

"It was no problem."

"Where does everyone think you are?"

"My dad and Jenny, my cousin, know I'm with you. We told my mom I was helping Jenny with her baby."

They keep things from her mother, he thought. *I wonder if she'll eventually tell me why*. "How old is Jenny's baby?"

Olivia's face softened. "Six months."

"And you adore him."

"I'm mad for him." She looked up at him, shyly. "Jenny wants me to bring you over for dinner tomorrow night. If you want to…"

"That sounds like fun."

"That's because you haven't met Jenny."

He laughed. "I'm not sure how I'm supposed to take that."

"Let's put it this way—she already has us married."

Again he should have been undone by the mere mention of a word he had studiously avoided, but he wasn't. "Is that so?"

Her cheeks went pink with embarrassment, and Cole decided she had never been lovelier.

"You can see why I'm not sure that taking you there would be such a good idea," Olivia said.

"She's important to you. I'd love to meet her."

Olivia's brown eyes turned up to gauge his sincerity.

He hated that she felt the need to question it. "What do you feel like doing?" he asked.

"Would you mind if I took a shower?"

"Of course not." His hand on her chin, he tilted her face up so he could see her. "You're not my guest here, honey. This is *our* room. If you want to take a shower, take a shower. I want you to relax and do exactly what you feel like doing."

Apparently, what she felt like doing at that moment was wrapping her arms around his neck and sliding her lips over his.

Cole held back, letting her take the lead, curious to know where she would take him. But when her tongue skimmed over his bottom lip, he couldn't keep a gasp from escaping. His hand found the small of her back, and he brought her closer to him. Still he fought the burning urge to plunder.

"I thought you were going to take a shower," he whispered.

"I am," she said but made no move to go.

"Is it your intention to kill me first?"

She laughed, a full laugh that engaged her eyes.

The impact hit him like a punch to the gut. He tilted his head, found her neck with his lips, and could have drowned in her scent.

Her head fell back. "Cole," she sighed.

"Hmm?"

"I'm going to the shower now."

"Okay," he said, but he continued to drop hot, open-mouthed kisses on her neck.

She giggled and gently pushed him away. "I'll be quick," she promised.

"Please."

Picking up her bag, she left him with a smile.

"Are you hungry?" he called through the closed door.

"Sort of."

"What do you feel like?"

"Whatever you want is fine with me."

She was easy to be with, undemanding, pleased with the little things another woman might have taken for granted. If he wasn't careful, he would be halfway in love with her before the weekend ended.

If he wasn't already.

That thought finally brought him up short, causing him to stand perfectly still in the middle of the living room. The only sound was that of the shower running in the bathroom. Was he already in love with her? Was that even possible so soon after meeting her? Had he loved her, maybe, from the instant he first looked up and saw her there, tending to him, waiting for him? Is that why none of the other women he'd dated recently held an ounce of appeal anymore?

A minute, maybe two, passed before his buzzing cell phone brought him back to reality. He realized he was still holding the room service menu, still standing in the middle of the room, frozen in place.

If I don't already love her, I could, he acknowledged. *I could very easily love her like I've never loved anyone else. I could very easily see myself rearranging my life and my priorities to make room for her, if that's what it comes to.*

He ran his life with single-minded focus, without regard to what anyone else wanted or needed, and he regularly took off on trips that kept him away from home for days at a time. Was there room in that life for someone as important as Olivia could be to him? And what kind of life would there be now if she wasn't somehow a part of it? No one had ever been important enough for him to reorder his priorities, so he had no answers to his own questions.

Cole shook his head, took a deep breath, and forced himself to focus on the room service menu. He settled on two kinds of pasta they could share, two bottles of the white wine he knew she liked, and remembering his pledge to pamper her, he ordered chocolate cake for dessert. What woman didn't love chocolate?

While he waited for her, he finally checked the caller ID on his phone and confirmed his worst fears. Natasha. Natasha. Natasha. His hand shaking ever so slightly, Cole called Tucker.

"Hey, man, what's up? I thought you were away this weekend."

"I am, but Nutty Natasha is stalking me. Sixteen calls in the last hour."

Tuck groaned. "Are you *shitting* me?"

"I wish I was." Cole glanced nervously at the bathroom door and lowered his voice even though the shower was still running. "Tuck, you gotta help me out. She can't be calling me. Not this weekend."

"Why? What's going on?"

Since Cole still hadn't told his friend about Olivia, he said, "It's just really important that she give me a freaking break this weekend. Will you talk to her?"

"No way! If I go over there, she'll grill me for an hour about every detail of your life. I can't deal with her."

"Tucker, *please*. I need your help."

"Call her parents again. That worked last time."

"They swore to me last week that I'd never hear from her again," Cole said bitterly. In the bathroom, Olivia shut off the shower. "Tucker, please," he said in a quiet but urgent tone. "*Do something*."

"All right," Tucker said begrudgingly. "I'll talk to her, but when you get home, you're going to tell me what was so all-fired important about this weekend. You got me?"

"I will. I promise."

"I'll let you know what happens when I talk to her."

"Text me."

"You owe me for this one, Langston."

"No question about that."

As the hair dryer went on in the bathroom, Cole ended the call and tried to calm his rattled nerves. He couldn't take much more of this crap from Natasha. More than once over the last few months he'd considered getting the police involved to finally expunge her from his life.

Wanting to avoid the humiliation of going public with

a relationship that had gone very bad, he'd avoided that route. But it was getting to the point where he couldn't avoid it for much longer. If that crazy woman messed things up with Olivia… Ugh. He couldn't go there or he'd lose his mind.

Still trying to calm himself, he fished his iPod out of the duffle and stretched out on the bed, hoping to relax his racing mind before she rejoined him.

—⁓—

Emerging from the bathroom in soft pajama pants and a silky tank top, she found him on the bed, his eyes closed, his hand gripping the sleek silver iPod. She wished she could draw him just like that. The energy that usually vibrated from him had calmed, but he was every bit as appealing in this state as he was at full tilt. It was another layer, another aspect to add to a growing list of attractive qualities.

Watching him, her heart ached. She wanted him. Not just physically, but that was definitely part of it. No, she wanted *him*. She wanted to know him, wanted to know he was hers and that she could come home to him, depend on him, be there for him.

All her life she had kept a tight rein on what she allowed herself to hope for. As a child, her Christmas and birthday lists would consist of the one item she couldn't live without, knowing her father would find a way to get it for her. By putting more on the list, she feared not getting the one thing she desired above all the others. She never risked asking for more than she felt she deserved.

So it was reckless of her to want this man the way

she did, to place him first on the list without knowing anything more than his name, his passion for flying, and a few random facts about his family and his life. What she wanted most, though, was to always feel the way he made her feel just by lying there on the bed, humming softly to himself. Safe. Content. Alive. Finally, *finally* alive.

He opened his eyes and caught her studying him. Smiling, he reached out, closed his fingers around hers, and pulled.

With a squeal, she landed on top of him and was imprisoned by strong arms. Breathless with surprise and desire, she glanced down to find startling blue eyes looking up at her.

His full, sensuous lips curved into an amused expression. "How was the shower?"

Olivia kept her focus on those fabulous lips. "Great. I feel much better."

"Mmm, you smell so good." He cupped her cheek and brought her in for a soft kiss. "Dinner should be here soon."

Realizing he had decided to let her set the pace, Olivia shifted slightly on top of him to gain better access to those lips of his. The new position also put her in direct contact with his erection. Her eyes flipped up to meet his.

He grinned sheepishly and shrugged. "Doesn't mean anything more than you turn me on, but you know that by now."

Full of her own power, Olivia brought her mouth down on his and put her heart and soul into the kiss.

His arm tightened around her, and his other hand

tunneled into her hair as their tongues mated, caressed, danced.

She released a startled gasp when he suddenly reversed their positions while clinging to the kiss. The weight of him on top of her was among the most exciting things she'd ever experienced. Her hands slipped under his sweater to discover his warm, smooth back.

He trembled from her touch.

She tilted her hips and sent a groan rumbling through him.

A knock on the door startled them. They pulled apart but stared at each other, stunned by the ferocity of their passion.

Glancing down at the noticeable ridge under the soft denim of his jeans, he smiled. "You'd better get that."

With a nervous giggle, Olivia reached for a sweater to cover nipples that stood at full attention, ran her fingers through her damp hair, and opened the door.

Chapter 8

"DO YOU THINK HE KNEW EXACTLY WHAT WE WERE doing?" she asked the minute the door closed behind the waiter.

Her cheeks were flushed, her lips swollen and deep red from kissing him. A rush of desire took his breath away. "I'm sure he suspects you were working me over, since I was flat out on the bed."

"*Cole!*"

He found her outrage even more adorable than the sexy dishevelment. Sitting up slowly, he moved to the edge of the bed and gazed at her, wanting to take in every detail, every nuance.

"What?" she asked when the heat of his stare got to her.

"I know you'll think this is another line, but you're just so very beautiful. I find it hard to look away."

She moved to him, wrapped her arms around him, and rested her cheek on the top of his head.

His hands found her waist, and he pressed his lips to her belly through the thin fabric of her tank top.

"Ready to eat?" she asked in a voice that was shakier than it should have been.

The sound of it sobered him, reminding him of his vow to take it slow and easy with her.

"Yep." He stood up, kissed her, led her to the table by the window, and held the chair for her. When she was settled, he opened one of the bottles of wine and poured them each a glass. He started to sit down but stopped abruptly.

"Wait a sec. Something's missing."

Confused, she looked around. "What?"

He went to his duffel and returned with a shopping bag that contained two tapered candles and a pair of heavy plastic candlesticks that were still in the packaging from the store.

Speechless, Olivia watched him.

Cole unwrapped the candles, lit them, and arranged them on the small table.

"You brought candles," she finally said.

"I liked looking at you in the candlelight the night we had dinner together," he said with a shrug.

Sitting back in her chair, she stared at him.

"I don't mean to freak you out... I just liked you in candlelight—"

"It's just the sweetest thing. I didn't realize you were such a romantic."

He groaned. "Don't stick me with that."

"Why not if it's true?"

"No one's ever said that about me, so it must be your influence."

She smiled and her brown eyes went soft with what looked an awful lot like love.

He cleared the emotion from his throat. "So what do you say we eat before it gets cold?"

Olivia nodded and he pulled his chair around so he could sit close to her. They fed each other and ate off each other's plates like they'd been eating together for years rather than twice.

"Which one do you like better?" he asked.

"The shrimp."

"Me, too."

"Have the rest. I'm done."

He refilled their wine glasses. "I hope you saved room for dessert."

"*Now* you tell me."

"It'll keep until you're ready for it."

Standing up, she stretched her arms up over her head. "Maybe later." She reached for the iPod he had left on the bed and glanced at him. "May I?"

"Sure."

"Let's see what you've got on here." She brought it with her when she returned to the table. "AC/DC, Aerosmith, Alanis Morrisette—one we agree on—America, Bach, the Beatles, Boston, Bob Dylan, Bob Seger, BTO. Buffalo Springfield? Who the heck is that?"

He grinned. "*Stop, children, what's that sound…*"

She raised a hand to cut him off. "Anything from this decade?"

"Alanis, Sheryl Crow, Green Day, Matchbox Twenty, among many others. My taste is eclectic."

She laughed. "If that's what you want to call it. What's your all-time favorite song?"

He took the iPod from her, cycled through until he found what he was looking for, and handed it back to her.

As she positioned the ear buds, she kept her eyes trained on him until the song seemed to transport her right out of the room. When it was over, she turned off the iPod and set it on the table. "Does that describe you? Are you a desperado?"

"I guess I have been. In the past."

It seemed to take courage for her to ask, "And now?"

He reached for her hand and brought it to his lips. "I'm tired of my feet being cold in the wintertime, and I'm starting to think the Queen of Hearts might've been on to something."

She held his gaze for a long moment before she released his hand and got up to look out the window.

He followed her. Resting his hands on her shoulders, he kissed the top of her head. "What about you? What's your favorite song?"

"'Big Girls Don't Cry.'"

"Don't they?" he asked, turning her to face him.

Her chin tilted defiantly. "The foolish ones do."

"Are you really so cynical, Olivia?"

She shrugged. "I've had reason to be."

He raised his hand to caress her face. "I'd like to show you that you can be foolish and safe at the same time, but you'll have to take a leap of faith. You're going to have to trust me and believe just a little bit."

"I don't know if I can," she said softly. "It's not that I don't want to because I do. I wish you knew just how badly I want to believe it's possible."

The yearning radiated from her. How could he *not* know?

"But things like this don't happen to me."

"Just because it hasn't happened before doesn't mean it can't." He brought his other hand up to her face. "Do you feel something when I touch you? Like this?"

She nodded—a small nod, but a nod just the same. "A jolt," she whispered.

His hands froze on her face. "You do?"

"It goes right through me."

"When I was on the floor in the airport with a concussion and a banged-up shoulder and you touched me… When you put your hands on my face, I felt it everywhere." Taking advantage of her speechless state, he stole a kiss. "Do you think that happens to me every day?"

"I don't know. Does it?"

He shook his head. "Never before, so I understand what you're feeling."

"You think so?" she asked, her expression skeptical.

"You're here with me now because you're as curious as I am about the instant connection between us, but your head is telling you to run as far and as fast as you can."

Her eyes widened with amazement. "How do you know that?"

Laughing softly, he nuzzled her cheek. "Because my head is telling me the same thing, but somehow I can't seem to make myself listen. As I got on the plane to come here today I was asking myself, 'What're you doing?' Do you know why I came when my better judgment was telling me to run?"

She shook her head.

"Because I meant it when I said I couldn't wait to see you. I thought of you constantly this week, and I needed to see you again to find out if what happened the other times I was with you would happen again."

"And did it?"

Nodding, he trailed his lips up her neck. "Even more so than before." Her skin was soft, so soft, and the scent of her shampoo lingered in her hair. He couldn't get enough of her. "Do you think you could try, just *try* to take that leap with me? I don't know about you, but I really want to see where we'll land."

"I'm scared," she confessed.

"I won't hurt you. I promise."

As she studied him he could almost see the thoughts—and the fears—spiraling through her mind. He had to remind himself to breathe as he waited and hoped.

"I want to take the leap. I do."

"Then let's take it together."

He wasn't sure who moved first, but suddenly she was in his arms kissing him without reservation, without fear, and the impact almost knocked him off his feet. He lifted her and groaned when she wrapped her legs around him.

"Olivia," he sighed as he held her tight against him. "I like the way you leap."

For once her laughter was free and easy. "And I like the way you catch me when I land." She kissed him again, a sweet brush of her lips over his.

His breath got caught in his throat. The feelings she stirred in him were almost painful.

"Cole? What is it?"

He shook it off. "Nothing," he said with a smile, letting her slide back down to her feet. "Want to get a movie?"

A hint of disappointment clouded her eyes. "If you want."

"Don't look at me like that, honey," he said as he tried to remember his vow to go slow, to keep it easy—for now. "You're taking the leap, and I'm so glad—and *so* relieved. But that doesn't mean we have to also leap right into bed, does it?"

"No," she said, fiddling with his hair. "We don't *have* to."

"But you want to?"

She looked up at him, her heart in her eyes. "Don't you?"

"What do you *think*? But I don't want to rush you—"

"How about we watch a movie… in bed?"

"Do you consider that a compromise?" he asked, contemplating her impish expression.

"Of sorts."

He smiled, delighted by her bravery in the face of so many fears. "You're on." Pulling the sweater over his head, he tossed it onto a chair and reached for the button to his jeans. Olivia, who had been watching him with interest, blushed and went to turn down the bed.

They took turns in the bathroom, and when he finally slid into bed wearing only a pair of gym shorts, he reached for her. "Did you find something you want to watch?" he asked, guiding her head to his chest.

"Yep." She flipped to the movie channel and chose what could only be called a chick flick.

"*For real?*"

"You can pick the next one," she said, giggling at his distress.

"I'll make sure there's lots of stuff blowing up to get back at you for this."

"Shh. I can't hear it over all the noise you're making."

Cole had good intentions. Really, he did. But the movie wasn't half as interesting to him as she was. That pale-pink tank top had been driving him crazy since she first appeared in it after her shower. He slid a hand under it and ran a finger slowly down her backbone.

Her short inhale was the only sign she gave that she was aware of him. Then her lips moved on his chest, and

Cole's heart skipped a beat. When her tongue flicked his nipple, the last of his good intentions was overtaken by desire that blazed through him like wildfire.

"Watch your movie," he said, his voice hoarse.

"I don't want to."

"I'm trying to watch it, but you're bothering me."

She laughed softly against his chest. "Liar."

"Olivia…"

She propped herself up so she could reach his chest. "What?"

"The movie."

With her lips pressed to his belly, she glanced up at him, her eyes alight with amusement. "I've seen it before." She held the remote behind her back to turn off the TV.

"You *tricked me* into bed?"

"I had to do something. You asked me to leap, and then when I did, you wanted to watch a movie."

He laughed so hard he had tears in his eyes. "You little witch. Here I am trying to be a good guy and not rush you. Turns out you're manipulating me."

"It sounds so sordid when you put it that way," she said, hovering over him.

He combed his fingers through her hair. "I feel used."

Laughing, she leaned down to kiss him. "I have a feeling you'll get over it."

With his arms tight around her, he held her still and kissed her. He came up for air, breathless with longing.

"I want you," he whispered. "I want you like I've never wanted anything. Ever."

"I want you just as much."

"We should wait."

"Probably. But if we didn't want to… wait, that is… do you have a condom?"

He swallowed hard. "If I say yes, it'll look like I was expecting this, and I told you I wasn't."

"*Please say yes!*"

"Yes," he said, laughing. "Yes!"

Chapter 9

THEY FELL TOGETHER IN AN EXPLOSIVE BURST OF passion that made Olivia's head swim. His hands were everywhere, and his tongue plunged into the depths of her mouth like he wouldn't be able to get enough if he had a lifetime to try.

As he turned them so he was on top, her every sense went on full alert. His cologne, her shampoo, the bristle of his whiskers against her face, the soft mattress below her, the cool sheet that covered them, the weight of his leg between hers.

He finally broke the kiss and buried his face in her neck.

She cradled his head in one hand while using the other to caress the huge, fading bruise under his right shoulder. "Oh, Cole, your shoulder. It must've hurt so much."

"It did. Worse than the face, if you can believe that."

Being careful not to hurt him further, she gently smoothed her hand over the area around the bruise.

He released a contented sigh. "Feels good. Where were you when I needed a nurse?"

"I was right here, wondering how you were doing and wishing I could see you again."

Raising his head, he found her eyes in the candlelight. "Did you really wish for that?"

She held his gaze while her hands continued to stroke his back. "There was a jolt."

"Right," he whispered. "The jolt." He kissed her

again, this time softly, his lips moving over hers in an easy rhythm that seduced and inflamed.

With her fingers buried in his hair, she held him right there as one endless kiss faded into another, neither of them in any rush to move on.

"God, I could kiss you all night," he said.

"Luckily, we have all night."

"So we do." Holding himself up on one elbow, he put his other hand flat against her belly under her shirt. "You have the softest skin. It's like silk." He pushed the shirt out of the way and replaced his hand with his lips.

Olivia gasped. "Cole…"

"Do you think we could get rid of this?" he asked, tugging on the tank top.

With only the briefest of hesitations, she sat up and pulled the top over her head. When she glanced at his face, she discovered cool blue eyes gone hot with desire.

He reached for her. His chest hair tickled her breasts, and he trembled.

Knowing he was as affected by her as she was by him infused her with tenderness and desire and love. Yes, there was love. To deny that would be foolish, and Olivia wasn't foolish. At least she hadn't been before this, before him.

He relaxed his hold on her just enough to cup her breasts and run his thumbs over her nipples. Then he dipped his head and sucked hard on one of them.

Olivia cried out, which startled him.

"Don't stop," she pleaded.

"I think I've found something else I could kiss all night," he murmured against her breast.

That she could laugh just then came as a total shock

until he went back for more, and her laughter faded into a moan. The firm weight of him on top of her gave her no choice but to lie there and feel—his lips, his tongue, the warmth of his mouth. She squirmed under him until she had worked her legs free. Arching her back, she pressed against his erection.

He responded by closing his lips tight around her nipple. She clutched fistfuls of his hair.

His wince got her attention, and she relaxed her grip. "Cole."

"What, honey?"

"I feel like I'm burning up," she panted.

"Maybe if we got rid of the rest of these clothes, you'd cool off."

"Somehow I doubt that's going to help," she said, lifting her hips so he could get rid of her pajama bottoms and the scrap of lace she wore beneath them.

He sat back and gazed at her. "When I was stuck at home for two weeks, I had all these fantasies about the girl in the airport," he said softly as he crawled back up to her. "But nothing I imagined could've prepared me for the reality of the woman—the beautiful, smart, funny, incredibly talented, and amazingly sexy woman she turned out to be."

Moved beyond words, she kissed him and hooked her fingers into the waistband of his shorts to push them down.

Kicking them the rest of the way off, he shifted to his side and brought her with him.

She wanted to touch him everywhere she could reach. His skin was smooth, his chest hair dark and soft. She liked that he was muscular but not bulky. Her fingers trailed over rippling abs and then lower until her hand closed around his pulsing erection.

His eyes fluttered shut. He exhaled a long, deep breath and seemed to be working hard to stay still so she could satisfy her curiosity.

And she was really, really curious as she stroked him, touched him, felt him.

"Liv," he sighed.

The sound of her nickname coming so naturally from him, especially just then, went straight to her heart.

The more she stroked him, the harder he seemed to get. "Does it hurt?" she whispered.

"No. It aches." He lifted her leg over his hip. "For you."

Olivia was breathless with anticipation as his fingers danced lightly over her leg and inner thigh. Without realizing what she was doing, she tightened her hand around him, drawing a deep groan from him.

His fingers slid through the slick heat between her legs, teasing, touching, rubbing.

She was teetering on the edge when he pushed two fingers into her and sent her hurtling over.

"Oh *God, Cole*." Her body was completely out of her control as sensation after sensation pounded through her. Gulping for air, she clung to him and slowly returned to earth.

"Wow," he whispered, his expression awestruck. "Is it always like that?"

"No," she managed to say. "Never."

Brushing the damp hair off her forehead, he pressed a soft, lingering kiss to her lips.

"Let me get a condom."

Reluctantly, she let him go, but only because she

knew he would be right back. She lay on the bed waiting for him, her body alive with aftershocks that reverberated from the soles of her feet to the palms of her hands, to her lips, to her breasts, and between her legs.

He sat on the edge of the bed to roll on the condom. When he turned to her, she wrapped her arms around him, and he started all over with kisses that, on their own, were almost enough to send her flying again. By the time he perched over her, Olivia thought she would go mad if she had to wait another minute.

"*Please*, Cole," she said between deep breaths. "Now."

As he began to push into her, he cradled her face in his hands and dropped soft, damp kisses on her cheeks, her nose, her forehead, and then her lips. His tongue traced a path from her bottom lip to her top. He thrust his hips again, and when he met with resistance, he froze and looked down at her, shocked.

"Don't stop." She looked up at him. "Please, don't stop."

The realization seemed to knock the wind out of him for a minute, but then he rallied. Moving slowly, so slowly, he worked his way past the barrier.

Olivia waited for pain that never came. There was only pleasure unlike anything she had ever imagined. Her hands slid down to cup his backside, pulling him tight against her. For a long, breathless moment they stayed just like that, joined but still.

"Are you okay?" he whispered, gazing down at her with concern all over his handsome face.

"*So* much better than okay."

His smile was a relief.

"You won't hurt me if you want to, you know, move

a little," she said, her eyes widening as her encouragement caused him to throb inside her.

A nerve in his cheek twitched with tension. "Are
you sure?"

She nodded.

He moved slowly at first and then faster when she
met each of his thrusts with the lift of her hips. Reaching
beneath her, he gripped her bottom to better angle her.
The new position put the focus on just the right place,
and before long she was climbing toward another release. He lowered his head to tug her nipple into his
mouth, and that was all it took. She cried out, tightened
her legs around his hips, and held onto him as he came
with a cry of his own.

He pushed hard against her one last time before he
collapsed on top of her, his forehead and back damp
with sweat.

Olivia held him close, so close she could feel the
pounding cadence of his heart, and was filled with satisfaction, knowing she had done that to him.

———∾———

His head spun with questions. Where to even begin?
What to say? *Why didn't she tell me?*

Her fingers made lazy circles on his back.

*How does a woman get to be twenty-seven in this day
and age without ever—*

"Are you mad I didn't tell you?" she asked in a small
voice that tugged at his heart.

"Of course not. I'm a lot of other things, but mad is
definitely not one of them."

"What kind of other things?"

He lifted his head and pressed his lips to hers. "I'm surprised and full of questions, but mostly I'm honored."

"You are?"

Nodding, he kissed her again. "Very much so. But why didn't you tell me? I would've been more careful—"

She stopped him with a kiss. "You were perfect. I'm sure it was no good for you, but next time—"

"What're you talking about? *No good?* That was best sex I've ever had in my life."

"You don't have to say that."

"Olivia," he said, exasperated. "I'm not just saying that. It's true." He withdrew from her and sat up to pull the covers over her. "I'll be right back. Don't go anywhere."

Her face lifted into a tentative smile. "I won't."

Cole went to the bathroom, got rid of the condom, and splashed cold water on his face. He looked in the mirror for signs of the changes he felt occurring inside but saw nothing new on the outside. How was it possible to feel so much and not have it show? His face should have been lit up like a Broadway marquee.

He reached for a bottle of her lotion and breathed in the scent that was so uniquely hers. The smell was enough on its own to turn him on. Returning the lotion to the counter, he took a couple of deep breaths and stared at his reflection.

"Tread lightly," he whispered. "Don't screw this up."

He went back to the bedroom to find her turned away from him, looking out at the darkness through the window they had left uncovered. Her hair flowed freely on the pillow, and the sheet had dipped to her waist, leaving the curve of her back exposed. Just looking at her made him want her again. Making an effort to keep his own needs in check, he got back in bed and snuggled up to her.

"What're you thinking about?"

"Dessert."

He laughed. "I would've guessed a hundred other possibilities."

"I'm kind of a sucker for chocolate."

"I figured you might be. Do you want it now?"

"Uh-huh."

"Coming right up." He brought the wine and cake back to bed.

Olivia rested against the pile of pillows and held the sheet over her breasts.

Cole fed her the first bite.

"Oh, that's *good*," she said, wincing as she shifted into a more comfortable position.

"Does something hurt?" he asked, alarmed.

"Not really."

"Why don't I believe you?" He took a bite and fed her another one. "Are you sore, honey?"

"A little."

"I'll draw you a hot bath. That'll help."

"Only if you join me."

"Twist my arm."

They ate the cake in companionable silence, but all the while Cole's mind raced with things he wanted to ask her if only he could find the right words.

Pouring wine into the glass he had put on the table next to her, she took a sip and studied him. "What do you want to know?"

Startled that she had read him so easily, he looked over at her.

"You have questions."

He shrugged. "A few."

"You can ask, Cole."

He gave her the last bite of cake and put the plate on the table. "I'll ask in the tub." Getting up, he went into the bathroom and turned on the water. In the closet, he found a robe and brought it to her since she might not be ready to walk around naked in front of him.

"Thank you."

Waiting until she was settled in the tub, he transported the candles into the bathroom and shut off the light. "Got room for me in there?"

She scooted forward so he could get in. "Sure do."

When he had arranged his long legs around her, she relaxed against him.

"Is the hot water helping?" he asked.

"Mmm."

"I hate that you're hurting because of me."

"It's a good hurt. The best kind."

Rubbing soap over her breasts, he watched her nipples spring to life. "Why haven't you ever done this before, Liv?"

"I haven't had much luck in the romance department." Tilting her head back so she could see him, she added, "Until lately, that is."

"I can't believe there hasn't been someone important before now."

"There've been two, actually. One I dated for a year when I was nineteen, and the whole time I was working up the nerve to take the next step with him. I was almost there when I found out he'd been doing it with someone else while pressuring me to 'prove my love.'"

Cole tightened his hold on her and forced himself to stay quiet.

"The second one got tired of waiting and decided to take what he wanted."

"No."

"Fortunately, I'd grown up with two older brothers and knew how to defend myself."

"Jesus," Cole uttered under his breath. The thought of her in danger made his gut clench with anxiety.

"I heard it was months before he stood up straight again."

"Remind me to stay on your good side."

She giggled. "Needless to say, it took me a while to venture back into the dating pool after that disaster. I've had a lot of first dates that never materialized into anything special."

"Their loss," he said against her ear.

"You're giving me goose bumps," she said with a shiver.

"You should see what you're doing to me."

"I can *feel* what I'm doing." She reached back to hook her arm around his neck and bring him down for a kiss. "I'm so glad I waited for you."

His heart contracted. "So am I," he said, his hands coasting up over her ribs to cup her breasts. "I feel like the luckiest guy in the world to have been your first." He wanted to add "and only" but didn't. At this point, he could only hope. "How's the soreness?"

"Much better."

"Ready to get out?"

"In a minute."

Resting his head back against the tub, he closed his eyes and realized he was completely and totally relaxed. There was nowhere else in the world he wanted to be, nothing else he could have wanted. This is what contentment felt like. He finally understood what had been missing with all the others. When he remembered he had to leave her on Monday, he ached. Who knew when they would get another chance to be together like this?

The water had grown cold by the time he finally stood up and reached for towels. He tied one around his waist and then held another for her. Wrapping it around her, he surprised her when he scooped her up and carried her back to bed.

"And you say you're not romantic." She kept her arms around him and brought him down with her. "That was right out of *An Officer and a Gentleman*."

Cole laughed. "I was an officer, but there're a few women out there who might dispute the gentleman part."

"Have you left a trail of broken hearts in your wake?"

"Define 'trail.'"

Olivia cracked up and looped her arms around his neck. "More than fifty?"

"*No!*"

His indignation fueled her laughter. "I'll bet there're hundreds you don't even remember."

He rolled his eyes. "No way."

"I shared my dirty laundry. It's only fair…"

Glancing at her with a worried expression, he bit his bottom lip. "Do you promise you'll still like me after?"

She raised her little finger. "Pinky swear."

"Huh?"

"God, you *are* old." She reached for his hand and hooked her pinky around his. "It's a very solemn promise."

"In that case," he said, amused by her, "I had a

girlfriend during my last two years of college, and we lived together senior year. I wanted to marry her. In fact, I even asked her."

"What happened?"

"She turned me down."

"Seriously?"

"Yup."

"A woman seriously said no when you asked her to marry you?"

"Yes," he said, laughing at her amazement.

"She must've been blind, deaf, and dumb."

"I hate to disappoint you, but she had all her faculties," Cole said, pleased by her irritation on his behalf.

"So why did she say no?"

"She didn't want to be a Navy wife."

"She hurt you," Olivia said, caressing his face.

"Mostly she disappointed me. I thought we really had something, but I guess it was one sided. Otherwise she wouldn't have cared what I did for a living, right?"

"That's right."

"I think about her sometimes, though. It amazes me to realize if she'd said yes, I'd have had a whole different kind of life. We'd be married fourteen years by now—if it'd lasted—and I'd probably have a bunch of kids."

"Do you wish you had kids?"

"Sometimes. But when you live the way I do for as long as I have, you start to wonder if there's room for a family."

"I can see how that would happen when you're on the go all the time." Her finger traced circles around his nipple. "So that's one…"

He nibbled on her neck. "And then I met you."

She poked him in the ribs, causing him to jolt. "Nice try."

"You're not going to let this go, are you?"

"Afraid not."

"I'll tell you, but you have to remember you did that pinky thing and still like me after."

"I remember."

Releasing a deep sigh, he looked up at the ceiling. "I guess I'm one of those guys women call toxic. I avoid commitment like the plague, but I'm always honest about it. I tell every woman I go out with that I'm not interested in anything serious, and it never fails that they think they're going to be the one to change me or housebreak me. There've been a few who'd call me an asshole for being exactly what I said I was, especially since everything happened earlier this year."

He finally risked a glance at her and found her looking pensive. "You're freaking out, right?"

"No, but I am wondering something."

"I'm almost afraid to ask."

"It's just that you didn't say that to me."

"You noticed that, huh?"

"Uh-huh. In fact you said the exact opposite, with the leap speech and all of that."

"Is that what we're calling it?" he asked, laughing. "The leap speech?"

"That's the official name."

He took her hand and brought it to his lips. "When I told you earlier that I want you more than I've ever wanted anything?"

She nodded, her lips parted in breathless anticipation.

"I didn't mean just physically. I want *you*. In my life for as long as it feels good to both of us."

"That's an awfully big step for a commitment-phobe, isn't it?"

"It's huge. But it seems to be a night for big leaps."

"Yes, it does."

Chapter 10

OLIVIA AWOKE BEFORE DAWN WITH COLE'S ARMS TIGHT around her and her face pressed to his chest. They never had gotten around to closing the drapes, so faint light filtered into the room where her whole life had changed in the course of one unforgettable night. Pursing her lips, she skimmed them lightly over his chest before she pulled back just far enough to see his face.

He sighed and shifted onto his back but didn't wake up.

As she studied him, the urge to draw him while he slept became overwhelming. Moving slowly, she slipped out of bed, put on the T-shirt of his that hung from the foot of the bed, hit the bathroom, and then went to grab her sketch pad.

She had almost finished when he stirred.

"Hey," he said, his voice hoarse and sleepy. "What're you doing?"

"Drawing you."

He looked like he wasn't sure whether to be touched or embarrassed. "Can I see?"

"In a minute."

"Am I allowed to get up and pee?"

She laughed but didn't look up from her pad. "Feel free."

When he got out of bed, she couldn't resist a peek at his muscular butt. She wondered if he'd let her draw him in the nude sometime. By the time he returned and got back in bed, she had finished the drawing but was suddenly shy about showing it to him.

He reached out to her. "Come back. I'm lonely."

Unable to resist him, she brought the pad with her when she got into bed.

"First things first," he said, leaning in to kiss her.

He tasted of toothpaste, and what started out as a quick kiss turned into a lingering event.

"Mmm," he murmured against her lips. "Good morning to you, too."

In the course of two or three minutes, he had ruined every future morning that didn't begin just like that.

He eased the pad from her hand and held it up to study her work.

Olivia's heart beat fast as she waited to hear what he thought of it.

"I've never seen myself asleep before."

"You're quickly becoming my favorite subject."

"Do you know what I love about this?" he asked, his eyes still fixed on the drawing. "Somehow you managed to capture the intimacy between us. Anyone who looked at this would know I'm your lover."

His insight amazed and delighted her. That he got it, that he got *her*, was such a special gift in the midst of everything else he had brought to her life.

"When you say those things, you make me believe I could really be an artist."

"You *are* an artist. Do you paint at all?"

"Watercolors. I like to do outdoor stuff."

"If you could paint anything, what would it be?"

"The Golden Gate Bridge," she said without hesitation. "I have this secret fascination with San Francisco."

"It's a beautiful city."

"Of course, you've been there."

"A few times."

"You're so lucky that you get to travel so much."

He picked up the pad again. "This is really so good."

"I want to do you nude sometime."

His eyes lit up with unrestrained lust. "Any time."

"I meant *draw* you."

"That, too?"

Laughing, she let the sketch pad slip to the floor and reached for him. His mouth devoured hers as he pinned her to the bed.

"I want to feel your skin against mine," he whispered, helping her out of the T-shirt. "Oh, yeah, that's better."

His lips traveled from her neck to her breasts where he dragged his tongue in circles, denying her what she craved.

She pulled on his hair, hoping to redirect him, but he wouldn't be rushed.

By the time he finally grazed her nipple with the tip of his tongue, Olivia was panting with desire.

He teased and tugged and sucked. "Would you mind if I just spent the day right here?"

Breathless, she said, "I can't take much more of that."

"Spoilsport," he grumbled, moving to her belly and leaving a damp trail around her belly button with his tongue. When he scooted down further, Olivia tried to sit up.

"Don't," he said, holding her in place.

"What're you doing?"

"Loving you," he said against her inner thigh.

His words sapped her of any resistance. At his

insistence, her legs fell open. When he ran his tongue over her most sensitive place, she almost launched off the bed.

He held her still and sank his tongue into her.

Oh, God…

"I changed my mind," he said between deep strokes.

No! Don't stop now!

"I think I'd rather spend the day here, instead." He set his focus on the spot that throbbed for him and slid a finger into her.

Over and over again he took her to the precipice and then backed off, leaving her sweating and panting and desperate.

"*Please*… Cole…"

This time he didn't back off, and she came with a cry of release so intense it frightened her. She was still breathing hard when he kissed a path from her belly to her breasts to her neck.

"I love the way you do that," he whispered, holding her tight against him.

"It's embarrassing," she murmured into his shoulder. Her whole body felt hot and flushed—and satisfied.

"Don't be embarrassed. I love it."

She wrapped her arms around him and pushed her pelvis against his erection. "What about you?"

"I'm good."

"I can't leave you in that condition," she said with a sly smile as she slid her hand down to stroke him. "It wouldn't be fair."

"You don't have to," he said, but he moaned when her hand tightened around him.

"Did you only bring one condom?"

"No, I have more, but you're sore from last night."

"Not anymore."

"But you will be—"

She found his mouth and sent her tongue in search of his. Urging him onto his back, she stretched out on top of him and pressed her breasts to his chest. "I really, really want to do it again," she said, nipping at his lips.

Looking up at her with a dazed expression, his hands coasted down her back to cup her bottom. "As soon as my head stops spinning, I'll find a condom."

Olivia laughed and angled her head for another deep kiss as her hips moved against his in an increasingly urgent rhythm.

"Condom," he gasped. "Now."

She let him up.

When he came back, he reached for her.

"Can I go back to where I was?" she asked shyly. "On top?"

He closed his eyes and took a deep, unsteady breath. "You're sure you've never done this before?"

With her hands on his chest, she pushed him down and straddled him. "Positive."

"I like this aggressive Olivia. She's very hot."

"Only for you."

"Even better."

"Tell me what to do, Cole," she said as she slid her moist heat over his hard length. "I don't want to hurt you."

"Instead you're killing me," he choked, guiding her as she took him in.

"*Oh*," she gasped when he was fully sheathed in her.

"Like it?"

"Yeah." She tossed her head back and tilted her hips.

He groaned and clutched her waist.

"Does that hurt?"

Biting his lip—hard—he shook his head.

Olivia wasn't sure if she was doing the right things, but he seemed to like it when she rocked back and forth and then raised herself up and came down on him again. If the tightening of his grip on her waist was any indication, he liked *that* a lot.

His eyes were closed, his lips slightly open, and his breathing choppy.

She leaned forward to kiss him softly.

He held her there with a hand in her hair, his hips moving in time with hers.

Olivia couldn't believe it when she felt herself climbing toward another orgasm. Tearing her lips free of his, she concentrated on the sensations as they built to a shocking crescendo.

With a hand on her lower back, Cole held her still as he came right after her.

Olivia lay on top of him like a boneless pile of Jell-O. The hand he still had in her hair massaged her scalp, sending a shiver straight through her.

"Amazing," he whispered.

"Was it?"

"Beyond amazing."

"I'm not going to like waking up alone after this weekend."

"I'm not either."

"We won't see much of each other," she said with a sigh.

"We'll figure it out."

She lifted her head off his chest so she could see his eyes. "You haven't even left yet, and I already miss you."

He framed her face with his hands. "I love you, Olivia."

Inhaling sharply, she gazed at him, her eyes shiny with tears. "You do?"

He nodded. "I really do."

"I love you, too."

His kiss was soft, sweet, and devastating. Then he gathered her up in his arms, and her heart tripped erratically.

"Aren't you afraid I might try to housebreak you?"

Chuckling, he said, "Nah."

"What're we going to do, Cole?"

"Well, today we're going to have some fun, and tonight we're going to Jenny's. When we get home, I'm going to make love to you all night long. Then we've got tomorrow and tomorrow night...So let's not think about Monday until we have to, okay?"

"I'll try," she promised, but even as she said the words she wondered if she could do it.

Cole woke up a second time, glanced at the clock, and discovered it was almost eleven. Olivia was curled up to him, her leg wedged between his, her hand resting on his chest. Nuzzling her silky hair and breathing in her scent, he was hit by a surge of love that left him weak. After the love came panic. The day was almost half over, and they had so little time. Suddenly, having her sleeping in his arms wasn't enough.

Shifting to gain access to her lips, he woke her with a kiss. He watched her eyes fly open and then soften when she saw him hovering over her.

"Scared me," she whispered.

"I'm sorry, but I couldn't wait another minute to talk to you."

"About what?" she asked, alarmed.

"Anything. Everything. Nothing."

She reached up to caress the stubble on his jaw. "I felt the same way when I woke up before you earlier."

"What should we do today?"

"We could take the Metro into the city and play tourist."

"Why would we take the Metro when we have a perfectly good car?"

She laughed. "Because it's impossible to park downtown."

He wrinkled his nose. "Do *you* want to do that? You're there every day."

"I love showing off my favorite city."

"If you want to, that'd be great. I haven't been here as a tourist since my senior year of high school."

"*That* long ago?"

He tickled her, and she dissolved into squealing laughter.

A rap on the door startled them into quiet snickers.

"Housekeeping."

"Shit," Cole muttered. "I forgot the privacy thingie last night."

The maid knocked again.

"We need some more time," Cole called, his hand over Olivia's mouth to silence her laughter. He replaced his hand with his mouth and sank into a deep kiss. "Do you think you can be quiet now?"

Chastened, her mouth quivered with laughter. "No."

"Here's the plan—shower, breakfast—or I guess it's lunch now—and then we'll head into the city. Good?"

"As long as there's coffee in there somewhere, that sounds perfect."

———

Olivia couldn't remember a day she had enjoyed more as they traipsed from the Air and Space Museum to the Hirshhorn Museum and Sculpture Garden to the row of monuments, beginning with Lincoln and ending at Jefferson. They sat on the steps at the Jefferson Memorial, overlooking the Tidal Basin, and shared a snow cone. The trees were alive with fall color and the water full of fallen leaves. Bright sunshine was no match for the nip in the cool, crisp air.

"Those are Washington's famous cherry trees," Olivia said, pointing them out to him. "When they bloom in April, it's the prettiest thing you've ever seen."

"I don't know about that." Cole smiled and tucked a strand of hair behind her ear. "Have you painted it?"

"Only a hundred times. But I never seem to be able to capture the full majesty of it."

"I'll bet your paintings are as spectacular as your drawings. Will you show me sometime?"

"Sure."

"I want to see everything you've ever done."

"Even my childish scribbles?"

"Everything."

"I have to put together a portfolio to get into art school." She stopped herself and laughed. "I still can't believe I'm saying that."

"Believe it."

She ran her hand over his leg. "Maybe you could help me decide what to include in the portfolio."

"I'd love to."

Olivia thought of her mother and their mess of a house. "What's wrong?"

She skimmed her foot back and forth over the smooth marble step.

"Liv?"

"I want you to help me, but I don't want to bring you to my house."

"Why not? The parents usually like me."

"I'm sure they do," she said with a sad smile. "It's just… my mother, she's…"

"What, honey?"

"She's an agoraphobic. Do you know what that is?"

"She doesn't leave the house."

Olivia shook her head. "Not in nine years."

Cole laced his fingers through hers. "That must be tough for you and your family."

A giggling young girl approached them. "Are you Captain Incredible?" she asked.

Olivia felt a shudder of revulsion go through him over the hated name and suppressed the urge to giggle herself.

"I suppose I am," he said reluctantly.

The girl thrust a small notebook at him. "Can I have your autograph?"

Olivia could tell he was annoyed by the interruption, but he smiled warmly at the child.

"Sure. What's your name?"

"Cecile."

Olivia watched him write, "To Cecile, Aim High, Dream Big. Cole Langston," and hand the pad back to the girl. She said a hasty thank you and went running back to her waiting family.

"Sorry about that," he said.

"I like what you wrote."

He shrugged off the praise. "We were talking about your mom and how tough her condition is on your family."

"Unfortunately, the agoraphobia is only part of it. She also shops compulsively—online, home shopping networks, and over the phone. Our house is full of crap. There's no other way to put it." She glanced at him. "I can't take you there. I just can't."

"Then tomorrow take the car, go get what you need, and bring it back to the hotel. We'll figure out the portfolio there."

"Are you sure?"

"Whatever you want is what I want."

"And you don't care that I don't want you to meet my parents—or, I should say, my mom? My dad is really great. He'd like you."

Cole brought their joined hands to his lips and kissed hers. "I'd love to meet him so I can tell him what a beautiful daughter he has."

"He tells me that all the time. To be honest, he's the real reason I still live there—I could never leave him to deal with her by himself. He's my first love."

"I thought I was," Cole pouted.

"You are," she whispered. "You know you are."

He nuzzled her neck. "Can we go back to the hotel and make out for a while before we have to be at Jenny's?"

She checked her watch. "We might have time for a quick kiss or two."

He stood up, tugged at her hand, and bolted down the stairs, pulling her with him. "Taxi!"

"Cole! Cabs are too expensive. We can take the Metro."

"That'll take too much time we can spend on better things—much better things."

Chapter 11

"WHAT DO YOU WANT ME TO WEAR TO JENNY'S?"

Olivia loved the way his soft chest hair felt against her face. "Jeans."

He brushed his fingers through her long hair. "I can do better."

"No need. They're casual."

"What if she doesn't like me?"

"She'll love you."

"We need to get going."

"I know," she said but made no move to get up. "I wish we could stay in again tonight."

"You don't want to go?"

"I do."

"But?"

"We're running out of time."

"Baby, this is just the beginning. We'll have more time soon. I promise."

"Weeks, probably."

"Two."

She lifted her head. "Really?"

"In two weeks I have another weekend off. Do you think you could be packed and ready to go by Friday?"

"Ready to go where?"

"That's for me to know and you to find out. Can you do it? With work and school?"

"I can bank some extra hours at the store."

"Friday night to Tuesday night maybe?"

"I'll miss a class."

"Will that kill your grade?"

"I have no idea. I've never missed one before."

"*Never?*"

"Not one."

"Oh, my God! I'm in love with a geek!"

She sighed. "Do you think you could say that again?"

"What?" he teased. "That you're a geek?"

"No, the other thing."

"That I'm in love with you?" He leaned in to kiss her. "That part?"

"Mmm."

"You like that, do you?"

"Oh, yeah."

"So then you'll run away with me in two weeks?"

"Will you tell me where we're going?"

"Nope."

"Then I'll have to think about it."

Astounded, he stared at her. "You will?"

"No," she said, laughing. "You're so easy."

His eyes flashed as he wrestled her under him.

"We don't have time for this," she reminded him, giggling nervously at the sinister look he attempted to pull off.

"You're lucky your cousin is expecting us."

"You don't scare me. Now get off me so I can take a shower."

"Make me," he said against her lips.

She smoothed her fingers over his back in a gentle caress that turned him to putty under her hands. Then she sank her fingertips into his ribs and sent him launching off her. Taking advantage of his surprise, she flipped him onto his back and brought her lips down so they almost touched his, whispering, "Two older brothers. Don't mess with me."

His eyes darkened with desire. "Very impressive," he said, reaching for her. "And *very* sexy."

She dodged him and poked his ribs again. "Get up."

―――

The first things Cole noticed when he stepped into Jenny and Will's townhouse were the framed drawings over the mantel, one of the couple on their wedding day and another of their son, Billy, both obviously done by Olivia. While Olivia had dark hair and eyes, her cousin was blonde with hazel eyes. Yet there were similarities. Upon closer inspection, he decided they shared gestures and expressions more than physical characteristics.

He enjoyed watching Olivia light up with delight when Jenny passed baby Billy to her. The blond baby was as happy to see Olivia as she was to see him. His pudgy fingers clutched a handful of her hair.

Will intervened before the baby could hurt her. "Be nice," he said to his son, who chortled in response.

"What a cutie," Cole said, reaching out to tickle the baby's foot.

"We've decided to keep him." Jenny steered Olivia toward the kitchen. "Come help me get drinks."

After the women left the room, Will glanced at Cole. "So it wasn't enough that you had to be a good-looking pilot," he said with a teasing grin. "You had to have the whole 'American Hero' thing going for you, too, huh?"

"It's my burden in life."

"Sure it is," Will said, laughing. "You've probably got a black book the size of the Bible."

"I recently burned it." Cole gestured to the closed kitchen door. "Are they talking about me in there?"

"What do you think?" Will replied dryly. He seemed pleased with Cole's comment about his womanizing days being behind him. "Be glad they at least left the room. When they talk about me, they do it right in front of me."

Cole laughed. "I'm sensing it's not easy being you around here."

"You don't know the half of it. What's not fair is I'm stuck out here with you, so I have to wait until later to hear what they said about you."

"Since we're stuck together for who knows how long, let me ask you… Where should I take Olivia for dinner tomorrow night? Somewhere nice. Where would she want to go?"

"That's easy. She loves the Chart House in Old Town but doesn't get to go very often."

"Good to know. Thanks."

―――∾∾―――

"Did you sleep with him?"

Still holding Billy, Olivia nibbled on a carrot she'd stolen from the cutting board. "We're sharing a hotel room. Where do you think I slept?"

Jenny sighed with exasperation. "That's not what I meant, and you know it."

Olivia laughed at her cousin's irritation. "Yes, I *slept* with him."

"Ohmygodohmygod*ohmyGOD*! *Finally!* How was it? He's *so* hot. Smoking hot."

"Is he? I hadn't noticed."

"You're being such a brat." Hands on her hips, Jenny said, "We can do this the hard way or the easy way. What's it going to be?"

"Why go easy when hard is so much fun?"

Billy picked that moment to unleash a deep belly laugh.

"See, even your son thinks it's fun."

Jenny tickled the baby's pudgy belly. "Traitor." She took him from Olivia and settled him in his high chair.

He shrieked in protest until his mother gave him an animal cracker to gnaw on.

"Come *on*, Liv. Spill it!"

"It was… indescribable."

"*Oh, my God!*" Jenny squealed.

"Pipe *down*, will ya?" Olivia hissed. "He's going to hear you and know exactly what I'm telling you."

Ignoring that, Jenny said, "So was it, you know, painful?"

"Not at all like I expected it to be."

"Did you tell him? Before?"

Olivia shook her head. "I wanted to. I really did, but there just wasn't a good time to say, 'By the way, Cole, I'm a twenty-seven-year-old virgin.'"

Jenny snickered. "So did he figure it out?"

"Um, yeah… you could say that."

"And?"

"He was freaked out at first, but he was cool about it. He said he was honored."

"Which, of course, was the perfect thing to say."

"He seems to have a knack for saying the perfect thing at the perfect moment. I told him about Gary and Steve, so at least he understood *why*."

"Are you glad now you waited?"

"*So* glad. It makes such a difference when you love the person you're with."

Jenny let out another "*Oh, my God!*" but this time she made an effort to keep her voice down.

"Remember how I agonized about sleeping with Gary and Steve?"

Jenny rolled her eyes and poured them each a glass of wine. "Do I *ever*."

"With Cole there was no decision because it was just right. And now that I know what it's like to really love someone, I can see I didn't love them at all."

"How does he feel?"

"He loves me, too," Olivia whispered as if she were afraid he might hear her spilling their secrets.

Jenny's eyes went misty. "Oh, Liv, oh *really*?"

Olivia nodded. "He's a dream come true in every possible way."

Jenny launched herself at Olivia. "This is so fabulous! I told you he was it, didn't I? You didn't believe me, but I told you!"

"*Shh*, will you? I don't want him to hear us acting like fools in here."

"That's what we do. He may as well get used to it if he's going to be hanging out with us."

"Yeah, I guess."

"What? What's that face?"

Olivia shrugged. "Everywhere we go..."

"What?"

"Women. They throw themselves at him, and if they have to push me out of the way to get to him, they don't even care."

"I bet he cares."

"It infuriates him, but it terrifies me. He has so many opportunities…"

"That doesn't mean he'll act on any of them." Jenny took her by the chin. "You're still thinking about how it's going to end, aren't you?"

"Not really."

Jenny raised a skeptical eyebrow.

"All right. Maybe."

"*Why?*"

"I can't help it," Olivia said. "I love him so much, it's scary."

"That's how it's supposed to be."

"But he lives in Chicago. He has a whole life there, and when will we see each other? I can't bear the idea of him leaving the day after tomorrow. I can't bear it," she said, finishing on a whisper.

Jenny ran her hands up and down Olivia's arms. "If it's meant to be, you'll work it out. You need to relax about the details and just go with it."

"That's what he says, too."

"He's right."

Olivia nodded. "I know."

Will and Cole came into the kitchen.

"We're thirsty, and you're taking too long," Will announced as he got beers for himself and Cole, who had stopped short at the sight of Olivia obviously upset about something.

He went over to her. "What's wrong?"

"Nothing," she assured him with a smile, her heart flip-flopping at the sight of him. "Nothing at all."

"Are you sure?"

She nodded and closed her eyes against the intense wave of emotion that struck when he kissed her cheek.

He put his arm around her and drew her close to him. Olivia looked up to find Jenny gazing at them. "What?"

"You two are *so* cute together."

"*Jenny*," Will groaned. "Leave them alone, will you?"

"What did I say? Just the truth."

Smiling, Cole looked down at Olivia.

"What's for dinner?" she asked, hoping to change the subject.

On the way back to the hotel at midnight, they had the usually jammed corridor between Springfield and Alexandria all to themselves.

Cole glanced over at her a couple of times, wondering why she was so quiet. "Jenny and Will are great. I really liked them."

"They liked you, too. Did you mind having to tell the story again?"

"Nah. It's no biggie. Why so glum over there? Didn't you have a good time?"

"It was fun. I'm glad you got to meet them."

"You and Jenny are so funny," he said with a grin. "You're like a teenager around her." But rather than being complimented by his remark, Olivia seemed embarrassed, which he hadn't intended. He reached for her hand. "I meant that in a good way."

"I know."

"What's wrong, Liv?"

"Nothing," she said quickly—a little too quickly.

He let it go until they got back to the hotel. When they were in their room, Olivia went straight to the bathroom and closed the door. Perplexed by her sudden withdrawal, Cole opened the second bottle of wine from the night before and turned on the radio.

He unbuttoned his shirt and sat down to wait. And worry. Something was up. Had she changed her mind about them? About him? The thought terrified him. She couldn't. Not when he was taking this huge gamble with his heart.

Cole had just enough time to work himself into a full-on panic attack before she opened the door and stepped into the room wearing a long, midnight blue, silk nightgown. The sight of dark silk over ivory skin sucked every thought right out of his head, leaving his mouth hanging open.

She fiddled nervously with the fabric.

He got up and went to her.

Her big, brown eyes, when they turned up to meet his, were shy and uncertain.

His heart hammered.

"I asked Jenny if she had something sexy she could loan me," she said so softly he wouldn't have heard her if he hadn't been standing right in front of her.

"You're so beautiful, and I love this." He smoothed his hands over her silk-clad back. "But you don't need any help to be sexy."

"I wanted to be sexy for you."

He held her tight against him. "Were you nervous about putting this on? Is that why you were so quiet before?"

"Not really."

"Then what's wrong? I can tell it's something."

She looked up at him, her smile shifting from shy to coy. "Do we really have to talk?"

As all the blood drained from his head and made for points south, Cole tilted her face up. "Yes, we have to talk."

"I put this on for you…"

"Olivia, honey, I *love* you, and as dazzled as I am by how you look right now, if you're upset about something, I want to know what it is. I want to help."

"It's just…"

"What? Tell me."

"When I think about you leaving on Monday, I feel sick. Physically sick. I know we said we wouldn't ruin the time we have with that, but it's all I can think about."

He released a deep, pained sigh and wrapped his arms around her.

"I want to enjoy this. I want to enjoy *you*, but all I can see are the roadblocks in our way. It just makes me wonder how this can ever work."

"Do you want it to work?"

"You know I do."

"I do, too. So we'll make it work. We'll figure out a way."

"You make it sound so easy."

He guided her to the bed and stretched out so he faced her. "It won't be easy. There'll be times when being apart will totally suck." Caressing her face, he added, "But the good times will be so good we'll forget all the bad times."

She captured his hand and pressed a kiss to the palm. "You're very convincing."

"Then why do you still look so uncertain?"

"I'm trying really hard to be optimistic, but this is all so new for me." Her cheeks blazed with color. "Not just the sex part. All of it."

"I know, sweetheart." He slipped an arm around her waist to draw her closer to him. "Believe it or not, it is for me, too. I certainly wasn't expecting to find you and to feel the way I do about you."

She smiled at him, but she still looked uncertain.

"What? You don't believe me?"

"I do."

"But?"

"Half the women in this country would like to be where I am right now. How can I compete against that?"

"You don't have to, honey. You're the only one I want, the only one I can think about."

With a sigh that sounded like relief, she reached up to brush the hair off his forehead.

"Maybe we're moving too fast—"

"No," she said, leaning in to kiss him. "No."

He held her tight against him and trembled with pleasure and contentment as her lips skimmed over his chest. Then her tongue circled his nipple and all thoughts of slowing things down deserted him. Somehow he ended up on his back trying to contain the urge to reclaim the upper hand.

Since it seemed important to her just then to be in control of something, he stayed still so she could feather kisses over his chest. He stopped breathing altogether when she toyed with his nipples and handled the surge of desire by clutching the duvet. Taking a ragged, deep breath, he forced himself to breathe when her hair grazed his stomach. Her lips soon followed.

"Liv," he gasped, reaching for her.

"Let me love you, Cole."

His head fell back on the pillow, his eyes closed tight against the pain of desire.

Her fingers trembled against his belly as she reached for the button to his jeans.

Breathe.

The zipper traveled slowly down, getting stuck on the hard ridge of his erection. For the first time in years, he hovered on the verge of an embarrassing accident. A groan escaped through his gritted teeth as she pushed his clothes out of the way.

She stroked him—slowly at first, so slowly he could have died from wanting more.

"I didn't get a chance to really look before," she said, her eyes devouring as her hand drove him crazy.

Then she bent and kissed the very tip, and Cole sat straight up. "I can't," he said, the words coming out as a pant. His fingers buried in her hair, he tried to bring her back to him. Her silky gown brushed against him, causing him to jolt from the contact. "*Jesus.*"

Olivia laughed and pushed him back to his pillow. "I'm not finished yet," she said with a playful pout as she returned her attention to the task at hand. "It's all slippery. Did I do that?"

"What do you think?" he choked out.

Her fingers skimmed through the pearly fluid. "Oh. It's so hard, and then it gets harder. I can't believe that doesn't hurt."

"Olivia," he said, breathless. "You're going to make me come if you don't stop."

"Isn't that the goal?" she asked, glancing up at him through sable lashes.

"Not without you."

"Just this once?" Before he could answer, she bent her head and took him into her mouth. And then her tongue swirled over the head, and he had to hold his breath to keep from losing it. Without being told, she did it just right—keeping up the firm strokes of her hand even as she took him deep.

"Liv... stop," he said, trying desperately to hold back.

"Don't want to," she whispered.

With a groan of defeat, he abandoned the fight and gave into the need blazing through him. The release was more intense than it had ever been before. Nothing could compare to the complete and utter surrender.

Her eyes, when they connected with his in the aftermath, were victorious. She was back in the game, and the relief was even more overwhelming than the shattering release had been.

He reached for her and brought her up to lie on top of him. His heart pounded so hard, he could hear it fluttering in his ears. All at once, he too was petrified about what Monday would bring. How could he just leave her here and go back to his life? Was he to pretend his whole world hadn't shifted on its axis the first time he lost himself in her?

Her breathing was slow and steady, and he wondered if she had fallen asleep.

Tightening his arms around her, he kissed her forehead. The tremble that shuddered through her told him she was still very much awake.

He rolled them over.

She opened her mouth to speak, and he took advantage of the opportunity to sink into her moist heat. He feasted on her mouth and was gratified to feel her arms encircle his neck to hold him there. For the longest time, he was satisfied to be exactly where he was. He wanted nothing more than what he had right then.

But she seemed to have other ideas. At first, she clung to him, her nails biting into his back. Then her hands slid down to pull him tighter against her.

He shifted his attention to her neck.

"Cole."

"Hmm?"

"I want you."

His lips flew over her warm, soft skin. "I'm here."

She gripped his backside and lifted her hips against his erection. "Now."

Startled, he looked up at her to find her eyes huge and hot with desire.

"Please."

He moved fast to get a condom. When he turned back to her, she was reaching for the hem of the nightgown. He stopped her.

"Let me."

Beginning with the soles of her feet, he kissed his way up, taking the nightgown with him. He left no sensitive spot unvisited on the journey. The stroke of his tongue over her, into her, sent her soaring.

Desperate for more, he decided that getting rid of the nightgown wasn't as important in that moment as driving into her. That he could want her this much again, so soon after the last time, came as a surprise. Would he ever get enough?

She reached for his hand, laced her fingers through his, and smiled up at him.

He kissed her, a light touching of lips, a mingling of breath. Her scent, a combination of lavender and vanilla and something else not as easily identified, filled his senses. Raising their joined hands over her head, he bent to lave at her nipple through the silky nightgown.

Moaning, she wrapped her legs around his back and took him deeper.

The next time he glanced at her, he found her watching him with a mixture of awe and wonder in her eyes. That he had the power to do that to her both humbled and frightened him.

"I love you," she whispered. "I love you so much."

He withdrew almost completely from her. "I love you more."

She shook her head and arched into him, seeking him. "Not possible."

"Olivia," he sighed as he went deep again. The sudden quickening of her breathing and the trembling in her thighs told him she was close, so he picked up the pace.

Her eyes flickered shut and then shot open in shock as the climax slammed into her, catching her off guard. She cried out, clung to him, and dragged him down with her into a freefall from which he suspected he'd never fully recover.

Chapter 12

AFTER A LONG, LAZY MORNING IN BED, COLE HANDED her the car keys the next afternoon. "There are two things besides your artwork that you need to bring back with you."

"What?" she asked, perplexed.

"A bathing suit."

"For?"

"Duh. To swim? In the hotel pool?"

"Oh, okay. I forgot there was a pool. What else?"

"Something to wear out to dinner tonight. Something a little… fancy."

She shook her head. "I don't want to go out tonight."

"What if I want to take you out?"

"It's our last night."

Resting his hands on her shoulders, he said, "*This* time. Not ever."

"I don't want to."

"Bring it just in case." He tipped her chin up so he could see her eyes. "For me?"

She could deny him nothing when he asked liked that, and he knew it. "Okay."

"One more thing," he said, touching his lips to hers.

"What?" she asked, breathless.

"Hurry back."

—*w*—

The moment she was out the door, Cole picked up his cell phone, furious with himself for not taking care of this sooner. He dialed a number that, for now, was programmed into his speed dial.

Brenda, his bartender girlfriend in Miami, picked up on the third ring. "Hey, baby," she said with the sultry purr that used to fire him up. Now it just left him feeling panic-stricken that Olivia might find out he had other women in his life. *Had* being the key word. By the time she returned, they'd all be history.

"Hey," he said, as the reality of what he'd failed to do hit him hard and fast. He should've cleared his decks *before* the weekend with her—not during. His only excuse was that he'd never expected to fall in love with Olivia—or anyone else, for that matter.

"I hope you're calling to tell me you're in town."

"Um, no. I'm not in Miami."

"Oh, poo."

Cole could picture her pretty mouth forming a perfect pout. Thinking of her thick, auburn hair and sultry, green eyes, he tried to remember what he'd found so enchanting about her. Oh yeah, right… She was a tiger in bed. He swallowed the lump in his throat and pushed those memories aside.

"So, listen, I hate to do this over the phone, but—"

"It's over, huh?"

"I'm afraid so."

"I figured something was up when you stopped calling."

Cole winced. He hadn't given her a thought in weeks. "I'm sorry."

"What happened? I thought we had a pretty good thing going."

Cole rubbed the back of his neck, hoping to loosen the tight ball of tension that had lodged there. "I met someone."

"We aren't exclusive. Why start now?"

"Because." After a long, pregnant pause, Cole said, "Are you still there?"

"Don't tell me you're actually planning to give monogamy a whirl."

"So what if I am?"

She laughed. Hard. "I give it a week. Maybe two."

He closed his eyes and conjured up Olivia's lovely face. Brenda was wrong—very, very wrong. What he had with Olivia would last a lot longer than that. Maybe even forever if he played his cards right. "I enjoyed the time we spent together."

"Yeah, yeah, yeah. Save the 'I wish you the best of luck' speech."

"I do."

"I've got customers. Gotta go."

"Bye, Brenda."

The click of the call ending served as her reply. He removed her name from his speed dial before scrolling through the list again and hitting "Send."

"Hey, Diana, it's Cole."

⁓

In the still new-smelling rental car, Olivia drove the short distance to her parents' house in a dreamlike state as she relived the night with Cole. And the morning. She shivered with delight. Dark clouds hung over the area, but she barely noticed. Until she remembered that by this time tomorrow, he would be gone and she'd be on her way to work—just another Monday after the most extraordinary weekend of her life. Would he think of her as he went through his days? Would she invade his thoughts as he navigated jetliners through the sky? Oh, how she hoped so.

She pulled onto Commonwealth Avenue and found a spot on the street. With a double beep, she locked the car and went up the stairs. Inside, she heard voices coming from the kitchen and started toward them. Just outside the door to the kitchen, her father's raised voice stopped her.

"*Goddamn it, Mary!* I can't *believe* you did this!"

"You took away my other one," her mother said petulantly. "What was I supposed to do?"

"I took it away because we're on the verge of bankruptcy, and you're spending money like I'm printing it on a press in the basement!"

"The card is in *my* name. I don't get why you're so mad."

"*Your* name!" he roared. "*Our* credit!"

"None of this would've happened if you hadn't lost your job. Why couldn't you have just shut up and done what they told you to do?"

With a hand over her mouth, Olivia muffled a gasp. She glanced into the room and saw a stack of what appeared to be bills on the table.

"Because those cars were crap, and I couldn't, in good conscience, tell my valued customers to buy them."

"So instead you got yourself fired. I hope your good conscience is pleased with itself."

"Must be nice to be you, Mary." Olivia had never heard such bitterness in her father's voice. "You sit in this house

day after day, year after year, hiding from life. No respon-
sibilities to anyone but yourself, accountable to no one."

"You know I can't help it," she spat back at him.

"I know you *won't* help it. There's a difference. A
big difference. We have to sell the house. It's the only
way we can fend off the creditors until I get a new job.
And you can't buy a goddamned thing. Do you hear me?
No trinkets, no do-dads, no *nothing*. I'll buy food, but
nothing else."

"We're not selling the house." Mary sounded truly
frightened. "We can't."

"We don't have any choice."

She began to cry. "What about Olivia?"

"I'll take care of her, just like I always have."

Olivia stepped into the room. "You lost your job?"

Stunned, Jerry spun around, and the devastation on
his face broke Olivia's heart. "Honey," he said. "How
long have you been there?"

"Long enough." Olivia glanced down at the papers
on the table, most of them stamped with "Overdue" in
bright red ink. "When did this happen?"

"A month ago," Jerry said with a sigh.

"Why didn't you tell me?"

"I didn't want you to worry." He ran a weary hand
through his gray hair. "I thought you were away for
the weekend."

"I came by to get something."

"I don't want you to worry, sweetheart," he said more
emphatically this time. "We'll work this out."

"How?"

"I've got a few irons in the fire with some of the other
dealers in town. I'm hoping something will open up in

the next few weeks. But even if that happens, there's no way we can hold on to the house."

"Maybe Alex or Andy could help," Olivia said, referring to her brothers.

Jerry shook his head. "Andy's getting slammed with alimony, and Alex just bought a house. I've already asked them."

He looked so defeated and humiliated that Olivia crossed the room to put her arms around him.

"I'm sorry you had to find out this way," Jerry said, smoothing a hand over Olivia's long hair.

Mary's sniffles grew into sobs. "There has to be something else we can do."

"There isn't," Jerry snapped as he stepped back from Olivia. "I tried to tell you a year ago that you had to stop spending money or we were going to end up exactly where we are."

"Sure, blame me. Like you mouthing off to your boss had *nothing* to do with it."

"It *is* your fault!" Olivia said to her mother. "All *he* does is work and all *you* do is buy worthless shit that no one wants or needs! Now we have a houseful of crap but no house. I hope you're satisfied."

Mary stared at her daughter with hard eyes. "This is none of your concern. A woman your age shouldn't still be living at home anyway. It's time for you to grow up and get a life."

Olivia gasped.

"Shut up, Mary," Jerry said in a tone Olivia had never heard before. "My daughter is welcome in my home for as long as she wishes to be here. No matter where I live, there'll be a place for her. You, I'm not so sure about."

"What's that supposed to mean?"

"Figure it out." He guided Olivia from the room. "I'm so sorry, honey," he said when they were out of earshot of the kitchen. "I hate that you were blindsided by this."

"You're leaving her?" Olivia whispered. "What happened to 'for better or worse?'"

"That was before I found out she'd run up twenty-five thousand on yet *another* credit card I knew nothing about. She's got us a hundred fifty thousand in the hole, Liv."

Olivia blanched. "*What?*"

Jerry's face was grim as he nodded.

"So even if you sell the house—"

"It probably won't be enough to stave off bankruptcy."

Olivia sat down hard on the bottom step. "God." She dropped her head into her hands and tried to absorb it all. "What're you going to do?"

"First, I'm going to sell the house. Then, I'm going to get her into a treatment place, which is something I should've done a long time ago. After that, I have to find another job. And fast."

"I wish I could help," Olivia said. "There's absolutely nothing I can do."

He sat down next to her and put his arm around her. "There *is* something you can do."

"Anything."

"Stay in school, get your degree, live your life. This is *not* your problem." He kissed the top of her head. "There'll be a place for you wherever I end up."

"She was right about me still living at home at my age."

"Don't listen to her," he scoffed. "You're living here

to save money while you go to school. That's the wise thing to do."

"I've gone to such great lengths to avoid loans. I didn't want to live outside of my means the way she does. But maybe it's time to look into some loans."

"Don't do anything drastic just yet. Nothing's going to happen overnight."

She rested her head on his shoulder for a long time before she looked up at him. "Are you going to be all right?"

"Sure I am," he said with the charming smile that had helped him sell a lot of cars over the years. "I always land on my feet. You know that." He squeezed her shoulder and whispered, "Where's your pilot?"

Olivia couldn't believe she had forgotten she was supposed to hurry back. "At the hotel. I just came by to get some stuff."

"Go ahead, honey. You don't want to keep him waiting."

"Will you let me know what's going on or if you need anything?"

"You'll be the first to know. I promise."

With a kiss to his cheek and a heavy heart, Olivia stood and trudged up the stairs. She felt like a robot as she packed the things she had come for. *How could all of this have happened right under my nose? Am I so self-absorbed that I failed to notice my father had lost his job?*

She included the best of her paintings as well as the sketches she had put aside the other night for possible inclusion in the portfolio. She grabbed a swimsuit, and after a few minutes in her closet, found something she could wear to dinner, although she still hoped she could convince Cole to stay in. Five minutes later, she went back downstairs where her mother waited for her.

"Where'd you get that car?"

"I borrowed it."

"Did Jenny get another new car? Must be nice to have all that money."

Her mother's rants about Jenny's parents and their money were old news to Olivia. Jenny's father was a corporate attorney, and their family had always been well off compared to Olivia's. It was something she and Jenny had never let come between them.

"It's not hers."

"Then whose is it?"

"My boyfriend's," Olivia said, raising her chin defiantly.

"Boyfriend," Mary scoffed. "Since when?"

"A couple of weeks."

"And you've already gone from kissing him on the street to sleeping with him?"

Olivia was glad her hands were full. Otherwise she might've been tempted to smack her mother. "That's none of your business."

"Men don't respect girls who give it up too easily."

"Save your maternal advice," Olivia snapped. "It's too little, too late."

"If he's so special, why didn't you bring him with you?"

Olivia snorted as she looked around at the chaos. "Yeah. Right."

Her face set into a hard expression, Mary opened the door. "Don't let me keep you."

Olivia started out the door but stopped to face her mother. "You need help, Mom," she said softly. "You can't live like this anymore. None of us can."

"Go to your boyfriend, Olivia."

With the heat of her mother's glare on her back, Olivia went down the stairs and loaded her things in the car. As she got into the driver's seat, she glanced up to find Mary still watching her from inside the house she had made her prison.

If Olivia had driven home in a dreamlike state, she returned to the hotel in shock. Could her timing for a quick trip home have been any worse? She found a parking space on the street in front of the hotel and rested her head on the steering wheel. The whole situation was so ridiculous, so ridiculously pathetic. She had no idea how much time passed before the driver's side door suddenly swung open, startling her.

"Baby, what's wrong?" Cole's arms slid around her. "What happened?"

Unable to speak, she fell against him but couldn't find the words she needed.

"Are you hurt?" His hands coasted frantically over her face, almost as if he was taking inventory. "Did someone hurt you?"

She shook her head and held on tight to his hand.

"I walked down to the Giant to get some beer, and I was on my way back when I saw you sitting here." His voice had gone from anxious to soothing. "I couldn't get to you fast enough."

"Sorry," she said, breathing in the clean, fresh smell of him in an attempt to cleanse herself of the ugliness.

"Liv, you're kind of scaring me here."

"I just need a minute."

"Come on." He eased her out of the car. "Let's get you inside, and you can have all the minutes you need."

"The stuff is in the back."

"I'll come back for it."

He kept an arm tight around her but didn't say anything as they made their way inside. In the lobby, a woman wearing a predatory smile approached them.

"Not now," Cole snapped.

"Jeez, what a jerk," the woman muttered as she walked away.

Once they were in their room, he settled Olivia on the sofa. "Can I get you anything? Some water? A stiff drink maybe?"

Against all odds, she smiled. "Water would be great."

He disappeared into the bathroom, reappearing seconds later with a glass of water. After handing it to her, he sat down next to her.

"Thanks." She took a sip and put the glass on the table. When she sat back, he slipped his arm around her and guided her head to his chest.

"Want to talk about it?"

"Not really."

"Okay."

Because he didn't push, because he didn't insist on knowing, she found herself telling him anyway—from the twin babies her mother lost when Olivia was five to the scene she had interrupted at home. And by the time she finished, the room had grown darker but still he held her.

"Do you know what I wonder sometimes?" she said softly.

"What's that?"

"What would've been different if they had lived? I would've had a sister and another brother. I always wanted a sister. I had Jenny, but that wasn't the same. She had two of her own sisters, and even though she was closer to me, they came first, you know?"

"Yeah, I can see what you mean."

"I also wonder what kind of mother I would've had if they hadn't died. I remember little snippets from before. There was a birthday party once. I'm not sure if it was for me or one of my brothers. My mother was laughing and carrying a cake that blazed with candles. There were no more parties after she lost the babies. There was no more of anything."

"Liv," he sighed. "I'm so sorry."

"I never understood why the three kids she had couldn't have been enough. I can only imagine how devastating it was for her to lose the twins, but did she want them so badly that she could just forget about the three of us after she lost them?"

"I don't know, honey. Grief does funny things to people. I've seen that in my own family since my mother died."

Olivia gasped. "I can't believe I'm saying all these awful things about my mother when yours died so tragically."

"One has nothing to do with the other. Everyone has different experiences with their mothers."

"I was sure lucky to have Jenny's mom. She's my father's sister, and she was always there for me when I needed her. But she had five kids of her own."

"So you never came first with her, either."

Olivia shrugged. "It was better than nothing."

With his hand on her chin, he turned her face up. "You come first with me."

His eyes were bluer than they had ever been and

full of love—for her. She was still getting used to the miracle of that.

"Always," he added.

How could he know what that meant to her? How could he ever know?

"Thank you," she managed to say.

"Do you know what you need?" he asked.

She shook her head.

"A swim."

"Now?"

"Why not? You'll feel better if you get your mind off all of this for a while."

"I'm sorry." She sat up. "I'm ruining our last day. I didn't mean to—"

He stopped her with his fingers on her lips. "Don't do that. Don't apologize for leaning on me when you needed me. I don't know what I can do for you, other than make sure you have some fun because I think you need it. That's the only reason I suggested a swim."

She caressed the cheek she had watched him shave that morning. "I love you."

"Good," he said, his voice heavy with emotion. "Because I love you, too. And I hate to see you unhappy."

"I'm a lot better now that I'm back with you."

He kissed both her hands. "Will you be okay for a minute if I run out and get your stuff?"

She nodded, and with a quick kiss, he left her.

While he was gone, Olivia went into the bathroom to freshen up. *What am I going to do?* She washed her face and smoothed on some moisturizer. *You're going to apply for student loans and get an apartment of your own.* As much as it pained her to admit it, her mother was right. It was time for her to be out on her own. A few loans to get her through the last year or two of school wouldn't kill her.

Satisfied she had a plan for herself, her thoughts shifted to her father and the enormous task he had ahead of him. Whatever he needed, she would be there for him, she vowed, just as he had always been there for her.

By the time Cole returned with his arms full, Olivia felt a little better. It always helped to have a plan.

"I'm dying to look at all of this," he said, holding the bag that contained her artwork. "But not until we have some fun." He handed her the other bag of extra clothes. "Is it too much to hope there might be a bikini in there?"

She smiled. "Nope."

He nudged her toward the bathroom. "Hurry."

His playful mood helped to further improve hers as she changed into the skimpy, black, crocheted bikini Jenny had bought her as a joke for her birthday the year before. Olivia had never worn it but had brought it knowing Cole would like it.

As she tied the top behind her neck, she worried that maybe it was too skimpy for a hotel pool. With a nervous laugh, she adjusted the tiny triangles that made up the bottom half of the suit, amazed by how uninhibited she had become after only a couple of days with him—albeit a couple of monumental days.

When she emerged from the bathroom, Cole was checking the messages on his cell phone. He had changed into navy-blue board shorts and had a dark T-shirt tucked under his arm. Olivia walked up behind him and kissed his back.

He startled. "Hey, I didn't hear you come out."

Slapping the phone closed like he had just gotten caught doing something dishonest, he put it back in his duffle bag and turned around.

"Everything all right?" she asked.

"Yeah," he said, but there was… something… in his eyes.

Her stomach twisted. "Cole?"

"It's nothing." His eyes skirted over her as he finally noticed what she was wearing—or what she wasn't. "*Wow*."

"Yes, you said that."

"Did I?"

She waved a hand in front of his face. "Hello? Swimming?"

"Right. Swimming."

When he still didn't move, she wrapped her arms around his neck and went up on tiptoes to kiss him. "Or not."

He fell into the kiss with abandon that made her head spin. Lifting her to him, he made her breathless with deep, sweeping thrusts of his tongue. Then, all of a sudden, he stopped and pulled away.

"What is it?"

"I'm sorry." He rubbed a hand over his mouth. "We were going swimming."

Olivia looked up at him as she laced her fingers through his. "We don't have to."

He smiled, but it seemed forced. "I promised you some fun."

She slipped on a T-shirt and a pair of flip-flops and followed him from the room, still wondering what was going on with him.

The pool was deserted when they arrived.

"Hot tub or pool?" he asked.

Olivia eyed the hot tub.

"Hot tub it is."

"Oh, I like this," she sighed, easing into the steamy water.

Cole flipped a switch on the wall to turn on the jets before he joined her.

"Feels good, huh?"

Tilting her head back, she said, "Mmm."

"Are you doing a little better?"

She opened her eyes and nodded. "Thank you. For listening and everything."

"That's what I'm here for."

"You know…" She ran a finger along his jaw and down his neck. "I'm here, too. For you."

"I know."

"You're sure everything's all right?"

"Well, let's see." He reached for her. "I have you wearing a barely there bikini and a hot tub all to our-selves." He guided her onto his lap so she faced him. "So yes, everything's all right. In fact," he said, cupping her bottom and pulling her tight against his erection, "I've never been better."

As the water bubbled around them, Olivia reveled in the moment. Being in love was a heady rush of emotion: excitement and fear and dread. The thought stopped her cold. *Where had that come from?* Sitting here, with his arms tight around her, was everything she had ever dreamed of. So why the dread? Because she worried it would end somehow, someday. That he'd find someone he liked better.

Cole rested his head on her shoulder.

She curled her arm around his neck. His hair brushed against her face, and his lips coasted over her shoulder.

"I really, really want to take you out tonight," he said softly, his kisses sending shivers through her.

"You don't have to. I'm perfectly content to stay in and do nothing as long as I can do nothing with you."

"Humor me?" he asked, sliding his hands up over her ribs, stopping just under her breasts.

Olivia clung to him, wanting him desperately. "You really want to?"

"Uh-huh."

"Okay," she said with a sigh.

He slanted a crooked smile at her. "You're not over-whelming me with your enthusiasm."

"I'll work on it."

"While you're doing that, we also need to work on your portfolio."

She tightened her arms around him. "Five more minutes?"

"How about ten?"

Chapter 13

COLE HELD UP A PAINTING OF CHERRY BLOSSOMS framing the Tidal Basin in front of the Jefferson Memorial. Olivia's paintings were more abstract than her drawings, but still he could almost smell the blossoms as he studied the painting.

"This one. Definitely."

She darted around the room, full of nervous energy, while he looked at one remarkable piece after another. He had no idea how she would ever narrow them down to the twenty the school had requested.

"Why not this one?" She held up the same scene done from the other side of the basin that included the memorial.

"I like the one that focuses only on the trees," he said, quickly adding, "I love them both, but if you can only have one, I'd use this one."

Pursing her lips in an expression he found completely adorable, she studied the options. "You're right."

"I like the way you say that, as if it's a surprise that I could be right about something," he said with a grin.

She rolled her eyes at him.

Laughing, he reached for a painting of autumn foliage. "When did you do this?"

"High school. I went camping with some friends at Skyline Drive in southern Virginia."

"Even back then," he said reverently. "I can't believe you were capable of this in high school."

"This was junior high." She held up a beach scene. "Ocean City."

"Amazing." His mouth watered as he imagined the smell of fried dough and hot dogs wafting from the boardwalk. "You have to include it."

Studying the painting as if she was seeing it for the first time, she shrugged. "I wasn't sure."

"It's fantastic. It makes me want a hot dog."

Olivia laughed. "Room service might have one."

With his hands on her hips, he drew her closer to him. "I'm so proud of you, Liv. For taking this step, for believing in your talent enough to try."

She combed her fingers through his hair. "I never would've done it if you hadn't given me the push I needed."

"I have a good feeling about this."

"Are we still talking about art school?" she asked with a coy smile.

"All of it—art school, you, me, us. I have a good feeling." Even though her gaze never wavered, her smile faded just the slightest bit. "You don't?"

The rally attempt was just as obvious. "Of course I do."

"But?"

She returned the painting to the pile on the table. Glancing back at him over her shoulder, she said, "No buts."

His heart in his throat, Cole got up and went to her. "Have you really made the leap, Liv?"

She turned to him, her eyes flashing with anger and emotion. "I've been to bed with you, made love with you—only you. And you can *ask* me that?"

Cupping her face in his hands, he held her still,

keeping his own fury in check. "You're waiting," he said softly, "and anticipating disaster. You're waiting for me to turn into a jerk because you don't believe it's possible I could love you with no conditions, no reservations."

"Cole—"

He brought his mouth down on hers in a hard, fast, furiously possessive kiss. He felt her clutch his shirt, but she didn't push him away. Rather, she kissed him back as if she had something to prove to him—and maybe to herself. Lifting her tight against him, their tongues tangled in a battle of wills.

By the time he pulled back from her, his heart pounded. He finally ventured a glance down at her and was appalled to find fear in her eyes. He hated that he had put it there.

Olivia looked away. "I'm, um, going to take a shower."

"Liv," he said, taking her arm. "I'm sorry."

"For what?"

"I don't know, exactly. For whatever it is that's giving you all these doubts."

"I love you, Cole. I have no doubt about that." She caressed his face and reached up to kiss him before she went into the bathroom and closed the door.

He watched her go, wishing he felt more comforted by her words.

—◆◆◆—

Olivia stood under the pulsing water of the shower to rinse the conditioner out of her hair. She couldn't believe how easily he had tuned into the doubts she was working so hard to keep hidden from him. *You always have been a terrible actress.* Her father used to tell her that she couldn't lie to him because her face lit up like a Roman candle whenever she tried.

Turning off the shower, she reached for a towel and then the robe she had hung on the hook behind the door. She used the towel to clear the steam from the mirror and went through the motions of preparing for a night out even though her heart wasn't in it. After she dried her hair, she opened the door to find Cole stretched out on the bed, listening to his iPod and wearing only his bathing suit.

He's so beautiful, she thought with a deep sigh of pleasure. *And he's mine—for now, for however long it lasts*.

She bent over to press a kiss to his belly.

He sucked in a deep breath of surprise.

"Bathroom's all yours."

He rolled off the bed. "Love your notification system."

After he closed the bathroom door, she slipped into a form-fitting red dress with a plunging neckline. Jenny always said red was Olivia's color because of her dark hair and pale complexion. She slid into two-inch heels and checked the ensemble in the mirror.

A few minutes later, Cole stepped out of the bathroom with a towel wrapped around his waist. The steam curled around him. Their eyes met in the full-length mirror. "Wow."

"Is that your favorite word?" she asked, smiling as she secured the back of an earring.

"When it comes to you, apparently it is. Let me see the front."

She turned around.

"Wow," he said on a long exhale, his eyes fixed on her cleavage.

Bending down to meet his eyes, she said, "I'm up here."

"Uh-huh."

"Cole?"

"Uh-huh?"

"Up here, honey." She used her fingertip on his chin to tilt his face up.

"Oh. Right." He licked his lips. "You were saying?"

"I'm sorry about the doubts. I wish I didn't have them." Her hands cruised through his damp chest hair to rest on his shoulders. "I want to close my eyes and just leap. And I thought I could. I really did. But that's not me. I wish it was, but I'm cautious and plodding and the least spontaneous person you'll ever meet. I dream about being free and loose and easy. Maybe someday I'll get there. For now, this is all I'm capable of." She hesitated before she added, "If it's not enough for you, I'll understand if you want to—"

"What? Walk away? Is that who you think *I* am?"

"The thing is, I really don't know, do I?"

His expression incredulous, his eyes hard, he turned away from her to get dressed. "That's just great."

Frozen in place, pain and longing and loss cut through her, leaving her breathless. *How had that gone so wrong?*

They left the hotel in silence.

As he held the car door for her, she remembered him leaning in to kiss her before they left the airport, and again the loss was paralyzing.

She wanted to reach for him but didn't. Her heart beat hard, so hard she could feel the flutter of it in her throat. This was the most important thing that had ever happened to her, and she was ruining it.

With his face set in a grim expression, he made no move to start the car.

"I'm sorry," she whispered. "You didn't deserve that. You've been nothing but honest and sincere."

"It's my fault."

"How can you say that?"

"I pushed for too much too soon. We shouldn't have spent the weekend together. You weren't ready."

"I was. I *am*. I want this, Cole." She looked down at her hands. "I want *you*, more than I've ever wanted anything. That's what scares me so much."

"You *have* me, honey." He reached over to grasp her hands. "I don't know how many different ways I can say that. I love you, Olivia."

She kept her eyes down.

"Look at me."

Reluctantly, she turned to him.

"I *love* you."

Tears flooded her eyes. "I know."

"I want you to know that I've only ever said that to one other woman, and that was years ago." He caressed her cheek. "Are they just words to you?"

"No." She risked another glance at him. "They're everything to me."

He reached for her.

"I'm sorry," she whispered into his shoulder. "I hurt you, and I didn't mean to. That's the last thing I'd ever want to do."

"Don't give up on us, Liv."

"I won't."

"Good, because I am going to take *you* to your favorite restaurant."

She lifted her head off his shoulder. "How do you know my favorite restaurant?"

"I have my sources." He started the car. "And for the right incentive package I might divulge them later."

She laughed softly. "Cole?"

"What, honey?"

"Thank you for taking me out tonight."

He brought her hand to his lips. "My pleasure."

—⁓—

Actually, it was *her* pleasure—the wine, the meal, the candles, him. Especially him. She liked the way he'd kept his hand on the small of her back as they followed the maître d' through the restaurant and how he had held her chair until she was settled.

Olivia noticed that every head in the room—especially the female heads—turned to look at Cole, not that he noticed. But she did. She hated the way other women looked at him with raw hunger on their faces. *Hands off*, she wanted to shriek. *He's mine!*

Olivia could see why he attracted such attention and figured he'd probably gotten just as many hungry looks before he was famous. He wore a black shirt with gray pants that fit him like they were made for him. His cuffs were turned back to reveal an elaborate silver watch with little dials that he said kept time in four different zones. The band of metal around his wrist struck her as ridiculously sexy.

She found herself fascinated by the way his hands moved as he buttered bread or toyed with the stem of his wineglass. He used those same hands to bring her to the most amazing orgasms and to fly airplanes. The thought made her giggle.

"What's so funny?"

She shook her head as the giggles escalated to laughter.

"Olivia, come on. Tell me."

"I was just thinking about your ability to... multitask."

His eyebrows knitted with confusion. "I have no idea what that means, and I'm not sure I want to."

She was saved when their meals were delivered— teriyaki chicken for her and salmon for him.

"How is it?" he asked.

"The best. My favorite meal."

"So I heard."

"We'll be discussing that later."

"Mmm, dessert."

She raised an eyebrow. "Mud pie?"

His fork went still in midair. "Not what I was thinking, but sure, if that's what you want."

"Maybe I could have both?" She slid her hand up his leg, and when she reached her destination, he choked on a mouthful of water. "Is that a yes?"

While he coughed, she glanced around to make sure no one was looking. Luckily, the busy restaurant couldn't have cared less that he was throbbing under her hand.

"Um, what are you doing?" he asked.

"Just trying to decide between the mud pie and the other very interesting dessert options. What do you think?"

"Not thinking too much at the moment."

She leaned in to whisper in his ear. "I love how your eyes get really dark blue when you're turned on."

He grabbed her hand. "Liv... That's enough."

"And your lips. They part ever so slightly, just

enough for me to do this." She leaned in to dab her tongue between them.

"Olivia, please. I'm starting to sweat over here."

A victorious smile lit up her face.

"Which is, of course, the goal," he mumbled.

"I think I'll pass on the mud pie."

"I was going to take you for a walk through the Torpedo Factory," he said, his voice gruff and controlled.

"I've been there."

"Not with me."

Her whisper was breathy against his ear. "The places I go with you are *so* much better than any old factory." She kissed him again while under the table she dragged a fingernail along his throbbing length.

He tore his lips free of hers and signaled to the waiter. "Check, please."

Cole all but dragged her to the parking lot. The moment they reached the car, he pressed her against it and plundered. She had driven him mad with her flirtation in the restaurant, and now as her arms curled around his neck and her mouth opened under his, he gave her everything he had. Her taste was an exotic combination of wine and the sweetness so unique to her, a flavor that could drive a man mad as surely as it could drive him to take what she offered so willingly.

Need pounded through him as he pushed his erection into the welcoming V of her legs. Her dress impeded him, so he pushed it up.

"Cole," she gasped, as much from the cold as the insanity of what they were on the verge of doing.

Breathing hard, he rested his forehead against hers for a moment before he opened the door for her. When he was settled into the driver's seat, he put his head back, seeking some semblance of control. No woman had ever had such an effect on him, and he was beginning to realize that no one else ever would.

Her hand on his leg got his attention. "I can't take any more of that, Liv. You're making me crazy, and you're not ready for crazy."

"Take me back to the hotel. I want to be with you."

He turned to her. "You don't have to do this to show me—"

"That I love you?"

"I know you do."

"Drive, Cole."

It took six minutes to get back to the hotel. The instant the door to their room clicked shut behind him, he pounced. He reached for the hem of her dress and took it right up and over her head. Underneath he found a black bra with matching panties and sheer hose that ended abruptly at mid-thigh.

"*Wow*," he said.

She giggled and the joyful sound went straight to his heart. After the difficult, emotional day she'd had, he wanted to make her forget, even if just for a little while. As he pressed her back against the wall, her expression shifted from delighted to wary and expectant. Starting with her neck, he set out to kiss every inch of soft, pale skin he could reach.

Her fingers clutched his hair. He loved how she did that, how she needed to touch him while he loved her. His lips skimmed over the tops of plump breasts still contained in the lacy bra while his hands skirted over her smooth, flat belly.

"*Cole*."

The sound of his name coming from breathless, parted lips fueled his desire. "What, honey?"

"My legs are all wobbly."

"We can't have that, now can we?" He quickly removed the scrap of panties and flipped open the front clasp of her bra. Shrugging out of the shirt she had unbuttoned, he dropped it to the floor.

"Don't move," he said as he crossed the room to get a condom. When he returned, he put the condom in his pocket and resumed kissing his way down the front of her. He left a hot path from neck to breasts to belly button and beyond. Using his feet to slide hers further apart, he dropped to his knees in front of her. His fingers found her slick with desire. The discovery made him throb almost painfully. Another part of him wanted in on this and soon, but not yet. Not quite yet.

Lost in the scent and taste of her, he pushed his fingers into her warmth as he flicked his tongue over her. Within seconds, he could feel the signs of her impending climax. He loved how easily she came for him, as if she had been made for him and only him.

She groaned, her legs trembled, and she cried out as the orgasm surged through her.

Cole glanced up at her and saw her head thrown back against the wall, her lips parted, her breasts flushed to a rosy red from the heat they had generated together. He got up, quickly shed the rest of his clothes, and fumbled with the condom. Reaching for her, he lifted her up and onto his straining erection.

He felt the whoosh of air escape from her at the moment of impact. Almost as if he were outside himself watching someone else, he took her hard and fast, right there against the wall.

Her fingers clutching his shoulders, her legs wrapped tight around his waist, she held on for the ride.

The desire, the passion, the *heat* was overwhelming, so overwhelming he had no choice but to take everything she offered. Sweat rolled down his back, and his lungs screamed for air, forcing him to tear his lips free of hers and suck in deep, greedy breaths. He pushed hard into her and felt her clutch him from within and then cry out again as she reached another peak. When she arched into him, he rode the wave with her and then let himself go, pouring forth with a great surge of release that left him stupid and weak in its wake.

With his forehead resting on her shoulder, he concentrated on breathing. Her arms were tight around him, her fingers massaging his neck. He trembled. And then suddenly he was ashamed. Two days ago she had been a virgin, and he'd just taken her against a wall like a madman. Lifting his head, he brushed his lips over hers in a gentle caress. "Sorry."

"For?"

"Being so rough with you. For—"

She kissed him. "I loved it," she whispered, a faint blush appearing on her cheeks. "Don't apologize. Please don't."

Holding her tight against him, he carried her to the bed and lay her down before he finally withdrew from her. Gazing down at her, he smoothed the hair back off her forehead.

"I promised myself I'd go easy with you, but there

was that black bra and this." He ran a hand over the thigh-high hose he hadn't taken the time to remove. "You make me so crazy, Liv. I've never lost control like that before."

Her eyes brightened with pleasure at his confession. "Really?"

Raising his little finger, he said, "Pinky swear."

Smiling, she wrapped her pinky around his and kissed him.

"Be right back." In the bathroom he flipped on the light, reached down to remove the condom, and did a double take when he saw a small but unmistakable hole.

"*Shit!*"

Chapter 14

OLIVIA CRAWLED UNDER THE COVERS, HER BODY languid and satisfied. They'd made love many times over the course of the weekend, but when she looked back on their time together, she'd remember the wall. *Who knew you could do it against a wall?*

As she relived the encounter, her nipples tightened and the place between her legs tingled. Already she wanted him again and wished he would hurry up in the bathroom.

By the time he finally emerged, she was more than ready for him.

He slid into bed.

Olivia shifted onto him. "I missed you."

"I see that," he said, looping his arms around her.

"Can we do it again yet?"

"Liv…"

"Oh," she said, embarrassed. "You don't want to." She moved off him. "I didn't mean to be so forward."

He turned onto his side and pulled her close. "Baby, you can't be too forward with me. If you want something, all you have to do is reach out and take it."

"What's wrong, Cole? I can see it on your face."

"Honey…"

She propped herself up on one elbow. "*What?* You're scaring me."

"The condom, the one we just used?"

·She nodded.

"It kind of… ripped."

Her heart stopped. "What does that mean?"

"Well, I guess it's possible you could've gotten pregnant, but that's all you'll get from me. I just had a full physical for work. I'm totally healthy." The words came out in a rush, like he was trying to get them said before she lost it.

She flopped down onto the pillow and stared up at the ceiling. "Does that… I mean, they rip?" she asked in a small voice. "Does that happen?"

"Never to me, but I've heard of it happening to other people."

"Do you think it was enough for me," she swallowed, "to get pregnant?"

"I don't know."

They fell silent, both absorbed in their own thoughts.

"What if—"

"Do you know—"

He reached for her hand and laced his fingers through hers. "You first."

She turned her head so she could see him. "I was just going to ask what we'll do if I am pregnant."

"I guess we'll have a baby."

His tone might have been flippant, but his hand was damp and clammy.

After another lengthy silence, she turned to him again. "What were you going to ask me? Before?"

"I wondered if you know how the timing works out."

"Since it's never been an issue for me before, I have no idea. Jenny would, though." Olivia glanced at the clock to find it was nearly eleven.

"You can ask her tomorrow."

"Yeah. Or I could call her now."

"Isn't it too late?"

"She'll be up." Their eyes met and held. Olivia finally looked away and reached for the phone. "Hey. It's me."

Cole rolled over, put his arm around her, and rested his head on her shoulder so he could hear Jenny.

"What's going on, Liv?" Jenny asked.

Olivia told her.

"Oh, no," Jenny said.

"How do I know about the timing?"

"When was the first day of your last period?"

Olivia thought about that for a moment. "Two weeks ago, I think."

Jenny was silent for a long moment.

"Jen?"

"The timing would be ideal," she said, adding quickly, "but that doesn't mean anything, Liv. You can't freak out until you miss a period."

Olivia absorbed the information, and despite what Jenny advised, she fought the immediate urge to freak out.

"Are you okay?" Jenny asked.

"Sure," Olivia said with a small laugh. "I finally decide to give sex a whirl, and look what happens."

"Must've been *quite* a whirl."

Olivia squeezed Cole's hand. "It was."

"I'll need details tomorrow."

"Good *night*, Jenny." Olivia put the phone on the table and turned to Cole. "Did you hear all that?"

"Yeah." He paused for a moment before he said, "Liv, if you are… pregnant, we'll handle it. Together. I promise. You can count on me."

She played with his fingers. "Does it scare the hell out of you? The idea of a baby?"

"Not if you're the mom."

As he once again said the right thing at the right moment, her panic was suddenly replaced by foolish hope. A baby. *His* baby.

"Would you have it?"

Her eyes connected with his. "Of course I would."

"I'm sorry. I thought so, but I wasn't sure."

He'd reminded her that they still had much to learn about each other, and now there might be a baby, too.

"This has been quite a day," she said with a sigh.

"All I wanted was to pamper you a little this weekend."

"You did." She snuggled into his embrace. "This has been the most wonderful weekend of my life."

His lips brushed over her hair. "Will you still think that if you're pregnant?"

"Things happen for a reason," she decided. That was better than freaking out, right? "I believe that. You were punched in my store so we could meet."

Amused by her theory, he spooled her hair through his fingers. "And what would be the reason for a baby?"

"Maybe it would keep me from ruining what fate was so kind to arrange for us."

He laughed softly. "Maybe so. Are you going to be afraid to ever make love with me again?"

She caressed his face. "Well, since the damage might already be done…"

Smiling, he kissed her sweetly, gently.

"Cole?"

"Hmm?" he murmured against her lips.

"I don't want you to go easy with me."

He stopped and looked at her. "What do you mean?"

Olivia felt her cheeks heat with embarrassment. "What you said before. I want to make you…"

"What, honey?"

"Lose control again."

The surprise registered on his face. "You liked that?" he asked, his voice hoarse with emotion and desire that she could see in the darkening of his eyes.

She nodded shyly.

"So did I." He lowered his mouth to hers.

The next morning, after they'd both showered and packed, they had breakfast in their room. Olivia fought through a riot of emotions, highs and lows so extreme she found herself wanting to laugh one minute and cry the next.

Cole studied her over the top of his coffee mug. He took a drink before he put the cup down and reached for her hand. "I've been thinking about something and I want to ask you about it, but you don't have to answer me now, okay?"

Intrigued, Olivia said, "All right."

"Before I say anything else, I want you to know this was the very best weekend ever. I love you, I love being with you, and I hate the idea of spending even one minute without you now that I've found you."

Tears pooled in her eyes as she wrapped her hand around his. "Cole."

He kissed her hand. "I know things are kind of weird at home right now, and you're making this big change at school. What I want you to know is that I'd love to have you come live with me in Chicago."

He rested a finger over her lips to keep her from saying anything. "It would be a big move, I know. Your life is here—I know that, too. But we have art schools in Chicago—good ones that would be lucky to have you. And you wouldn't have to work if you lived with me. You could focus only on school and finish that much sooner. I don't want you to say anything now. Just think about it. We can talk about it the next time we're together."

"You're so sweet to even ask," she said, overwhelmed by him.

"I have a big place, and you could do whatever you wanted to it." He grinned as he sweetened the deal. "And lots of friends who would love having you around. Of course, I'd still be gone four or five nights a month for work, but you could get all your homework done then so you could play with me when I'm home."

She smiled at the picture he painted. It was so tempting to just say yes, to take what he offered without a thought to the implications.

"Will you think about it?" he asked, his heart in his eyes.

Nodding, she leaned over to kiss him. "Thank you for asking."

He brought her onto his lap and into his arms, holding her close for several minutes. "I hate to say it, but we have to go. I need to catch the noon flight back to Chicago so I'm ready to fly at four."

"I know," she said but didn't let him go.

"A week from Friday," he reminded her. "Four whole days together."

"That's years from now."

He laughed as he kissed her neck. "Coffee on Wednesday around four? I'll have about half an hour between flights if everything's on time."

"Whoo-hoo. Half an hour."

"Better than nothing?"

"I guess so."

"I'll call you tonight. I'll call you every night."

Knowing she couldn't delay any longer, she got up from his lap, zipped her suitcase, and rolled it over to the door.

He got up and crossed the room to her. "This is just the beginning."

She stepped into his embrace and held on tight.

"It's going to be great. I promise."

"Thank you," she whispered. "I had the very best time."

"Me, too."

———

They drove to the airport in silence. In the passenger seat, Olivia felt like the air was being squeezed from her lungs as she tried to breathe.

"Keep the car for as long as you want," he said.

"I'll turn it in when I go to work this afternoon."

"Whatever you want."

In no time at all, he pulled up to the curb at the departures level. Her heart beat fast and her stomach twisted as she fought hard not to cry. She wasn't going to cry. Later, for sure, but not now.

He retrieved his bag from the back of the car.

Olivia got out and met him at the curb with a smile that she hoped didn't look too forced. "Until Wednesday?"

When he nodded, his jaw shifted ever so slightly, which was the only indication he gave that he was fighting his own emotions. He drew her into a tight hug.

"Love you," he whispered.

"Love you, too."

"Just remember that any time you start to think it's hopeless."

"I will."

With his eyes open and fixed on hers, he cradled her face in his hands and kissed her, just his lips on hers, nothing more. Just enough. He pulled back, took a long last look at her face, and then kissed her forehead. "See you next time."

"I'll be here."

"Counting on it."

She did her best to smile as she watched him go.

From inside the terminal, he turned and waved. And then he was gone.

Still struggling to breathe, Olivia got back in the car and called Jenny's cell phone. "Hey, where are you?" Olivia asked when her cousin answered.

"Just got home and put Billy down for his nap. What's going on?"

"Cole just left."

"Are you okay?"

"Not really."

"Come here, Liv. Right now."

"I have to work at three."

"You can get changed here. Come on."

Since the last place Olivia wanted to be was at home with her mother, she agreed.

—◦—

Jenny was waiting at the front door when Olivia arrived. She fell into her cousin's embrace and held on tight, determined to get through this without completely falling apart.

"It's all right, sweetie," Jenny said softly. "Everything's going to be fine. He's wild about you. Even Will said so the other night."

"So much happened this weekend," Olivia said when she had recovered some. She followed Jenny into the kitchen and filled her in on what was going on with her parents.

"A hundred and fifty *thousand*?" Jenny gasped.

"That's what my dad said."

"Jesus. Are they getting divorced?"

"He didn't use that word, but he inferred he was done with her."

"I can't say I blame him."

"Me, either. I don't know how he's tolerated her this long."

"He's such a sweetheart," Jenny said. "He deserves to be happy."

Olivia took a sip of the coffee Jenny had poured for her. "Cole asked me to come live with him in Chicago."

"*Shut up!* What did you say?"

"Nothing yet. We're going to talk about it the next time we're together."

"When's that going to be?"

"A week from Friday. We're going away for four days."

"To where?"

"He won't tell me. He wants it to be a surprise."

"He's lovely, Liv."

Olivia smiled. "Isn't he?"

"Are you happy?"

"When I'm with him, there's nothing else in the world I want. But watching him leave today was so hard. The hardest thing ever."

"What do you think about moving there?"

"I don't know. He just mentioned it this morning. I haven't had two seconds to think about it."

"You don't have to decide anything right away." Jenny reached for her hand. "You've waited such a long time for this. I want you to enjoy it. Even if you're not with him, he's out there and he loves you, Liv. He really does."

"I know."

"It's amazing, isn't it? To be loved like that?"

"I never thought it would happen to me. Not like this."

"Well, it has, so try to relax. It'll work out."

Olivia sighed. "You're right, and I'll try. It's just…"

"What, honey?"

"You should see the way other women stare at him. Everywhere we go. They're like predators. I hate it."

"What does he say about it?"

"He doesn't even seem to notice it most of the time."

"Then you shouldn't worry about it. His mind is clearly on you, Liv." Jenny raised an inquisitive eyebrow. "So what happened with the condom?"

"It ripped."

"That doesn't just happen. You must've given it a hell of a workout." Jenny's expression shifted from inquisitive to amused. "Do tell."

"There was this black bra and a wall."

"Holy shit! Against a *wall*?"

Olivia's face burned with embarrassment.

"How was it?"

"Better for me than it was for the condom."

Jenny howled with laughter. "You know the odds of you being pregnant are really low, right?"

"Yeah, but part of me kind of hopes—"

"That you *are*? Pregnant?"

Olivia shrugged. "Is that awful?"

"You want a baby? You've never said that before."

"Someday, I guess. I've been so focused on school that I haven't really thought about it much. What I *do* want is Cole, and having a baby together would kind of seal the deal, you know?"

"That'd be an awful lot of pressure on a new relationship," Jenny said. "What will you guys do if you are?"

"He said we'd handle it together, and that I shouldn't worry about it."

"That's probably good advice until you know you have something to worry about."

"Somehow I think that'll be easier said than done." Olivia stood up and went to the sink to rinse her mug. "I should get home and drop off my stuff before I have to be at work. I've got to turn in the rental car before my shift."

"Liv, why don't you stay here until you figure out what you're going to do? We've got the guest room all ready, and I hate the idea of you having to deal with Aunt Mary every day."

Olivia contemplated Jenny's offer. "It's too far from the Metro."

"I can take you to the station and pick you up. I wouldn't mind at all."

"Sometimes it's pretty late."

"So what? Stay, take a breather here for a while—for as long as you want."

"What about Will?"

"He'd love hearing all our gossip real time, rather than post-call recaps."

Olivia laughed. "Could you at least *pretend* you don't tell him everything?"

Jenny shrugged sheepishly. "So what do you say? Let us be your safe house for a while."

"I'd love to," Olivia said with a hug for her cousin. "Thank you."

Chapter 15

OLIVIA'S CELL PHONE RANG WHEN SHE WAS ON THE Metro that night. She saw Cole's number on the caller ID, and her heart skipped a happy beat.

"Hi," she said.

"Hey, honey. How's it going?"

"Better now. How are you?"

"Fogged in." He sounded annoyed and tired.

"Where?"

"Cleveland."

"Are you staying there tonight?"

"We're giving it another hour before we bag it. How was your day?"

"All right. Nothing special."

"No one got punched out in the store?"

"Not today," she said with a laugh. The sound of his voice had lifted her spirits. "I'm hoping that was a once-in-a-lifetime event."

"Once was just enough, right?"

"Absolutely."

"I miss you. Bad."

"Me, too," she said softly. "I was just thinking about you when you called."

"What about me?"

"About the wall, actually." Her cheeks heated, and she was glad no one was sitting near her on the train.

"Don't talk about that! I'm at work."

She giggled at his distress. "I'm not."

"Behave. So where are you?"

"On my way to Jenny's on the train. She invited me to stay with them for a while until I figure out my living situation. I can't stand to be anywhere near my mother right now, not after what I found out about her yesterday."

"I don't blame you. I'm glad you're going to Jenny's. That's a great idea."

"She offered me a 'safe house' until I make some plans."

He laughed. "Cute."

"My dad thought it was a good idea, too. He's going to bring me what I need from the house."

"Don't forget my offer."

"How could I?"

"I know we said we wouldn't talk about it until next time, but are you leaning in any direction on that?"

"Not yet."

"I'm sorry. I shouldn't have asked."

"You can ask." She paused and then added, "You know I want to, right?"

"Do you?"

"Cole… Of course I do. Watching you leave today was so hard." Her voice caught. "The hardest thing ever."

"We could be together every day, baby. *Every day*." His tone was urgent. "God, I'd love that."

"So would I, but I just need to—"

"What, honey?"

"I think I need to be on my own for a while. How can I go from my father's house to your house without ever knowing if I can take care of myself?"

"You don't have to take care of yourself. I war. to take care of you."

"And I love you for that, but I need to do this for me. Will you hate me if I want to live by myself for a while before we decide anything?"

"Yes."

Olivia was speechless.

He cracked up. "I'm kidding. Did I scare you?"

"Nah. I knew you were kidding."

"You did not!"

"Come back, will you? Fly through the fog and come back. I need you."

"Don't say that," he whispered. "You're killing me."

"It's not like you don't have a plane available, right?"

He laughed softly. "Are you encouraging me to commit a plane-napping?"

"How much time would you do?"

"I think it could be a pretty long stretch."

"More than two weeks?"

"Much more."

"Damn."

"Hang on a sec, hon."

Olivia heard him consulting with someone in the background.

"Hey, I've gotta go. We just got clearance."

"To go where?"

"Chicago."

"Will you call me when you're safe?"

"I'm safe in the plane."

"Safe on the *ground*."

"It'll be late."

"I'll wait."

"All right."

"Love you."

"Love you, too."

—⁂—

Olivia was in bed at Jenny's house when the phone rang two hours later.

"Safe," he said.

"On the ground?"

"Yes, and on my way home. Finally."

"Oh, good," she said.

"Hey, I don't want you worrying about me when I'm flying. It's as natural to me as breathing or driving a car."

"Only without the breakdown lane."

"It's much safer than driving a car. Far fewer people die in planes than in cars every year."

"But people *do* die in planes."

"I'm not going to," he said firmly. "Just put that right out of your head, or being with me is going to make you nuts."

"Too late."

He sighed. "You've got to be tired. What are you doing still awake?"

"I was waiting for you to call, and I'm having trouble getting used to sleeping alone again. Thanks for ruining that for me, by the way."

"Happy to help."

She heard him choke back a yawn. "You're beat, huh?"

"Yeah, it was a long day, and I had someone messing with my sleep the last few nights."

"You loved it."

"You bet your life I did."

"What time are you working tomorrow?"

"Noon flight to Orlando, then Atlanta, D.C., and back to Chicago."

"You're going to be in D.C.?"

"Very briefly. It's a short turnaround time, so I won't see you."

"That's *so* not fair."

"I shouldn't have told you."

"No, you shouldn't have. Let's talk about something else. What's your house like?"

"It's a town house. Three floors, three bedrooms, two bathrooms. Nothing special."

Nothing special? It sounded like a palace to her.

"Like I told you," he said in a cajoling tone, "there's plenty of room."

"If I were going to take on a roommate, you'd be my first choice."

"You're really going to do this? Get a place of your own?"

"I think I am."

"Don't sign anything more than a six-month lease. Will you promise me that?"

"Is that long enough to prove my point?"

"Actually I think one month would do the trick."

"Not long enough. Just think, though, if I have my own place you won't need to stay at the Sheraton on your D.C. overnights."

"Well, there is that. And maybe I could hang out with you on some of my weeks off."

"Really?"

"Why not?"

"I'd love that."

"I'd have to figure out how that would work with my other gig, though."

"What other gig?"

"I, ah, fly kids and young adults with cancer to their treatments a couple of times a month."

"That's amazing. Why didn't you tell me?"

"I don't know. It's just something I do since my mother died. Something I can do to help the cause."

"Do you always take the same people?"

"Most of the time. I have one I take to Sloan-Kettering in New York and another to MD Anderson in Houston. I can't always take them because of my work schedule, but I see them most often."

"You must get attached to them."

"I try not to."

"And how's that going?"

"Not so well," he confessed. "They're great kids, and despite what they're going through, they always have a big smile and a hug for me. It's very rewarding."

"I imagine it is. Where do you get the planes to fly them?"

"Several companies here in Chicago donate their corporate jets whenever they're not using them. I'm checked out on three different planes so I can be ready to fly whatever's available."

"Just when I thought I couldn't love you more I find out there's this whole other side of you."

"It's no big deal, Liv."

"It is to the people you're helping."

"A lot of people helped us when my mother was sick."

"Was she sick for long?"

"Four months from diagnosis to death."

"God," she sighed. "What kind of cancer did she have?"

"Pancreatic. It was the most shocking thing. She went from perfectly healthy to terminally ill in a month's time. I took a leave of absence from the airline and moved home to help take care of her. I'm so glad now I had that time with her."

"You must've been so devastated when she died."

"To be honest, the diagnosis was more devastating. By the time she died, it was almost a relief. I know that must sound weird, but the highs and lows of the treatment and the doctors' appointments—where there was never any good news—just sucked the life out of us."

"I can understand that. How's your dad doing?"

"He's surprised us all. He never lifted a finger at home, and now he's doing his own laundry and grocery shopping. He even took a cooking class at one of the local churches. He has a lot of good friends who keep him busy, and my nieces and nephews are always over there."

"Do you think he'll ever get married again?"

"Nah. I don't think so. They were very happy together for almost forty years."

"Would you care if he did?"

"People ask me that a lot. I wouldn't mind as long as he found someone who wouldn't try to reorder his whole life. He likes it the way it is." Cole yawned. "I hate to say it, but I've gotta go to bed, hon. I'm fading fast."

"Me, too. I'm hugging a pillow, but it's a poor substitute."

"I hear ya. I'll call you tomorrow."

"Can't wait. I love you, Cole."

"I love you, too. Sleep tight."

She closed the phone and held it tight against her chest. When she woke up in the morning, it was still there.

Chapter 16

THE NEXT EVENING, COLE ARRIVED HOME AT ELEVEN to find Tucker waiting for him.

"I've given out way too many keys to this place," Cole grumbled, even though he was happy to see his friend.

"You owe me some information, so I figured if I bribed you with a six pack, you'd spill it."

"You figured right." Cole went to the fridge and grabbed a bottle of Sam Adams. "Need another one?"

"Twist my arm."

Cole opened two bottles and brought them to the living room. He handed one to Tucker, put his on the table, and pulled off his tie. Reaching for the top button of his uniform shirt, he glanced at his friend. "So what do you want to know?"

Tucker put Sports Center on mute and raised an eyebrow. "Whatever you're not telling me."

"What makes you think I'm not telling you something?"

Tucker rolled his eyes. "Let's examine the evidence, shall we? It all begins with a mysterious weekend in Washington, followed by an urgent phone call to sidekick and best pal Tucker pleading with him to deal with Nutty Natasha before she screws something up for our fearless hero. Screws up what, exactly, our hearty sidekick would like to know. The evidence points to a romantic liaison for our dashing hero, but *why*, the sidekick wonders, wouldn't the hero spill the deets when he knows his feckless friend lives vicariously through him?"

Cole couldn't help but smile. Tucker had that effect on people. "You've figured me out."

"Ah ha! I knew it! Who is she?"

"Olivia," Cole said with a smile. Just saying her name made him happy.

"And when did you meet Miss Olivia?"

"The day I got punched in the airport."

"And you've waited *all this time* to tell me about her? What's that about?"

Cole shrugged. "I wanted to keep it to myself for a while. Since when is that a federal crime?"

"I'm wounded."

"You'll recover."

Tucker studied Cole for a long moment.

"What?"

"Something's different about you."

Cole couldn't deny that so he didn't try.

"Would this *Olivia* have anything to do with why Brenda called me crying her eyes out because you ended it with her?"

Cole swallowed hard. "I guess." He hated to hear Brenda was that upset. In fact, it surprised the hell out of him. They'd never been serious.

Tucker rubbed the whiskers on his jaw. "Acting mysterious, holding out on poor old Tucker, breaking up with longtime ladies… This is sounding serious."

"It is," Cole said without hesitation.

Tucker stared at him, apparently too astounded to speak. "Wanna run that by me one more time?"

"The thing with Olivia. It's serious."

Tucker shook his head, as if he hadn't heard Cole correctly. "So you mean to tell me you plan to be like, what, *exclusive* with this girl?"

"Yep."

"Man, that must've been some head injury. It totally rebooted your computer."

"Very funny."

"You honestly think you can pull this off?"

"Pull what off?"

"The one-woman-man act."

"It's not an act. I love her."

Tucker nearly choked on the mouthful of beer he was attempting to swallow. "Did you just say… You did not just say… *Shit*."

Cole laughed at his friend's reaction.

"I absolutely have to meet this girl as soon as humanly possible."

"What's the rush?"

"She's managed to do what no woman before her has even come close to doing."

"And what is that, exactly?"

"She's got *you* chasing *her*. That's a freaking miracle, man. I need to meet this wonder woman so I can bow down before her."

Cole chucked a throw pillow at him. "Shut up."

On Wednesday morning, Olivia spent extra time on her hair. And rather than the khakis she usually wore with her royal blue uniform shirt, she tossed a short black skirt into her tote bag to change into before work. Jenny dropped her at the Metro an hour before she was due on campus for a study group meeting for her international finance class.

After the meeting, she couldn't have said what had happened. She hadn't heard a word of it but had several items on her "to do" list that she had no memory of writing down.

"I'm losing it," she whispered to herself with a laugh as she walked across the quad on her way to the art department. The adviser she had met with wasn't in, so Olivia left her portfolio with the department secretary. She cast a nervous glance over her shoulder and caught the secretary tossing the leather case into a pile on her desk, as if it didn't contain the most important work Olivia had ever done as an artist.

Deep breaths. Whatever's going to happen will happen. It's out of my hands now. Outside, she checked her watch. She had to be at work in forty-five minutes, and in just four hours she'd see Cole. The thought made her want to skip to the Metro station. *It's only for thirty minutes*, she reminded herself. *Thirty minutes!* She couldn't wait.

———

Olivia watched for him at the end of the concourse, where the flood of people pouring into the terminal blocked her view. On tiptoes, she strained to see over the hoards coming from the gates. Her eyes finally connected with his, and his face lit up with a big grin.

Trying to be patient, she let him make his way to her, but she was out of patience after waiting all day to see him.

Then he was in front of her, and she stepped into his outstretched arms. Relief flooded through her as she breathed in the masculine scent that was so uniquely his. The crowd parted around them, but they didn't move for a long time.

Finally, he released her and looked down at her. "Come on." Keeping an arm tight around her, he steered her through the terminal to the Capital Airlines lounge. Inside, he flashed his ID at the dumbfounded attendant.

"First Officer Langston," the attendant said, giddy with excitement. "It's such an incredible thrill to have you here."

"Oh, um, thanks," he muttered, clearly embarrassed by her effusive welcome.

"If there's *anything*, anything at all I can do for you, just let me know."

Behind Cole's back, Olivia rolled her eyes. Could the woman *be* any more ridiculous? Even as she dismissed the bottle blonde as foolish, Olivia's stomach ached at the thought of how often he probably received such attention. How did he react when she *wasn't* with him?

"Thanks," Cole said, steering Olivia into the room.

Forcing herself to shake off the sickening insecurity, she looked around at the luxurious lounge, which was empty of other customers at the moment. Sofas—in Capital red and blue—were arranged into sitting areas, a wide variety of beverages were available on the bar, and a row of TVs were tuned to most of the major news channels.

"I've always wondered what it was like in here."

"As you can see, it's very exciting," Cole said dryly. He helped himself to a Coke and offered her one.

"Diet, please."

They sat on a sofa around the corner from the prying eyes of the attendant.

Cole put their drinks on a table and whispered, "Kiss me, will you?"

"Happy to."

He cupped her cheek as his lips moved softly over hers.

Olivia's hand rested on his chest, inside his uniform coat. He seemed to be making a huge effort to keep the kiss light and undemanding, but after days without him Olivia wasn't interested in light *or* undemanding. She teased him with flicks of her tongue over his bottom lip. When he finally pulled back from her, his eyes had darkened to a deep, navy blue.

"There's no way I can wait until next Friday to make love with you again," he whispered as he put his arm around her shoulders and pulled her close.

"I'm afraid you'll have to."

"Maybe not."

She raised her head off his shoulder. "What do you mean?"

"I'm trying to trade flights with one of my coworkers so I can get the overnight leg here next Tuesday. No promises, though."

"I'm not going to even think about it until you know for sure."

"I'll have to sleep," he warned her, his eyes dancing with amusement.

"I might allow some of that."

He captured her lips in another soft kiss that had her craving much more.

The attendant walked over, startling them. Cole withdrew his arm from Olivia's shoulders and sat up straighter.

"Can I get you anything?" the woman asked with a flirtatious smile as her curious eyes shifted from Cole to dismiss Olivia before she returned her attention to him.

"No, thank you," he said.

"Let me know if you change your mind," she said as she walked away, her statement heavy with double meaning.

Olivia felt sick again.

His entire demeanor had changed in the course of the brief encounter with the attendant.

Chilled by the sudden distance he had put between them, Olivia said, "What's wrong?"

"I shouldn't have brought you in here."

She couldn't believe it was possible, but she needed to know. "Are you… ashamed… to be seen with someone who has kind of a menial job in the airport?"

His expression shifted from remote to shocked. "*What? Ashamed? Of you?* Jesus, Olivia. I'm not ashamed of you, but I'm supposed to maintain a certain decorum while in uniform. Getting caught making out with my girlfriend in the company lounge hardly counts. And the reason I shouldn't have brought you in here is because all I've thought about today is kissing you. I thought it might be more private in here than in some corner of the terminal. I was wrong."

"Oh." She was ashamed of *herself* now. Her stomach sank, and her heart ached. "I'm sorry, I just… I didn't know." She saw anger in his eyes and in the firm set of his jaw. Somehow she had managed to hurt him—again.

He checked his watch. "I need to go."

"*Already?*"

"By the time I get back, they'll be boarding."

"Don't leave like this." She rested her hand on his arm. "Please. I didn't mean to offend you."

"I know you didn't, Liv, but it *does* offend me that you could think that of me, and I *hate* that you've got it in your head that you're not good enough for me."

Tears filled her eyes. "I'm sorry. I love you so much, and I just keep messing it up. That's the last thing I want to do."

With both hands on her face, he kissed her—properly—with no regard to the prying eyes of the attendant. By the time he pulled back from her, Olivia's head was spinning.

"Does that take care of any remaining questions?" he asked, his eyes dark and fixed on her.

"Yeah," she said breathlessly. "I think that'll do it."

"I look at you, and I'm useless," he said in a quiet but urgent tone. "I think about you from the minute I wake up in the morning until the second I close my eyes at night. I. Love. You. Stop trying to talk me out of it, will you?"

Overcome by his emotional outpouring, she could only nod.

He kissed her again. "Walk me back?"

With his hand wrapped around hers, she followed him past the nosy attendant and back into the crowded terminal. Just before they reached his gate, he stopped and drew her into a tight hug.

Olivia wrapped her arms around him under his coat and held on tight. "So, um, you called me your girlfriend back there."

He drew back from her so he could look at her. "Well, duh. What do you think you are?"

"I liked it."

Kissing her forehead, he held her close. "Then I'll have to say it more often." He glanced over his shoulder at the door to the Jetway where a Capital representative had begun boarding the plane. "I've got to go, hon. See you next time."

"I'll be here."

"I'm counting on it." He kissed her cheek and left her with a smile.

Olivia stood at the window and waited until the plane pulled back from the gate. In the cockpit, Cole wore sunglasses and talked into a headset. Moving to the other side of the door for a better view, she kept her eyes on the shiny blue-and-red plane as it taxied to the end of the runway where it sat for several minutes.

She sucked in a deep breath when the plane suddenly lurched forward, hurtled down the runway, and lifted into the air. It was out of sight before she released the breath she'd been holding in one long sigh. She couldn't imagine what that moment—when the plane lifted off the ground—was like for the people onboard. Did they hold their breath, too? She was sure she would.

She got back to work ten minutes late, but it had been worth it—so totally worth it.

—∿∿—

By the time Cole brought the plane to a stop at the gate in Chicago, it was nearly eleven. He was exhausted and grateful to have the next day off. He planned to sleep all day.

Next to him, Jake Garrison worked on the paperwork while the flight attendants said good night to the passengers. Without looking up from what he was doing, Jake said, "So who's the looker at DCA?"

"What?" Cole asked, startled.

"The *girl*, Langston," Jake said, laughing. "The one you were wearing like a necklace at the gate?"

Cole took the clipboard from him, signed on the line below Jake's signature, and handed it back to him. "She's my girlfriend."

"You have an actual girlfriend."

"That's what I said."

"A girlfriend who works in the airport?"

Cole looked over at him. "What's wrong with that?"

"Not a thing," Jake said, holding up his hands.

"She's working there while she goes to school."

Raising an eyebrow, Jake said, "You're dating a coed?"

"She's twenty-seven, Jake."

"What's she still doing in school?"

"Thanks to some family issues, she's done a few years at the school of hard knocks. She's a gifted artist who's finally starting to believe in her talent." He looked up to find Jake watching him with interest. "What?"

"Nothing."

Cole sighed. "Just say it. Whatever it is."

"What happened to your harem?" Jake asked in a teasing tone.

"Those days are over."

"Seriously?"

"Yep."

"Hmm."

"What does that mean?"

"Oh, nothing," Jake said. "I just don't see you as a one-woman kind of guy."

"Well I am now." Jake was the second person in as many days to make that observation, leaving Cole to wonder just how awful his reputation had become. His womanizing had definitely gotten worse since his mother died, as if he was trying to fill the void or something. Whatever the reason, it hadn't worked until he found Olivia.

Irritated by Jake's comments, Cole took off his seatbelt and slipped out of his seat. He grabbed his uniform coat and backpack. "See ya." He was halfway up the Jetway when he heard Jake calling him.

"Langston! Wait. Come on. Wait up."

Cole stopped, took a deep breath, and turned around.

"What're you so pissed about?" Jake asked.

"Who's pissed?"

"Oh," Jake said with a knowing smile. "I get it."

"I'm tired, Jake, and I have no idea what you're talking about."

"Don't you?"

"As exciting as this conversation has been, I'm afraid I'll have to catch you later." He turned away and started back up the Jetway. "My bed is beckoning."

"You love her, huh?"

Cole stopped but didn't turn back. "Yeah, something like that."

"I'm sorry for what I said. I was out of line."

"Don't sweat it, man. See you later." Cole walked through the terminal thinking that Jake was a good guy who'd always been great to work with. Cole wouldn't hold Jake's comments against him, but it *had* pissed him off to hear Olivia dismissed as nothing special. Although, after the way he'd lived the last few years, he shouldn't be surprised that his friends were noticing the rather significant changes he'd begun to make lately.

On the shuttle to the parking lot, he checked his watch. He wanted to call Olivia, but it was after one in the morning her time. Since she was at Jenny's, he was afraid he'd wake up the baby if he called this late. Rather than risk Jenny's wrath, he decided to wait to call in the morning.

It was just as well. Between what had happened earlier with her and his conversation with Jake, Cole was in a foul mood. But he really wanted to talk to her, to say good night, to hear her voice. So he sent her a text message that said, "Call me if U R still up."

He sank into the soft leather seat of his new black Mustang GT and sat there for a minute hoping she would call before he fired up the car and made quick time of the ride home. Driving as fast as he dared, he beat his personal best by two full minutes—a satisfying end to an otherwise crappy day. Well, other than that one amazing kiss with Olivia. That had been worth getting up for.

How he wished she were waiting for him at home.

He pulled into the complex and parked in front of his townhouse. Glancing up, he noticed a light on in the living room. "What the hell?" he muttered on his way up the stairs.

"Cole! Wait!" Tucker called from his front door.

"Who's in there?" Cole asked, gesturing to his own door as his cell phone rang. No doubt Olivia was calling, but he couldn't take it until he dealt with whatever was going on in his house.

Tucker bounded down his stairs and up Cole's. "I was gonna call the cops when I saw her, but I didn't know if you'd want me to."

Cole's entire body went rigid. "Saw who?"

Pained, Tucker looked away. "Who do you think?"

"*She's in my house?*"

"I didn't know what to do."

Cole charged up the remaining stairs and unlocked the door to find Natasha in all her naked glory stretched out on his sofa with a red rose positioned between her ample breasts.

"Thought you'd never get home, lover," she purred.

"Tucker," Cole said through gritted teeth, "make that call."

Olivia let the phone ring until his voicemail message picked up. Then she tried again, but he still didn't answer. "That's weird," she said, re-reading the text message. He had sent it half an hour earlier when she was in the shower. Wide awake and frustrated by his failure to answer the phone, she took her cell with her and went downstairs to get some water. She was surprised to find Jenny in the kitchen.

"What are you doing up?" Jenny asked.

"Cole sent a text asking me to call him, but he's not answering his phone."

"He probably went to bed."

"Yeah, I guess. What's your story? Can't sleep?"

"Not feeling too good."

"What's the matter?"

"Nauseous."

Olivia eyed her cousin with interest. "The last time you were nauseous in the middle of the night—"

Jenny held up a hand to stop her. "Don't say it. Don't you dare say it." Jenny burst into tears, startling Olivia.

"Hey! What's wrong?" Olivia wrapped her arms around Jenny's shaking shoulders.

"I *cannot* be pregnant again already. I can't."

"Is that wishful thinking? Or something else?"

"Liv, I can barely handle Billy. How in the world will I deal with *two* in diapers? We were going to wait until Billy was three."

"I thought you were on the pill."

Jenny shook her head. "I'm still breastfeeding Billy, so I didn't want to start back on it until after that was done. So much for breastfeeding as birth control."

"You're a great mom, Jen. You'll be just fine with two."

"I wish I could be as optimistic."

"What does Will say?"

"I haven't told him yet. I just took the test today. It didn't even have the decency to take ten seconds to pop positive."

Olivia was unsuccessful in suppressing a giggle.

"Your amusement is interesting since you might be in the same boat."

"Thanks for reminding me," Olivia said, sobering.

"You gonna tell me what happened today? You hardly said a word when you got home tonight."

"I screwed up. Again." She told Jenny about the incident in the Capital lounge. "He was so mad."

"I can't say I blame him. Why is your first impulse to think poorly of him when he's done right by you since the first instant you met him—when, I might add, he was out cold after taking on a guy who was hassling you?"

"I can't seem to help it. This whole thing is straight out of a fairy tale, you know? I just keep waiting for the clock to strike midnight and my coach to turn into a pumpkin. I don't want to be that way, but that's me."

"It's your mother's fault," Jenny said bitterly. "She's made you into a total pessimist. That's going to poison this thing with Cole if you don't get it under control."

"It already has. Twice now I've really hurt him by doubting his sincerity."

"Don't do it again, Liv. It's not his fault that your mother's a miserable old bitch. Don't let her ruin this for you. She's not worth it."

"No, she isn't. I want so badly to let go of all the fear and the worries."

"Then do it. My gut's telling me he's worth it."

"Mine, too. He says the most amazing things to me. Today he said he looks at me and he's useless."

"Wow," Jenny sighed. "That's so romantic."

Right in that moment, Olivia made a decision. "What the hell am I doing? He loves me. I love him. Maybe it won't end. Maybe it'll last forever. I'm just going to go with it."

"I'm sure he'd appreciate that."

"Yes, he would. Are you going to be all right?"

Jenny shrugged. "What choice do I have?" she asked glumly. "I guess we also need to get busy looking for a bigger house if we're going to have another baby."

"Aren't there twins in Will's family?" Olivia teased.

Jenny's horrified face sent Olivia into another fit of laughter.

Chapter 17

OLIVIA TRIED SEVERAL TIMES TO REACH COLE THE next morning, but his phone went straight to voicemail each time. She read his text message from the night before yet again. "No, I'm not imagining things," she muttered. "He did ask me to call him, and then he disappeared."

"Talking to yourself, Liv?"

Olivia turned around to find Jenny leaning against the door frame holding two coffee mugs. She handed one of them to Olivia.

"Thanks. I just can't figure out where he is. I know he's off today, but he's not answering his phone."

"Maybe he's *sleeping*, like you would be if you were off."

"Probably," Olivia said, savoring her first sip of coffee. "I thought you gave up caffeine when you're pregnant."

"One last day," Jenny said with a sigh. "So what are you up to this weekend?"

"Except for working Saturday during the day, not a thing. What about you?"

Jenny sat on Olivia's bed. "I'm trying to figure out a way to break the news to Will. Any suggestions?"

Olivia sat down next to her. "Why don't you take him out for a nice dinner, ply him with many drinks, and then spring it on him. Quick and dirty."

After pondering that for a moment, Jenny said, "I like

it. I'd already decided that significant amounts of liquor would be necessary to take the edge off."

"I'll watch Billy."

"Are you sure? I can ask my parents."

"I'd love to spend the evening with my favorite little man."

"Thanks."

Olivia's phone rang, and she pounced. "Hello?"

"Olivia, this is Leslie Chambers from the Studio Art Department at AU."

"Oh," Olivia cast a glance at Jenny, who put both their mugs on the bedside table. "Dr. Chambers. How are you?"

"Well, to be honest, I'm stumped."

Olivia's stomach dropped with disappointment. "I'm afraid I don't understand."

"What the hell are you doing in business school?"

"Oh, um, well…"

Dr. Chambers laughed. "Olivia, your portfolio is very, *very* impressive. There's a maturity and a depth to your work that really spoke to me."

"Oh. It spoke to you?"

"Loud and clear. Have you completed your transfer paperwork?"

Olivia's tongue was tied in knots. "I, ah, turned it in to the registrar's office last week."

"Good, because we're very pleased to welcome you into the program as of January. Congratulations."

"Oh." Tears blinded her as she tried to absorb the enormity, the sheer magnitude of the moment.

"Olivia? Are you all right?"

"Um, yes. I'm just overwhelmed."

"You have a rare talent, Olivia. I'm looking forward to seeing where it'll take you."

"Thank you," Olivia whispered. "Thank you so much."

"You'll get an official acceptance letter, and I'll be in touch."

Olivia thanked her, closed her phone, and looked over at Jenny.

"*What?* What'd she say?"

Shell-shocked, Olivia said, "I got in."

"In?"

"To art school."

Jenny shrieked and launched herself into Olivia's arms. The two of them were screaming and hugging on the bed when Will appeared at the door holding Billy.

"Just when I think you two can't get any weirder, you top yourselves."

"*Liv got accepted to art school!*"

"Oh, my God!" Will said. "Really?"

Olivia nodded, and Jenny let out another whoop of joy.

"That's awesome, Liv," Will said. "Congratulations."

"What're you doing here anyway?" Jenny asked her husband.

"Spilled coffee on my shirt so I came home to change and discovered that you two fools had disturbed his nap." He tickled Billy's feet.

Jenny reached for the giggling baby. "I'm sorry, buddy, but Livvie and I were celebrating."

"And you and I have a hot date on Saturday night," Olivia said to the baby.

"My son doesn't date yet," Will informed her.

Jenny tugged on Will's tie to bring him down for a kiss. "No, but you do. Seven o'clock on Saturday. Don't be late."

Will looked from Jenny to Olivia and then back to his wife. "What are you two up to?"

"Nothing," Jenny said innocently. "Date night. Got a problem with that?"

Still looking suspicious, Will said, "I guess not, but something's up. My radar's getting a huge reading here."

"Don't you have a job to get to?" Jenny asked.

With his hand on Jenny's chin, he tilted her face up. "You underestimate me at your peril."

"I'm oddly turned on right now," Jenny said with an animated growl.

"And that," Olivia said to Billy as she scooped him up, "is our cue to get the heck out of here."

"Don't bother," Will said with one last pointed look for his wife. "I'm going, but this isn't over."

"Have a nice day, dear," Jenny called after him.

They waited until they heard the front door close before they collapsed on the bed in another fit of laughter.

———✦———

When noon came and went without a call from Cole, Olivia decided to try a different tactic, one that made her feel like the kind of clingy, needy girlfriend she swore she'd never be. She called Chicago information to see if he had a home number listed and was disappointed that he didn't. Refusing to call his cell phone again, she went about her day trying not to think about why he wasn't calling her.

She had forgotten all about her decision the night before to relax and go with it and had to admit she was mad at him. This was exactly the kind of grief she didn't want in her life. His message from the night before followed by twelve hours of silence made her question everything. He said he didn't want her doing that, but if that was the case, then why didn't he call? It had also crossed her mind that he could be hurt or sick, which scared her more than she cared to admit.

By the time he finally called at two, she had gone past scared and was well on her way to furious. "Hey," she said, trying to sound casual and unaffected.

"Hey, hon. I'm so sorry I missed your calls. I had some shit to deal with when I got home last night, and by the time I was free, it was too late to call you. I was up really late so I slept in today."

"What kind of shit?"

He sighed. "Would you believe me if I told you that you really don't want to know?"

"Actually no, I wouldn't."

After a long pause, he said, "You're pissed."

Her stomach ached. "Yeah, kind of."

"Liv, I'm sorry. I really am."

"I don't like the feeling there's something going on that I don't know about. You tell me I can trust you, and then I can't reach you when you're the one who asked *me* to call. What am I supposed to make of that?"

"You *can* trust me, Olivia. I swear it."

"I want to."

"Liv…"

"Why did you send that message last night?"

"Because I was missing you and wanted to say good night."

Almost against her will, the ice around her heart began to thaw. "I would've liked that."

"Can we pretend it's last night and try again? Please?"

She was tempted to let him charm his way out of it because she hated being mad with him, but this was too important to let him off that easily.

"Feeling edgy and uncertain about the man I love is not a fun way to spend a day, Cole, especially after a sleepless night."

"It won't happen again. I promise."

Wanting desperately to believe him and to get things back on track, she took a deep breath. "Something kind of big happened today."

"What's that?"

"I got into art school. Officially."

"Liv! Oh, my God, that's great! I'm so proud of you."

"Thanks."

"Such amazing news."

"I just… I really wanted to tell you."

"I'm sorry. I wish I could take you out to celebrate tonight."

"Next week."

"Yes, we're going to celebrate this. So, um, I hate to say it, but Tuesday night's a bust. I couldn't get anyone to swap with me."

Olivia swallowed her disappointment. "That's okay. I need to get my homework and everything done before our trip next weekend. Where are we going anyway?"

"I'm not telling, and you can't trick me by sliding that in there."

"If you were here, I'd be able to get it out of you."

He laughed. "You think so, huh?"

"I *know* so."

"Do you still love me after I made you feel sick all day?"

He sounded so sweet and so genuinely concerned that she decided to forgive him. "I guess so," she teased.

"That wasn't very convincing."

"Is all your so-called 'shit' dealt with now?"

"I really hope so."

"And you haven't been off with your wife or your other girlfriend for the last twelve hours?"

"There's only you, Liv."

"Then I still love you."

"Good," he said, sounding relieved. "Because I love you. A whole lot."

"Call me later?"

"I will."

And he did. He called that night and the again the next night while she was baby-sitting Billy.

"Hey," she said, breathless from carrying the baby.

"What are you doing?" Cole asked.

"Well, at the moment, I'm soaking wet from attempting to give Billy a bath. I'm not even sure he got wet. He's a madman."

Billy squealed with delight and pulled her hair.

"He's definitely large and in charge tonight." Olivia put the baby down on his play mat on the floor. Exhausted, she sat on the sofa and put her feet up. "He's killing me."

Cole laughed.

"I don't know how Jenny makes it look so easy."

"Lots of practice, I suspect."

"She's out telling Will there's going to be another one, which I gather is a bit of a surprise."

"Ouch."

"No kidding—two babies, fifteen months apart. Makes me shudder just thinking about it."

"Speaking of babies… Any developments on our front?"

"Not yet. Jenny says the odds are in our favor, though."

"Yeah, I guess."

"Why do you sound so bummed?" she asked.

"I've never really given much thought to having kids, but now that it's possible, it doesn't freak me out as much as it probably should."

"I know what you mean."

"Really?"

"Really."

"So you're saying you kind of hope you're pregnant?"

"I guess maybe I am," Olivia confessed. "I know it would throw my whole life—and yours—into such an uproar, but then I look at Billy, and the possibility of having one who looks like you…"

"Or you," he said softly.

"This is nuts," she said with a nervous laugh. "We hardly know each other, and here we are hoping we're having a baby together."

"We know each other, Liv."

"Well enough to have a baby together?"

"Definitely."

"What would we do, if I am, you know, pregnant?"

"You'd have to move out here to live with me."

"Or you'd have to move here to live with me."

"Either way."

"You'd do that? Move here?"

"If that's what you wanted."

Amazed, Olivia had no idea what to say. It had never occurred to her that he'd pick up and move to be with her.

"Still there?" he asked.

She cleared the emotion from her throat. "Yeah. I should probably get Billy to bed."

"I can't wait to see you next weekend."

"I can't, either."

"Talk to you tomorrow?"

"I'll be here."

"I don't want you to worry about anything, okay? If there is a baby, we'll figure it out."

"I know."

"Love you."

"Love you, too."

———

The next week was one of the longest of Olivia's life. She studied for three tedious days for her international business midterm, telling herself all the while that she just had to get through this semester. Once she began taking art classes, her academic life would finally become interesting. Leaving the exam on Wednesday, she felt good about how she had done, but school was the last thing on her mind. Cole was due in at four, and they'd have thirty minutes together.

She headed for the airport in high spirits, which were dashed when she learned his flight was delayed. There would be no visit today.

She was slogging through her shift at the store when he called from the gate.

"Can you talk?" he asked.

"For a second."

"Sorry about today." He sounded equally disappointed. "I was really looking forward to it."

Her eyes filled. "So was I."

"Two more days until Friday," he said brightly.

"Nice try."

"Not working?"

"Not so much." Knowing he was so close but out of reach did nothing to bolster her spirits.

"I hate to say it, but I've got to run. Call you tonight?"

"All right."

"Olivia?"

"Yeah?"

"I'll see you next time. Pinky swear."

She smiled. In only two days, they'd have four days together—*four whole days*. That is, if she didn't die from missing him in the meantime.

"I'll be here."

"Counting on it."

Chapter 18

OLIVIA PACED AS NERVOUS ENERGY AND EXCITEMENT dueled with the butterflies storming around in her stomach. Being this excited to see a man was wrong on so many levels, but she couldn't seem to help it. And then there was the matter of her first airplane ride. To where she still had no idea. But did it really matter? She'd be with him, and that was all she cared about.

Back and forth she went in front of the gate where she was due to meet him. They had announced his flight was "in range." Whatever that meant. She had picked up the ticket he had arranged to have waiting for her at the Capital Airlines counter, and despite her burning curiosity she had kept her promise not to look at the destination. When she'd handed her boarding pass to the security screener, she'd fought the urge to glance at it. As she navigated the security line for the first time as a traveler, she had realized it was no wonder she was so excited. Seeing him *and* flying. This was quite a day!

He had told her to pack warm clothes—jeans, sweaters, a coat, something to wear out at night, and something sexy to wear to bed. "It won't be on for long, so don't go to too much trouble," he had said.

Olivia smiled as she recalled the conversation they'd had the night before during which he had spelled out exactly what was going to happen the instant they arrived at their destination. A bolt of heat went right through her as she recalled his low, sexy voice describing in intimate detail where he wanted to lick her. She took a deep breath and glanced around at the people waiting in the gate area, all but certain her heated cheeks were announcing her thoughts to the world.

Drawn to the window, she watched three Capital flights land in rapid succession. Two of them came toward the gate where she waited and then dashed her hopes by continuing on to other gates.

They finally announced the arrival of the flight from Chicago a few minutes later. A stream of passengers disembarked, but there was no sign of him. After a long lull, the flight attendants came up the ramp pulling suitcases behind them. Olivia wanted to ask them how much longer he'd be, but she couldn't bring herself to interrupt their conversation.

The crew for the next flight arrived, and announcements were made that boarding would begin shortly. *Where is he?* Just when Olivia thought she would lose her mind if she had to wait another minute, she saw him coming up the Jetway while talking to an older pilot. The other pilot said something that made Cole laugh, and the sight of his smiling face made Olivia's heart dance with excitement and love and impatience. *Oh, he looks so good!*

His eyes connected with hers, and his smile got even bigger.

She wanted to play it cool and wait for him to come to her, but she found herself moving toward him anyway.

The other pilot watched the scene with amusement as Cole and Olivia did a poor job of hiding their desire to leap into each other's arms.

"Um, Jake, this is Olivia," Cole said, drinking her in with his eyes.

She tore hers off him long enough to say hello and shake hands with the other pilot.

"I haven't seen her in nine days, so you'll have to excuse me," Cole said. "Because I can't wait another second to do this." He wrapped his arms around Olivia and lifted her right off her feet.

Startled, she clung to him.

"Well, don't let me get in the way," Jake said with a laugh. "I've got a flight to catch."

Cole's "see ya" was muffled by Olivia's hair. He held her for a long time before he eased her back down. He pressed his lips to her forehead. "Let me go get changed so I can kiss you the way I'm dying to."

"Hurry up," she said, pushing him toward the men's room.

He squeezed her hand. "Don't go anywhere."

"Not without you." She watched him go and then checked the time. Their flight was leaving at seven o'clock, and she'd soon find out where they were going. She couldn't wait.

A few minutes later he returned, wearing faded jeans with a long-sleeved, maroon button-down shirt he'd left un-tucked. "Come on." He reached for her hand, and with both of them dragging luggage behind them, he steered her through the concourse to a deserted gate area.

"Don't we need to get to our gate?" she asked, her heart hammering as he maneuvered her up against a big pillar so his back was to the crowd.

"It's right there," he said, bringing his lips down on hers. "We'll hear them."

Her arms encircled his neck.

His fingers dug into her hips as he brought her up tight against his instant erection for a hot, urgent, carnal kiss. He tasted of toothpaste and sin.

Olivia didn't even care that people might be watching them—she wasn't letting him go until she'd had her fill.

The sweep of his tongue against hers made her knees go weak with desire. She tunneled a hand into his thick hair and held on. By the time he finally slowed the kiss to a more manageable sliding of his lips over hers, Olivia was ready to say, "To hell with the trip—let's find a hotel!"

A shudder rippled through his big frame, and she loved that she'd done that to him.

"God, I want you," he whispered, dragging his lips from her throat to her ear where he lingered.

This time, Olivia trembled. Her hands fell to his chest where she could feel his racing heart. "We could skip this whole trip thing and be in a hotel in twenty minutes."

His agonized groan made her smile. "Don't tempt me."

"But I love tempting you."

"And you do it so well." He tilted her face up, seeking out her eyes. "I love you, and I'm literally dying to make love with you. But I really, really want to take you on your first flight to somewhere you've never been before."

"Oh, *all right*," she teased. "If you're going to be that way about it."

"But once we get there," he said, nipping at her bottom lip, "watch out."

She released a choppy, ragged breath. "Yes, you mentioned that last night."

He hugged her tightly. "I'm never going to make it. I might have to indoctrinate you into the Mile High Club."

Olivia looked up at him. "Do I even want to know what that means?"

His smile was as sinful as his kisses. "Think about it. A mile up, a bathroom… Are you getting a visual?"

Rolling her eyes, she said, "What I really want to know is whether *you* are already a member."

He laughed. "I'll never tell."

She pinched his butt. "Give it up."

"Hey! Get your hands off my ass."

"I love your ass." To prove her point, she let her hand slide down to cup one muscular cheek. "So have you? Done it on a plane?"

Amazed by her audacity, he stared down at her. "I've done a lot of things in an airplane, but that's not one of them. Now what *I* want to know is where has my shy Liv gone?"

"She's history."

"You're making my blood boil," he hissed.

She smiled, delighted by the effect she was having on him.

He reached for his back pocket and withdrew his iPod. "Before they call our flight and blow my surprise," he said as he placed the buds in her ears, "I need to get you wired for sound." As he dialed through the songs to find the one he was looking for, he added, "And no peeking at the signs in the gate area."

She was surprised and pleased to hear Fergie's "Big Girls Don't Cry," the song she had once told him she loved.

He raised his eyebrows to ask if she approved of his choice.

"Thank you," she said softly. She closed her eyes and rested her head against his chest.

He kept his arms around her as they leaned against the pillar and waited to board the plane.

Olivia listened to three songs before he nudged her to signal it was time to go. Suddenly, she couldn't move. Her stomach lurched and her heart pounded.

Sensing her anxiety, he brought their joined hands to his chest and mouthed the words "Trust me."

Because she did and because she couldn't wait to know what it felt like to fly, she let him lead her to the gate.

He handed their boarding passes to the agent and shepherded Olivia down the long Jetway.

With a deep breath for courage, Olivia stepped onto an airplane for the first time in her life.

After storing their bags in the overhead bins, Cole gave her the window and settled into the middle seat.

Olivia pointed to the headphones, asking if she could take them off.

He raised both hands to say ten more minutes.

She watched the people getting on the plane, stowing their belongings, and acting as if they did this every day. A lot of them probably did. Rubbing her sweaty palms on her jeans, Olivia looked out to the tarmac where the ground crew loaded luggage into the belly of the plane while two other men disconnected a long hose from the wing. She nudged Cole and pointed to the wing, raising an eyebrow in question.

"Gas," he mouthed, reaching beneath her to find the other half of her seatbelt, which he fastened tight around her.

A few minutes later, he removed the headphones and

turned off the iPod. "I think we're safe. The pilot just said he expects a smooth flight."

"That's a relief."

"This is one of the best times of year to fly—very few thunderstorms and no snow."

"Good."

"You're tight as a drum, Liv," he said, running his hand up and down her leg. "What're you feeling right now?"

"Excited, curious, scared."

He held her hand between both of his. "Don't be scared. Remember what I told you—it's safer than being in a car."

"And remember what I told *you*—there's no break-down lane."

He smiled and rolled his eyes.

When the flight attendants began the preflight safety spiel, Olivia reached for the brochure that outlined the features of the Boeing 757.

Cole snorted with laughter.

"What?"

"No one ever pays attention to the flight attendants. They should, but they don't."

"Why not?" Olivia asked, horrified. "What if something happens?"

"Nothing ever does. That's what I've been trying to tell you."

"The pilot could have a heart attack."

"You think you're funny, don't you?"

"Be quiet," she said. "I want to hear about the oxygen masks." She paid intense attention to the instructions. "So if we lose pressure in the cabin, I should help myself before I help you?"

"Yeah, *right*," he drawled. "I'll be too busy cleaning up after you pee your pants."

Olivia laughed and then shushed him so she could learn how to use her seat cushion as a flotation device in the event of a water landing. Pondering the notion of the big plane splashing down, she was scared again.

Cole brought her hand to his lips. "Not going to happen, honey."

"Tell that to the people who landed in the Hudson."

"A once-in-a-lifetime occurrence."

Trying to think about anything other than landing in the Potomac, she returned the brochure to the seat pocket, pulled out the barf bag, and glanced over at him.

"For wimps."

"In that case…" Olivia put the bag on her lap.

"You won't need it."

"Could you fly this plane?"

"If I had to."

"What does that mean?"

"I'm not checked out to fly passengers on a 757, but in an emergency I could get it down."

"That makes me feel a little better."

Amused, he asked, "How do you know I'm any good?"

"Because you've told me—often," she said, laughing at his offended expression. As the plane rolled back from the gate, Olivia gasped.

"Deep breaths," he said. "You can do it. We're going to taxi to the runway for a few minutes, so no need to panic yet."

"What happens then?" she managed to ask.

"Just like I told you last night, the pilot will come on to tell us we've been cleared for takeoff."

"Do you know them? The pilots?"

"Nope."

She swallowed hard.

"Baby, do you think I'd be on this plane or would've brought you on it if I wasn't sure it was totally safe?"

"No," she squeaked.

"Then please try to relax and just enjoy it, will you?"

"Um, sure… easy for you to say. You've done this what? A million times?"

Laughing, he raised the armrest between them and put his arm around her.

Grateful for the gesture, Olivia rested her head on his shoulder and focused on breathing.

"Make sure you look out as we lift off. The view of D.C. at night is unbelievable."

"I'll be too busy trying not to pee my pants."

"It never occurs to me that there might be people on my flight who've never flown before. It's so rare these days."

She watched the dazzling array of lights on the taxiway. "As rare as a twenty-seven-year-old virgin?"

"No," he said softly against her ear. "That's in a league all its own. How lucky am I to be able to share all these amazing firsts with you?"

Feeling like the lucky one, Olivia raised her head to reward him with a warm smile.

"Good evening from the cockpit," came a voice over the loudspeaker. "We've been cleared for takeoff. Two hours and three minutes to Denver. Flight attendants, please be seated."

Cole winced.

"Denver, huh?"

"*Shit*," he groaned.

Olivia laughed at his distress. There were other places she'd rather go, but she wasn't going to complain about an adventure like this.

"We were *so* close!"

"It's all right. I don't care where we go as long as we go together."

The plane lurched forward, and Olivia tightened her grip on his hand.

He kept his other arm around her as they hauled ass down the runway.

"*Oh, my God*," she whispered, watching the airport buildings whiz by.

"Keep your eyes open, honey."

Olivia had to make an effort to do just that as they lifted into the air. Below she saw the U.S. Capitol, the Lincoln and Jefferson Memorials, and the lights from thousands of tiny cars on the Beltway. It was the most amazing sight she'd ever seen, and she was utterly captivated until a bang from below the plane stopped her heart.

"Just putting the wheels away," Cole said, his voice calm and soothing.

"It's so…"

"What? Tell me."

"Magical."

Over her shoulder he looked out the window. "I guess it is, isn't it?"

"That something this big can just lift into the air and soar through the sky."

"It's all about aerodynamics—"

She patted his knee. "Don't ruin it."

He nuzzled his nose through her hair until he found her ear. "Kiss me."

Glancing over his shoulder, she saw they had the entire row to themselves. Besides, after their demonstration in the airport, what did she care?

With her hand on his face she kissed him softly, dodging his efforts to get more. She teased him with little darts of her tongue until he all but begged her to have mercy.

Cole took the opportunity to anchor her face and kiss her with a kind of desperation he hadn't shown her before.

Olivia was on fire. With her ears already popping from the altitude, she held fast to a handful of his shirt hoping to gain some equilibrium.

"I love kissing you." He trailed his lips over her face. "It's quickly becoming my favorite thing to do."

"Better than flying?"

"Mmm, flying's got nothing on you. What was I thinking taking you so far away? We should've gone to Newark. One hour." He cruised down to her neck. "Up, down, then in, out."

Olivia laughed and arched her neck to give him better access. "I've heard great things about Newark," she teased.

"It's nothing special."

"I bet it has hotels with big soft beds and doors with 'Do Not Disturb' signs."

He closed his teeth over the spot where her neck met her shoulder.

She moaned.

"Uh-huh, and what else have you got to say?"

Her answering sigh made him laugh. "So I'm not the only one who's suffering here?" he asked.

"No. There's enough to go around."

"What do you think of flying so far?"

"On the lists of firsts, it's a very close second to sex," she said, tilting her hip against his erection.

He sucked in a harsh, deep breath that he banked when a flight attendant walked by. "You're going to get me fired," he whispered.

"Fired up."

"Already there."

"How many more hours until Denver?"

He checked his watch. "Hour and forty."

"We can handle that, right?"

"Sure, no problem. We've already waited almost two weeks. What's another couple of hours?"

"An eternity?"

"Next time Newark. Definitely Newark."

Chapter 19

LANDING WAS ALMOST AS EXCITING AS TAKING OFF. THE captain had warned them to expect a few bumps as the plane descended through the clouds, so Olivia clutched Cole's hand and listened to his soft words of comfort. He equated the bumps to potholes on a dirt road, and the visual helped to keep her from panicking. They finally broke through the cloud cover and there was Denver, laid out in the distance below.

"The airport is quite a ways from the city," Cole said. "There's a whole lot of nothing out here, which is why it's so dark."

Olivia watched the darkness below as she felt the plane going down. Whispering a silent prayer that the pilots knew what they were doing, she had to remind herself to keep breathing.

"Remember what I told you about landing—a bump on impact and then a big roar when they deploy the thrusters to slow the plane."

"Right," she said. "A roar."

He looked out the window to see where they were. "There're the approach lights, so any second now."

The runway lights came into view next, and the plane suddenly slowed in the moment before a smooth touchdown. But despite Cole's warnings, the roar of the thrusters still startled her.

"Perfect landing," he said, kissing the hand that gripped his.

"Ladies and gentlemen, welcome to Denver where the local time is seven o'clock," the flight attendant announced.

"That's so weird," Olivia said. "We took off at seven and landed at seven."

"Two time zones."

"It's weird."

"For those of you continuing on with us to San Francisco, please stay seated until our Denver passengers have deplaned. San Fran passengers will have about twenty-five minutes if you wish to get off and stretch your legs. We just ask that you stay close to the gate area, as this'll be a quick turnaround. If Denver is your final destination, we thank you for choosing Capital. Come back and see us again soon. Your Denver-based flight crew wishes you a good evening and safe travels."

Olivia sighed wistfully. How she wished they were going to San Francisco. But since he had gone to so much trouble to arrange this trip, she wasn't going to let him see an ounce of disappointment.

When the plane pulled up to the gate, Olivia reached for her purse.

Cole stopped her with a hand to her arm.

"What?"

"We're not getting off here, honey."

Her eyes widened. "We're not?"

He shook his head.

"We're going to San Francisco?" she whispered.

"I hope that meets with your approval."

Stunned, she stared at him.

"Denver's pretty, but it's not where you told me you wanted to go."

"No one's ever done anything like this for me," she said, still whispering.

"I want to do everything for you."

As the other passengers gathered up their belongings and left the plane, Cole held her tight against him. "You know what this means, though," he said after a long period of silence.

"What?"

"Several more hours until the hotel."

"I promise you'll be *richly* rewarded once we get there."

Rendered momentarily speechless, he finally recovered his senses. "Since there's no way I can think about that, let alone talk about it, tell me what you want to do in San Fran."

"I want to ride the cable cars, go to Alcatraz, and paint the Golden Gate. I want to see the Coit Tower and the Ghirardelli chocolate factory and eat at Fisherman's Wharf and in Chinatown. Oh! And the crooked street—I want to see that, too."

"You've given this significant thought," he said, delighted by her enthusiasm.

"I've been wanting to go there since I was a little girl. You have no idea what a dream come true this is—all of it, but mostly you."

"We'll do it all," he said, his voice heavy with emotion as he leaned over to kiss her. "Let's take a walk."

"What if we miss the flight?"

"We won't. They're doing a crew change, so we have plenty of time." He unbuckled her seatbelt, tugged her up, and led her from the plane into the terminal.

They shared a pretzel and a beer before their flight

was called. As "through" passengers they were allowed to board first.

Once they were settled in their seats, Cole turned to her. "I meant to ask you, what did Will have to say about the new baby?"

"Jenny said he was so shocked that she almost had to call the paramedics to administer first aid."

Cole laughed. "Poor guy."

"Yeah, except the poor guy was there when it happened, so you can't feel *too* sorry for him."

"That's true. At least he's not in my boat. At the rate I'm going, I'll be coaching Little League at fifty."

"Being fifty won't slow you down."

He raised an amused eyebrow. "You don't think so?"

"Nah. You're too full of energy to be slowed down by a number."

"I guess we'll find out, won't we?"

Her eyes flicked up to find him watching her with interest, waiting for her reaction. "I don't know."

"You don't want to be around when I'm fifty?"

"I don't want to get ahead of myself."

"Yeah, I guess that wouldn't be wise," he said, failing to keep a hint of bitterness from creeping into his tone.

"Cole. Don't do that."

"Why not? You are."

"You're not being fair. A little over a month ago, I didn't even know you. I'm sorry if I'm not ready yet to talk about forever."

"Do you think you'll ever be?"

"I hope so." She reached for his hand. "You're the very best thing that's ever happened to me, but among my many worries is that we're at different places in our lives. You're ready to settle down, and I've still got stuff I need to do before I'll want that."

"Why can't you do both at the same time? Do you think I'd ever stand in the way of you finishing school and having a career?"

Olivia sighed. This was not the conversation she wanted to be having now, not when they were on their way to San Francisco and four precious days together.

The plane pushed back from the gate. Takeoff was a little less magical the second time, without Cole's arm around her. He was too busy brooding to remember this was just her second flight. She kept her hands clenched in her lap as the plane hurtled down the runway. When she began seeing dancing dots, she realized she was holding her breath.

Cole reached over and put his hand on top of hers.

"I want to be with you, Cole," she said softly as the plane lifted into the air. "I want that more than anything else. Can't that be enough for now?"

"I guess it'll have to be."

Olivia rested her head against the seat. "I'm not the only one who's holding back."

He turned to look at her. "What's that supposed to mean?"

"Well, let's start with more than twelve hours of silence during which you had some 'shit' to deal with that I'm better off not knowing about."

"That's not the same thing."

"Isn't it?" she asked when she wanted to scream, *Why are we fighting*?

"You don't know what you're talking about."

"No, I don't, because you won't tell me."

She found out then that desire wasn't the only thing that made his eyes get darker.

"Do you really want to hear about an ex-girlfriend who refuses to accept that I'm involved with someone else now?"

Olivia looked down at her hands, folded in her lap. "Not really."

"I didn't think so, which is why I didn't tell you."

"Why are we doing this?" she asked softly. "I've been living for this time with you, and I didn't imagine we'd spend it fighting."

"I don't want to fight with you either, Liv. That's the last thing in the world I want."

"Can we call a truce so we can enjoy our trip?" She forced a smile. "No serious talk for four days?"

He studied her. "Three and a half."

"So we'll only ruin the last day?"

The left side of his face lifted into the sexy half smile that made her mouth go dry. "That's the plan."

She extended her hand to him. "Deal?"

He curled his pinky around hers, brought her hand to his lips, and said, "Deal."

"*Cole?*" A squealing female interrupted the moment.

Olivia watched his face change from relaxed to startled to embarrassed in a fraction of an instant as he looked up at the flight attendant standing in the aisle.

"I thought that was you." The pretty blonde's hungry blue eyes moved from Cole to Olivia and then back to him again.

"Tara," he said in a strangled tone that sounded nothing like his usual voice. "How are you?"

"Great." Her tone was full of playful invitation. "I've missed you! Where ya been?"

Olivia watched the exchange with growing dismay and discomfort.

"I've been around. Um, this is Olivia. Olivia, Tara."

"Nice to meet you," Olivia said.

"Uh-huh." Tara returned her attention to Cole. "You said you'd call, and then I never heard from you." Pouting, she rested her hand on his shoulder. "And I used to defend you when people called you Love 'Em and Leave 'Em Langston."

"I've just been really busy," Cole said tightly.

Olivia wanted to disappear into the seat.

"Busy," Tara said with a giggle. "I'll bet you keep *plenty* busy. We should get together the next time you're in Denver."

Olivia couldn't believe the other woman's audacity.

"I'm with Olivia now."

"So?"

"So I'm not seeing anyone else."

"Well, you know where I am when you get tired of her."

His expression hardened. "Please take your hand off me and get back to work. I'd hate to have to complain to your supervisors about your inappropriate behavior."

"Clearly, a little bit of fame has gone right to your head," Tara said tersely, but she removed her hand from his shoulder. "Best of luck to you, *Olivia*. You're going to need it."

As Tara stalked off, Olivia's heart raced and her stomach surged.

"I'm sorry about that." Cole's jaw was tight with tension. "We hung out once, and apparently she had some idea that it was more."

"What does 'hung out' mean?"

Exquisite discomfort radiated from him as he shrugged. "You know."

"You slept with her."

"One time."

"And then you didn't call her?"

"I thought we both knew the score going into it. I told her I wasn't looking to get involved."

"You should've at least called her."

"You pinky swore that you wouldn't hate me for my past," he reminded her.

"That was before I was confronted with it in person."

"So what? Now you're disgusted by me?"

"No, I just feel sorry for her."

"She just totally disrespected you, and *you* feel sorry for *her*?"

"I would've been really sad if you hadn't called me after we spent the weekend together."

"That's different, Liv," he said with a sigh. "Everything about us is different."

"Why?"

"All I know is that I need you in a way I've never needed anyone else. I can't explain why it's different with you. It just is."

Processing what he'd said, Olivia rested her head on his shoulder.

"Do you believe me?"

"I really want to."

He pressed his lips to the top of her head. "I love you," he whispered. "You and only you."

Olivia closed her eyes and tried to calm her racing heart. He'd had other women. Love 'Em and Leave 'Em Langston. Okay, many other women. But he said he wanted only her. For however long it lasted, she would try to enjoy it.

—✺—

Olivia's mouth fell open when they pulled up to the Fairmont Hotel on Nob Hill. "We are *not* staying here."

"Well, this is where I'm staying, and I sort of hoped you'd stay with me."

She kept her hand over her heart, as if that would stop the furious staccato that was two parts excitement, one part nerves. "Cole."

"Are you coming?" he asked, reaching for her hand.

Olivia linked her fingers through his.

He helped her from the cab and paid the fare as a uniformed bellman retrieved their bags from the trunk.

Inside, the opulent lobby and famous grand staircase were almost too much to absorb all at once. Soaring marble pillars, lush potted plants, soft lighting, and gilded accents. Even the ceiling was outfitted with elaborate moldings. Olivia had never seen anything more beautiful.

"As you requested, Mr. Langston, we have you in a Signature Room in The Tower, which looks out over the city and San Francisco Bay," the front-desk clerk was saying when Olivia tuned into the check-in proceedings.

Cole handed the woman his American Express card. "With a king-sized bed, right?"

"That's correct, sir."

"Thank you very much."

They followed the bellman to a bank of elevators. Their room, like everything else she had seen so far, was elegant and huge. She went straight for the windows, gasping at the view of the city stretched out before her.

The bellman wished them a good evening, and the door clicked shut behind him.

Cole came up behind her and rested his hands on her shoulders. "What do you think?"

"It's overwhelming." She turned to him. "I can't believe you did this."

"I wanted it to be special for you."

"This is beautiful—in fact it's so far beyond beautiful I don't even have the words. I hope you know I would've been just as happy at the Holiday Inn."

He put his arms around her. "I do know that, which is why it was fun to raise the bar a little."

She snorted. "A *little*?"

"Okay, a lot."

"I feel like Cinderella." She went up on tiptoes to kiss him. "What's going to happen when the clock strikes midnight?"

"You might wake up and find yourself at the Holiday Inn."

Laughing, she kissed him again. "The trip, this amazing hotel… It's the loveliest thing anyone has ever done for me, Cole. Thank you."

"It's my pleasure."

"Speaking of your pleasure…" Slowly, she unbuttoned his shirt, nuzzling each new bit of skin as she uncovered it.

"Liv." He took her hands to stop her. "Aren't you hungry?"

"Nope." She tugged on the button to his jeans. "You?"

"I was."

"And now?"

"I seem to have lost my appetite for food."

Taking a step back, she dodged his attempt to take over her seduction. "No touching."

"What? Why?"

"Because I'm in charge." Pushing his shirt off his shoulders, she walked around him dropping soft kisses on his back. "Mmm, I do so love the way you're put together."

He trembled. "Liv. Come on."

"Where do you want to go?"

"You *know* where I want to go."

"We'll get there, sooner or later."

"I vote for sooner."

Pushing his jeans down, she ran her hands over his muscular thighs. "My vote's for later, and since I'm in charge, my vote wins."

Groaning, he let his head fall back.

She walked him to the high bed and rested her palm on one of the mahogany posts as she eyed him.

"Don't even think about it."

"Oh, such a dirty, *dirty* mind. I like that."

"Remember—payback's a bitch, and you won't be in charge for long."

"Maybe not, but I'm in charge right now."

"So you've said. Now that you have me, whatever will you do with me?"

As he watched her every move, she tugged her sweater over her head. "I wasn't sure how I felt about a lavender bra." She trailed a finger over the lace cups. "What do you think?"

His Adam's apple bobbed, and his eyes burned holes through the bra. "Have I mentioned I love lavender?"

"Excellent," she said as her jeans joined the pile of clothes on the floor.

"Especially when it comes in sets. Is that a, ah, thong?"

"Uh-huh."

"Oh, my God," he said, releasing a long, jagged breath.

With her hands on his shoulders, she eased him back on the bed and kissed him. Sweeping her tongue into his mouth, she reveled in the strangled sound that came from his throat.

"Let me touch you, Liv," he said, his voice hoarse with desire.

"Not yet." She left damp, open-mouthed kisses along his jaw and neck. Moving down to his chest, she flicked her tongue over his nipple. His hands, she noticed, clutched the duvet, and his breathing was labored. Smiling, she continued on to his toned abdomen, making sure her breasts grazed his chest on the way.

"Remember when I said you'd be richly rewarded?"

"Yeah," he choked out.

"I'm trying to decide the best way." She got rid of his boxers and tossed them over her shoulder. "There are so many options. Like this, for starters." Wrapping her hand around his straining erection, she bent to skim her tongue over the head.

His hips surged up off the bed. "Liv," he hissed as he broke out in a sweat. "Please."

She took him into her mouth, keeping her hand and tongue moving in synch.

His harsh breathing told her she was doing something right. Suddenly, he gripped her shoulders. "Baby, wait."

"Why?"

"Come here." He brought her up to him.

"I wasn't finished with your reward," she pouted.

"Don't you think the lavender thong was enough?" Placing his hands gently on her face, he kissed her. "Are you done being in charge?"

"For now."

He flipped her onto her back so fast she had no time to prepare before he ravished her. The lavender bra flew across the room. Cupping her breasts, he sucked hard on one nipple and then the other.

"*Cole!*"

"Hmm?" His tongue made circles on her breast.

Like useless noodles, her arms dropped to the bed. "I forgot what I was going to say."

"You have the world's most perfect breasts. Have I ever told you that?"

"Ah, no, I don't think so."

"And the way they fit my hands like they were made for me. Have you noticed that?"

She reached for him. "Make love to me, Cole."

"Back in charge?"

"My powers only work when you obey me."

"Happy to." He rolled over and got up, returning with a condom. "Extra strength, you'll be glad to know."

Olivia laughed and held out her arms to him. "Who knew they came in extra strength?"

"Not me, that's for sure." He slid her thong off and held it up for a closer look. "I might need you to model this for me again later."

"I have a few of them."

Those vivid blue eyes she loved so much went dark with desire. "With you?"

"Well, they wouldn't do me much good in a drawer at home. Now, are you going to talk all night or are we gonna get on with it?"

"Oh, we're gonna get on with it. And then we're gonna get it on."

"Thank God."

Chapter 20

OLIVIA CAME THREE TIMES. BEFORE COLE HAD PROVEN otherwise, she wouldn't have thought that was possible. But he'd set out almost relentlessly to make her into a trembling, quivering wreck, and they hadn't even gotten to the best part yet. Olivia was so sated and loose she would have drifted off to sleep if he hadn't chosen that moment to finally enter her.

As she hooked her legs around his hips to take him in, she watched him. Something was different, and if she hadn't been so busy having mind-altering orgasms, she might have noticed it sooner.

He was holding back.

Even as he made passionate love to her, he kept a firm grip on his control. There was no sign of the reckless, abandoned lover who had taken her against a wall in Washington.

Saddened by the realization that he felt the need to protect himself from her, Olivia caressed his face and brought him down for a deep, searching kiss. "Turn over," she whispered.

He shook his head.

"Yes," she insisted, pushing at his shoulders until he gave in and did as she asked.

He kept his arms tight around her and turned them so she was on top.

Olivia pulled out all the stops to break him. She went

slow, dragging her nails over his chest as she arched her back and took him deep, her eyes fixed on his while she waited and hoped. When slow didn't work, she gave fast a whirl.

His breathing changed and his fingers dug into her hips, but there was still an aura of control about him that frustrated her. Even when he finally climaxed, it wasn't the all-consuming event it had been the last time but rather a civilized ending to a rather civilized round of sex.

Olivia wanted to scream. She didn't want him civilized. She wanted him the way he'd been before when he'd loved her with everything he had, before she'd given him reason to hold something back so he wouldn't be left with nothing if she walked away.

Why shouldn't he be afraid? She'd certainly given him ample reason to be concerned. *I'm skittish and hesitant, so why shouldn't he be, too? I can't have it both ways. I can't commit only halfway and expect him to be in it all the way. He'd have to be stupid to take a risk like that, and he's anything but stupid.*

He caressed her back as she rested on top of him, drinking in the scent of his cologne mixed with a hint of perspiration that actually smelled good coming from him.

"Are you okay?" he asked.

"Mmm. You?"

"Never better."

"You must be hungry."

"A little. We can order something."

She slid off him and pulled the covers up over them. "Whatever you want."

"What's wrong, Liv?"

Startled, she glanced over at him. "Nothing."

Lying on his back, he ran a hand through his hair and stared up at the ceiling. "Are we going to play games now?"

"No, we're not."

He sat up. "Okay, well you know where I am if you want to tell me what's bugging you." He stalked into the bathroom and closed the door with a loud thwack.

Olivia hugged a big fluffy pillow and battled the huge lump in her throat. *How was this going so terribly wrong?*

———————

She awoke to the sound of "Ode to Joy" the next morning. Since Cole had slept on the far side of the big bed, she didn't disturb him when she got up. In the large, dark hotel room, she fumbled to find her purse before the phone woke him. Once she had the phone in hand, she didn't take the time to check the caller ID before she flipped it open.

"Hello?" she whispered. On the way into the bathroom, she glanced at the clock and found it was five forty-five. She closed the door softly.

"Hi, honey. Did I wake you?"

"Oh, hey, Dad." She rubbed the sleep from her eyes and stifled a yawn as she put a thick Fairmont robe on over the silk nightgown she had slept in. "That's okay. What's up?"

"Where did you end up on your mystery trip?"

"San Francisco."

"Oh, you must be thrilled, Livvie! You've always wanted to go there. How is it?"

"What I've seen so far is beautiful."

"Crap, it's really early there, though!"

"Don't worry about it. My body is still on East Coast time. What's going on?"

"Well, honey, I hate to do this to you while you're away, but I wanted to let you know that Mom's committed herself to a treatment place. It's a nice facility in southern Virginia that we've heard good things about."

Astounded, Olivia sat down hard on the closed lid of the toilet. "When did this happen?"

"Yesterday afternoon."

"*Why didn't you tell me?*" she cried. "I would've been there with you!"

"Her doctor called on Thursday to say they had a spot opening up, so it happened fast. I knew how much you were looking forward to your trip."

"Dad! You should've told me!"

"Believe me, Liv, you were better off not knowing."

"Why?" she asked, hesitantly. "What happened?"

"Let's just say she didn't go easily."

"Oh, God," she sighed.

"She signed the paperwork willingly, but then she lost it as we were helping her out of the house. They ended up having to sedate her." His voice caught. "It was a horror show."

Olivia's eyes filled. "Daddy…"

"I'm okay, honey. We should've done this years ago."

"How long is she going to be there?"

"Thirty days to start with. They're going to re-evaluate her after that."

"Can you go see her?"

"I doubt she'll want to see me. She thinks I'm the root of all evil right about now since I didn't give her much choice. I told her it was this or a divorce."

"You're just trying to do what's best for her."

"She doesn't see it that way. I'm so sorry to dump this on you right now, but I didn't want you to hear about it from your brothers or Jenny."

"Do you want me to come home? I can be there this afternoon if you need me."

"No, honey. That's not necessary, but thank you. I'm fine. In fact, I have a second interview next Monday at a Cadillac dealer in Springfield. I have a feeling it's just a formality, and the job's mine."

"They'd be lucky to have you. That's your line."

"It is indeed. I'm also meeting with a Realtor today about the house, and I found someone who'll clean out the place for cheap. She'll get what she can for all the junk, so at least it won't be a total loss."

"I hate that you're dealing with this by yourself. I can help with the house when I get home."

"Don't worry about it, Livvie. Andy's coming home this weekend to help me move the furniture I'm going to keep in storage until I get a new place. The rest is crap. We'll either trash it or sell it."

"Jenny and I looked at an apartment the other day that'll work for me until I figure out what I'm going to do. They said I can move in at the end of the week." She glanced at the door, thought of Cole sleeping in the next room, and remembered him asking her to live with him. She wondered if the offer was still on the table. "I'll get my stuff out of the house as soon as I get home."

"There's no rush. I'm sure it'll take a month or two to sell."

"So what happens with you and Mom when she gets out?"

"I guess that'll depend on whether or not the treatment works."

"No matter what happens, you know you have me, right? And Andy and Alex, too. We're always here for you."

"Thank you, sweetheart. They said the same thing. I'm blessed to have three great kids who somehow turned out beautifully despite how they grew up."

"Will you let me know if you need anything?"

"I sure will. Please don't worry about any of this. It's all going to work out. I promise."

"I love you," she said.

"And I love you. Have a great time with your pilot, you hear me? Tell him your old man wants to meet him the next time he's in D.C."

"I will. Bye, Daddy." Olivia closed the phone and curled her hand tight around it as she absorbed the news from home. She had no idea how long she sat there before she realized she wasn't alone.

"What's wrong?" Cole asked from the doorway.

Olivia cleared her throat. "That was my dad. My mother is in a 'very nice facility' as of yesterday. I know it's for the best, but he sounded awful."

Cole took her hand and led her from the bathroom to a big easy chair by the window. He brought her down onto his lap and put his arms around her. "Do you want to go home? I'd totally understand if you wanted to."

"He'd flip if I went home on his account."

"What can I do for you?"

Resting her head on his shoulder, she said, "This is pretty good."

"I woke up, and you weren't there," he whispered

as his lips brushed her forehead. "I was worried until I heard you talking in the bathroom."

"Did you think I'd run away?" she asked in a teasing tone.

"I wasn't sure."

"I'm not going to run away, Cole. I hate that you're worried I might."

"We still have three-and-a-half days until serious talk is allowed," he reminded her.

"That's true." She ran her fingers through his hair and lifted her head off his shoulder to kiss him.

"Do you want to go back to bed for a while?"

"To sleep?" she asked, trying to coax a smile from him.

"Whatever you want."

"I'm seriously torn between you and a spot right in front of this hotel."

His eyebrows knitted with confusion. "What spot?"

"The only place in the whole city where all the cable car lines come together."

He laughed. "Well, since I wouldn't dare try to compete with the cable cars, what do you say we get an early start?"

They returned to the hotel twelve hours later, laden with bags and souvenirs.

"You're going to need another suitcase to get all this stuff home," Cole said as he dumped his portion of the haul on the sofa.

"I went totally nuts, didn't I?"

"You had fun. That's what matters."

She shrugged and studied the mountain of bags.

"What?"

"I just…"

"What, honey? Talk to me."

"I don't want to end up like my mother, you know? I shouldn't have blown so much money on stuff I don't really need."

He came over to her and put his hands on her shoulders. "When was the last time you did something like this?"

She thought about it. "Um, never?"

"So there you go. A one-time splurge does not make you like your mother."

"I suppose you're right."

"Now I have a very important question for you."

"What's that?"

"Do you have any more of that dark chocolate, or did you eat it all?"

She smiled. "I might have one more piece I could share with you." She found the bag from Ghirardelli and sat down next to him on the sofa. Breaking off a piece of the chocolate, she fed him a bite.

"Mmm, that's *so* good." He leaned his head back on the sofa. "What was your favorite thing we did today?"

"I liked Alcatraz a lot. Can you imagine escaping from that place?"

"No way. Have you ever seen the movie?"

"Nope."

"We should rent it sometime. It's a great story."

"I loved the cable cars, too."

"By the fourth ride, I figured you were liking them."

"The hills are amazing, aren't they?"

"I'm still recovering from the trek *up* Lombard Street.

While everyone else was walking *down* the crooked street, we had to walk up."

"I wanted the full experience."

"You're going to feel the full experience in your calf muscles tomorrow."

She shrugged. "It was worth it to beat you to the top. You were really showing your age up there, old man."

"Shut up," he snorted, poking her ribs.

Smiling, she added, "Union Square was cool, too. Can we go back to Fisherman's Wharf tomorrow? I'd like to do some sketching."

He dug through the pile of bags. When he found the one he was looking for, he pulled it from under the others and handed it to her. "You mentioned you want to paint the bridge, right?"

Olivia peeked inside the bag and let out a happy squeal when she found professional-grade watercolors, brushes, and a packet of oversized paper. "When did you get this?"

"While you were in that jewelry store in Union Square."

She threw her arms around him and sprinkled kisses on his face. "You're so thoughtful."

His face twisted with dismay. "That's almost as bad as romantic."

"You're both."

"If you say so."

Olivia got up, put the bag on the table, and turned to straddle his lap.

"Well, well, what's this?" he asked with a grin as he cupped her bottom and pulled her tight against him.

"This," she said, touching her lips to his, "is me telling you that *this* was the very best day of my whole life."

"The very best day?"

She nodded. "And I have you to thank for it."

"Any day I get to spend with you is the best day."

"I love you, and I'll never, ever forget this," she whispered as she brought her mouth down on his.

A groan rumbled through his chest when he met her questing tongue with thrusts of his own. He filled his hands with her breasts and ran his thumbs over her nipples.

Olivia gasped.

"I was thinking we should go out to dinner," he said, his lips moving on her neck. "We need to celebrate your art school news."

"Could we maybe do that tomorrow?"

"I suppose we could." He rolled her earlobe between his teeth. "What do you want to do tonight?"

"How about we get naked and spend the whole night in bed?"

He went completely still. "I can't stand it when you mince words like that, Liv."

She laughed and tugged at his shirt while rolling her pelvis over his erection. "Is that a yes?"

In answer to her question, he surged to his feet and carried her to the bed. Coming down on top of her, he molded his lips to hers. They rolled over the bed, locked in a passionate embrace that was only broken when Olivia dissolved into a fit of laughter.

"What the hell is so funny?"

"I've seen that done in movies, but I had no idea people could actually roll across a bed without breaking the kiss."

His sexy smile stopped her heart. "Wanna do it again?"

"Uh-huh."

This time they ended up perilously close to the edge.

"That's a big fall," he said, looking down at the floor.

Her lips coasted over the stubble on his unshaven jaw. "Cole?"

"Yeah?"

"Can we get to the naked part now?"

"I suppose if we have to."

Olivia laughed and pulled his shirt over his head.

Chapter 21

COLE'S PLAN WAS FAILING MISERABLY. EVER SINCE their argument on the plane, he'd tried to build a protective fence around his heart. Just in case. But she made it impossible to remain aloof. Her infectious joy at discovering a city she had dreamed about visiting, the playful race up Lombard Street, and her worries about being like her mother had combined to knock down his sad attempt at fence building, leaving him defenseless as her lips slid over his belly.

He'd waited all his life for this woman, but he hadn't imagined there would be so many complications and challenges when he finally found "the one" for him. If he pushed too hard, he'd lose her. He knew that for certain. So he'd tried to hold back and had failed at that, too, because she'd picked up on it and had been hurt.

Maybe he had to roll the dice. If he gave her everything and she ended up walking away, at least he wouldn't have to wonder if there was more he could have done. It was a risk, for sure, but one he was willing to take for her.

He watched her finish undressing him and reach for her sweater. She had no idea what an erotic picture she painted with her milky white skin, waterfall of long dark hair, and full breasts spilling out of a lacy yellow bra. When she reached back to unhook her bra, he stopped her, brought her down next to him on the bed, and hovered over her.

"Let me," he whispered.

Her cheeks were flushed, and her breathing slowed as she waited to see what he would do.

Cole dipped his head and found her nipple through the lace. The alluring scent of her lotion fueled his desire as he tormented her. Finally, when he couldn't bear to wait another minute for the real thing, he reached behind her and flipped open the bra with one hand. Nudging it out of his way, he gazed down at her. He loved how her pretty pink nipples darkened to a deep, dusty rose when they made love.

He dragged his tongue in lazy circles designed to drive her mad. Apparently, it was working.

She combed her fingers into his hair, trying to direct him to where she wanted him. "*Cole.*"

"Hmm?"

"Come *on*," she pleaded.

He laughed against her breast but made no move to give her what she wanted.

"You're not being nice."

He glanced up at her. "No?"

"You know you're not."

"Well, if you're going to pout about it." He closed in on one of the pebbled buds. Using his tongue, teeth, and lips, he gave her everything she wanted and then some. Judging by her moans and pants, she was done pouting. He gave her other breast the same treatment before he moved down. She was so ready for him that just a few sweeps of his tongue sent her flying.

He rolled on a condom and slid into her to ride the last waves of her orgasm.

Her eyes were closed, her lips parted, and her hands open and resting on either side of her head. So complete was her abandon that Cole had to look away for a moment to keep from coming too soon. He wanted more from her before he let himself go.

"Hey," he whispered.

"Mmm."

"Look at me."

She opened her eyes.

"That's better," he said, bringing his lips down on hers for a light kiss. "I don't want you going to sleep." He pushed hard into her.

Her laughter mixed with another moan. "As if I could sleep right now." She curled her arms around his neck and sought out his mouth.

Cole slowed the motion of his hips and sank into the kiss. Her breasts were flat against his chest, her ankles hooked around his back as her tongue curled around his. The combination made his head spin and his cock throb.

The kiss went on forever. Holding nothing back this time, he drank in her sweet taste like a starving man.

She squirmed under him, asking him for more.

Without ending the kiss, he began to move again, swift strokes in and out.

Olivia tore her lips free of his and took a harsh deep breath.

He felt her tremble and went deep, knowing she was close.

Her fingers clutched his backside.

A bead of sweat pooled at his brow. "Come on, baby," he whispered. "Come for me."

She cried out a minute later, and he let go—of his control, of his attempt to stay removed, of his plans to build a fence. He poured into her knowing he had lost the battle and acknowledging that if she left him now, he'd be ruined.

―⁓―

It had been different this time. *He* had been different, more like the man she'd made love with in Washington. Olivia sighed with contentment. They had gotten past the bump in the road, and she couldn't be more relieved.

After the day they had spent together, she was more determined than ever to make this relationship work, despite the obstacles that stood in their way. So there was some geographical distance and a few years between them. And yes, they were at different places in their lives. But none of that mattered when stacked up against her love for him.

She opened her eyes and took another visual tour of the extravagant room. He had done this for her. His arms were wrapped tight around her from behind, his breathing slow and steady. As she wove her fingers through his, she wondered if he was asleep.

He squeezed her hand. "What are you thinking about?" he mumbled.

"You."

Stifling a yawn, he drew her closer to him. "What about me?"

"Just how much I appreciate this trip and everything you did to make it happen."

"I'm glad you're enjoying it."

"I know you've been here before, so it might not be as much fun for you—"

"Watching you see it for the first time is about the most fun I've ever had."

She moved onto her back so she could see him. "I was sure you were asleep."

"I was on my way, but I could hear your wheels turning."

"Are they loud?"

"Very," he said, shifting to use her for a pillow. "Spill it."

Cradling his head against her chest, she played with his hair. "I'm afraid of ruining our good mood."

He went still. "Are you going to tell me you're through with me?"

"No," she said with a soft chuckle.

"You've been faking all those orgasms?"

She smacked his shoulder. "Definitely not."

"Then whatever it is, I think I can handle it."

She tilted his face up so she could see him. "I signed a lease on an apartment the other day."

"You said you might, so I'm not totally surprised. How long?"

"A year, but I can get out of it with a month's notice."

"I guess that's reasonable."

"You're not mad?"

"Of course not. I'd rather have you living with me, but I understand why you need to do this."

"You do? Really?"

"Sure I do." Amused by her distress, he twirled a lock of her hair around his finger. "So you were pretty worried, huh?"

She nodded. "You took me on this amazing trip, and you made me such a lovely offer to come live with you. I'd hate for you to think I don't appreciate it."

"I know you do. And I didn't take you on this trip to convince you to come live with me. That's a whole other deal, and you're not ready. I'm cool with it."

"The apartment is in Alexandria so you can stay with me whenever you're in town."

"And maybe you could come to Chicago during your Christmas break? Check things out? See what you think? For later, of course."

His attempt at restraint drew a smile from her. "I'd love to."

"When are you moving in?"

"They said I could have the place at the end of the week."

"Want some help moving?"

"Really?"

He shrugged. "I'm off this week, so I could spend a couple of days in D.C."

"What about the kids you fly to treatments?"

"I only do that on Tuesdays, so I had already let them know I was unavailable this week because we were going to be here."

She squealed and flung her arms around him.

"I take it you're pleased?"

"Yes," she said, rewarding him with a deep kiss.

After a minute, he pulled back from her. "What if there's a baby?" he asked tentatively.

"We'll have plenty of time to prepare for that."

"I won't want to miss a thing." He laid his hand on her flat belly. "I'd want to be there for every second."

Olivia covered his hand with hers. "Are you planning to quit your job?" she asked with a smile.

"No, but if you're pregnant with my baby, I want us to live together so I can take care of you. Both of you."

She studied him for a long moment. "Am I going to wake up one of these mornings to find that my carriage has turned into a pumpkin and this whole thing was a dream?"

He pulled her tight against him. "No way."

Pressing her lips to his chest, she relaxed into his embrace. "If it *is* a dream, it's a dream come true."

"For me, too, honey. For me, too."

——⁓——

They rented a car the next morning and drove across the Golden Gate Bridge to Marin County. In Sausalito, they parked to walk through the artsy town. Olivia gazed into the window at a gallery that featured abstract paintings and sculptures.

"Do you want to go in?" Cole asked.

She shook her head.

"Why not?"

"I get so jealous in those places," she confessed. "They're like private clubs I'll never be allowed to join."

"That's *crazy*! You've got more talent in your little finger than some of those people have in their whole bodies. Look at that." He pointed to a sculpture. "What the hell is it?" Leaning in for a closer look, he snorted. "Twenty *grand*? For that?"

Olivia laughed at his indignation.

"Once you get into art school, you'll get all kinds of connections and opportunities. I bet you'll have your own showing in less than a year."

"You're very good for my self-esteem."

He hooked his arm around her. "Let's go in there and laugh at the outrageous prices they're charging. We can figure out how much you're going to be worth someday."

They hit every gallery in town. "I guess I can retire," he concluded after they were seated for lunch. "You're going to be loaded."

"Are you going to let me keep you?"

"I'll be Mr. Mom to our five kids."

"*Five?*"

"Why not?" He studied the menu. "You've got lots of years left before your clock starts ticking."

"You're high if you think I'm having five kids."

"All right. Four then."

"Two if you're lucky."

He smiled victoriously. "You just agreed to have two kids with me."

"Hey! You tricked me!"

"Whatever it takes."

"So let me get this straight—you're going to give up flying to stay home with our two kids?"

His smile faded. "By give up flying, do you mean—"

Olivia howled with laughter. "I didn't think so."

"How did that just backfire on me?"

"Clearly, you're not as clever as you think you are."

He sulked through lunch, which Olivia seemed to find hilarious. When the check arrived, she reached for it.

"Give me that," he said.

She held it out of his reach. "Oh, let me. It's the least I can do after you agreed to give up flying so I can pursue my dreams."

"I have a feeling I'm going to live to regret this," he mumbled as he followed her from the restaurant.

"Don't worry, *honey*. You've got nine months—or I guess it's more like eight now—to fly your little heart out before Junior arrives and brings you solidly down to earth."

He glowered at her. "Are you enjoying yourself?"

"I'm having a blast." She hooked her arm through his. "What's next?"

Half an hour later, Cole waited outside for Olivia while she browsed through a shoe store. The day was clear and warm, the sky a bright, vivid blue. San Francisco's famous fog had decided to take the day off from blanketing the area, and Cole had never experienced a more glorious northern California day.

Of course, his enjoyment of the day was largely due to his companion, who made every day feel like Christmas. They'd also noticed that people tended to recognize him but didn't approach him here the way they did back East. West Coasters were no doubt more used to celebrity sightings and handled them with more aplomb.

"Cole."

He brought his eyes down from the sky and made eye contact with Chelsea Harper. *Oh, God. Does any man alive have worse luck than me?*

"Chelsea."

The striking redhead hugged him, and as he returned the embrace Cole's heart tripped with anxiety. He could only imagine how this would look to Olivia.

"It's so great to see you," Chelsea said. "You look fabulous, as always."

"Likewise. How've you been?"

"A little better." Her pretty face lifted into a small, sad smile. "I miss you, but I'm trying to move on."

"I'm so sorry about what happened."

"We were caught up in all the Captain Incredible magic," she said with a rueful expression. "I've come to see it was doomed from the start."

Cole had no idea what to say to that, so he asked the obvious question. "What're you doing here?" The last he knew, she lived in Portland, Oregon.

"I decided I needed a new start. My sister lives here, so I moved last month. I'm working at one of the galleries." With a shy smile, she added, "And I'm writing again."

He was surprised they hadn't run into her earlier when they were visiting the galleries. "I'm so glad to hear that. I've thought of you—"

Her hand on his arm stopped him. "Please don't say what you think I need to hear. That won't help me."

Humbled by her quiet grace, Cole met her green-eyed gaze, remembering how hard he'd tried to fall in love with this gem of a woman.

"Um, Cole?"

Olivia's voice blasted him out of his reverie and returned him to his present predicament. But before he looked away, he saw the flash of hurt that dashed through Chelsea's eyes.

He put his arm around Olivia. "This is Olivia Robison. Olivia, Chelsea Harper. We met after the blizzard landing. She was a passenger on the flight."

"I remember reading about the two of you." Olivia's expression remained neutral as she shook hands with Chelsea. "Nice to meet you."

"You, too," Chelsea said.

Cole's stomach constricted at the tension he heard in Olivia's voice. She had to be getting tired of running into his ex-girlfriends. What if she decided she'd had enough of it? The thought sharpened the pain circling in his gut.

"Well," Chelsea said, "I'd better be getting back to work. It was really great to see you, Cole."

"You, too."

Chelsea's gaze took in both of them. "Take care."

Cole watched Chelsea until she ducked into a door on the next block, and then he ventured a glance at Olivia whose eyes were fixed on the building down the street.

"She's very beautiful."

"Yes."

"She was in love with you."

"Yes again."

Olivia crossed her arms and finally looked up at him. "What happened?"

"I didn't love her," he said with a helpless shrug. "I wanted to, but I just didn't."

"Why not? She seems perfectly lovely."

"She was. I mean, she *is*. But something was missing." He tucked a strand of Olivia's hair behind her ear and caressed her cheek, hoping to allay the fear he felt coming from her. "It bothered me, you know? Here was this woman who was so perfect for me in every way, and yet I couldn't love her. That was the first time I really thought something was wrong with me, that I was deficient in some important way. But that wasn't it."

"What was the problem?"

He looked again at the gallery where Chelsea worked before he lowered his gaze to Olivia. "She wasn't you."

"Cole."

"I know you probably think I'm feeding you a line because of what just happened, but I swear I'm not. I never understood what was missing until I met you." He gestured toward Chelsea's building. "She wanted more than I was willing to give. After it was over, I remember thinking that if I couldn't love Chelsea, what hope was there for me? You know? When she walked away, I told myself I should be sad or lonely or disappointed. But I wasn't. I wasn't anything."

He cradled Olivia's face in his hands and gazed into her eyes. "If you walked away, I'd never get over it. That's how I know everything about us is different."

"I want so badly to believe that."

Cole experienced a surge of panic. "You *can* believe it. I swear to you, Olivia."

"I'm not going to lie to you and tell you your past doesn't bother me because it does. It's hard picturing you with other women."

"Then don't. Picture me with just you because that's the only place I want to be, Liv." He tilted her face so he could see her eyes. "Do you believe me?"

"I'm trying," she said softly. "But I'm still scared."

"Of what?"

"That you'll find someone you like better—"

Oblivious to the other people passing on the sidewalk, he captured her mouth in a quick but passionate kiss. "It'll never happen."

"You have women throwing themselves at you everywhere you go." She looked away. "So many opportunities."

"None of which would ever tempt me." Cole suddenly realized this was the most important conversation he'd ever had. "Not when I have you in my life. Not when I finally have everything I've ever wanted."

The obvious battle she was waging with her emotions touched his heart. He hated that she now had one more reason to doubt his love for her.

"How about we get back to our day?" he asked, forcing a cheerful tone. "Ready to paint the bridge?"

Despite her nod, he still saw concern lingering in her expressive eyes.

"Everything's going to be okay, Liv. I promise."

She attempted a smile. "Let's go."

They drove to Golden Gate Park where the bright sun kept the fog from consuming the bridge.

"Do you want to paint it from this side or the other?" Cole asked.

Mesmerized by the view, Olivia said, "This is fine."

He came up behind her, put his hands on her shoulders, and rested his chin on the top of her head. "Want me to disappear for a while?"

"You don't have to."

"You don't want me watching."

"I wouldn't mind if you did."

"Really? I thought you artist types were very secretive about your works in progress."

"Other artist types maybe. But not me." She went up on tiptoes to kiss him. "And not if it's you who's watching."

"I'm honored." He stole another kiss and went to get her supplies from the trunk of the car. "I should've gotten you an easel, too," he said, surveying the picnic table she had chosen.

"And how would we have gotten that home?"

"I do have a few connections with the airline, you know."

"The table is fine."

"Do you need anything else?"

She cracked open the bottle of water they had bought for her to use with the watercolors. "Not a thing."

"And you're warm enough?"

"I'm *fine*," she said with a giddy grin. She couldn't believe where she was and what she was about to do. "I hope you aren't going to be bored."

He bent down to kiss her cheek. "Take your time. Minutes, hours, whatever you need."

Squeezing the hand he had placed on her shoulder, she said, "Thank you," and got busy setting up the table to her satisfaction.

"Are you *sniffing* the paint?"

"I *love* the smell of new paint." She held it out for him to take a whiff.

His face crinkled with disgust. "Ew."

"It's an acquired taste."

"Apparently. I'm going to take a walk so I don't mess with your groove."

"You don't have to."

"I know." He kissed her nose. "Have fun. I'll be back in a bit."

"Okay." Olivia watched him go and then turned her attention to the bridge.

She studied the span for several minutes as her mind wandered back to the incident in Sausalito. Another woman from Cole's past. They seemed to be just about everywhere. If she were wise, she'd run from him as fast as she could before he could do to her what he'd done to them.

As she puzzled over the situation, Olivia kept coming back to a saying of her father's: call 'em like you see 'em. In other words, judge people by the way they treat you, not by what others say about them. If she were to judge Cole solely based on the way he'd treated her, he'd get a gold star.

Here she was sitting in Golden Gate Park about to paint the bridge she'd dreamed of seeing in person for most of her life. He'd done that for her. He'd brought her here, bought the paints, and given her all the time she needed to indulge her passion. On top of that, he'd encouraged her to apply to art school. That was the Cole she knew. That was the *only* Cole she knew. And that was the Cole she would love and believe in, unless he gave her a reason not to.

Determined to have faith in him—and in *them*— Olivia dipped her brush into the paint and got busy.

Chapter 22

COLE WALKED FOR AN HOUR ALONG THE SCENIC PATH that overlooked the bay, all the while resisting the urge to go back to see what Olivia had gotten done. But he kept walking because he wanted to give her time to work without any distractions.

Along the way he thought about Chelsea and the brief but passionate affair that had followed the landing in the snow. The media had gone wild over the romance between the hero pilot and the grateful passenger. They'd been on the covers of two magazines and were recognized everywhere they went. In the midst of all the madness, they'd struggled to find time alone together, and Cole had struggled to figure out why he was unable to feel even the most basic of emotions for a wonderful woman who adored him.

The affair had ended as suddenly as it began when Chelsea came right out and asked him if he loved her, or if he thought he ever would. When he'd said nothing, she'd had her answer. For a long time afterward, he'd thought about the stricken expression on her face when she realized he didn't feel the same way she did. He hadn't seen or heard from her since then. Until today. And of course, it had to happen when he was with Olivia.

Cole was ashamed of many of the meaningless interludes in his past, but he didn't regret anything about his time with Chelsea. He'd tried as hard as he possibly could to make it work. At one point, he'd almost had himself convinced he was in love. The niggling feeling that something elemental and necessary was missing had kept him from saying the words she'd needed to hear. It took meeting Olivia to understand what had been lacking with Chelsea, and now that he had it, he'd do whatever he could to keep it.

He looked up to realize he'd traveled further away from Olivia than he had intended. Turning around, he headed back. As he got closer to her, he saw an older man talking to her. A small white dog on a leash waited patiently at his feet while the man talked with animated hands. Olivia hung on his every word.

Cole's heart began to beat faster, and he broke into a run. *What was I thinking? I shouldn't have left her for so long in a strange place.*

"Hey!" he called to let her know he was coming.

Olivia looked up at him with a bright smile. "Cole! You won't believe it!"

He arrived at the picnic table and moved to position himself between her and the tall, distinguished man with white hair and warm blue eyes. He looked nothing at all like the predator Cole had conjured up from a distance.

"This is my, um, boyfriend, Cole." Olivia's cheeks flushed with color. "This is Victor James. He walks his dog here every Sunday."

Still eyeing him warily, Cole shook the other man's hand.

"I know you from somewhere," Victor said, his eyebrows furrowed in thought as he studied Cole.

"He's the pilot who landed the plane in the blizzard and then saved the captain's life," Olivia said proudly.

"Captain Incredible!" Victor cried. "Of course!"

Cole cringed. If he never heard that stupid nickname again, it would be too soon. "Guilty as charged."

"Well, it's a great honor to meet a true American hero," he said, shaking Cole's hand. "I was just telling Olivia that I have a large collection of San Francisco area art, and I love her view of the bridge. She's wonderfully talented."

"Yes." Cole's heart tripped with excitement for her. "She certainly is." He glanced down at the table and did a double take. The painting was magnificent. It was the bridge, but it was so much more. Hues and textures and depth. And that she'd managed to do it in just an hour's time. "Oh, Liv. *Wow*."

"My sentiments exactly, young man. In fact, I was just about to offer your lovely lady a thousand dollars for it."

Olivia gasped. "*What?*"

Victor took another long look at the painting. "You're right," he said thoughtfully. "A thousand's not enough. How about three?"

"She accepts," Cole said when he realized Olivia had gone mute. "Three thousand it is."

Victor reached into his breast pocket. "I only have a thousand in cash on me. Will you take a check for the rest?"

"She'd be happy to."

Cole accepted the ten one-hundred-dollar bills and spelled Olivia's last name for Victor, who tore the check out of his checkbook and handed it to Cole.

"But," Olivia sputtered, "it's not finished."

"I love it exactly as it is," Victor insisted.

"Sign it," Cole said softly.

Dazed, Olivia glanced at him. "What?"

"Sign it," he said through clenched teeth.

"Oh. Right." She dipped her brush into the blue paint and put her name in the corner.

Only Cole noticed the slight tremble of her hand. He lifted the painting off the table and held it for Victor. "Give it a minute to dry."

When Victor's white toy poodle realized they were about to resume their walk, it began to dance around at his feet.

"Nice doing business with you, Olivia." Victor held out his card. "I'd be interested in seeing more of your work, especially anything local."

Since Olivia now seemed paralyzed as well as mute, Cole took the card from Victor and handed over the painting. "She's working on something at Fisherman's Wharf, too. I'll have her manager get in touch."

"See that you do." Victor made a kissing sound that got the dog's attention. "Come along, Tootles. We need to hit the frame shop."

After they had walked away, Cole let out a loud whoop, hauled Olivia into his arms, and swung her around.

"Oh, my God," she whispered as she clung to him. "Did that seriously just happen?"

"What? You making three grand or introducing me as your boyfriend? I'm not sure which part I liked best."

"Cole, he paid me *three thousand dollars* for my painting. That's the first time…"

"I know, baby." Wiping a tear from her cheek, he smiled. "You've got a client. A real, live client." Leaning in, he kissed her softly and then reached for her hand, putting the stack of bills and the check on her palm and curling their joined hands around it. "I'm so proud of you I could bust."

"Before you bust, do you mind answering two questions for me?"

"Shoot."

"Who exactly is my manager, and how much of a cut is he expecting?"

Cole tossed his head back and roared with laughter.

Olivia floated on air. She had relayed the story four times now—to her dad, both her brothers, and Jenny, and it hadn't gotten old yet. *Three thousand dollars for something she had created!* It was beyond her wildest dreams, and the money gave her a financial cushion that would be a huge relief as she moved into her apartment.

Cole, who was just as excited, waited patiently while she made her calls. When she hung up with her brother Andy, Olivia crossed the room to flop down next to Cole on the sofa. The wad of bills and the folded check sat on the table in front of them.

"I still can't believe it," she said, staring at the money.

"Just think, we have all day tomorrow, too. You can do Fisherman's Wharf, Chinatown, Pacific Heights. At the speed you work, I'll bet you could triple your take in the time we have left."

"I wouldn't know what to do with that kind of money."

"The first thing you're going to do is pay your taxes."

"I am?"

"You'll need to file a 1099 with the IRS."

"A ten ninety what?"

"Don't worry about it. I have a friend from home who's a CPA. I'll get you hooked up with him."

"It's only three thousand dollars, Cole. I don't need an accountant."

"It's just the start, Olivia, and you *do* need an accountant."

"If you say so."

"Hey, I'm your manager, right? You need to listen to me."

"How much is this piece of advice going to cost me?" she asked warily.

His face lifted into a lascivious grin. "I'll let you pay me back in trade."

She rolled her eyes. "Oh, gee, lucky me."

"No, lucky *me*. I'm sleeping with the art world's next big thing."

"I don't like to mix business with pleasure, so if you're going to be my manager, we'll have to cool it in the bedroom."

"In that case, I quit."

Olivia laughed and reached for him.

He brushed his lips over her cheek in a soft caress. "Are you happy?"

"I never knew it was possible to be this happy. You've changed my whole life. You know that, don't you?"

He shook his head. "I didn't do it. You did."

"You had faith long before I did."

"Maybe, but it's your talent that's opening these doors for you, and tonight we're going to celebrate you and all your good news."

Her tongue danced lightly down his neck. "Could we maybe have a private celebration first?"

"What'd you have in mind?"

She whispered her suggestion in his ear.

He cleared his throat. "We might be able to fit that into the schedule."

"Now aren't you glad you're my ex-manager?"

"Oh, *yeah*."

Cole emerged from the bathroom wearing a dark blue suit with a starched white shirt and a royal blue tie.

Olivia stared at him.

"What?"

"As you would say, *wow*."

"Same to you, my love." He nibbled on her neck and dragged a finger into the plunging neckline of her black dress.

She hoped he wouldn't notice that it was the same dress she'd worn to their dinner at the airport. However, he didn't seem to be noticing anything but her cleavage at the moment. "Where are we going?"

"Somewhere the concierge recommended. Asian fusion cuisine—whatever that is."

"Sounds good to me."

He wrapped a shawl around her bare shoulders. "You look gorgeous, Liv. Every guy in the place will be checking you out."

"You'll turn a few heads yourself—like you always do." She adjusted his tie and then reached up to kiss him. Wiping the lipstick off his lips, she studied his handsome face.

"You're staring again," he said with that half grin she loved so much.

"I can't seem to get enough of you."

Putting his arms around her, he brought her in for a kiss that quickly spiraled out of control. He appeared dazzled as he pulled back from her.

"Just say the word and we can stay in," she said.

"No. We're going out to celebrate."

She stopped him with a hand on his arm. "I don't need anything more than you to have a celebration."

"I love you." He kissed both sides of her face and then her lips. "Have I mentioned that lately?"

"Not in the last half hour or so."

"I don't mean to be slacking off."

"That's all right. You did a pretty good job of showing me a little while ago."

"Mmm," he growled into her ear. "Just pretty good?"

She giggled. "*Very* good." The thought of it made her want more, but since he was determined to go out, she turned him around and pointed him toward the door.

After dinner, they went dancing at the Top of the Mark Sky Lounge. "I'd love to paint this," Olivia said wistfully as she swayed with him to the sounds of a jazz band. Over his shoulder, she took in the sparkling lights of the city that stretched for miles below the nineteenth-floor landmark.

"We could probably arrange to get you up here tomorrow."

"I meant the night view."

"Could you commit it to memory and paint when we get back to the room?"

"You wouldn't care?"

"Why would I? I have to learn to take the bad with the good if I'm going to be your kept man."

Olivia laughed softly. She had been delighted to

discover he was a smooth, graceful dancer. Their bodies were locked together in sensuous movement that wasn't all that different from lovemaking. His cologne, a dark and spicy scent that suited him perfectly, filled her senses as his arousal pressed against her, an ever-present reminder of the passion they shared.

"Remember when I told you yesterday was the best day of my life?" she asked.

"Mmm-hmm."

"I can't believe it's possible, but today was better."

Cole tightened his hold on her. "I wonder what tomorrow has in store for you."

Glancing up, she found his eyes closed and his face relaxed. "Nothing could top this."

He opened his eyes and dipped his head to kiss her. "You never know."

They had apple martinis and danced for an hour at the Sky Lounge before they strolled back to the Fairmont. In the elevator, Cole kept his arm around her. She rested her head on his chest. "Thank you for yet another unforgettable evening."

"Congratulations on all your good news."

She choked back a yawn. "It wouldn't be half as good if I couldn't share it with you."

"Are you too sleepy to work?" He opened the door to their room and ushered her in ahead of him.

"I told you that second martini wasn't a good idea."

Cole pulled off his tie and unbuttoned his shirt. "What you need is some sleep to recharge. You can get up early in the morning and get to it."

She reached up to caress his face. "You're right. It's too late to start anything now."

He raised an eyebrow. "Anything?"

Laughing, she said, "Too late to paint."

"Better."

As he took off his suit coat, Olivia went into the bathroom to change into the last of the silk nightgowns she had bought for the trip. This one was black with lace trim and fell to mid-thigh. She slipped on the matching thong and washed the makeup off her face. Filled with giddy anticipation, she brushed her hair and teeth.

Every time with him felt like the first. That she could be with such an amazing, loving, thoughtful man any time she wanted was something she was still getting used to. And that he loved her. Really loved her. Maybe she had finally taken that leap after all. One thing she knew for sure—faced with the choice, she would gladly give up all the other incredible things that had happened recently if it meant she got to keep him.

When she emerged from the bathroom, she discovered he had lowered the lights and removed his shirt. He stood in front of the big window with his hands in his pockets. For a moment, she took in the delicious sight of broad, muscular shoulders, a narrow waist, and tight buns.

Oh, how I love those buns, she thought, resisting the urge to giggle. She slipped her arms around him and pressed her lips to his back.

"What are you thinking about?"

He surprised her when he said, "My mother." Putting his hands on top of hers, he added, "She would've loved you. I'm sorry you'll never get to meet her."

"So am I."

"I want you to meet my dad and the rest of my family

when you come out after Christmas." He turned to her. "Would that be okay?"

"I'd love that. My dad wants to meet you, too."

"Another big leap," he said with a teasing smile. His eyes darkened when he finally noticed what she was wearing. "Oh, *man*." He tilted his head for a better view. "Wow."

She smiled. "Your favorite word."

"Only since I met you."

Winding her arms around his neck, she skimmed her tongue along his bottom lip. "I want you," she whispered.

He pulled her tight against the hard ridge of his erection. "You have me. I'm all yours."

"Let's go to bed."

"When there's a perfectly good wall right here?"

"I've learned that walls are nothing but trouble."

Grinning, he brought his lips down on hers for a hot, desperate kiss full of longing. He lifted her into his arms and wrapped her legs around his hips.

"Speaking of trouble," she whispered against his lips. "Is it midnight yet?"

Perplexed by the question, he glanced at the clock. "Ten after. Why? Do you have a curfew?"

"No, but I *am* late."

His eyebrows knitted with confusion. "Late?"

"Officially *late*."

Watching his face soften with awareness was among the best in a string of unforgettable moments with him.

"Yeah?" he asked, his voice gruff with emotion.

Nodding, she moved her hand to his chest in time to feel his heart flutter.

"Does that happen sometimes?"

"Never. I'm like clockwork."

This time his kiss was fierce—and possessive. "Maybe we scared it off with all our 'activity' this weekend."

She laughed. "I doubt it. I'll give it another day or two, and then I'll take a test."

"Do we *have* to wait that long?"

"I'm only one day late. And you're supposed to be having a meltdown, not hoping it's true."

"Who says? I want it to be true. I want it so much."

"So do I."

For a long time they held each other, absorbed in thoughts and dreams Olivia had certainly never imagined might come true for her.

"Cole?"

"Hmm?"

"It only took ten minutes for today to top yesterday."

Chapter 23

HE LAID HER DOWN ON THE BED AND HOVERED ABOVE her, teasing her with light touches of his lips to hers. "What do you want?"

"You." She reached for him, trying to bring him down on top of her. "Just you."

He shook his head and then kissed her neck. "You have to tell me."

"*Cole…*" She moaned when he added his tongue to the action on her neck.

"What?" he whispered in her ear.

Olivia squirmed under him as he drove her wild with just the tip of his tongue against her ear. The sensations rocketed through her, causing her nipples to tingle and heat to pool at her core. She caressed the hard muscle of his chest and shoulders.

"I need you. Don't tease."

"Why not? It's so much fun."

She closed her eyes tight against an almost painful wave of desire.

"*For who?*"

Laughing softly, he rolled his lips over her nipple through the silk nightgown.

Olivia, who hadn't seen that coming, almost flew off the bed. She clutched a handful of his hair to anchor him to her chest.

"Tell me," he urged. "Tonight is all about you, so I need to know what you want."

She felt the flush of longing from her breasts to her face. "I want you." Her voice was small when she added, "In me."

"What part of me?"

Her wail of dismay echoed like a sob as he continued to toy with her nipple. "All of you."

Nudging aside the flimsy silk of her thong, he pushed two fingers into her, and she came instantly. As she rode the wave, he sent his tongue plunging into her open mouth, mimicking the motion of his relentless fingers.

"God, Liv," he whispered. "You're so hot."

The two-pronged assault on her senses made her head spin and her heart pound. She was aware of him removing the nightgown and thong as well as the rest of his own clothes. And when his hot mouth closed over her sensitive nipple, Olivia almost came again. She reached for him and curled her hand around his straining erection, but he stopped her before she could stroke him.

"Don't, baby," he rasped. "I'm hanging by a thread here."

"Then don't wait," she said, urging him to enter her.

"Not yet." He kissed his way down to her belly. "You haven't gotten everything you asked for."

Pushing her knees as far apart as he could get them, he teased her with endless strokes of his tongue on her thighs that stopped just short of where she wanted him. Finally, he gave her his tongue in soft but determined caresses.

Olivia clutched the duvet and lifted her hips in answer to his questing strokes. She was so hot she feared she would combust if he kept it up much longer. The heat built until it was almost unbearable. And then she shattered into a million pieces. He stayed with her throughout the tumult and only let up when she had returned softly to earth, her eyes closed tight against the rush of emotion. That it was possible to feel so much, even more than ever before, amazed her.

He sat up to reach for a condom on the bedside table, but she stopped him.

His eyebrow arched in a questioning look.

"I want to feel you." She tugged at him. "Just you."

"Liv, we shouldn't."

"What does it matter now?" She sat up, eased him onto his back, and straddled him.

"Wait, honey."

"Shh." Olivia leaned forward to kiss him and slid her hot wetness back and forth over his hard length.

He groaned, held her still, and surged up and into her in one smooth move.

Olivia gasped at the impact and struggled to accommodate him. She tossed her head back, reveling in the sensation of being filled by him. For a long time she stayed still, her hands on his chest supporting her weight. Then she began to move the way she knew he liked.

She looked down to find his eyes closed, his lip between his teeth, and his forehead damp with sweat. Reaching for his hands, she laced her fingers through his and held on tight as she pivoted her hips back and forth.

"*Liv*," he gasped. "*You're killing me.*"

"Good," she said, keeping up the pace.

He squeezed her hands as his eyes flew open and found hers in the soft light.

She raised their joined hands and brought them down on either side of his head. Leaning forward, she kissed him softly, all the while keeping her eyes fixed on his and her hips moving.

He surprised her when he suddenly turned them over without losing their connection.

As he pounded into her, she was exhilarated to realize she had once again broken his control. This was how she loved him best—wild and driven to take and take and then take more. Everything.

He dipped his head and sucked hard on her nipple, sending her into a climax that ripped through her like a freight train. Then his hands were under her, holding her tight against him as he went deep one last time and let himself go with a cry of release ripped straight from his soul.

Looping her arms around him, she closed her eyes and drifted off to sleep, still joined with him in every possible way.

—⁓—

Cole worried he might be crushing her. He dropped a kiss on the side of her breast as her chest rose and fell in an easy cadence.

"Am I hurting you?" When he received no answer, he raised his head. "Liv?"

He smiled when he realized she was asleep. It was no wonder she was exhausted. She amazed him. He had never been with a woman who could be counted on for no fewer than three orgasms every time they made love. He wondered if that was just another sign of a perfect match. Maybe he'd never experienced such a thing because he had been making love to—or, he should say, having sex with—the wrong women.

He'd also never in his life had unprotected sex, and now that he knew what he'd been missing… well, it would be damned hard to go back to using condoms after experiencing what it was like to bury himself in her with nothing between them but love and desire.

As he planted a kiss on her breastbone, he watched her pretty pink lips part and then move as if she were dreaming. Was she dreaming of him? He certainly hoped so. Withdrawing from her, he reached for the soft chenille blanket at the foot of the bed to cover her. He kissed her cheek, and just in case she wasn't completely asleep, he whispered, "I love you."

She mumbled and turned into him.

He held her for a long time before he got up to take a shower.

Standing under the pulsing massage of the hot water, he thought of her joy at selling her painting, the way her face had lit up when she told the story to her loved ones at home, her almost childlike enthusiasm for the exotic food they had shared over dinner, and the awestruck reaction she'd had to the Top of the Mark. He loved her so much. And now there might be a baby to love, too.

For the first time since his college girlfriend rebuffed his proposal, he could imagine asking the question again. He laughed to himself when he thought of what his mother—who had long ago given up on ever seeing her oldest child settled down—would've said about him being ready to take the plunge with a woman he'd known only six weeks. Yes, she would have enjoyed this.

Time hardly mattered in a situation like this, he reasoned. He had known instantly that Olivia was special, just by the tender way she had cared for him after the incident in the store. She had shown him her heart in those first few minutes, and nothing that had happened since then had detracted from that crucial first impression. If anything, she had demonstrated time and again that he'd been right to go back to find her after thinking about her for two long weeks.

Being in love like this made him feel dizzy and breathless, just like flying fighter jets when every move had to be carefully considered. The last thing in the world he wanted was drive her away by pushing for too much too soon.

She was right when she said they were at different places in their lives. Now that he had her in *his* life, he was ready for all the things he had disdained for so many years. But that wasn't what she wanted. Not yet anyway. If they were having a baby, though, that would move things along. Olivia wouldn't bring a child into this world out of wedlock if she could avoid it. Of that he was fairly certain.

He turned off the water and wrapped a towel around his waist. Using a hand towel to dry his hair, he wandered into the bedroom, anxious for reassurance that she was still there.

She slept on her side with her hand under her cheek. Her silky dark hair was fanned out on the pillow, in sharp contrast to the snow-white sheets.

Cole wanted to wrap himself around her and never let go. For a guy who had spent most of his life avoiding commitment, the feeling was new and unexpected. He had also taken meticulous care to ensure there would be no unplanned children. But because of her, none of that frightened him anymore. No, the only thing he was truly afraid of now was that he would somehow manage to push her away by wanting her too damned much.

Olivia woke up thirsty at two thirty and was disoriented for a moment. The last thing she remembered was making crazy love with Cole and then... nothing. Had she really conked out right after? That was kind of embarrassing. *I hope he doesn't think I didn't like it or that I was bored. Nothing could be further from the truth.* He looked so adorable and peaceful, asleep on his back with an arm thrown over his head. She wanted to wake him up to apologize for falling asleep, but she couldn't bring herself to disturb him.

Getting up, she went to find some water and was surprised to feel a rush of sticky wetness between her legs. *Oh, no! No, no, no!* The disappointment overwhelmed her. She'd had no idea until that very second just how badly she wanted the baby she wasn't even sure she was carrying. Then she remembered they hadn't used a condom, and maybe, just maybe, it wasn't her period but something else.

She closed her eyes and whispered a prayer, "Please, please, please." Her eyes opened slowly and took a moment to focus. She had to look again to be certain. It wasn't her period. The relief was so overwhelming that she closed her eyes to absorb the feeling. By the time she had showered and changed into a clean T-shirt and panties, she was wide awake and full of nervous energy.

As she took a drink from a bottle of water, she decided to work for a while until she felt sleepy again. She set up her paints at the wide desk and got busy.

That's where Cole found her at eight o'clock the next morning. Drying paintings occupied every available surface in the room.

"Jesus, Liv," he uttered as he picked up her take on the view from the Top of the Mark. "Have you been at it all night?"

Startled, she looked up at him. "What?"

"Have you been working all night?"

"Just since three."

"After the way you passed out on me, I figured you were down for the count."

"I'm so sorry about that. I hope you didn't think—"

He smiled. "That I'd worn you out?"

Her face heated with embarrassment. "Well, you did."

"Don't sweat it," he said, trailing a finger over her cheek. "So you couldn't sleep?"

"I woke up, and I thought…"

He traded the painting he'd been holding for one of Fisherman's Wharf. "Thought what?"

"That I'd gotten my period."

His eyes flew up to meet hers. "And you didn't?"

"No."

She saw the relief on his face and understood exactly how he felt.

"Good." He leaned down to kiss her forehead. "How about some coffee?"

She smiled up at him. "I'd love some."

"I'll call."

"Cole?"

He turned back to her.

"Are they any good?" She bit her lip. "The paintings?"

"Let me put it this way—after I call for coffee, I'm going to give your client a ring. He's going to want to see what you've done here."

—∿∿—

Victor invited them to dinner at his home, a contemporary built into one of the hills above Sausalito that overlooked the bay, the bridge, and the city in the distance. Victor and his partner, Paulo, had lived in the house for more than fifteen of the twenty years they had been together, and after Paolo made a big deal about meeting Cole, the first thing they did was show Olivia her framed painting on the wall of their study.

Seeing it displayed so prominently as part of their vast and eclectic collection made Cole's heart race with excitement for her. His hand closed around hers and their eyes met. Sharing the delight only made the moment sweeter.

"We understand there's more," Paolo said, rubbing his hands together. He had dark hair, a deep olive complexion, and a thick Spanish accent, even though he said he'd lived most of his adult life in the United States.

"Victor comes home from his walk yesterday all excited about the new artist he discovered." With Paolo's accent, "Victor" became "Veektor." "We were so happy to hear from you today."

"You'll have to excuse Paolo." Victor rested a hand on the other man's shoulder. "He went nuts over your painting, so he can barely contain himself waiting to see what else you've got."

Cole handed Victor the portfolio they had bought earlier in the day to transport her latest work. As Victor and Paolo pored over the paintings, Cole kept his arm tight around Olivia.

At one point Paolo looked up at Olivia, his eyes gleaming.

Cole felt her tremble so he leaned in and brushed a kiss over her cheek.

Finally, they reached the end of the portfolio. "We'll have a show," Paolo declared.

"A show?" Olivia stammered.

"At our gallery in town," Paolo said. "Let's see, what is it now, November? We'll do a show in March. Do you have more?"

Olivia had gone mute again, so Cole answered for her. "She has a huge collection of paintings. She does amazing drawings, too."

"What kind of drawings?" Victor asked.

"All kinds but mostly portraits," Olivia managed to say.

"Why don't you show them, Liv?" Cole said. All eyes shifted to him. "Give her fifteen minutes, and you'll have something you'll treasure forever."

"I didn't bring my sketch pad," Olivia stammered.

"We have one," Victor said, "but only if you're game. We didn't invite you here to work."

"I'd love to draw you both."

"She probably thinks you have good bone structure," Cole added dryly.

Both men laughed.

"That's what I said about him. He's still trying to decide if it was a compliment."

"Let's go into the library," Paolo suggested. "Victor

set a fire before you arrived, and it should be nice and warm in there."

With the toy poodle skipping along at their heels, Cole and Olivia followed them through the single-story house where one room flowed into another. They had used an intriguing mix of antiques and contemporary pieces to create a warm but stylish environment dominated by art of all kinds.

The library boasted two floor-to-ceiling walls of books. The other walls were windows that had been situated to take full advantage of the view of Sausalito below and San Francisco in the distance. The sunset and fire cast a cozy glow over the room.

"What an amazing house!" Olivia said.

"We love it," Victor said. "We can hide out if we want, yet we're close enough to both towns to be there in minutes."

"Oh, here's Marta," Paolo said as a young Hispanic woman came into the room. He introduced her to Cole and Olivia as their cook, housekeeper, and life manager.

Cole noticed Marta's startled expression when she recognized him, but she refrained from comment.

"How about some of Napa's finest?" Victor suggested.

When Cole and Olivia nodded in agreement, Marta left to get the wine.

"Now," Paolo said, "where do you want us?"

Olivia took a look around the room and decided on the love seat.

Victor produced a sketch pad and professional-grade pencils and pens that Olivia practically drooled over. "Will this work?" he asked.

"Um, yes," she said with a smile.

"Do we need to stay still?" Paolo asked, excitement all but radiating from him. "I've never posed before."

"Just be natural." Olivia settled on the sofa across from them.

Cole stood behind her so he could watch but not be in her way.

"So how long have you owned the gallery?" Olivia asked as she began to draw.

The two men looked at each other. "Ten years?" Victor asked his partner.

"Eleven."

"Yes, you're right. I always forget. The gallery is Paolo's baby. I'm just a silent partner."

Paolo rolled his eyes. "Silent, my ass."

They shared a laugh full of love and admiration. Cole had no doubt that Olivia would capture that.

"What do you do, Victor?" she asked.

"I manage the business end of the gallery to keep Paolo free to deal with the art side of the house. He's the one with the real eye for talent."

"I don't know about that," Paolo chimed in. "Who discovered Olivia Robison?"

"Well," Victor said modestly, "I've picked up a few things from you over the years."

Paolo, the more openly affectionate of the two, patted Victor's knee. "He has a keen eye. Don't let him tell you otherwise."

"You won't hear us arguing," Cole said, and they laughed.

Marta came in with the wine as Olivia's hand continued to fly over the crisp white page.

Victor poured three glasses of the '92 merlot. Olivia had declined, and Cole smiled to himself when he realized she wasn't drinking because she might be pregnant.

"I also do some financial planning for a number of clients in town," Victor said.

"He's wildly successful," Paolo said. "You'll want him managing your money when we start raking it in."

Olivia's hand went still, and she looked up at him. "Raking it in?"

"My dear," Paolo said with a big, charming smile, "I'm going to make you a *ton* of money."

"Shall we drink to that?" Victor asked.

As he touched his glass to theirs, Cole looked down to find a dazed expression on Olivia's face.

Chapter 24

COLE WOKE UP FACE DOWN AND ALONE IN BED ON their last morning in San Francisco. His head pounded, and his tongue was stuck to the roof of his mouth. On the bedside table was the bottle of champagne they had polished off after returning from Victor and Paolo's house with a twenty-five-thousand-dollar "down payment" on Olivia's future earnings. Since Olivia had taken just a taste, Cole figured he'd consumed most of the bottle himself. His stomach surged in agreement, and he fought back the need to puke.

Since Olivia was in the bathroom, he groaned his way through a second wave of nausea. When was the last time he had puked from drinking too much? Years ago. Determined to get his mind off his throbbing head and aching stomach, Cole thought about the evening they had spent with the colorful Victor and Paolo. How many bottles of Napa's finest had the three of them polished off? He had lost count. No wonder he felt so sick today.

They had gone nuts over Olivia's portrait, which had reduced Paolo to tears. Over a gourmet meal served by Marta, he had outlined his elaborate plan for Olivia's career. She had been so overwhelmed that Cole wondered if she had managed to swallow a single bite of food. As a result, the small amount of champagne had gone straight to her head. He had never seen her as giddy—or as uninhibited—as she had been after receiving that hefty advance check from Paolo.

Twenty-five thousand dollars! Well, twenty-eight if they counted the other three she had gotten from Victor. That kind of money would give her a cushion she'd never had before. Maybe she could work less and take more classes so she could get through school faster. Since he had resigned himself to waiting until she got her degree to propose, that thought lifted his spirits but did nothing to quell the need to puke.

He sat up slowly, hoping the new position would work with gravity to settle his stomach. His head pounding, he sat still to ride the wave of pain. Over the water running in the bathroom he heard another sound. Wracking sobs. He bolted for the door and gritted his teeth against the blast of pain in his head as he knocked.

"Liv?" When there was no answer, he knocked again. "Honey?" She still didn't answer, so he opened the door to find her sitting bent in half on the closed lid of the toilet. "Hey." He dropped to his knees in front of her. "What's wrong?"

She startled.

"Are you sick? From the champagne?"

Hugging the hotel robe tight around her, her face was so pale that she blended into the white robe. "There's no baby," she whispered, her eyes flooding with new tears.

"Oh, honey," he sighed. "Come here." As she broke down again, he held her tight against him. "It's okay. When the time is right, we'll have as many babies as you want."

"I wanted this one. I know there're a million reasons why it wasn't a good idea right now, but I wanted it."

"I know. I did, too." Surprised by just how disappointed he was, he sat on the bathroom floor with her for a long time, but her sobs didn't let up. "Honey, you're breaking my heart. We'll have a baby. We can try as soon as you want to. Who cares about the logistics? We'll figure it out."

"I wanted to do this for you. You've done so much for me. This was something I could do for you."

Deeply moved by her, he brushed the hair back from her face and the tears off her cheeks. "Liv," he whispered. "You've already given me so much that I've never had before. We've got all the time in the world to have babies."

"I was so sure I was pregnant. I was *sure*."

"You got your hopes up."

"Yes, especially after you were so excited about it." Glancing up at him, she asked, "Are you sad?"

He nodded. "I got my hopes up, too. But guess what?"

"What?"

"There's always next month."

"So we just throw caution to the wind and go for it?"

"Why not?"

She laughed through her tears and studied him, seeming to really see him for the first time since he came into the room. "You're green."

"I have the worst hangover I've ever had in my life."

"Me, too, and I only had a little because I thought I was pregnant. I even puked."

"I've been trying not to for the last half hour."

"Next time we celebrate, no champagne."

"That's fine as long as we get to do the other stuff." He wiggled his eyebrows. "I've never seen you quite so wild."

She cringed. "I can't even think about it. It's so embarrassing."

"I'll never forget it," he said with a dirty grin. "Especially the striptease."

Groaning at the memory, she said, "Success does funny things to me. Did they really give me twenty-five grand last night, or was that a champagne-fueled dream?"

"I *love* the things success does to you, and yes, they really did. I'm not sure if you remember the details since you were in such a daze, but that was the only way they would keep your portfolio."

"Aren't they the most adorable couple you've ever met?"

"I never thought I'd be saying this about two guys, but they really are. I feel like I've known them forever after just a few hours with them."

"I do, too."

"Your career will be in good hands with them, Liv."

"I know."

"I wish I could think of some way to cheer you up. This should be another one of your best days ever."

She rested her head on his shoulder. "It will be. Just give me an hour or two."

"I can do that. Is there anything else you want to do today before we go home?"

"Not really. What time do we have to leave for the airport?"

"Two."

"Then let's go back to bed for a while."

Olivia was subdued as they winged their way across the country that night. So much had happened in the last four days. She would need a while to fully process it all.

"How are you doing over there?" Cole asked.

"Better since I could finally eat something and keep it down."

"Same here." He paused before he added, "How about the other thing?"

"I was just thinking that I suddenly have a better idea of how my mother felt after she lost the twins. I wasn't even actually pregnant, but the sense of loss is so profound. Imagine what it must've been like for her."

"I can't."

"That doesn't mean I get why she treated us the way she did, but still, I can see how losing two babies would do something to your heart."

Cole held her hand between both of his. "I wonder how she's making out in the rehab place."

"I don't know. My dad can't have any contact with her for the first week." She paused and glanced at him. "I have no idea what he's going to do if this doesn't work. There's no way he can stay with her the way she's been the last few years. He's got too many years left to be living like that."

"Well, let's hope it works."

She smiled at him.

"What?"

"I like how you said that, like you have a stake in it."

"I do. I want you to be happy, and I think you mother's problems have been a huge cloud hanging over your life."

"Yes, they have." She caressed his face. "I love you," she whispered. "Thank you so much for this trip, the Fairmont, everything. I'll remember it always."

"So will I." He reached for the hand she had placed on his face and kissed her palm. "And you'll be back there in no time to get ready for your show."

"I hope you can come with me. I can't imagine being there without you."

"You'll be so busy with your work that you won't have time for me."

"I'll always have time for you."

"That's what you say now. Just wait until you're a globe-trotting sensation. Then I'll have to make an appointment with your people just to have a nooner with you."

Laughing, she pushed at him. "Shut up."

He slipped an arm around her and nibbled on her ear. "Is Jenny going to mind that you're bringing home a guest?"

"Not at all. She's one of your biggest fans. And besides, it's only for a day or two until we can move into my place."

"True. We'll have to keep it down, though. We wouldn't want Jenny to find out you're a screamer."

She rolled her eyes. "We're out of business for a few days, don't forget."

"What do you mean?"

"Hello? The monthly event?"

"You think that's going to get in our way?"

She shot him a wary glance.

"Think again, baby."

They tiptoed into Jenny and Will's house after midnight, leaving everything but the essentials downstairs to minimize the noise, but Olivia was hit with the giggles as they crept up the stairs.

Cole clamped a hand over her mouth and followed her into the guest room. He shut the door behind him. "All the way over here in the cab you're lecturing me about being quiet, and then you're the one making a racket."

"I couldn't help it," she snickered. "I felt like a teenager sneaking my boyfriend into my bedroom while my parents are sleeping."

He hooked an arm around her neck. "Your *horny* boyfriend."

"I thought you were sick." She took a step back from him. "The champagne and all that?"

"I'm fully recovered."

"Cole, wait."

He dropped hot, passionate kisses on her neck. "Get naked, will you?"

"I am *not* having sex with you when I have my period. Forget it."

"I won't forget it, and you *are* having sex with me. Right now." He started pulling at clothes until he found soft skin. "Mmm, that's what I've been dreaming about sitting next to you for hours breathing in that Olivia scent that drives me wild."

Even though her heart beat fast with desire, she tried to wriggle free. "I don't want to," she said, which sounded lame, even to her. Apparently, it did to him, too, because when he ran his thumbs over her nipples they hardened, and she couldn't stop a shudder from rippling through her.

"Liar."

She looked up to find his eyes dark with amusement

and longing and determination. No way could she do this. Could she? With her hands on his chest, she tried once more to disengage, but he was having none of it. "I really don't want to."

"Hey." He waited for her to look up at him. "Do you trust me?"

"You know I do. Don't ask me that."

"Then get naked. I promise you'll like it."

Because she also saw love mixed in with the desire and determination in his eyes, she reached for the hem of her sweater and pulled it over her head. She swallowed hard, unbuttoned her jeans, and slid them off. He never took his eyes off her as she reached behind her to unfasten her bra.

"This isn't fair," she said when she faced him wearing only panties. "You haven't even taken off your coat."

He shrugged off his leather jacket and let it fall to the floor. "Happy now?"

"No." She crossed her arms over her breasts. "More."

With a rakish grin, he unbuttoned his shirt and then his jeans. When he was down to just his boxers, he reached for her, sighing as she wrapped her arms around him. "Now that's what I'm talking about."

Breathing in his warm, masculine scent, Olivia couldn't help but smile at the relief in his voice. In a thick, Cockney accent, she said, "Am I permitted a quick trip to the loo, my lord?"

Cole cracked up. "Only if you hurry up. Your lord's boner requires your immediate attention."

"Then I shan't make him wait." Olivia surprised him when she stroked him through his underwear.

He gasped.

She kissed his cheek. "Be right back."

As he fell on the bed with a loud groan, Olivia suppressed a giggle and scooted into the adjoining bathroom. She returned a few minutes later to find he had turned down the bed and waited for her under the covers.

When she hesitated, he held out a hand to her. "You're trusting me, remember?"

Olivia took his hand, got into bed, and snuggled up to him. "Not quite the bed we had at the Fairmont, is it?"

"We don't need a big bed. We only use a fraction of it."

"That's true." Olivia's stomach tightened with nerves while she waited to see what he had planned for her.

"Relax," he said softly as his hand coasted from her belly to her breasts and back again.

"I can't. You've got me wound so tight I might spontaneously combust."

"That's the goal."

Olivia couldn't help but laugh. "You're out of your mind. You do know that, don't you?"

"So I've been told." He shifted so he was above her and brushed his lips over hers in a caress so light she wouldn't have been sure he had kissed her if she hadn't been watching him so intently. "Kiss me."

She lifted her hands to his face and brought him down for a kiss that sapped the energy from her limbs and sent heat straight to where she lived.

His tongue explored her mouth as his hand cupped her breast.

Olivia arched her back, seeking him.

He tore his lips free and turned his attention to her breast.

She discovered the sensations were even more intense, more acute than usual, perhaps because of her cycle. Clutching handfuls of his hair, she kept her eyes closed against the dizzying array of feelings and needs. She still couldn't believe she had let him talk her into this. But what she really couldn't believe was the climax she felt building as he swirled his tongue around her hypersensitive nipple.

"Is this okay?" he asked, looking at her with dark blue eyes.

"Mmm."

He flashed a cocky smile, but she expected nothing less from him. Through her panties, he pressed his erection into the V of her legs and returned his attention to her breast. Pushing hard against her and then letting up, he simulated intercourse with his hips and the motion of his tongue against her nipple.

Breathless, Olivia moved with him, higher, *higher*, and then she soared.

He brought his mouth down on hers to muffle the cry that erupted from deep inside her and stayed with her until the crisis had passed. Burying his face in her hair, he whispered, "Now *that's* what I was talking about."

Her laugh was weak and her breathing labored. "I don't know how you did it."

"A magician never reveals his secrets."

"You must be a magician. I can't imagine anyone else could make me feel the way you do."

His smile lost some of its cockiness as he looked down at her.

She traced a finger over his lips. "What?"

"Are you going to wonder?"

"About?"

"What it would be like with other guys?"

"Cole," she sighed, bringing his head down to rest on her chest. "Why in the world would I wonder when I have you?"

He shrugged. "It's only natural that you'd be curious."

"I'm not the slightest bit curious. In fact, I know now why I waited so long."

"You do?"

"I was waiting for you, and I don't have an ounce of curiosity about how it would be with someone else. I never will."

"That's good, because I've loved you from the instant I saw you leaning over me that day in the airport, and the thought of you with someone else—"

She silenced him with a kiss. "Not going to happen." Another kiss. "You've really loved me that long?"

He nodded. "What about you? How soon did you know?"

"When I put my hands on your face and felt the jolt. Instantaneous."

"Like being hit by lightning."

"Just like."

"This is special. What we have." He looked down at her with eyes so blue she could easily get lost in them. "You know that, don't you?"

"Yes."

"Are you still worried about how it's going to end?"

"Not like I was."

"I won't be happy until you say not at all."

She nudged him onto his back and leaned over him. "I'm getting there."

"What's this?" he asked as she left a trail of kisses from his chest to his belly.

"This, my lord, is what's known as your turn."

Chapter 25

WITH THE HELP OF COLE, HER FATHER, JENNY, AND Will, Olivia moved out of her parents' house and into her own apartment later that week. Her father had given her a sofa, end tables, and the dining-room table and chairs from the house. She also brought her bedroom set and TV. The apartment was perfect for one person—a large combination kitchen–dining room–living room, a newly remodeled bathroom, and a nice-sized bedroom.

Olivia quickly put her unique stamp on the small apartment. Under her direction, Cole painted the living room a dark taupe and the bedroom a pale pink. He hung her favorite city posters in the bedroom and several of her watercolors in the living room. On the mantel, she propped a framed copy of her favorite sketch of Cole and surrounded it with the fleet of tiny cable cars she'd bought in San Francisco.

The best part, though, was the wide patio off the living room. Olivia planned to do a lot of painting out there when the weather permitted. In the meantime, she set up her easel in front of the big window in the living room.

"You'll have good light there in the afternoons," Cole said.

"Uh-huh."

He slipped an arm around her and kissed the top of her head. "Cheer up, will you? You've got this great place all to yourself. It's another dream come true. You said so yourself."

"I know, but I wish you didn't have to go." They had spent a week together, and now that it was over, Olivia was anticipating the crash from the high she'd been on for days.

"I'll be back in just over a week." His brows furrowed into a comically stern expression. "By then I expect you to be completely unpacked."

"I appreciate all your help. I know this isn't what you wanted—"

He placed a finger over her lips. "I want whatever you want. If you need to do this for a while, that's fine. I'm not going anywhere."

"Well, you're going back to Chicago," she said with a pout. "Any minute now."

"That's not what I mean, and you know it. Whenever you're ready to take things to the next level, you know where I am."

"Thank you for understanding. I need this for me, you know? I lived at home for far too long, and I know I'd regret it if I never had my own place."

"I get it, honey. Don't worry."

She smiled up at him. "That doesn't mean I'm not willing to share." Withdrawing a key from her pocket, she pressed it into his hand. "So you can come and go as you please."

"For midnight booty calls between flights?" he asked with a devilish grin, clearly pleased by her gesture.

"I'll take whatever you're dishing out."

"Thank you," he said, leaning in to kiss her. He held her close for a long, quiet moment. "Have you decided what you're going to do about work and school?"

She took a deep breath and expelled it. "I'm going to take another big leap and drop to part time at work so I can take three classes next semester. If I can keep that up, I should be able to graduate in a year—if I go all summer, too."

"You should be fine, especially if Paolo's predictions come to pass. After your show, you might be able to quit your job altogether and go to school full time."

She shook her head. "I can't bank on that."

"I think you can. Victor and Paolo think you can. Your dad thinks you can. Need I go on?"

"I don't need you and my dad ganging up on me."

"Why not? Jer and I know what's best for you."

"You might want to tell your new best friend that I can take care of myself, thank you very much."

His smile was all charm when he said, "But why would you want to when you've got us?"

She wrapped her arms around his neck and kissed him senseless. "Do we have time for a quickie before you have to go?"

His groan rumbled through both of them. "I hate to say it, but we need to head out if you're going to insist we take the Metro rather than a cab."

"Cabs are too expensive."

"Spoken by the woman who made twenty-eight grand this week."

"And you probably spent half that much at the Fairmont."

"Not even close," he scoffed.

"Metro."

"If we take a cab, we have time for a quickie."

"Really?"

"Ah, ha! I see your frugality only goes so far."

She flashed a saucy grin. "I do have my priorities."

His eyes went dark, and his jaw clenched with tension. "Stop it. We don't have time."

Sliding her hands over his chest and up to his shoulders, she planted kisses on his neck. "We could be so quick." She nibbled on his bottom lip. He was tempted. She could see that. But then he snapped out of it to remind her they really didn't have time. Sighing, she released him and followed him into the bedroom.

"So if you're only working part time," he said as he zipped his bag, "no more coffee dates in the airport, huh?"

"Why do you say that?"

"You won't be there as much."

"I'll be there if you're there. In fact, I'll make sure Wednesday afternoons are free when I do my schedule for next semester."

"Good answer. I'm off next week. Should I plan to hang out here?"

"Absolutely! What about Flights for Life?"

He slipped on his coat. "I'm going to tell them my schedule has changed, and I'll have to go week to week on my availability. They appreciate whatever I'm able to do, and a lot of other pilots volunteer." He zipped his coat. "Ready to go?"

"No."

Cole got her coat and held it for her. "I'll be back before you have time to miss me."

"No, you won't."

He put his arms around her. "Why don't you just stay here, hon? There's no need for you to go to the airport."

"It's another half hour together."

"You don't have to."

She pasted on a smile. "I want to. Let's go."

They were quiet on the brief Metro ride to the airport, each absorbed in their own thoughts. Because she wasn't working, she couldn't accompany him to the gate.

"So hopefully I'll see you Wednesday around four," he said as they approached the security line.

"I won't get my hopes up."

"Think positive. Capital has the best on-time record of any airline in the business."

She rolled her eyes. "Save the commercial."

Smiling, he reached for her. "I'll miss you."

"Thank you," she whispered. "For the trip, for painting, and helping me move. Everything."

"It was fun—every minute of it. Think about where you want to go next. Maybe New York?"

"You must have a limit on the number of flights you can dole out."

"Unlimited for me, twelve a year for friends and family."

"You should give them to your family."

"My dad has no interest in traveling. I sent my brother's family to Disney last year and my sister's the year before. So this year's flights are all yours." He checked his watch. "I hate to say it."

She hugged him. "Call me when you get home?"

"I will."

"Is it just me, or does this get harder every time?"

"It's not just you." With his hands on her face, he kissed her softly. "See you next time?"

"I'll be right here."

"Counting on it." He kissed her once more. "Love you."

"Love you, too."

She pulled on his hand and went up on tiptoes for one last kiss, and then, with great reluctance, she let him go.

Over the next month, they fell into a routine of Wednesday coffee dates on the weeks he was working followed by Friday night reunions that lasted well into the next week.

On one of his brief overnight stays in Washington, Cole let himself into the apartment, slid into bed, and made passionate love to her. He was asleep thirty minutes after he arrived and was gone when she woke up the next morning. Since he spent so much time at her place, Olivia bought him a lamp and an alarm clock for his side of the bed. The situation wasn't ideal, but they spent more time together than some couples who lived in the same city. For now, they were making it work.

Her parents' house sold in early December. Olivia and her brothers helped their father move into the modest townhouse he was renting until he got back on his feet. Her mother had consented to a second month in rehab, and Jerry reported that Mary seemed to be making some progress.

Olivia hadn't been able to bring herself to visit her mother. Cole had offered to go with her the next time he was in town, and she'd agreed to think about it. Things were going so well in her own life just then that she hated the idea of letting her mother's drama detract from her happiness.

Three days before Christmas, Olivia took the final exam in her international business class and bid adieu to her friends and professors in the business school. She skipped down the stairs of the Kogod Building, wishing she could scream at the top of her lungs that she was now officially an art major!

Since she couldn't very well do that, she called Cole to share the news.

"How'd it go?" he asked.

"Who cares? It's over!"

"You care, or you wouldn't have studied like crazy."

"How are you feeling?" A bad cold had grounded him for a week, and he had been miserable and grumpy every time she talked to him.

"Terrible."

"Poor baby. I'll be there soon to take care of you. Three more days."

"That's too long."

Olivia smiled at his petulant tone. Whoever coined the adage that men made lousy patients had never met a sick pilot. "Good thing you had next week off anyway so you can recover."

"Yeah, I guess. Flights for Life called today to ask if I'd take a flight on Tuesday."

"Will you be able to fly by then?"

"God, I hope so. How do you feel about Houston?"

"Hard to say since I've never been there."

"It would be an overnight since they're admitting the child for a night. Want to go with me? Be my co-pilot?"

"So, like, you would fly us to Houston?"

A cough cut off his laughter. "That's the idea. But if you're not up for it, I'll tell them I can't do it."

"You've missed so many weeks already because of me. I don't want you to miss another."

"Is that a yes?"

"Sure," she said with more confidence than she felt. "Why not?"

He laughed at her reluctance. "You might get a reprieve if this goddamned cold doesn't clear up in time."

"Are you still going home for Christmas?"

"Yeah, my dad would be heartbroken if I didn't go."

"We'll have our own celebration when I get there."

"You bet we will. Hurry up, will you? I need you to rub Vicks on my chest and make me chicken soup."

She snorted. "I'm an artist, not a nurse."

"Well, listen to you."

"What? I was only kidding. I can't wait to take care of you."

"I meant listen to you calling yourself an artist. That wouldn't have happened a couple of months ago."

"You're right," she said, surprised by the revelation and the notion that she now considered herself first and foremost an artist.

"Have you talked to Paolo?"

"Briefly this morning. The show's set for March 18."

"I'll put in for some time off so I can be there."

"That'd be great. Everyone here is talking about going out for it."

"I should hope so. It's a huge deal."

"My stomach hurts just thinking about it."

"It'll be awesome. Don't worry." He was hit with a fit of sneezing.

"Bless you," she said with a wince. "I should let you get some rest."

"I'll call you later."

"Don't worry about it. Focus on getting better."

"I hope you don't catch it from me."

"Just to be safe, I won't kiss you."

"The hell you won't."

Olivia laughed at both his gravelly voice and fierce tone. "Talk to you tomorrow."

He sneezed again and said, "Sleep tight."

———⁓———

On Christmas night, after his brother and sister and their families had left, Cole sat in his mother's recliner in the family room and closed his eyes, hoping to calm the pounding in his head.

"You look like hell, son," his father said as he came into the room with a cup of steaming tea. With a sheepish grin, he added, "I thought this might help."

Touched, Cole accepted the lemon tea his mother had always made for them when they were sick. "Thank you."

"Mother always said lemon tea could cure any ill."

"Yeah," Cole said, his throat tightening with emotion as it had many times throughout the long day at home. He'd noticed his father's attempts to replicate his mother's holiday decorating style. The tree was right where it always was, to the left of the fireplace, her acorn wreath hung on the front door, and battery-powered candles lit every window. Cole appreciated the effort his father had made to make the holiday seem normal, and he knew his siblings did, too. Nothing about it, however, was normal, and they were all painfully aware of that.

Cole put down the tea and got up. "I'll be right back." He went into his old bedroom and returned a minute later with a wrapped gift that he handed to his father.

"*Another one?* Are you made of money these days?"

Cole smiled. "I got this one for free."

"Is that so?" Joe tore the paper off the gift. "Oh. Oh, wow. Well, will you look at that?" Uncovering the framed drawing Olivia had done of his son, his eyes went glassy with tears.

"What do you think?"

Joe brushed imaginary dust off the glass. "The person who did this certainly knows you."

"She didn't know me all that well at the time."

"Yet she captured you. Right down to that arrogant little grin."

Cole laughed. "I knew you'd love that."

"This is wonderful." Joe couldn't stop staring at it. "She has a real gift."

"That's what I keep telling her."

Setting the picture on the table next to his chair, Joe turned to Cole. "Who is she?"

"Olivia." Just saying her name sent a rush of longing through him. How he wished they could have spent the holiday together. Maybe next year.

"And this Olivia is someone important?"

"Very."

Joe's face lit up with delight. "You don't say. Well, it's about damned time!"

Cole laughed, which made him cough. "I had a feeling you'd say that."

"When do I get to meet this very important Olivia?"

"She's flying out tomorrow. I thought maybe I'd bring her home next weekend if that's okay with you."

Joe reached over to rest his hand on top of his son's. "That's more than okay."

———

Olivia arrived in Chicago the following afternoon. "Oh," she sighed when she saw him leaning against a wall outside security. "You look awful."

"Nice to see you, too, babe." He scooped her into a big hug and kissed her cheek.

"You're burning up! You should've stayed home. I could've taken a cab."

"Since you don't take cabs and there's no train to my house, I figured I'd better pick you up." He took her bag and led her to the escalator. "How was the flight?"

"Kind of scary."

"Why? Was it bumpy?"

"Not really."

"Then why were you scared?"

"I didn't have my own personal pilot with me to explain every weird noise."

Smiling, he put his arm around her. "There's nothing to be scared of." He was so congested he didn't even sound like himself. "I've told you that."

"Sure, if you're *you*, there's nothing to be scared of."

His laugh was interrupted by a deep, hacking cough. "God, I'm a walking germ factory. You should stay as far away from me as you can get."

"No way."

"Good answer," he said, leading her to the parking garage. "I'm so bummed. I had all kinds of things I wanted to do when you were here, but I don't feel like doing shit."

"That's all right. I'll be perfectly happy to curl up with you on the sofa and watch movie after movie until you feel better."

"Sounds good to me." He dug his keys out of his coat pocket.

Olivia's eyes widened when she saw the taillights flash on a shiny black Mustang GT. "No way."

"Yes, way."

She ran a hand over the tailfin. "*Oh!* It's *gorgeous*."

"I love it," he confessed as he stashed her bag in the trunk. "I've always wanted one, and I finally took the plunge last summer."

"I should've figured you for a muscle car," she teased. "Your need for speed and all that. Do you want me to drive? Since you're not feeling good?"

He held the passenger door for her. "Ah, no. That's okay."

Crossing her arms, she studied him. "You don't trust me with your baby, do you?"

"I never said that. It's just that no one else has ever, well…"

Olivia laughed. "You've never let anyone else drive it, have you?"

"No," he said sheepishly.

"Hmm." She held out her hand. "Prove your love?"

"Liv."

"You're sick. I'm here to take care of you. The least you can do after I've come *all* this way is let me drive you home."

"I don't know about this."

"Keys, please."

"When was the last time you even drove?"

She had to think about that. "The weekend you rented the Toyota in D.C."

"Then you're out of practice."

"And you're high on cold medicine. Which is worse?"

When he had no answer for that, she played her trump card. "I thought you trusted me."

"I do, but not with—"

"Your car?" She took the keys from him and walked around to the driver's side.

"*Liv.*"

God, he was a whiner when he was sick!

"Come on," he pleaded.

"Are you just gonna stand there, or are you coming with me?"

"Since you have no clue where you're going, I guess I'm coming with you."

With a victorious smile, Olivia got into the driver's seat and got busy rearranging all the mirrors. She heard him groan under his breath.

"Go easy with the clutch. It's temperamental."

"Don't worry, honey. I've been driving a stick since I was fifteen. My dad's into cars, remember?" She fired up the car and sat back for a minute to listen to the roar of the powerful engine. "Wow. Tell me we get some interstate action on the way home."

This time when he groaned, he made no effort to hide it.

"Oh, goodie!" She shifted into reverse and left some rubber on her way out of the parking space.

"If I was sick before," he muttered as they pulled up to the tollbooth, "I'm dead now."

"Shut up and pay the man."

—⁓—

By the time they reached his complex, twenty-six minutes later, Cole was even paler than he'd been before.

"That was *so* awesome," Olivia sighed as she cut the engine and returned his keys.

"Yeah," he said, dripping with sarcasm. "Awesome. I hope you enjoyed taking advantage of a sick person because you won't get away with that twice."

"It was *so* worth it. I've never driven such a cool car."

He softened somewhat at that. "You do have a way with a stick."

She flashed him a huge grin and followed him up the stairs to his townhouse. "Are we still talking about the car?"

He laughed so hard he ended up coughing. "*Don't make me laugh.*"

"I'll try not to," she said, forcing a solemn expression. She was so damned glad to see him she didn't even care that he was a walking germ factory. "Oh, this is beautiful!" Walking ahead of him into the living room, she took in the dark leather furniture, glass tables, and flat-screen TV. Everything about the place was masculine, but there were feminine touches, too, like the silk flowers on the dining-room table and the window treatments. "Did you do this?"

"With a little help from my mother and sister. But most of it was me. You like?"

"I love."

"So you could—maybe *someday*—see yourself living here?"

"Tell me the truth—did you have the place profession-ally decorated so I'd want to move here immediately?"

"No," he said with a grin, "but that would've been a good strategy." He wrapped his arms around her. "I missed you so much."

"Me, too."

He kissed her neck, her jaw, and her cheek, and nibbled on her earlobe, but he was careful to avoid her mouth. "I want to take you straight upstairs to bed, but I don't think I've got it in me tonight. Will you be disappointed if we just chill?"

"Of course not." She helped him out of his coat and led him to the sofa. "I'll make us something to eat while you take a nap."

"You don't know where anything is."

"I'll figure it out." Brushing her hand over his eyes, she urged him to close them. "Sleep."

He kept his eyes closed. "I don't want to sleep when you're here. I want to be with you."

"We have a whole week. I'm not going anywhere."

"Pinky swear?"

She kissed him lightly on the lips and wrapped her finger around his. "Pinky swear."

Chapter 26

OLIVIA TOLD HERSELF IT DIDN'T COUNT AS SNOOPING. After all, he knew she was there and had to figure she'd be curious, right? She decided her whole apartment would fit in his dining room and kitchen, which had stainless steel appliances, brown granite countertops, and dark wood cabinets. Running a hand over the smooth granite, she paused to look at the photos on the refrigerator.

The Langston family Christmas card from three years earlier had been signed "with love from Joe, Irene, and Family." In the picture, Cole held a blond child in each arm. From the other four young adults, she found the two she figured for his brother, Josh, and sister, Amanda. She looked forward to meeting them next weekend.

Olivia took a moment to study his mother, a robust, smiling woman who seemed full of life. In her eyes, Olivia saw a hint of the mischief she loved so much in Cole. She decided he favored his mother.

In another photo of him with his parents, Cole wore a flight suit and a tan Navy uniform hat with a gold pin on the side. The rest of the space on the refrigerator was dominated by school photos of his three nieces and two nephews, and candid shots of Cole with the kids, who clearly adored their uncle.

When she went back into the living room she found him out cold. *Poor guy*, she thought as she played with his hair. He was always so full of energy that it

was strange to see him flattened like this. Figuring he
would be asleep for a while, she took her bag upstairs
where there were three bedrooms and a bathroom off
the hallway.

In the first bedroom, she found a home gym and a sofa
that probably doubled as a guest bed. The second room
housed a meticulous computer workstation. On the walls
were photos, plaques, and mementos from his ten years in
the Navy. She stopped for a closer look at a photo of him
sitting in the cockpit of a fighter jet that had "Lt. Cmdr.
Cole 'Jackpot' Langston" scrolled in cursive on the body.
She'd have to ask him how he got that nickname!

Sitting on the desk, she noticed what looked like a
scrapbook and decided to take a quick look. Inside the
front cover she found a brief inscription: "To Cole, who
was a hero to us long before the rest of the world caught
on. Love, Dad."

Moved by his father's sweet words, Olivia flipped
through the pages of coverage that had followed Cole's
heroic act the previous January. He'd been on the covers
of *People*, *US*, *Time*, and *Vanity Fair*. Articles, including several about his brief but dramatic relationship with
passenger Chelsea Harper, had been clipped from major
newspapers across the country.

The final item was a photo of Cole with his arm
around the captain he'd saved, the two of them sporting
huge grins. The captain had autographed the photo, "To
my new best friend Cole Langston. I owe you everything. Bob Greenman."

"Wow," Olivia said as she took a second slower trip
through the scrapbook. She'd managed to compartmen-
talize his national hero status, but seeing it all spelled

out in black and white was a daunting reminder of just how famous he'd become. After the second look, she closed the book and continued on to the next room.

Throughout the house, she noticed framed artwork and other souvenirs he had brought back from his travels. She wanted to know the story behind each one of them.

His bedroom was done in shades of tan with red accents. The dark cherry headboard on his king-sized bed was so pretty that Olivia couldn't resist touching it to see if it was as smooth as it looked. It was.

She couldn't imagine owning a home as lovely as this. She had expected it to be nice, but she hadn't predicted such a finely tuned sense of style. In hindsight, she should've known he had it in him by the way he could make jeans and a sweater look like a *GQ* ad. She left her bag in his room and checked out the large master bathroom.

Another flight of stairs from the hallway led to the third floor, which was used for storage. Boxes of all shapes and sizes were stashed in the open loft.

Her curiosity satisfied—for now—Olivia went downstairs to poke around in the kitchen and discovered he'd been to the store in anticipation of her arrival. She threw together a salad and boiled some pasta. Since she had to search for everything she needed, it took nearly an hour to make the simple meal.

As she was setting the table, his cell phone, which was plugged into the charger on the counter, rang. Olivia stared at it as she debated whether or not she should answer it. Finally, she reached for it.

"Hello?" Silence. "*Hello?*" Oddly, she felt like someone was there—someone who was choosing not to speak. A weird prickling sensation danced down her spine as she ended the call and looked at the caller ID. The number was unavailable. She shook off the strange feeling and lifted the lid on the pot to see if the pasta was done.

When it was ready, she went to check on Cole. Squatting down next to him, she caressed his face and pressed her lips to his warm forehead.

He awoke with a start. "Hey," he said, rubbing a hand over his face. "What time is it?"

"Almost seven."

Wincing, he tried to shake off the stupor. "Sorry."

"Don't be. Feel any better?"

"A little." He reached up to twirl a lock of her hair around his finger. "I'm having déjà vu."

She smiled. "I still feel the jolt."

"Me, too."

Unable to resist for another minute, she leaned in and kissed him.

"Liv, honey, wait. I don't want you to get sick."

"I'm willing to take my chances." She flicked at his lips with her tongue. "Besides, you're probably not contagious anymore."

He buried his fingers in her hair and brought her down for an easy, gentle kiss.

But after not seeing him for nearly two weeks, she wasn't interested in easy or gentle so she sent her tongue to find his.

He pulled away. "I can't do this to you. It's misery."

With a smile, she got up and stretched out on top of him. "I remember saying that same thing once, and I seem to recall a certain lord of the manor *insisting* I could."

He wrapped his arms around her. "This is different. You could get sick."

"I just want one decent kiss, and then I'll feed you and nurse you."

His eyebrow lifted into a rakish expression. "Nurse me how?"

"If you don't kiss me, you won't find out."

"Oh, all right. If I *have* to, but don't tell me I didn't warn you."

"The sacrifices you make for me."

Laughing, he cupped the back of her head and gave her what she wanted.

—⁓—

After dinner, they exchanged Christmas gifts. Olivia had found an elaborate book on biplanes that she thought he would like and a sweater she hoped would fit him. And there was one more she couldn't wait to give him.

He opened the first two gifts with childlike glee. The book was a huge hit, and when he would have dived right into it, she had to remind him there were others. He opened the sweater and put it on over his T-shirt.

"Oh, good," she said, pleased to see the color complemented his eyes just as she had hoped it would. "It fits."

"Perfectly. I love it. Thank you."

"There's one more."

Picking up on her excitement about the gift, he shook it, listening intently to see if there were any clues.

"Just open it, will you?"

With a smile, he tore the paper off and went still. "Oh, wow." The framed sketch showed the two of them together over a backdrop of all the highlights of their San Francisco trip. "This is just *amazing*. You've got everything in there—the bridge, the cable cars, the Top of the Mark, the Fairmont, Victor and Paolo, Sausalito. Unbelievable."

He studied it for the longest time and then reached for her. "Second to you yourself, this is the best gift I've ever gotten. Thank you."

"I'm glad you like it."

"I *love* it. Just when I think I've seen the full scope of your talent, you go and top yourself." Getting up from the floor, he removed the map of Egypt that had hung over his mantel and replaced it with her sketch. "What do you think?"

"It looks like it belongs there."

"Yes, it does, and I'm glad to see you signed it, too."

"My manager is a pain in the ass about that. He insists I sign all my work."

"A wise man." He picked up two small packages from the coffee table. "Your turn. This one first."

Olivia teased him by shaking it the way he had done to hers. Then she tore off the red foil paper. "Oh! An iPod! I've wanted one forever!"

"I thought you could use it on all those long flights you'll be taking to your gallery in San Francisco."

She threw her arms around his neck and kissed his cheek. "Thank you! Of course, I have no idea how to use it."

Amused by her delight, he tweaked her nose. "I put a few songs on there I thought you might like, but I'll show you how to do it." He picked up the other present and handed it to her. "Open this one."

"You've got that look you get when you're up to something."

He raised his hands in innocence. "I'm not up to anything. Just open your present."

Something about this one felt significant. Her hand trembled ever so slightly as she tore the paper off a jeweler's box. She looked up at him. "What's this?"

"Open it."

With a deep breath to calm her racing heart, Olivia flipped open the box. Inside were diamond earrings. *Big* diamond earrings. She gasped. "*Cole!*"

"Do you like them?"

"They're spectacular, but this is too much. I got you a sweater."

"Olivia," he said softly, "I want you to have them." He took the box from her and removed the earrings. "I'd put them on for you, but I wouldn't have a clue how to do it." Reaching for her hand, he dropped them into her palm. "You do it."

With unsteady hands, Olivia removed her earrings to replace them with the new ones.

Cole tipped his head. "Let me see."

She gathered her hair into a ponytail and held it back.

"Gorgeous," he said, looking satisfied. "Will you wear them to your show? For luck?"

"I'll never take them off."

His face lifted into the sexy half smile that melted her bones.

"Thank you."

"You're welcome. Thank *you* for my gifts."

They sat there, drinking each other in, for a long, breathless moment before he moved toward her. The next thing she knew, she was under him, and he seemed to have forgotten that he was worried about getting her sick. As he devoured her, a wild surge of desire left her lightheaded. The kiss went on for what felt like forever, and she wrapped her legs around him to bring him tight against her.

"Let's go to bed," he finally said.

"I thought you didn't have it in you tonight," she teased.

He pressed his erection against her as he dropped kisses on her face and neck. "A little sleep, a little food, a little you, and I'm a new man."

He might have been a new man, but his eyes were still bright with fever. "We don't have to. You're not feeling well."

"I feel much better just having you here. And," he said, leaving more hot kisses on her neck, "I want to see you wearing nothing but those earrings."

"Cole?"

He was busy tasting her neck. "Hmm?"

"While you were sleeping, your phone rang. I didn't know if I should answer it, but when I did no one was there. Or I should say, someone was there but they didn't say anything."

He went still and lifted his head to look at her. "How do you know someone was there?"

She couldn't miss the stricken expression on his face. "Just a feeling I got," she said as a weird knot of fear twisted in her belly. "I'm sorry. I probably shouldn't have answered it."

"Of course you can answer it. I don't care."

"The number was unavailable," she added. "Do you know who it was?"

"No."

There was something about the quick, decisive way he said the single word—or maybe it was because his eyes changed as he said it—but Olivia had no doubt that he was lying. He knew exactly who had called.

Tucking her hair behind her ears, Olivia stood in front of the mirror in his bathroom and took another long look at the sparkling earrings. *God, they're gorgeous*. She tried to imagine him in a jewelry store picking out such an extravagant gift for her. They must have cost a fortune! How she wished their lovely evening hadn't been spoiled by a phone call and a lie.

She ran a brush through her hair. *Why would he lie to me? I wonder if it's that ex-girlfriend he mentioned, the one who won't leave him alone. If that's the case, why doesn't he just say so? Maybe I should ask him about her and let him know he can talk to me about it. No. If he wanted me to know, he would've told me. But I can't stand that he lied to me! I know he was lying.*

"Liv! What're you doing in there? I miss you."

"Coming."

The reflection darting off one of the earrings caught her attention. *He loves me. I know he does. I need to have faith that he'll tell me what's going on when he's ready to. In the meantime, I have to try to be patient.*

She opened the bathroom door to find him already in bed waiting for her.

"Everything all right?" he asked, holding out a hand to her.

"Yeah." She took his hand and slid into bed.

He tipped his head to study her. "Are you sure?"

Nodding, she rested her head on his chest. "You sound a little better."

"Drugs. It's a bitch when they wear off."

As her hand explored his chest and belly, she decided she had no patience where this was concerned. She needed to know. "Cole?"

"Hmm?"

She tried to work up the courage to ask the question. "What is it, honey?"

"If there was something going on in your life, something upsetting or difficult or just annoying, you would tell me, wouldn't you?"

His breathing slowed. "Why do you ask?"

"Because I get this feeling there's something you're not telling me—something big."

He sighed and ran a hand through his hair. "I had an issue," he said after a long pause, during which Olivia had no idea what he was going to say. "I've worked it out, and it's not something I want to spend two seconds of my precious time with you talking about."

Olivia considered that for a minute. "Is it possible this person you had the 'issue' with was the one who called earlier?"

"I hope not, but yes, I suppose it's possible." He turned on his side so he could see her. "Honey, please believe me when I tell you it has nothing to do with you or us."

"I don't want you treating me like I'm fragile and can't handle things. I've talked to you about my mother, my family, everything. You've helped me so much, and I'd like to do the same for you. I want you to feel like you can talk to me about anything."

"I do."

"But not this?"

He wanted to. She could see that.

"Not now, okay? Soon, though. I promise."

"Pinky swear?"

With a smile, he linked his finger with hers. "You got it."

Satisfied that he intended to tell her eventually, she decided to let go of the worries and enjoy being back in his arms.

"Hey." He nudged at her cheek with his nose. "Are we okay?"

"Yeah," she said, lacing her fingers through his.

"I hope so because I love you so damned much, Liv. I couldn't wait to see you today."

"I couldn't wait to see you, either. I hate being away from you."

He shifted so he was on top of her. "Any time you're ready for a change of scenery…"

Smiling, she reached up with both hands to caress his smooth face. "You don't give up, do you?"

"Not until you're sleeping here with me every night." Pushing her nightgown up to her waist, his eyes went dark with lust when he discovered she wore nothing underneath. He brought his lips down on hers for a kiss that reminded her of the many ways she loved him. And when he sank his fingers into her, he reminded her of the many ways she wanted him.

Gasping, she let her legs fall open in complete surrender to him.

"Liv, honey." His face was tight with tension. "I want you so much."

She curled her hand around his straining erection and guided him home to her.

"Wait," he said, his voice hoarse from the cold and the emotion. "No condom?"

"We're going for it, remember?"

"You're sure?"

If he'd asked her that question thirty minutes ago, she would've said no, she wasn't sure. But she had decided to trust him, to trust in the feelings they had shared from the first moment they'd laid eyes on each other. This was the real thing. Of that she had no doubt. "I'm sure."

He slid into her and sighed with completion. "*God,* nothing in the world feels as good as this."

Since he had succeeded in taking her breath away, she couldn't reply with words. Instead, she ran her fingers through his hair while her other hand caressed his back. Everything moved in slow motion, almost as if time had decided to stand still just for them.

His lips were soft against her neck as he whispered words of love that went straight to her heart.

Olivia floated. Surely this was a dream from which she would awaken any second.

As he withdrew from her, her eyes fluttered open to find his dark and fixed on her face, watching her. He went deep again, and she moaned as a climax rippled through her in soft, gentle waves that touched her everywhere. "*Cole.*"

"Tell me, Liv," he whispered. "Tell me."

"I love you. Only you. Always."

He filled her again and lost himself in her. When he had caught his breath, he raised his head off her shoulder and touched his lips to hers.

Their eyes met, filled with the awareness that something significant had occurred. They had made love many times before, but everything had been different this time, and they both knew it.

Chapter 27

ON MONDAY EVENING, COLE INVITED SEVERAL OF HIS closest friends over for pizza so they could meet Olivia.

Cole had warned her about Tucker's effusiveness, but nothing could have prepared her for the bear hug he gave her when Cole introduced them.

"You're a goddess," Tucker declared when he put her back down. "Of course, I knew you had to be some sort of mystical figure to succeed in taking this guy off the market."

Olivia glanced at Cole in time to catch the glare he directed at his friend. "Zip it, Tucker."

"What?" Tucker asked with an innocent smile that made Olivia giggle. "I only speak the truth." He put his arm around Olivia and guided her away from Cole. "Come, my sweet. Tell me all about how you did it. You cast some sort of spell on him, right?"

An hour later, Tucker cornered Cole in the kitchen. "Why did *you* get to meet her first?"

Once again, Cole glowered at his friend. "Hands off."

"She's amazing." Tucker raised his beer bottle in tribute to Cole. "I can totally see how she'd turn a player like you into a one-woman man."

"I'm glad you approve."

"I can't wait to dance at the wedding."

Cole smiled at him. "Neither can I."

Tucker shook his head in amusement. "Who'd a-thunk it, huh?"

"Not me. That's for sure."

Tucker's smile faded into pensiveness.

"What?"

He looked up at Cole with an expression far more serious than Cole had come to expect from him. "Can I ask you something?"

"I suppose," Cole said warily.

"It's about Brenda."

Taken aback, Cole said, "What about her?"

"Since you ended things with her, we've been, you know… talking. On the phone." Tucker's face flushed with color. "Almost every day."

Cole had never seen his happy-go-lucky friend so flustered. "And?"

"She's thinking about coming up. Maybe. For a visit."

"With?"

"Me. Who do you think?"

"Just making sure it wasn't with me," Cole said, only half in jest.

Tucker's mouth hardened. "Not everything is about you."

"I never said it was. I just hope she's not, you know—"

"Using me to get to you?"

Cole wouldn't have put it that way. Exactly.

Tucker released a disgusted snort. "It's not possible for you to believe that she could actually be interested in me, is it?"

"You're putting words in my mouth, Tucker. Why wouldn't she be interested in you? I just don't want to see you get hurt."

"She's not Natasha. That's not how she is."

"Of course, she isn't." Cole regretted his suspicion. His experiences with Natasha had made him paranoid. "I'd love to see you guys together."

Tucker brightened. "Really? You would?"

"Sure I would. The long-distance thing really sucks, though. Trust me on that."

"We've had some conversations about that. Depending on how things go, she might consider moving."

"From Miami to Chicago?" Cole made a distasteful face. "It must be love."

Tucker flushed again. "Could you *try* not to jinx me? Please?"

"I'll do my best," Cole said gravely, suppressing the urge to laugh.

"So you really wouldn't mind if I went out with her?"

Cole glanced into the living room and met Olivia's gaze. She smiled at him, and his heart skipped a beat. "I really wouldn't mind."

Cole had recovered enough from his cold by Tuesday to fly the Flight for Life to Houston. They packed an overnight bag and headed for O'Hare at ten that morning. Olivia had been amused to witness his preflight routine, which consisted of half an hour running on the treadmill, twenty minutes of free weights, and one hundred sit-ups followed by a shower, two scrambled eggs, two pieces of wheat toast, and two cups of coffee consumed exactly ninety minutes before takeoff.

"You do this every day?" she asked on the drive to the airport.

"When I fly in the morning."

"You're not right."

"There're a few other steps to it."

"*More?*"

He looked adorable and embarrassed. "You know, left shoe on first, button left cuff first."

"You're superstitious!"

"I wouldn't say *that*."

"You are! After all your speeches about how safe flying is. You're a fraud."

"I can't help it," he said with a sheepish grin. "Superstition is in my DNA. My mother was ridiculously superstitious."

"What else are you superstitious about?" she asked, intrigued by this new, unexpectedly vulnerable side to him.

"If I tell you, you'll never fly with me."

Olivia turned in her seat to face him. "Now you have to tell me."

"Pinky swear you'll still go with me today?"

She studied him for a long moment before she extended her pinky.

He wrapped his finger around hers and sent her a shy gaze that went straight to her heart. "Things happen in threes."

"Sometimes."

"Most of the time. My mother believed that with every fiber of her being."

"So?"

"So, I keep waiting for the third big thing. The blizzard, the punch in the face. That's two."

Olivia released his hand. "Now you're just freaking me out."

"You pinky swore! You can't back out now."

"I can't believe you'd tell me this minutes before I'm supposed to fly with you."

"Nothing's going to happen."

"I'm just *filled* with confidence."

"Forget I said anything," he said as he retrieved their overnight bag and locked the car. "I don't know what I was thinking, telling you this today."

Olivia shot him a dirty look and followed him into the bowels of the airport. They emerged on a tarmac and walked through a maze of planes to the PiperJet that awaited them. Olivia stopped short at the sight of the plane.

"What?" he asked.

"We're going in *that*?"

"Yeah. Why?"

"It's awfully small."

He laughed as he hooked an arm around her neck and hugged her. "Don't be a wimp. Wait here. I'll be right back, okay?"

"Sure."

Kissing her forehead, he added, "No thinking, you got me?"

"Right." She watched him go, focused on his cute denim-clad butt instead of the small plane she was leaning against—the small plane she was about to get into, the small plane he was going to fly with her in it. *No thinking*, she told herself.

Cole came back a few minutes later with a girl in a wheelchair. She was maybe ten, eleven at the most. With them were her parents and younger brother. Olivia's heart ached at the sight of the sick child, who was clearly delighted to see Cole and talking to him with animated hand gestures as he pushed her to the plane.

"Grace," he said, "this is Olivia. She's going to come along with us today."

"Is she your girlfriend?"

He looked down at the child. "Yeah, she is. Is that okay with you?"

"I guess. You're kind of old for me anyway."

"*Hey!*"

Grace's hollowed-out eyes danced with glee. "Nice to meet you." She extended a hand to Olivia.

"You, too. I love your earrings."

"You've got some pretty nice rocks of your own there. Christmas present?"

Smiling, Olivia said, "Yep."

Grace looked up at Cole. "Not bad."

"Glad you approve." He introduced Olivia to Grace's family and got everyone loaded into the plane. The four passengers sat two abreast, facing each other. Cole stashed Grace's wheelchair in the cargo bay beneath the plane.

From the co-pilot's seat, Olivia watched him walk around the plane checking and poking and kicking various parts. When he had completed his inspection, he went through the same process inside before he fired up the engines, typed something into the keyboard in front of him, donned a headset, and requested permission for takeoff from the air traffic control tower.

While he waited for clearance, he glanced over at her. "Okay?"

She nodded even as her stomach did cartwheels. *Things happen in threes. Stop!*

He picked up another headset and handed it to her. "Want to listen in?"

"I'd love to."

The plane rolled forward as he engaged a dizzying array of switches and dials and buttons while talking to the controllers.

Olivia couldn't follow much of the rapid-fire exchange between Cole and the controllers, but she gathered they had assigned him to a runway.

They taxied for several minutes behind a Capital 737, which took off just ahead of them.

Cole held the mouthpiece to the side, tipped his head, and called to the passengers, "We're cleared for takeoff. Ready?"

"Ready," Grace replied.

Olivia found takeoff to be a whole different experience from the front seat. Lifting into the air, she couldn't take her eyes off Cole as he guided the plane up and out of the busy air space around O'Hare. His handsome face was set with concentration, every movement deliberate and precise. She was full of admiration and respect, not only for the proficiency with which he flew the plane but for what he was doing for Grace and her family.

They were airborne for nearly thirty minutes before she heard his voice again and realized he was talking to her.

"Are you okay?"

"I'm doing great. I love the view from up here." They had found a sunny, clear day above a light layer of clouds. "I forgot to ask how long the flight is."

"Almost three hours."

"Why aren't you doing anything right now? Shouldn't you be driving or something?"

"Autopilot."

"And does this autopilot know what he's doing?"

He snickered. "I sure as hell hope so."

"So you get us off the ground and then turn things over to Mr. Autopilot. I see how this works."

"You were impressed. Admit it."

"For a minute or two, but I'm over it now that I know you don't really do anything."

"Then I'll let you tell Mr. Autopilot how to get us back down."

"Since you two seem to have a pretty good groove, I'll leave that to you."

He laughed and made an adjustment to one of the dials.

"Why did they call you Jackpot in the Navy?"

"How do you know about that?"

"The picture on the wall of your office."

His expression sheepish, he said, "It was because I never missed."

"Missed what?"

"My targets during training—landing, shooting, carrier landings."

"Ever?"

"Not often."

"Is that unusual?"

He shrugged. "I guess so."

"It's unheard of, isn't it?"

"I wouldn't go *that* far."

"I'll bet you never missed with the women, either, Jackpot."

"Whatever." He rolled his eyes. "That had nothing to do with the nickname."

"*Sure*, it didn't." Olivia laughed at his obvious discomfort with the conversation. "Were there a lot of them?"

"What? Targets?"

"Women. Before all the Captain Incredible business?"

He glanced over at her. "A few."

"Are we talking a dozen, two dozen, three?"

"What does it matter?" he asked. "There's only you now."

Olivia nibbled on her thumbnail, wishing she had the nerve to ask her many questions.

"What?"

"How long ago did you break up with the last one?" When he didn't answer, she looked over to find his jaw pulsing with tension.

"Recently."

Alarmed, she gasped. "*How* recent?"

"Look, Liv, I told you—I used to be kind of a dog." He reached for her hand and brought it to his lips. "But I've changed my ways since I met you."

"There hasn't been anyone else since we, you know—"

"No! God, no."

Olivia released a deep breath she hadn't realized she was holding. "What if you get bored being with just one woman after all that variety?"

"Baby, if I get to spend the next sixty years with you, it won't be long enough. I've never felt anything even close to the way I feel when I'm with you."

Delighted and relieved by his declaration, Olivia sat back in her seat.

"Are we okay?" he asked.

She squeezed his hand and then released it to retie her ponytail. "We're great. Thanks for answering my questions."

"Any time."

Olivia glanced over her shoulder at their passengers. "What's wrong with her? With Grace?"

"Leukemia," he sighed. "They thought they had it beat, but she relapsed about six months ago." He lowered his voice. "I haven't seen her in a while, and it was kind of shocking how bad she looks. She's lost all her hair—a second time—in the last month."

Olivia shook her head with dismay. "And yet she's still so upbeat and happy."

"I know. That's why she's one of my favorites. She's getting the best possible care at MD Anderson, so we're hopeful."

"It must be hard for you to be around people with cancer after what happened to your mother."

"It can be. It brings back all the memories of when she was going through treatments we knew were futile. But I hope she'd approve of what I'm doing. It feels good to help people, even if it's hard sometimes."

Olivia reached out to him.

He closed his hand around hers and looked over at her with one of the half smiles she loved so much.

She had worried about what it would be like to fly in a small plane, but as they soared through the sky holding hands, she realized she was in the midst of yet another unforgettable experience with him.

—⁂—

As they drew nearer to Houston, he talked to air traffic control again. After he got a weather report, he turned to Grace and her family. "We might have a few bumps going into Hobby. They've got rain showers in the area. Nothing to worry about, though."

"Okay," Grace's father answered.

"Keep those seatbelts on," Cole added.

Olivia could see the darker clouds in the distance. She clutched her damp hands together in her lap, trying not to think about the number three.

"Hey."

She glanced over at him.

"No biggie. Pinky swear."

Grateful for his attempt at levity, she forced a smile for his benefit, focused on breathing, and left him alone to do his thing. He had told her there were two primary airports in Houston—George Bush Intercontinental and William P. Hobby, which was closest to MD Anderson.

The plane bumped and rolled through the stormy clouds.

Olivia told herself over and over—*Jackpot never misses his targets.* If she hadn't been trying so hard not to embarrass herself in front of him, she would have cried like a baby. It was so dark inside the clouds that it might have been nighttime rather than two in the afternoon. Just when she thought she would go nuts if she had to hold it together for another second, they finally emerged from the clouds.

When she saw the runway through the rain, she wanted to sing a hallelujah. She felt the plane losing altitude and watched in amazement as Cole put it down right on the dotted line. Jackpot. Releasing a long, deep breath, she tried to relax as they taxied in. A car waited for Grace and her family, and Cole helped them off before he came back for Olivia.

He held out a hand to her. "No biggie, right?" he said with that cocky grin.

She took his hand and hoped her legs would hold up under her. "Of course not."

"Were you freaking out? I'd understand if you were. You can admit it."

"Freaking out is for wimps. I had full confidence in you."

He laughed and gently cuffed her jaw. "Whatever you say, tough guy."

They flew back to Chicago alone the next day. Grace's father had called Cole that morning to tell him they'd encountered a few complications and Grace wouldn't be released until later in the week. Cole had offered to come back for them whenever they were ready to go home.

"I'd wait for them," he told Olivia, "but the owner of the plane needs it tomorrow."

"So you'll fly a different one to get them?"

"Probably. I'm sorry this is taking up so much time this week."

"Please don't apologize. It's for a good cause." She paused, not sure if she should ask. "He didn't say what kind of complications?"

"No."

She could tell the news had depressed him, so she tried to get his mind off it. "Houston was great."

"It's a fun city."

"I've stayed in more hotels since I met you than I had in my whole life."

"Tomorrow I'll show you Chicago."

"Or we can stay home and do nothing. You don't have to entertain me. This has been enough of an adventure to last me a while."

"Oh, come on. This is nothing."

She raised an eyebrow. "Are we really going to have that conversation again?"

Chicago was blanketed in snow the next day, and since he was still coughing, Olivia insisted they stay home. With Tucker and most of Cole's other Chicago friends away on a holiday ski trip, they had nothing but peaceful time to themselves.

Cole checked with Grace's father that night and learned her grandfather had joined the family in Houston. Grace was to be released the next morning, so Cole made arrangements to meet them at noon.

"Shit," he grumbled when he hung up. "I can't take you with me this time. The grandfather is coming back to Chicago with us."

"That's no problem. I can hang out here and do some painting. I owe Paolo a few more pieces for the show, so don't worry about me."

"Are you sure? I'll be gone most of the day."

"I'm positive."

He buried his face in her hair and hugged her tight against him. "I don't want to be away from you for a minute, let alone a whole day."

Olivia rested her head on his chest, steeped in the simple magic that came with being in his arms and knowing there was nowhere else in the world she'd rather be.

"We'd better get to bed. You've got to get up early."

"It's only eight o'clock."

"I didn't say we were going to sleep."

"Oh, well, since you put it that way."

She cried out with surprise and laughter when he flipped her over his shoulder and carried her upstairs.

He was gone when she woke up the next morning. She shifted onto his pillow and drank in his scent, wondering how many hours she had to wait until she could be with him again. He had said he'd be back by five at the latest, but there was always a chance of delay.

Thinking about him, she stayed there a long time before she got up, showered, and put on the old T-shirt he had loaned her for painting. After breakfast, she spread newspapers over his dining room table and set up her paints.

A short time later, she heard a key in the front door. Her first thought was that Grace had developed another complication. Otherwise why would he be back so soon? Jumping up from the table, she went into the living room just as a tall, blonde woman rolled a suitcase into the house.

Dressed in a long, black, leather coat tied at her waist, she wore her hair in a fashionable twist and had diamond earrings that rivaled Olivia's in size. Over her shoulder she carried a dry-cleaning bag, and a wad of mail was tucked under her arm.

Dropping her keys on the table inside the door, she looked up and saw Olivia. "Hello," she said with a warm smile. "You must be Olivia, Cole's sister's friend from Washington, right? He mentioned you might be crashing here this week while you're working on a school project."

Olivia stood frozen in place.

"I'm sorry." She spoke with an accent that sounded Texan. "I've totally startled you." Extending a hand to Olivia, she added, "I'm Natasha. Cole's fiancée."

Mute with shock and confusion, Olivia let the other woman reach for her hand and shake it. *This could not be happening. Could it?*

"Where is he anyway? I thought he was off this week."

"Houston," Olivia mumbled.

"Oh, Flights for Life. That's odd. He usually goes on Tuesdays. And he's been so sick. I'm surprised he could fly."

Olivia never took her eyes off the other woman as she hung her coat in the hall closet. She was, without a doubt, the most striking woman Olivia had ever seen, and she was clearly right at home in Cole's townhouse.

"You look like you've just seen a ghost," Natasha said with a delicate laugh. "I'm sorry if I frightened you. He didn't tell you I'd be home today because he didn't know. I've been in Europe for the holidays with my family, but I missed him too much to stay gone through New Year's so I decided to surprise him. Besides, with the wedding in April, we have *so* much to do. I need to grab him when he's home. Trying to get that man to make a decision is like trying to nail down Jell-O."

Feeling like a thousand-pound weight had landed on her chest, Olivia struggled to breathe.

"Cole told me you're an artist." Wearing a plum suit that might have been Chanel, Natasha looked Olivia over from head to toe. "You must've been, um, working."

Feeling like a total frump in her oversized T-shirt and sweats, Olivia wanted to curl up and die from shock and disbelief.

"I'm afraid I don't understand," she finally managed to say. "He doesn't have a fiancée."

Natasha's jaw shifted into an unreadable expression. "We had a little fight a month or so ago." She waved her left hand dismissively. "But we'll get past it. We always do. When you've been together as long as we have, you're bound to have a dust-up every now and then."

Olivia's mouth fell open when she saw the huge engagement ring on Natasha's finger. *Oh, my God, please tell me this is a bad dream. Please.*

"Olivia? Are you all right?" Natasha rushed over and helped her to the sofa. "You look like you're going to be sick."

Since Olivia was trying hard not to be, it didn't take much encouragement on Natasha's part to get her to sit down.

"Oh, honey." Natasha's voice dripped with sympathy as she ran her hand up and down Olivia's back. "Do you have feelings for him? I mean, I can understand why you would. He's so amazing, isn't he?" Natasha sighed. "I hope he hasn't led you to believe... Well, men can be such pigs, can't they? Ever since I moved my stuff in here—those are my boxes on the third floor—he's been acting funny, but I wouldn't have figured him for a last fling. That's so disappointing."

"A last fling," Olivia stammered.

"I'm sure he even paraded you out in front of his friends. They probably acted like they love you, but trust me, they'll turn on you the second something goes wrong. They were only nice to you because they don't want him to marry me. Good thing we don't need their approval."

Everything inside Olivia had gone cold, and suddenly she knew if she didn't leave right away, she was going to be sick all over Natasha's Chanel suit. "Excuse me." She flew up the stairs. In Cole's bedroom, she changed into jeans and a sweater and stuffed the rest of her belongings into her bag. She left the new iPod sitting on his bedside table.

With shaking hands, she called information to get a phone number for a cab, telling herself all the while to stay focused on getting out of there. She could lose it later.

Fifteen minutes later, she heard the honk of the cab's horn outside and went downstairs. Pulling on her coat, she wondered where Cole's *fiancée* had gone. The smell of her French perfume lingered in the air, so she must have been close by. Olivia couldn't have cared less. She had heard more than enough. With one last look at the room where they had spent so many lovely hours together—and where the whole thing had come crashing down on her—she went out the door, down the stairs, and into the waiting cab.

Only when the car had pulled away from his house did she allow herself to collapse into tears.

Chapter 28

OLIVIA'S CELL PHONE STARTED RINGING AT SIX O'CLOCK, which was four o'clock in Chicago.

"You're not going to talk to him?" Jenny asked.

Olivia swiped at the endless stream of tears. "What's there to say?"

"I don't believe any of this. All this time he's had a fiancée? I don't buy it."

"You didn't see her. She came in like she owned the place wearing a big, old diamond on her left hand."

"If she's living there, why would he ask you to live with him?"

"Because he knew I wouldn't do it," Olivia said bitterly. "I've got school and my whole life here." She'd had ample time on the flight back to Washington—on another airline—to dissect every moment they had spent together, every moment of his last fling. "I *knew* something was going on. I never imagined this, but I knew there was *something*."

Her phone rang again.

"If you don't get it, I'm going to," Jenny said.

"Don't."

With a defiant look at Olivia, Jenny reached for the phone and turned on the speaker. "Cole, it's Jenny."

"Jenny?"

"Olivia is with me at my house."

"*What? What the hell?*"

"She met Natasha."

He gasped. "*Oh, my God*. Keep her there. I'm on my way." The connection went dead.

Jenny closed the phone and glanced at Olivia.

"I don't want to see him."

"Something about this stinks to high heaven, if you ask me. You owe him the chance to explain."

"I don't owe him anything!" Olivia broke down again into grief-stricken sobs. "I should've known something like this would happen. Everywhere we go, fabulously beautiful women throw themselves at him or reappear out of his past. How can I ever compete with that? I'm sick of trying!"

Jenny put her arms around her. "Liv, honey, I know this has been an awful day and you've had a terrible shock, but if you don't see him, you're always going to wonder what he might've said. I've seen the way he looks at you. He loves you. I'm sure of it."

"I was sure of it, too, but now I'm wondering how I'll know if anything he says is true."

"You'll know."

"I feel like I'm going to die," she whispered, resting her head on Jenny's shoulder. "My heart literally hurts."

"I know, sweetie. I know."

~~~

Cole came storming up the stairs to Jenny's townhouse at ten o'clock.

She opened the door for him and led him into the living room where Olivia slept on the sofa.

"Nothing she said was true, Jenny," he said, his tone quiet but frantic. "I swear to God."

"Unfortunately, I'm not the one you need to convince."

"She believed her." When Cole shifted his eyes to Olivia, he noticed her face was red and puffy from crying.

"I guess it was quite a performance."

"She's a total nutcase. I've been trying to get rid of her for months. Long before I met Liv."

"Can I get you anything?" Jenny asked. "Something to eat? A stiff drink maybe?"

"No, thanks. I'm sorry to come barging in here like this. If she'll go with me, I'll take her to her place. Would you mind if we borrowed your car? We'll get it back to you tomorrow."

"I'll get the keys."

She left the room, and Cole went over to kneel down next to Olivia. He brushed his hand over her silky hair and kissed her forehead. "Liv," he whispered.

Her eyes fluttered open, and she greeted him with a soft, dreamy smile. He watched her smile fade as she remembered what had happened earlier. She sat up and put as much space between them as she could. "You shouldn't have come here."

"We need to talk. Let's go to your place. Jenny's going to loan us her car."

"I'm not going anywhere with you."

A stab of fear lodged in his breastbone, making it difficult to draw a breath. "Yes, you are."

Jenny came back with the keys, which she handed to Cole.

"I'm not leaving until you talk to me. We can either do it here and maybe wake up Billy, or we can go to your place. But we *are* going to talk."

With great reluctance, Olivia got up and slipped on her shoes and coat.

Jenny hugged her and whispered something in her ear. Olivia nodded and went out the door.

"Thanks," Cole said to Jenny.

She squeezed his arm. "Good luck."

―⁓―

Neither of them said a word as he drove to Alexandria. When they arrived at her apartment, he used his key to open the door and held it for her.

Olivia went in ahead of him and dropped her coat on the hook by the door. Feeling like she was wading through quicksand, she went through the motions of making coffee to thaw the block of ice that had formed inside her.

Out of the corner of her eye, she watched him pace like a pent-up tiger in a cage, ready to pounce. She also couldn't help but notice how exhausted he looked, but she refused to feel any compassion for him. Those days were over.

"Are you ready to listen to me now?" he asked after a long period of silence.

She kept her back to him and took a sip of the coffee, but it did nothing to warm her.

"Olivia."

Turning to him, she forced herself to look at him. "Whatever you have to say won't matter, so why don't we skip this whole scene and call it a day? You've had your last fling. What more do you want from me?"

His face went slack with shock. "Is that what she said? Yes, you were my last fling—the last fling I ever planned to have before I married *you*, Olivia."

"What about your wedding? April, I think she said it was."

He shook his head in disbelief. "There is no wedding."

"She had a ring."

"Not that she got from me! I've never been engaged to anyone. The only person I want to be engaged to is you."

At that, Olivia snapped. "*She had a key and luggage and your mail!* She knew your schedule and that you'd been sick. *You expect me to believe there's nothing going on between you?*"

He came over to her and put his hand on her arm. "Will you sit down? Please? Let me explain."

She shook him off. "What can you possibly say that I'm going to believe?"

"There's nothing going on with her. Not anymore. Not since before I met you."

"So there was?"

"Sit with me." He led her to the sofa and sat down next to her. "I should've told you about her," he said with a deep sigh. "I know that. I almost did the other night when you asked me, but you've been so skittish and things between us were going so well. I didn't want to give you any reason to have doubts."

"Well," she snorted, "that backfired on you, didn't it?"

"Liv, she's a total freak. She latches on to guys, and when they break up with her, she goes nuts. I didn't find out until after I broke up with her that she's done this before."

Olivia wasn't sure she wanted to know, but she couldn't help but ask. "Done what?"

He ran a frustrated hand through his hair and released a deep, rattling breath from his congested chest. "I met her through some friends about two and a half years ago. We started seeing each other once in a while, nothing major. I told her the same thing I told everyone else— I'm not looking for anything serious, I just want to have fun, I don't want anyone to get hurt. For a while, things were okay. We were having a good time, you know? Then my mother got sick. Everything happened really fast. She went to the doctor because she wasn't feeling well. They sent her to a specialist, and the next day we found out she was terminal."

His pain was so acute, even after all this time, that Olivia wanted to reach out to him but didn't.

"I was in a big rush to get home to Indiana. I called Natasha and asked her to deal with my fridge and the mail and stuff. I put a key under the mat for her and left town. While my mother was sick, Natasha came to Lafayette a couple of times to bring me my mail and more clothes. She always brought food, too, and was really helpful, which I appreciated. When my mother died, she came to the funeral and everything. It was all such a blur that I hardly remember her being there.

"I stayed with my dad for two weeks after the funeral, and then I had to get back to work. I'd been on a leave of absence for almost five months by then. I was numb, and I really needed to focus on work for a while. Natasha didn't like that. She had waited months for me and wanted to get back to having fun.

"We were fighting a lot, which I didn't need just then, so I called it off with her. She totally freaked out. I mean she went nuts, which was the first sign that something wasn't right with her. I had just lost my mother, and she was making it about *her*?"

Olivia didn't want to be moved by his story, but she was nonetheless.

"I stopped taking her calls and ignored her messages. Maybe I didn't handle it as well as I could have, but I had other things on my mind. A couple of weeks went by without any word from her, and then she started showing up at my house at odd hours. Sometimes she was drunk, sometimes she wasn't, but it always led to a screaming match. My neighbors called the cops once, and they gave her a warning.

"This went on for months, until I couldn't take it anymore. I called her parents and asked them to talk to her. They were deeply distressed to hear about what'd been going on. That's when I found out I wasn't the first guy she'd latched onto in an unhealthy way. They got involved, and I didn't hear from her for more than a year. I thought I'd seen the last of her."

"What happened?"

"When I was home for those two weeks after I got punched in the store?"

Olivia nodded.

"She showed up again, crying and pleading with me to give her another chance. I decided to play hardball this time. I told her I'd met someone else, and I was in love with her."

Olivia gasped. "You said that before you even saw me again?"

He took her hand, held it tightly. "I already knew, Liv. You were it for me. I knew it then."

Tears flooded her eyes, but she shook her head. "You're only saying what you think I need to hear."

"I'm telling you the truth!"

"*How do I know?*" she cried, tugging her hand free of his grip.

His teeth gritted with anger and frustration, he was clearly struggling to stay calm. "Let me finish, and then you can decide."

She wiped at tears and buried her face in her hands. This was the most excruciating thing she'd ever been through in her life.

"The weekend we had dinner at the airport? Do you remember how I didn't call you until Sunday night, and you thought I wasn't going to call?"

Looking up at him, she nodded.

"I left the next morning on an eight o'clock flight to Orlando, and all I was thinking about was you and how much I'd loved being with you and kissing you. When I landed, I got an urgent message from the airline representative meeting the plane that Natasha's father was trying to reach me. I checked my cell phone and found four incoherent messages from her and two frantic messages from him. She was barricaded in her apartment threatening to kill herself if she didn't see me."

Shocked, Olivia stared at him. "What did you do?"

"I wasn't going to have that on my conscience, so I arranged for emergency backup, which did me no favors at work, I might add, and hopped on a flight back to Chicago. I spent the rest of that weekend talking her out of her apartment and into the hospital so she could get some help. Her parents thanked me profusely for coming and promised I wouldn't hear from any of them again. The first thing I did when I left that hospital was call you."

"*Why didn't you tell me this?*"

"Olivia," he said with a smile that didn't reach his

eyes. "Have you no memory of how it was between us at first? I was so busy trying to convince you the feelings I had for you were real and genuine that I wouldn't have dared drop this on you then. You would've gone running for the hills."

She couldn't deny that he had a point. "When we were together that first weekend, you got messages from her, didn't you? I came out of the bathroom, and you were checking your voicemail. I could tell you were troubled, but you said it was nothing."

He nodded. "She was whacked out on something, so I couldn't even understand what she was saying. You were upset about what had happened with your parents that day, so I wasn't going to lay this on you then, either. The night I sent you the text message asking you to call me?" He paused. "I didn't answer when you called because I got home to find her stretched out naked on my sofa with a red rose between her breasts."

Olivia gasped.

"That time I'd had enough. I called the cops, went to the station, and pressed charges against her for breaking and entering. But because she had a key, the cops refused to pursue it. I finally got the key back that night, and I was sure I'd seen the last of her. It never occurred to me that she would've had others made. I should've known. I'd planned to change the lock but never got around to it since I've been away so much lately. Somehow she found out you were staying with me. We have a lot of friends in common, and most of them have no idea what she's put me through. Anyone could've told her."

"She knew things about me."

"What kind of things?"

"That I live in Washington and I'm an artist."

"Stuff I've mentioned to my friends."

In a small, dead sounding voice, Olivia added, "She said you'd told her I was your sister's friend, and I'd be staying there this week while I did a school project in Chicago."

He hung his head with dismay. "Liv, it's all lies. I've never talked to her about you, except to tell her I'd met you and was in love with you. That's it. I swear to God."

"She said the boxes on the third floor were hers—"

His eyes flashed with rage. "Those *boxes* are things of my mother's that my father couldn't bear to have around the house and we couldn't bear to part with!"

"How did she know you were sick?" she asked as the awful truth began to sneak past the block of ice.

"She called one day this week while I was sleeping. I answered the phone thinking it would be you. She must've heard it in my voice." He stood up, hands on his hips, eyes flashing with anger. "What else? What other lies do I need to defend myself against?"

"Are you *serious*? If you had told me about her, we wouldn't even be having this conversation!"

He snorted with disbelief. "If I had told you about her, it would've been over between us long before now."

Something about the way he said that made her heart shatter into a thousand pieces. "I guess we'll never know, will we?"

"I guess not."

"So where does that leave us?"

Picking up his coat, he put it on slowly, never taking his eyes off her. "I can't be with someone who thinks I'm capable of this. It's not the only time your first impulse was to think the worst of me. Either you trust me, or you don't. Clearly, you don't, and I'm tired of trying to convince you that you can."

"That's not fair!" Olivia cried, standing up to face him. *"What was I supposed to think when she came waltzing in there claiming to be your fiancée?"*

"Maybe you could've picked up the phone and *asked me* instead of believing her and running away! Maybe you could've had a little faith in me after everything we've shared!"

"You could've had some faith in me, too."

"Well, I'm sorry for trying to protect you from something ugly after what you were going through with your family. I'm sorry I put your needs ahead of my own. I won't make that mistake again."

Taking her key off his ring, he put it on the counter and went to the door. With his hand resting on the doorknob, he turned back to her. "I wanted everything with you, Olivia. I wanted to marry you, have a family with you, share my life with you. I loved you that much. Congratulations. You've finally succeeded in talking me out of it."

"*Cole!*" His name caught on the huge lump in her throat. "Please don't leave."

He hesitated, but only for a moment. Then he opened the door and was gone.

Olivia slid to the floor and dissolved into helpless, heartbroken sobs.

The next day she woke up with the worst cold she'd ever had.

Chapter 29

SHE'D HAD NO IDEA IT WAS POSSIBLE TO HURT THIS much. Over the next month, Olivia slogged through her days without feeling, tasting, or seeing much of anything. School started up again, but for all she cared she might have been back in business school rather than pursuing her dream. Without Cole to share it with, what did it matter?

Most alarming of all, she hadn't drawn or painted a thing since their awful confrontation. Her talent seemed to have dried up and died right along with their love.

Had she ever noticed before that every song was about heartbreak or lost love? She found herself staring into the mirror with tears rolling down her cheeks at odd hours of the day and night. Apparently, she had lost weight because her dad and Jenny were after her to eat. But nothing appealed to her, so most of the time she didn't bother.

When she got her period, she experienced a new wave of grief for all the things that would never be. She dreamt of the dark-haired, blue-eyed babies they would've had together and woke up heartbroken every time.

Just over a month after their breakup, she received a box in the mail from Cole. Tearing into it, she found the painting she had been working on when Natasha arrived and ruined everything. Also in the box were her paints, brushes, and the iPod he had given her. That was it. No note, no word, nothing to tell her he missed her or was thinking of her.

She tore the painting into tiny shreds and dumped it into the garbage. Not able to bring herself to trash the iPod, she put it in the same drawer where she had stashed the diamond earrings and tried to forget they were there.

A week later, she received word through her father that her mother was anxious to see her. Olivia hadn't seen her mother since the terrible blow-up the previous fall. Mary had been home for a while, and from what everyone had told Olivia, the change in her was quite remarkable. Regardless, Olivia had to work up the courage to go to her parents' new home.

She almost didn't recognize Mary when she walked into the orderly, uncluttered house. "Mom?"

Mary stood up to reveal a figure that was at least forty pounds lighter than it had been the last time Olivia saw her. There was also a sparkle in her eyes that Olivia had never seen before. She knew she was staring, but she couldn't seem to help it.

Mary held out her arms to her daughter. "Livvie."

Olivia stepped into her mother's embrace and fought the urge to sob. She had cried enough lately to last a lifetime.

"It's so good to see you," Mary said as she released her daughter.

"Where's Dad?"

"Still at work. He's made three sales this week alone. They're thrilled with him. He's right where he belongs, selling Cadillacs."

"That's great." They sat together on the sofa. "You look wonderful. I can't believe it."

"I feel pretty good. I go out for a walk every day. Little by little, I'm getting there."

"I'm happy for you."

"But you're terribly unhappy, aren't you? I can see it in your eyes."

Olivia felt her chin quiver but refused to give into the despair again. It had to stop. "I'll survive."

"I'm so sorry things didn't work out for you and your pilot." When Olivia looked up at her with surprise, Mary said, "Daddy told me. Don't be mad at him."

Olivia shrugged. "It was my fault. I drove Cole away by not trusting him."

"He must've given you reason."

"Not intentionally. I was kind of looking for it the whole time we were together, so when something actually happened, I thought the worst. I hurt him."

"We all make mistakes, honey. If he loves you, he'll see that eventually."

She shook her head. "It's over."

"Dad's worried about you. He says you haven't been eating. I can see you've lost weight that you didn't have to lose."

"I can't seem to work up much interest in eating or anything else, for that matter."

"My poor baby." She reached for Olivia, who rested against her mother's chest like she had been doing it all her life. "May I give you some advice I probably have no right to offer?"

Desperate for some relief from the pain, Olivia nodded. "Please."

"Don't make the same mistake I did by letting grief destroy you. You've had a terrible disappointment, an awful loss, but you've got your whole life ahead of you and so much to look forward to."

As a sob erupted from her throat, Olivia gave up trying to fight the tears. "Not without him. I can't live without him."

"Unless you can figure out a way to fix things with him, you're going to have to."

"He doesn't want to fix it. I ruined it."

"Then you have to learn from it and go on."

"I don't know how. It hurts so much that I wonder how it's possible to keep breathing."

"Livvie, I'm so sorry. I'd give anything to be able to make that pain go away for you. But since I can't, you have to try. Focus on the things that give you joy—your art and baby Billy and school. If I had done that, if I had focused on you and your brothers rather than on the babies I'd lost, our lives would've been so much different. You have no idea how much I wish I had it to do over again."

Olivia wallowed in the comfort of her mother's embrace for a long time.

"Do you think you can try, honey? I can't bear to see you so sad."

"I suppose there's no other choice, is there?"

Mary chuckled. "Nope."

Olivia kissed her mother's cheek. "Thank you."

"I'm sorry if it's too little too late."

"It's not too late. In fact, it's just in time."

Overcome, Mary clutched Olivia's hand. "I have no right to ask you to forgive me, but I hope, in time, maybe—"

"There's nothing to forgive. It's in the past now."

Her father came home a short time later, and they talked Olivia into staying for dinner—the first real meal she could remember eating since that last breakfast at Cole's house.

By the time she got home, she was surprised to realize she felt a little better. Seeing her mother looking so good and acting for once, well, like a mother, had done wonders for Olivia's flagging spirits. She wandered over to her easel and picked up a pencil. Flipping it back and forth between her fingers, she studied the blank sheet of paper. After a long while, she lifted her hand to the page. Yes, it was a sketch of Cole, but at least she was drawing. She had to start somewhere.

That same night, Cole arrived home to snow after a fourteen-hour day. One weather delay after another had caused a ripple effect throughout the entire air traffic control system in the Midwest.

He cracked open a beer and flipped through the avalanche of mail that had accumulated on the counter over the last few weeks. Lately, the simplest things seemed to take more energy than he could bother to summon. Work was his primary focus, and when he wasn't working, he had picked up a few extra Flights for Life—anything to avoid sitting at home thinking about how badly he had screwed things up with Olivia.

He should have told her about Natasha. If he had, maybe she would've understood that it was a situation he couldn't control. At least then she wouldn't have been blindsided by Natasha showing up and filling her head with lies. If Olivia had known, she could have fought back.

He had heard from his friends that when Natasha's latest—and most dramatic—ploy to win him back had failed, she decided to move to New York. Cole felt like taking out a billboard in Times Square to warn the men in the city to be on the lookout for her.

Between his *Business Aviation* magazine and the latest issue of *Time* was a small cream-colored envelope. He picked it up and noticed his name and Capital Airlines written in Olivia's handwriting. Underneath, someone else had scrawled his home address. He took it with him to the living room, sat down on the sofa, and held it for a long time.

Gazing up at her sketch of their trip to San Francisco, he got lost in a sea of memories that made him ache with regret. He missed her so much. Sometimes he thought he'd lose his mind if he had to spend another day without her. He was also tormented by the idea that he might've left her alone and possibly pregnant.

He opened the letter. When he saw the date they met and her neat, precise words, his heart slowed to a crawl.

Dear Cole,

I wanted to thank you again for what you did today. I hope you weren't too badly injured. If you're receiving this note, it's because your airline wouldn't tell me anything about your condition and I couldn't let what you did go by without a proper thank you.

I also wanted to say that no one has ever done

*anything like that for me. That you were willing to risk
your own safety to defend me was brave, to say the least.
If you find yourself at Reagan National again, I'd love to
know how you are. Look for me at the NewsStop in the
main terminal. I'm there most afternoons.*

Sincerely,
Olivia Robison

He read the note over and over until the words ran
together. Then he dropped his head into his hands
and wept.

~~~

On Valentine's Day, Olivia shipped off the last of the
pieces Paolo needed for her show, which was now just
over a month away. She had worked all weekend to finish them and was hopeful that Paolo would like them.
Her new work had a definite edge to it since life had
ripped off her rose-colored glasses. She had no idea
what her mentors in San Francisco would think of them.

She was on the Metro between school and the airport
when Jenny called.

"Hey, happy VD," Olivia said.

"Liv, where are you?"

"Almost to the airport. Why?"

"Honey, listen, I hate to do this to you, but Cole's
plane has declared an emergency."

Olivia gasped. "What happened?"

"Apparently, they were getting ready to land at
Reagan and couldn't get the front landing gear to
deploy properly."

Olivia's heart literally stopped for a moment. "The third thing."

"What do you mean?"

"He believes things happen in threes. Oh God, Jenny, how do you know?"

"It's on CNN. They're making a big deal about Captain Incredible having another chance to be a hero. They've got cameras following the plane as it circles the airport. I guess they're trying to make a plan to get them down safely."

"What do I *do*?"

"Go to the airport and ask the people at Capital. Tell them you're his fiancée. If that freak show Natasha can do it, so can you."

"What if he dies? He could die without ever knowing how much I love him."

"He's not going to die. Pull yourself together, Liv. I'd come there to be with you if I could, but Billy's asleep and Will's in Richmond for the day."

"I'm getting off the Metro now. I'll call you when I know anything."

"Please do. I'll be praying for him, for both of you."

"Thanks."

Olivia sprinted into the terminal and ran straight for the Capital counter, which was mobbed with media and the frantic families of people on the plane. Since there was no way to break through to anyone who could help her, she took off for the Capital lounge.

Inside, she ran straight past the attendant to find a group of Capital pilots and flight attendants glued to the bank of televisions. Among them, Olivia saw Jake Garrison, the pilot Cole had introduced her to before their trip to San Francisco.

"Miss, you can't be in here," the attendant said to Olivia as she approached Jake.

"Excuse me." When he turned to her, she said, "I'm not sure if you remember me, but I'm Cole Langston's—"

"Girlfriend," he said. "Olivia, right?"

She nodded.

"It's fine," he said to the attendant who hovered next to Olivia. "She's my guest."

"Thank you. What's the latest?"

"We just got word they're going to divert them to Dulles. It's a bigger airport with a larger emergency-management capability."

"In case they crash?" Olivia asked softly.

"They won't. I've known the captain for years. He's a good friend of mine and one of the best pilots I've ever flown with. And I'll tell you the same thing I told CNN—if I was in this situation, there's no one I'd rather have in the right seat than Cole Langston."

"Jackpot."

"Pardon me?"

"That's what they called him in the Navy because he never missed his targets."

Jake smiled. "Suits him. He's an ace, honey. You've got nothing to worry about." He put his arm around her shoulders. "Since they've grounded us for the time being, some of us are catching a shuttle out to Dulles to meet the flight. Why don't you come along?"

Olivia hesitated. She had no idea how she'd be received by Cole if he managed to get through this unharmed. Then she realized she didn't really care if he'd be happy to see her. She needed to see him. "I'd appreciate that."

Olivia called in sick to work and boarded the shuttle with Jake. As she watched the miles fly by on Route 66 during the forty-minute ride, all she could think about was what must be running through Cole's mind at that moment. *They said there were eighty-nine passengers and six crewmembers on board. They must be so scared, but I'm sure Cole and the captain are doing all they can to reassure them.*

"The good news is they got a perfect weather day for something like this," Jake said. "No snow or precipitation of any kind. Rare in February."

"Yes," she said, appreciating his efforts to keep her spirits up.

"Of course, he'll hate all the renewed media attention," Jake added, chuckling. "Twice in just over a year with a punch-out in the middle. The guy lives on the edge."

Olivia nodded in agreement, but she yearned with all her heart for the sound of Cole's voice, for any sign that he was okay. When she couldn't bear it another minute, she dialed his cell phone number from memory and waited for his message to pick up.

"Hi, this is Cole. I can't take your call right now because I'm probably in the air. Leave a message, and I'll get back to you as soon as I'm back on terra firma."

Her eyes flooded as she waited for the beep. "It's Liv. I just…" Words failed her for a moment, and then she knew exactly what she had to say. "I love you. I needed you to know that. Please be safe. I couldn't stand it if anything happened to you. That's all I wanted to say. I love you."

She ended the call and held the phone tight against her chest as tears spilled down her cheeks.

Jake put his arm around her. "It's okay. He's going to be just fine."

Olivia was grateful for the comfort but couldn't help but wonder if Cole would care that she still loved him. Hopefully, she'd get the chance to find out.

—*w*—

They waited an endless hour as the plane circled over Dulles, which had been closed to other aircraft.

"Before they attempt to bring her down, they're going to fly by the tower real low so the controllers can get another look at the gear," Jake explained.

"Can they land without it?"

He nodded. "But because it's not fully deployed, it's going to want to collapse under the weight of the fuselage. The worry is that the metal will drag and cause sparks. That's why they're covering the runway with flame-retardant foam—as a precaution."

Olivia's heart lodged in her throat as she watched the flyby and listened to the speculation from the other pilots, who'd welcomed her into their tight circle after Jake introduced her as Cole's girlfriend. The pilots had gathered in a lounge that overlooked a runway lined with emergency vehicles. The passengers' families were in the room next door.

"Gotta keep all the weight on the back for as long as they can," one pilot said.

"And get everyone out of there stat," another replied.

Olivia couldn't listen to any more. She wandered away from them to the window in time to see the big jet banking up and away from the airfield. The addled wheel was obvious to her now, angled as it was at about thirty degrees.

"This is it," someone cried. "They're making one more loop and then bringing her in."

Olivia clasped her hands together and prayed like she never had before. *Please*, she begged, *just let him be okay. Let them all be okay. I'll do anything, give up anything. Anything at all.*

"Here we go," she heard Jake say. His voice was tight with tension. His eyes, when she glanced over at him, were glued to the runway. "Easy does it. That's the way."

Olivia held her breath as the back wheels touched down.

"Good," Jake said to no one in particular. "Keep that nose up."

Finally, as the plane slowed, they eased the nose down. Sparks and flames shot from under the wheel as it dragged along the foam-covered runway.

She gasped.

"Just the tires blowing out," Jake said. "That's to be expected."

"Oh, my God." Olivia looked away as fire trucks sped toward the plane to aim more foam at the smoldering front tires. She braced herself for a huge explosion that never happened.

"It's okay, honey," Jake said, his voice euphoric. "You can look now. They did it!"

Olivia took a deep breath before she allowed herself to look at the runway where the plane was surrounded by fire engines, ambulances, and other emergency vehicles.

"Jackpot," she whispered.

Chapter 30

ANOTHER HOUR PASSED BEFORE THE FLIGHT CREW WAS delivered to the terminal. Most of the other pilots had left, but Jake stayed with Olivia. After what they had been through together that day, he felt like an old friend. Over the last hour, she had told him about her breakup with Cole.

"No wonder why he's been such a grouch lately," Jake said. He jumped up when he saw Cole and the captain come through the door from the tarmac. "Damned fine job, you two," Jake said, hugging them both. "Damned fine."

"Thanks," Cole said, returning Jake's embrace. He looked up and froze when he saw Olivia standing there. "Liv?"

Jake stepped aside. "She's been waiting a long time to say hello. You'd have been proud of her today, Langston. She was a real trouper." He kissed Olivia's cheek.

"Thank you, Jake. For everything."

"The pleasure was entirely mine, honey. Tell him what you told me. He needs to hear it." Jake threw his arm around the captain's shoulders and walked away with him saying, "Now let me tell you how I would've done it."

Their laughter echoed through the hallway as Cole and Olivia stared at each other.

"What're you doing here?" he asked.

Olivia had never seen him looking quite so exhausted—or handsome. "I, ah, found Jake at Reagan. He remembered me and offered to bring me here."

"That's not what I meant."

She took another step toward him, her hands twisting with nerves. "I'm here because I love you so much, and when I thought you might die, I wanted to die, too," she said, not caring that she sounded like a blithering fool and must have looked like one, too, with tears cascading down her face.

"Liv," he sighed.

And then she was in his arms. She had no idea if he moved or if she did—or maybe they both did. Who cared? There was the scent that belonged only to him and the strong arms that held her just right, the way no one else ever could.

"I'm sorry you were so scared," he said.

She pulled back to look up at him. "Were you? Scared?"

"For the first time ever, I really was."

"At least you won't have to worry about that third thing anymore."

His face lifted into a small, tired smile. "True enough."

She reached up to frame his face with her hands. "I'm so happy to see you. I've missed you so much, and then when I thought I might never see you again…" Shaking her head, she couldn't continue.

He brushed the tears from her cheeks with his thumbs. "I hate to say it, but I have stuff I need to go do. The NTSB is waiting to talk to us," he said, referring to the National Transportation Safety Board. "They like to get to us while it's still fresh in our minds."

She let her hands fall from his face. "I understand."

"How will you get home?"

"I'll grab a cab."

"From here?" He raised an eyebrow. "That goes against everything you believe in."

"That's okay. Being here was worth it. If you need a place to stay after you're done, I'll leave the door unlocked."

"It's apt to be really late."

"Doesn't matter. I'll be there."

The captain he had flown with came around the corner. "Langston, are you coming?"

"Be right there." When Cole brought his eyes back to her, she noticed they were dark with fatigue and what might have been emotion. He kept them fixed on her for a long moment. "I've got to go."

"Okay," she said, even though she wanted desperately to kiss him. Just once.

He brushed his finger over her cheek in a gesture that left her breathless. "It was good of you to be here. I appreciate it." He attempted the half smile she loved, but his eyes were sad, so very sad. "I'll see you."

Heartbroken, she watched him walk away. For the first time, he hadn't said, "next time." She had poured out her love for him, but he hadn't clung to her and professed his undying love the way she had pictured during the endless hours she had spent praying for his safety.

In a daze, she walked through the deserted airport and into the freezing cold night to find a cab. Forty-five minutes and fifty dollars later, she arrived at home. As promised, she left the door unlocked for him, changed into her pajamas, and got into bed. She sat up all night, hoping he would come home to her. But by the time the sun rose the next morning, she had accepted he wasn't coming then or ever. The scent of his cologne still clung faintly to her hands as she realized it was really over this time, and somehow she had to find a way to go on without him.

—⁓—

Olivia decided to take her mother's advice and threw herself into her schoolwork over the next two weeks. Her classes were interesting and challenging, her professors supportive and encouraging, and in her classmates she discovered a network of likeminded artists who made going to school each day a joy.

Paolo had gone wild over her latest work and had reported the gallery was in full preparation mode for the Olivia Robison debut show.

Her parents, her brothers, Jenny, Will, and Billy were all flying to San Francisco for her big day. She tried to stay focused on the excitement and not dwell on the fact that Cole wouldn't be there, that nothing would be as they had planned.

Fifteen days had passed since she had seen him, and all she'd had of him since then was the new flurry of media coverage that followed his latest heroic episode. Obviously, he had made his decision where she was concerned, and she was determined not to let it ruin her life the way her mother had let grief ruin hers.

Someday she would find love again, and while it might never be like it had been with him, she'd make it work. With every passing day, she felt stronger and more determined to survive without him.

The last day of February dawned bright and

unseasonably warm. Jenny called as Olivia was getting ready to leave to do some work at the campus studio.

"What's up?" Olivia asked her cousin.

"We found it!"

"Found what?"

"A house! Oh, Liv, it's absolutely perfect—four bedrooms, two bathrooms, right in Del Ray. The neighborhood is full of kids and young families."

"I grew up down the street from there, remember?" Commonwealth Avenue ran right through the eclectic neighborhood. "I love Del Ray."

"I got the key from the Realtor, and I'm dying to show it to you. Will you meet me there? Do you have time?"

"Sure. I don't have class until later. What's the address?"

"Twenty-two East Custis."

"Thirty minutes?"

"I'll be there."

"See you then."

Olivia took the Metro to King Street and walked past her old house on Commonwealth Avenue. The new owners had painted the outside and put in some new shrubs. The place looked well cared for, and Olivia felt a twinge of melancholy as she glanced back over her shoulder for one last look. Despite the few highs and many lows, that house had been her home for a lot of years. But it wasn't her home any more. At some point during the last month, her cozy little apartment had become home.

She continued along Commonwealth toward East Custis, feeling the warm sun on her face. It could be months before northern Virginia would see another day as nice as this one, and Olivia planned to enjoy every minute.

As she approached the corner of East Custis, she noticed a black Mustang GT wedged in between two other cars and was flattened by the memory of cajoling Cole's keys from him in Chicago. With a look around to make sure no one was watching, she ran a finger over the bright black paint and gave herself permission to remember. Just for a minute.

After a deep cleansing breath to absorb the memories, she took another long look at the car before she turned the corner in search of number twenty-two. "Oh!" she said when she saw the house. "I *love* this one!"

The two-story gray-shingled house had a wide porch and big, open windows. A few years earlier, it had been completely renovated and updated, and she'd wondered what it looked like inside. Skipping up the front stairs, she turned the knob and found the door unlocked.

"Jenny, are you here?" Olivia wandered inside, marveling at the wide, knotty-pine floors that had been buffed to a gleaming finish. She ran her hand over the shiny white molding that surrounded the living-room doorway before she continued on to the kitchen where Cole leaned against the counter drinking a cup of coffee from St. Elmo's, looking for all the world like he had been waiting there just for her.

"Hello, Liv."

Rendered speechless with surprise, she could only stare at him.

Amused by her mute shock, his eyes twinkled. "How are you?"

"What are… What're you doing here?" she stammered, continuing to stare at him. He wore a faded denim shirt that made his eyes an even crazier shade of blue than usual. Had he ever looked so good? "Where's Jenny?"

"To answer your first question—I live here—or I will as soon as the movers get here with my stuff. As for your second question, I have no idea. Her job was to get you here. I'm not sure what her plans are for the rest of the day."

Confused, she tried to process what he'd said. "You live here? Get me here? For what?"

"For this." Putting down the coffee, he crossed the room, lifted her right off her feet, and kissed her.

He tasted like coffee and toothpaste and, *oh God*, he tasted like Cole, and she couldn't get enough of him.

When he came up for air several minutes later, he looked into her eyes. "You have no idea how badly I wanted to do that the last time I saw you, waiting for me at Dulles with a pale face and big brown eyes full of love."

"Then why *didn't* you?"

"Because I wasn't ready yet."

"Ready for what?"

He let her slide back down to her feet but kept his firm hold on her. "I wanted to do it right this time."

"You're making my head spin. Will you please tell me what the heck is going on here?"

Laughing, he helped her out of her coat and lifted her onto the counter to put her at his eye level. Standing between her legs, he ran his fingers through her long hair. "Before I say anything else, I have to know one thing."

"What?"

"Are you pregnant, Liv?"

She shook her head, feeling the genuine regret once again.

"We'll have to try harder."

Shocked and still confused, she tried to get her head around what he was saying. "We will?"

He nodded. "I wanted to ask you that so badly the night at Dulles, but I couldn't just blurt that out like it was the only thing I cared about." His fingers continued to spool through her hair. "I'm so sorry, Liv. I screwed everything up."

"No, you didn't. I did. Everything you said about me was true."

"And none of it would've happened if I'd been straight with you from the beginning, so that's what I'm going to do this time. The day after we got back from San Francisco, I put in a request to change my home base to Washington. I didn't say anything to you at the time in case they said no. But they approved it on the first of February. I got busy looking for a house, hoping that maybe if I lived here, somehow, over time, I could make it right with you. Jenny told me how much you love this neighborhood, so I focused my efforts here. I closed on this place the day after the Valentine's Day near-disaster."

"I don't understand. Why would you do all this when we were broken up?"

"Because the woman I love lives here, and it's going to take her a while to finish school. Since I couldn't bear to live halfway across the country from her for that long, I figured I'd better do something about it before she slipped through my fingers and forced me to spend the rest of my life longing for her."

"But that night," she stammered, "in the airport, you were so remote. I was sure it was over for good after that."

"The whole time I was circling that airport, all I could think about was getting through it so I could see you again. And then when you were there, waiting for me… What you said that night and the message you left on my phone… After that, I knew for certain I was doing the right thing by moving here. I love you so much, Liv, and I want us to date like normal people without all the pressures and drama of a long-distance thing. Can we please start over again and do it right this time?"

She shook her head. "No."

"*No?*" he asked, startled. "You don't want to date me?"

"I do *not* want to date you."

He groaned. "*Liv*. You've *got* to be kidding me. I picked up my whole life, drove halfway across the country, and you've changed your mind? It's only been *fifteen days* since you told me you still love me!"

Right then, she realized the Mustang she had admired in the street was his. "Shut up, will you? Will you please just shut up and kiss me again, you big idiot?" With both hands on his face, she molded her lips to his as her heart did a happy dance in her chest.

Between kisses, she said, "I want to live with you and marry you and have a family with you and share your life—all the things you said you wanted from me before I ruined it. So no, I will *not* date you."

"Well, you might have to for a while because when we get engaged, I'm doing the asking. You got me?"

"As long as you make it snappy."

"Yes, ma'am." He leaned his forehead against hers.

"There was another reason why I wasn't ready to tell you all this that night in the airport."

"What other reason?"

"Guess what today is?"

"Um, Tuesday?"

"Even better. It comes around once every four years. Last day of February? Ringing any bells?" He let that settle for a long moment before he curled his face into the half grin she loved so much. "It's leap day, baby."

Epilogue

OLIVIA FOUND A QUIET CORNER IN PAOLO'S OFFICE AND sank to the floor, her back propped against the wall. Sliding off the three-inch heels Jenny had talked her into, she stretched her feet and back, all of which were screaming from standing up for hours. The place was so packed she had lost track of Cole and her parents an hour earlier. Feeling overwhelmed and alone in a sea of admirers, Olivia had fled to the quiet office.

That's where Cole found her twenty minutes later. "There you are! Everyone's looking for the art world's latest sensation." He had a bottle of champagne tucked under his arm. Sitting down next to her, he reached for her hand. "You're a smash, honey. Paolo just announced that every one of your pieces has sold for the asking price. Apparently, there was a bidding war for one of them."

"*All of them?*" she squeaked.

"Every one. I'm so proud of you and so happy for you." He leaned over and kissed her softly. "You deserve this more than anyone ever could."

She caressed his face. "I'm so glad you're here to share it with me."

"Where else would I be?"

Amused by him, she glanced at the bottle. "So what's with the champagne? I thought we learned our lesson the last time."

He toyed with her earlobe, rolling the diamond earring between his fingers. "It was all I could find, and since I'm one step closer to my dream of being your kept man, I figured we needed to celebrate." Untwisting the cork, he let it fly across the room and sucked down the first blast of fizzy wine before he handed the bottle to her. "Madame?"

She took a sip and gave it back to him.

He rested his head against the wall and turned so he could see her. "How do you feel?"

"Happy—really, truly happy. This definitely qualifies as one of the best days of my life, and you're the one who made it happen."

"No way. This is all about you."

"This is all about *us*."

After pondering that for a second, he nodded. "Okay, I'll drink to that."

She nudged his shoulder with hers. "We make a pretty good team, huh?"

"The best. In fact, I was planning to do this when we got back to the Fairmont, but suddenly I don't want to wait."

"For what?"

Reaching into the pocket of his black pinstripe suit coat, he retrieved a huge square-cut diamond ring and slid it onto her left hand. "What do you say we make this partnership official?"

Tears flooded her eyes. "Do you promise to love me forever?"

His blue eyes went dark with desire and love as he nodded. "Forever and ever."

"Pinky swear?"

He smiled and wrapped his little finger around hers. "Pinky swear."

She leaned in to kiss him. "Then you've got yourself a deal."

Acknowledgments

I never imagined I'd have an idea for a book while sitting in an airport bar. While waiting for a flight at Reagan National with my husband a couple of years ago, I watched a woman run into the arms of an arriving pilot, and a novel idea was born—again in an airport. Yes, I do see the comedy: I, who hate to fly, writing two books that open in airports. Call it therapy!

I'm blessed to be surrounded by family and friends who are incredibly supportive of my writing career. Thank you to my husband, Dan, a retired Navy chief petty officer, who filled in some of the pieces of Cole's Naval career. My fabulous children, Emily and Jake, just seem to "get it," and that means the world to me. My dad, the retired aviation mechanic, answered numerous questions and ran the scenarios with me. Thanks, Dad!

To my pilot friend and former Naval aviator, Mike Deganutti, thank you for helping with Cole's military career. To my "baby" cousin Jennifer Barrera: Olivia's cousin Jenny is you, of course. Our 10 p.m. phone calls were a highlight of the baby years, and I never would've survived motherhood without the laughter. To my old pal, Lisa "Cat" Thatcher, thank you for helping me to navigate the American University campus.

To the rest of the home team: Julie Cupp, thanks for the help with the Alexandria details, for allowing me to use Cupp Condo as Olivia's place, and for once again chairing the character-naming committee. Proofreaders Christina Camara, Lisa Ridder, and Paula DelBonis-Platt help to keep it clean (well, the grammar anyway). To my most faithful readers: Arlene, Mary, Jeannie, Martine, and Lorraine, you ladies are the best. My mom had awesome taste in friends.

To my agent, Kevan Lyon, editor, Deb Werksman, and publicist, Danielle Jackson, thanks for all you do for me. And to the readers who write to tell me they enjoy my books: you'll never know what those notes mean to me. Thank you from the bottom of my heart. You all are the very best part of being a published author.

About the Author

Marie Force is the author of *Line of Scrimmage* and *Love at First Flight,* as well as *Fatal Affair* and *Fatal Justice,* the first books in her new Fatal Series. Of *Line of Scrimmage, Booklist* said, "With its humor and endearing characters, Force's charming novel will appeal to a broad spectrum of readers, reaching far beyond sports fans." Wild on Books said, *"Love at First Flight* by Marie Force is most definitely a keeper. It is an astounding book. I loved every single word!"

Since 1996, Marie has been the communications director for a national organization similar to the Romance Writers of America. She is a member of RWA's New England, Beau Monde, From the Heart, and Published Author Special Interest Chapters.

While her husband was in the Navy, Marie lived in Spain, Maryland, and Florida, and she is now settled in her home state of Rhode Island. She is the mother of Emily, 15; Jake, 12; and a feisty dog named Brandy.

Find her at www.mariesullivanforce.com, on her blog at http://mariesullivanforce.blogspot.com, on Facebook at www.facebook.com/pages/Marie-Force/248130827909, and on Twitter at twitter.com/MarieForce. Marie loves to hear from readers. Contact her at marie@marieforce.com.

An Excerpt From

Love at FIRST FLIGHT

Available from Sourcebooks Casablanca

The boss had picked a hell of a time to get chatty.

A bead of sweat rolled down Michael's back. As Baltimore City State's Attorney Tom Houlihan pelted him with a rapid-fire series of pre-trial questions over the phone, the departure time for Michael's flight to Florida crept closer. He needed an exit strategy, and he needed it now.

Travelers swarmed through the gate area while Michael struggled to stay focused on the call despite the chaos around him. Tugging on his burgundy silk tie, he released the top button of his shirt and watched a line form to board the flight.

"And Rachelle?" Tom asked.

"I saw her last night," Michael said. "She's antsy, but hanging in there." He flipped through some other notes on his laptop, hoping to anticipate Tom's next question.

"How antsy?"

"Well, she's a teenager stuck in protective custody. You've got daughters, so you can probably imagine."

An exotic scent filled Michael's senses, drawing his attention away from the call. He glanced at the seat next to him where a young woman with silky dark hair and an olive-toned complexion watched with dismay as a gate attendant slipped a "Delayed" sign over the flight number.

"Michael?" Tom said.

Michael tore his eyes off the woman. "I'm sorry. What did you say?"

"I asked if there was anything else you needed from me."

"We should be set until jury selection. I'll want your input then. George prepped the last of the witnesses today. We've covered all the bases, so try not to worry."

"Yeah, right," Tom said with a wry chuckle.

"I'll check in first thing on Monday."

"Enjoy the party. Hopefully, it's the only time you'll be engaged."

Michael laughed, relieved that Tom seemed satisfied—for now. "That's the goal. I appreciate the time off. Have a good weekend." He ended the call and caught the tail end of the gate attendant's announcement. "What did she say?" he asked the woman next to him.

She glanced over with a distressed expression on her stunning face. "Ninety-minute delay."

A jolt of desire surprised Michael. He was on his way to visit his fiancée and to attend their engagement party, so what was with the unexpected reaction to a pretty stranger? Pretty wasn't the right word. Strikingly beautiful was more like it. Since they now had ninety minutes to kill, he decided to indulge the curiosity. "Where're you heading in Jax?"

"Jacksonville Beach."

He noticed her eyes were fixed on the gate attendant who slid the updated departure time into a slot on the board.

"My boyfriend's working there for a year. How about

you?" She glanced over at him with soft brown eyes that drew him right in.

He couldn't remember the last time anything other than the upcoming trial had captured his attention so completely. "Amelia Island. My fiancée lives there with her parents."

"So you're doing the long-distance thing, too, huh?"

"Yeah, and it sucks. How long have you been doing it?"

"Almost seven months," she said with a sigh. "Five more to go."

"Six months down and eight to go for us. We're getting married in April."

"Well, at least we both know it won't last forever. I don't know how people do it indefinitely. That would make me even crazier than I am now."

"For real."

"What do you do?" she asked.

"I'm a prosecutor for the Baltimore City state's attorney."

Her eyes widened. "Wow, that's so cool."

"More like overwhelming—especially lately. What about you?"

"Nothing quite so exciting. I'm a hair stylist."

"That sounds like more fun than putting people in jail."

Her smile engaged her entire face, and his heart skipped an erratic beat.

"It is until someone hates their haircut, but fortunately that doesn't happen to me very often."

"What do you do when it does?"

"If they're truly upset, we offer them a freebie next time, but usually they come back telling us they got all kinds of compliments on their new look."

Hoping to keep her talking, he ran his hand through his mop of wavy brown hair. "I could use your services right about now."

"You should stop by the salon sometime."

"Where do you work?"

"Panache in the Inner Harbor."

"I wish I had time for a haircut. I'm going to trial in just over a week."

"Can you tell me about it?" She turned in her chair and pulled her legs up under her.

"It's the Benedetti brothers," he confided in a low tone, thrilled to have her full attention.

She gasped. "Oh my God!"

Gang members Marco and Steven Benedetti were accused of gunning down three teenaged boys in the city.

"My co-worker's cousin was one of the kids they killed. Timmy Sargant."

"We're going to get them."

"I hope so," she said softly. "I really do."

"Attention in the gate area. Announcing the arrival of Flight 980 from Providence with continuing service to Jacksonville. For those of you waiting for the Jacksonville flight, we'll begin boarding as soon as the thunderstorms clear out of the Jacksonville area."

"I wish I was going to Providence," he said.

"Why's that?"

"I'm from there. My family lives in Newport."

"How'd you end up down here?"

"I went to Georgetown Law and met my fiancée, so I ended up staying here. Then her parents moved to Florida, and here we are living apart. How'd you meet your boyfriend?"

"We went to high school together. We've been to-gether ten years, since junior year."

"So then you're… twenty-seven? You look older than that."

"You're not supposed to say that to a woman," she said, laughing at his sudden embarrassment.

"What I meant is that you look much too sophisti-cated dressed all in black to be only twenty-seven. Is that better?"

"Nice save," she said with a grin. "We wear black in the salon—it's the uniform."

"I'm Michael Maguire, by the way, and I'm thirty-two."

Smiling, she reached out to shake his hand, and an odd current traveled through him at the feel of her soft hand in his. He had to remind himself that he was sup-posed to let go.

"Juliana Gregorio. Nice to meet you, Michael Maguire, thirty-two."

"So how come you aren't married to that boyfriend of ten years yet?" he asked with a teasing grin, not sure why the answer suddenly mattered so much to him.

"We just haven't gotten around to it, I guess. I've been asking myself that question more often in the months since Jeremy's been gone."

"You'll get around to it."

"We'll see." She nibbled on her thumbnail. "For some reason, I feel like there's a lot riding on this weekend."

"Why do you suppose that is?"

"I don't know. Everything was going along pretty well for months, but he's been kind of remote on the phone the last few weeks. I can't figure out what's up."

"I'm sure it'll be fine when you see him. Paige's

parents are having an engagement party for us this weekend, which is the number one reason why I'd rather be heading north instead of south."

"You're not excited about the party?"

"I'm dreading it. It's so stupid when you consider all the same people will be at the wedding less than a year from now."

"That's true."

"It's a waste of time and money—two things her parents have way too much of."

Juliana smiled, and Michael found himself riveted by her every expression. Her face flushed under the heat of his scrutiny, and she looked away. He wondered if she thought he was one of those weird strangers women were taught to fend off in self-defense classes. She'd probably run for her life if he acted on the urge to lean in closer for a better whiff of the earthy, spicy scent that was driving him mad.

Reminding himself he was a grown man and not a hormonal teenager, he made an effort to keep the staring—and the sniffing—to a minimum and the conversation light. By the time the gate attendant announced their flight, he felt like he had known Juliana for years rather than an hour. Since the plane wasn't full, they chose seats together.

Her cell phone rang just as she took it out to turn it off. "Hi, Dona. I can't talk. I'm on the plane, and I have to shut my phone off soon."

While pretending not to hang on her every word, Michael watched her stiffen with tension.

"You promised me! You said you'd handle it!" Another pause. "I'll call Vincent." She ended the call and dialed another number. "Vin, you gotta help me out. Can you take dinner over and check on Ma tonight? Dona totally bailed on me." Pause. "Vincent, *I'm on an airplane.* You've got to do it." She lowered her voice. "Please."

Something about that softly uttered word tugged at Michael's already over-involved heart, making him wish he could fix all her problems. *What the hell is that all about?*

"Thanks, Vin. I really appreciate it. I'll talk to you Sunday." She shut the phone off, returned it to her purse, and stared out the airplane window.

For a long moment, Michael debated whether he should say anything. "Are you all right?" he finally asked.

"Yes. Sorry."

"Don't be."

"It's just my family. They drive me nuts. My mother, she needs… She has problems."

"That's tough. I'm sorry."

"I'm sorry I have to deal with it every day of my life."

"Do you have brothers and sisters?"

"Two of each, but they're much older than me and mostly useless. How about you?"

"I'm the baby, too. I have three older sisters."

"I'll bet they doted on you," Juliana said, seeming relieved by the shift in conversation away from her troubles.

He grinned. "Oh, yeah, nonstop torture. They were forever dressing me up as their living doll. Don't tell anyone that. It'll kill my image." Noticing how she clutched the armrest as the plane hurtled down the runway and lifted into the sky, he wanted to offer her a hand to hold but didn't.

"Are you close to your sisters?" she asked once they were airborne and she'd released the death grip on the armrest.

"Yeah, all of them. They're married with scads of kids who're the most adorable kids in the world, of course."

She smiled. "Do you see them very often?"

"I get up there every now and then, but it's harder since Paige moved to Florida. Whenever I have a free weekend, I end up down there."

"Is your family coming to the party this weekend?"

"They couldn't get away for it, but that's fine with me. My folks and hers don't have much in common."

"You must be excited about the wedding at least."

He thought about that for a minute. "I'd be more excited if it hadn't turned into such a circus. I've already heard enough about it to last me forever, and I've got eight months to go."

"Big to-do, huh?"

"The biggest of to-dos, which is not at all what I wanted. But she's their only child, so I gave in."

"It must've been hard for you to get away so close to the trial."

"We've been working weekends for months now, so my boss wasn't thrilled, believe me. But he's a good friend of the Admiral's. That's Paige's dad."

Juliana raised an eyebrow. "You call him 'the Admiral'?"

"*Everyone* calls him 'the Admiral.' He retired as superintendent of the Naval Academy last year."

The stewardess came to take their drink order.

"Can I buy you a drink?" he asked.

"Why not?" She ordered a gin and tonic, and he asked for a beer.

He paid for the drinks and saluted her with his can. "Cheers. Here's to a good weekend."

"I'll drink to that."

"Ladies and gentlemen, as we make our final approach into Jacksonville, we thank you again for choosing Southwest Airlines. Enjoy the weekend."

Juliana looked up, surprised by how fast two hours had passed as she chatted with Michael. The thought of seeing Jeremy in a few minutes filled her with nervous energy and excitement.

"Are you ready?" Michael asked.

He had the bluest eyes she'd ever seen and a sexy smile that made her tingle all over when he directed it at her. "As ready as I'll ever be."

"I'm sure you'll have a great time. Keep in mind that all guys suck on the phone. Paige is forever complaining that I never have anything to say."

Juliana appreciated his attempt to bolster her confidence.

"How about you? Ready to put on your best party face?"

"I don't have much of a party face."

"You've got five minutes to get one."

"When do you go back?" he asked.

"Seven on Sunday evening."

"Me, too!"

"We can compare notes," she said, oddly relieved to know she would see him again.

"I'll look forward to it."

They gathered their bags and walked up the Jetway and through the terminal together. When she spotted Jeremy waiting for her, she looked over to say good-bye to Michael, who had made eye contact with his fiancée, a waiflike blonde with porcelain features and big blue eyes. She looked like she would break if hugged too hard and wasn't at all what Juliana had pictured for him.

"I'll see you Sunday," she said to Michael.

"Have a good one," he said, walking toward Paige as she went to Jeremy.

"Who's that guy?" Jeremy asked when she reached up to hug him. He was eight inches taller than her and still built like the football player he had been in high school.

"Just someone I sat next to on the plane. How are you?" She looked him over for clues to what was troubling him lately, but he looked the same as he always did. He kept his curly blond hair cut short now that he was older, but when she met him it had been six inches high and unruly—a lot like he had been then.

"Fine," he said, leaning down to kiss her.

She turned away from the scent of stale beer on his breath. "Have you been drinking, Jer?"

"Just a few beers with the guys after work," he said with a shrug. "Your flight was late, so I had time to kill."

Judging by the glassy look in his eyes, Juliana could tell that he'd had more than a few and was disappointed he had done that on the night she was coming to visit.

Holding hands, they walked by Michael as he hugged Paige.

He glanced at Juliana, and the dismayed expression on his face made her sad for him.

Line of
SCRIMMAGE

BY MARIE FORCE

SHE'S GIVEN UP ON HIM AND MOVED ON...

Susannah finally has peace, calm, a sedate life, and a no-surprises man. Marriage to football superstar Ryan Sanderson was a whirlwind, but Susanna got sick of playing second fiddle to his team. With their divorce just a few weeks away, she's already planning her wedding with her new fiancé.

HE'S FINALLY FIGURED OUT WHAT'S REALLY IMPORTANT TO HIM. IF ONLY IT'S NOT TOO LATE...

Ryan has just ten days to convince his soon-to-be-ex-wife to give him a second chance. His career is at its pinnacle, but in the year of their separation, Ryan's come to realize it doesn't mean anything without Susannah...

978-1-4022-1424-0 • $6.99 U.S. / $8.99 CAN

Love at FIRST FLIGHT

BY MARIE FORCE

What if the guy
in the airplane seat next to you turned out
to be the love of your life?

JULIANA, HAPPY IN HER CAREER AS A HAIR STYLIST, IS ON HER way to Florida to visit her boyfriend. When he tells her he's wondering what it might be like to make love to other women she is devastated. Even though he tries to take it back, she doesn't want him to be wondering all his life. So they agree to take a break, and heartbroken, she goes back to Baltimore.

Michael is going to his fiancée's parents' home for an engagement party he doesn't want. A state's prosecutor, he's about to try the biggest case of his career, and he's having doubts about the relationship. When Paige pulls a manipulative stunt at the party, he becomes so enraged that he breaks off the engagement.

Juliana and Michael sat together on the plane ride from Baltimore to Florida, and discover they're on the same flight coming back. With the weekend a disaster for each of them, they bond in a "two-person pity party" on the plane ride home. Their friendship begins to blossom and love, too, but life is full of complications, and when Michael's trial turns dangerous, the two must confront what they value most in life...

978-1-4022-2006-7 • $6.99 U.S. / $7.99 CAN

Romeo, Romeo

～ BY ROBIN KAYE ～

Rosalie Ronaldi doesn't have a domestic bone in her body…

All she cares about is her career, so she survives on take-out and dirty martinis, keeps her shoes under the dining room table, her bras on the shower curtain rod, and her clothes on the couch.

Nick Romeo is every woman's fantasy— tall, dark, handsome, rich, really good in bed, AND he loves to cook and clean…

He says he wants an independent woman, but when he meets Rosalie, all he wants to do is take care of her. Before long, he's cleaned up her apartment, stocked her refrigerator, and adopted her dog.

So what's the problem? Just a little matter of mistaken identity, corporate theft, a hidden past in juvenile detention, and one big nosy Italian family too close for comfort…

"Kaye's debut is a delightfully fun, witty romance, making her a writer to watch." —*Booklist*

978-1-4022-1339-7 • $6.99 U.S. / $8.99 CAN

Breakfast in Bed

BY ROBIN KAYE

HE'D BE MR. PERFECT, IF HE WASN'T A PERFECT MESS...

Rich Ronaldi is *almost* the complete package—smart, sexy, great job—but his girlfriend dumps him for being such a slob, and Rich swears he'll learn to cook and clean to win her back. Becca Larson is more than willing to help him master the domestic arts, but she'll be damned if she'll do it so he can start cooking in another woman's kitchen—or bedroom...

PRAISE FOR ROBIN KAYE:

"Robin Kaye has proved herself a master of romantic comedy." —Armchair Interviews

"Ms. Kaye has style—it's easy, it's fun, and it has every-thing that you need to get caught up in a wonderful romance." —Erotic Horizon

"A fresh and fun voice in romantic comedy." —All About Romance

978-1-4022-1895-8 • $7.99 U.S. / $9.99 CAN

Too Hot to Handle

by Robin Kaye

HE SURE WOULD LOVE TO HAVE A WOMAN TO TAKE CARE OF...

To Dr. Mike Flynn, there's nothing like housework to help a guy relax, while artist Annabelle Ronaldi doesn't have a domestic bone in her body.

When they meet at her sister's wedding, Mike is sure this is the woman he wants to take care of forever. While Mike sets to work wooing Annabelle, she becomes determined to sniff out the truth of the convoluted family secret that's threatening to turn both their lives upside down.

PRAISE FOR *TOO HOT TO HANDLE*:

"Entertaining, funny, and steaming hot." —BookLoons

"A sensational story that sizzles with sex appeal."
  —The Long and Short of It Reviews

"Witty and enchanting." —Love Romance Passion

"From the brilliant first chapter until the heartwarming finale, I was hooked!" —Crave More Romance

978-1-4022-1766-1 • $6.99 U.S. / $7.99 CAN

HEALING LUKE

BY BETH CORNELISON

She can't escape her past...

Occupational therapist Abby Stanford is on vacation alone, her self-confidence shattered by her fiancé's betrayal. Romance is the last thing on Abby's mind—until she meets the brooding and enigmatic Luke…

He won't face his future...

Scarred by a horrific accident, former heartthrob Luke Morgan is certain his best days are behind him. Abby knows how to help him recover, but for Luke his powerful attraction to her only serves as a harsh reminder of the man he used to be. Abby is Luke's first glimmer of hope since the accident, but can she heal his heart before Luke breaks hers?

"Beth Cornelison writes intriguing, emotionally charged stories that will keep you turning the pages straight through to the end. Fabulous entertainment!"
—Susan Wiggs

"Healing Luke is a breath of fresh air for romance fans... a stirring novel and a five-star read!"
—Crave More Romance

978-1-4022-2434-8 • $6.99 U.S. / $8.99 CAN

The TREASURES of Venice

BY LOUCINDA MCGARY

"Bursting with passion."
—Darque Reviews

An Irish rogue who never met a lock he couldn't pick…

With danger at every corner and time running out, Keirnan Fitzgerald must use whatever means possible to uncover the missing Jewels of the Madonna. Samantha Lewis is shocked when Keirnan approaches her, but she throws caution to the wind and accompanies the Irish charmer into his dangerous world of intrigue, theft, and betrayal. As the centuries-old story behind the Jewels' disappearance is revealed, Samantha must decide whether Keirnan is her soul mate from a previous life, or if they are merely pawns in a relentless quest for a priceless treasure…

"Lost jewels, a sexy Irish hero, and an exotic locale make for a wonderful escape. Don't miss this charming story."
—Brenda Novak, *New York Times* bestselling author of *Watch Me*

"A brilliant novel that looks to the past, entwines it in the present, and makes you wonder at every twist and turn if the hero and heroine will get out alive. Snap this one up, it's a keeper!" —Jeanne Adams, author of *Dark and Deadly*

978-1-4022-2670-0 •$6.99 U.S. / $8.99 CAN

SEALed
with a *Kiss*

BY MARY MARGRET DAUGHTRIDGE

THERE'S ONLY ONE THING HE CAN'T HANDLE, AND ONE WOMAN WHO CAN HELP HIM...

Jax Graham is a rough, tough Navy SEAL, but when it comes to taking care of his four-year-old son after his ex-wife dies, he's completely clueless. Family therapist Pickett Sessoms can help, but only if he'll let her.

When Jax and his little boy get trapped by a hurricane, Picket takes them in against her better judgment. When the situation turns deadly, Pickett discovers what it means to be a SEAL, and Jax discovers that even a hero needs help sometimes.

"A heart-touching story that will keep you smiling and cheering for the characters clear through to the happy ending." —*Romantic Times*

"A well-written romance... simultaneously tender and sensuous." —*Booklist*

978-1-4022-1118-8 • $7.99 U.S. / $9.99 CAN

SEALed
with a
Promise

BY MARY MARGRET DAUGHTRIDGE

NAVY SEAL CALEB DELAUDE IS AS DEADLY AS HE IS CHARMING.

Professor Emmie Caddington's quiet intelligence and quirky personality intrigue him. When he discovers that her personal connections can get him close to the man he's vowed to kill, will their budding relationship be nothing more than a means to revenge…or is she the key to his salvation?

Praise for *SEALed with a Kiss*:

"This story delivers in a huge way." —Romantic Times

"A wonderful story that will have readers experiencing a whirlwind of emotions and culminating with an awesome scene that will have your pulse pounding." —Romance Junkies

"What an incredibly powerful book! I laughed and sniffled, was turned on and turned inside out." —Queue My Review

978-1-4022-1763-0 • $6.99 U.S. / $7.99 CAN

SEALed
with a
Ring

BY MARY MARGRET DAUGHTRIDGE

SHE'S GOT IT ALL...EXCEPT THE ONE THING SHE NEEDS MOST

Smart, successful businesswoman JJ Caruthers has a year to land
a husband or lose the empire she's worked so hard to build. With
time running out, romance is not an option, and a military husband
who is always on the road begins to look like the perfect solution...

HE'S A WOUNDED HERO WITH AN AGENDA OF HIS OWN

Even with the scars of battle, Navy SEAL medic Davy Graziano is
gorgeous enough to land any woman he wants, and he's never
wanted to be tied down. Now Davy has ulterior motives for
accepting JJ's outrageous proposal of marriage, but he only has so
long to figure out what JJ doesn't want him to know...

Praise for *SEALed with a Ring*:

*"With a surprising amount of heart, Daughtridge makes a
familiar story read like new as the icy JJ melts under Davy's
charm during a forced marriage. The supporting cast, including
one really unattractive dog, makes Daughtridge's latest one for
the keeper shelves." —Romantic Times*, 4 stars

978-1-4022-3698-3 • $7.99 U.S. / $9.99 CAN

GETTING *Lucky*

BY CAROLYN BROWN

Griffin Luckadeau is one stubborn cowboy...

And Julie Donovan is one hotheaded schoolteacher who doesn't let anybody push her around. When Griffin thinks his new neighbor is scheming to steal his ranch out from under him, he's more than willing to cross horns. Their look-alike daughters may be best friends, but until these two Texas hotheads admit it's fate that brought them together, running from the inevitable is only going to bring them a double dose of misery...

Praise for Carolyn Brown:

"A delight to read." —Booklist

"Engaging characters, humorous situations, and a bumpy romance... Carolyn Brown will keep you reading until the very last page." —Romantic Times

"Carolyn Brown's rollicking sense of humor asserts itself on every page." —Scribes World

978-1-4022-2436-2 · $6.99 U.S. / $8.99 CAN

MY
GIVE A DAMN'S
BUSTED

By Carolyn Brown

He's just doing his job...

If Hank Wells thinks he can dig up dirt on the new owner of the Honky Tonk beer joint for his employer, he's got no idea what kind of trouble he's courting...

She's not going down without a fight...

If any dime store cowboy thinks he's going to get the best of Larissa Morley—or her Honky Tonk—then he's got another think coming...

As secrets emerge, and passion vies with ulterior motives, it's winner takes all at the Honky Tonk...

978-1-4022-3928-1 • $7.99 U.S./$9.99 CAN/£4.99 UK

COWBOY Trouble

By Joanne Kennedy

*All she wanted was a simple country life,
and then he walked in...*

Fleeing her latest love life disaster, big city journalist Libby Brown's transition to rural living isn't going exactly as planned. Her childhood dream has always been to own a farm—but without the constant help of her charming, sexy neighbor, she'd never make it through her first Wyoming season. But handsome rancher Luke Rawlins yearns to do more than help Libby around her ranch. He's ready for love, and he wants to go the distance...

Then the two get embroiled in their tiny town's one and only crime story, and Libby discovers that their sizzling hot attraction is going to complicate her life in every way possible...

"I'm expecting great things from Joanne Kennedy! Bring on the hunky cowboys." —Linda Lael Miller, *New York Times* bestselling author of *The Bridegroom*

"Everything about Kennedy's charming debut novel hits the right marks...you'll be hooked." —BookLoons

978-1-4022-3668-6 • $7.99 U.S. / $9.99 CAN / £4.99 UK

One Fine COWBOY

By Joanne Kennedy

The last thing she expects is a lesson in romance...

Graduate student Charlie Banks came to a Wyoming ranch for a seminar on horse communication, but when she meets ruggedly handsome "Horse Whisperer" Nate Shawcross, she connection entirely...

Nate needs to stay foc from foreclosure, but sexy and brainy Char time Nate has finally tame his wild heart?

Praise for *Cowboy Tr*

"A fresh take on the tr There's plenty of wac mystery-laced escapad

"Contemporary Weste
—*Romantic Times*

"A fun and delicious r cowboys, you won't mystery, and spurs! Y

978-1-4022-3670-9 •